THE DRAGON KIN

TIANI DAVIDS

To the fighters.

Books by Tiani Davids

The Eldrasian Chronicles
The Dragon Healer
The Dragon Kin
TEC3 (coming spring 2023)

CHAPTER ONE

E LINTA PRESSED HER BACK into the wall by the palace front
doors, backpack slung loosely over one shoulder, and peered
out into the dimly lit courtyard. It was just before midnight and
Elinta was supposed to have met Prince Lorrin and their friend
Niles in the stables five minutes ago. But she'd been held up and
she needed to hurry. The gates would close for the night soon and
their plans would be ruined if they weren't outside them.

Relieved, Elinta sighed as she saw the path to the stables was
clear. She darted out, ignoring the pain from the cut across her
hip, a token from her fight with the mysterious Asali named

Mazen who'd attacked her only two nights ago and slipped into the cover of the dark stables.

"There you are! Where have you been?" Niles's voice whispered through the darkness. The boys hadn't lit any lanterns, keeping them from being noticed, and had saddled the horses by the faint light of the flames in the courtyard. Elinta could hardly make out her friend's face, but she knew it would be alight with excitement.

"The guard arrived early in the corridor outside the dining hall," she said in a low voice. "I had to wait for him to leave." She paused as a crunching sound came from Niles's dark figure. "Are you eating?"

"What? I'm hungry."

Lorrin's dim form appeared on her right, leading the mare, Ash, that Elinta would ride on the long journey they were about to take. "The guard didn't see you?" the prince murmured, ignoring the noise from Niles's direction as he continued to eat.

"No," Elinta said, thinking of the cramped little cupboard she'd hidden inside until the man's footsteps had disappeared down another corridor.

"Good." Lorrin handed her the reins. His hand brushed hers in the darkness before he hurried to retrieve his own horse, Bentley.

"Are we ready to go?" Elinta asked as she tied her backpack to the mare's saddle alongside the saddlebags. It was the same brown bag Raisa had given her in the White Mountains all those months ago when she'd first met Lorrin.

"All set," Niles said, and she knew he was grinning. After weeks of talking about it, they were finally on their way to see the Asali Council in the city of Liyarna. A thrill of nerves shot through Elinta.

"Just one more thing," Lorrin said, reappearing with Bentley behind him. He stopped beside Elinta and held out a long, thin, shadowed object in his hand.

"Did you fix it?" Elinta asked, reaching for it and feeling the familiar form of her sword in its scabbard. The blade had once been his.

She caught the vague movement of Lorrin nodding. "Like new."

Elinta grinned and fumbled in the dark to strap the weapon to her belt, feeling the familiar weight of it at her hip. The sword had been damaged by an *illayas* dagger in her fight against Mazen. The rare weapon had left nicks and dints along the length of her blade. Lorrin had kindly smoothed the damage out while she'd rested. Elinta made a mental note to check the blade over later.

"Can we go now?" Niles said, already in the saddle of his horse, Horse. "It's nearly midnight."

"Yes," Elinta said, pushing herself up onto Ash's back and wincing as the stitches in her forearm and hip pulled tight. But she had to stop herself from practically bouncing in the saddle once she'd settled. They were finally going. Things were finally going to change.

Elinta double-checked the bags were in place as Lorrin moved to the front of their line. Niles brought up the rear.

"Ready?" Lorrin whispered loudly.

"Yes."

"Yep."

They pushed their horses out into the courtyard and straight into a canter.

This was the one part of their plan they couldn't control. The guard at the gate. For fear the man would be punished, they'd decided not to approach him about looking the other way as they snuck from the palace in the middle of the night. So, despite the risk it posed to their plan, they were going for the less stealthy option, trusting that any chase after the prince would, according to him, take at least ten minutes to muster. And by then, they would have a good lead.

Air rushed against Elinta's face and there was a yell as the guard caught sight of them, jolting into action, but it was too late. They were nearly at the gate. Squeezing her legs into the side of the mare, Elinta urged the horse even faster and the three friends shot through and out into the night. The gate clanged shut belatedly after them.

Elinta counted away the seconds. Two full minutes passed before the alarm was raised and they were already near the border of the city. The bell echoed through the night on their heels, but she smiled anyway. They'd done it. They were on their way.

Niles shouted in elation as they passed the last straggles of Nevira, the sound of the bell fading far behind them. Elinta's grin widened, jostling the large bruise across her cheek from Mazen's backfist. But she didn't care about the pain. No one knew where they were headed, and they'd know soon enough whether they could outrun the men that would come after them, but right now it felt like they had.

Elinta patted Ash once before pushing her into a gallop and watching the night landscape whiz by. She turned up the collar of her jacket against the cold wind and ran her hand along the horse's neck again. She'd ridden the mare once before on a trip to visit Zhayra, the dragon that now excitedly awaited their arrival in the woods she'd been living in for several months. It was a good animal and would suit her well on the long trip ahead of them, especially at the speed they intended to maintain.

Though it was dark, the light of the moon and stars illuminated the smooth road enough that the three friends felt safe to keep up their fast pace. They moved single file, drawing ever closer to Zhayra and keeping the horses at a gallop until they were satisfied they'd put enough distance between themselves and the palace to drop back to a trot. Now at a slower pace, Elinta ran the plan over again in her mind to reassure herself. Zhayra would join them in the woods where they would turn west and travel for five days until they hit the Benhurst Ranges. They would head north after that, along the base of the mountains, until they reached the Calaza Forest where they would find the city of Liyarna. All in all, it would take them about a week to get there at the quick pace they were going to set. Then they'd finally be able to speak to the Asali Council. And there was so much that she wanted to talk to them about. So much she wanted to know.

Soon they reached the borders of the woods, and Elinta's excitement doubled as her eyes landed on the large, white form that shone in the moonlight filtering through the trees. Zhayra hummed. Her amber eyes shining, the dragon slipped out from under the trees, but there was no time to greet each other. Besides, Ash was too nervous around the dragon to allow her any closer.

Elinta cocked her head, listening for signs of pursuit from behind them. All was quiet, but they still had a big lead on their pursuers.

"Can you see if anyone's following us?" Elinta asked the dragon.

Zhayra spread her massive membrane wings and launched into the sky above them.

"Anything?" Elinta called.

Zhayra loosed a low growl, just loud enough for them to hear from the ground.

"I take it someone's following us," Lorrin said with a sigh.

Elinta nodded, glad for the dragon's keen sight.

"Let's go, girl," she called, and Zhayra angled in the dark sky to follow them.

The trio ducked under the trees and toward the Afonlin River, the darkness of the woods forcing them to keep to a walk. All the while, they strained to hear their pursuers, but there was still too much distance between them for their human ears. All they could hear was the steady drumming of their horses' hooves on the packed earth beneath them.

Zhayra's joy at being able to fly again shot through their bond, meeting Elinta's own happiness to be doing *something* about the dragon's plight and Mazen. But underneath Zhayra's excitement was a tinge of worry, which Elinta put down to several things, including their apparent pursuit, the secretiveness of their trip, and Elinta's near-death experience only two days ago when Zhayra had been unable to help.

The dragon had been angry and frightened by the fight with Mazen, but Elinta thought her trip to reassure the dragon the next day had calmed her. Apparently not. She sighed. At least now they could be together.

They paused on the banks of the Afonlin, listening for any signs of whoever followed them, but they couldn't hear anything over the rush of water. Elinta looked to Zhayra, thinking back to the time she'd heard a sound she shouldn't have been able to. If only she could work out how to access that again, she'd be able to hear whatever it was Zhayra could now, and they'd know how far ahead they were. She filed it away as another thing they could ask the Asali about.

"Do you think we'll lose them once we cross?" Elinta asked the dim outline of the boys. She squinted over her shoulder into the dark woods, expecting to hear the thunder of hooves at any moment.

"Maybe," Niles said, looking to Lorrin.

He shrugged. "Let's hope so."

They turned north, parallel to the river for some time before they found a place safe enough to cross in the dark. There was a bridge further south, but they didn't dare use such a common crossing. They wished to keep their path secret, including even the rough direction they'd taken if they could.

"We'll cross here," Lorrin said, looking out across the flat bank and river. The water didn't seem as deep here, and the moon reflected off its smooth surface. "I'll go first."

He nudged Bentley and the two crossed through the calm water. When he reached the other side, he called back to them. "It can't be more than three feet deep. You're next, El."

Elinta urged Ash forward slowly, feeling the smooth stones shifting under the horse's hooves as they entered the river. The water gradually rose up Ash's legs as they continued their crossing. Halfway across, the horse slipped and dropped deeper into the water, plunging Elinta's shoes into the icy river. Gasping at the cold, Elinta nudged the horse sideways, where it recovered, and she pushed it on.

"Are you alright?" Lorrin asked her quietly as they emerged up the opposite bank.

"Yeah. That water is cold!" She slipped her feet from the stirrups and shook them out, careful not to knock the horse, and sending droplets of water flying. "Go ahead, Niles," she called to the lone shadow she'd left behind.

Once Niles joined them, they urged the horses up the bank and through a smattering of tall reeds. Despite the threat of their pursuers catching up to them, a threat they felt had significantly lessened now they were across the river, they continued at a slow pace, having to pick their way across the landscape now they'd left the road behind. Soon they had to cross a smaller stream, a branch of the Afonlin, before they turned west. Elinta longed to study the landscape around her. Though Kethmere, her village, wasn't too far away to the south, she'd never been in this part of the country before. But shadows draped the land, so she turned her thoughts inward as they continued west, knowing she had a whole week ahead of her to study the new sights. They didn't stop until dawn.

Elinta dismounted stiffly, trying not to scrunch up her face at the pain in her hip. It'd only been two days since she'd received the wound, but it felt as fresh as the moment Mazen's dagger had sliced into her. It had been weeping again when she'd changed the dressing on it before leaving the palace, the droplets of blood slipping past the stitches holding her skin together. While the boys dug out food for a cold breakfast, Elinta pulled out the medicine the palace healer had prescribed and swallowed a large spoonful. She grimaced at the bitter taste and took a swig of water to rinse her mouth.

"Well," Niles said, sitting on the ground and taking a bite of bread. "We did it!"

Lorrin grinned.

"We did."

"Did you see that guard's face when he turned around to see us riding toward him? Priceless!" Niles laughed, running a hand through his blond hair, and making it even messier.

Elinta sat beside Lorrin, and they ate their meals in nervous excitement as the sun slowly rose and the air heated up around them. Soon it became clear that whoever had been sent to pursue them had indeed lost their trail, since they'd neither seen nor heard from them and some of Zhayra's nerves had dissipated. When they'd finished their small meal, Elinta stripped off her jacket, stuffing it into one of the saddlebags on the mare before they mounted again and continued on.

It was a long day of riding, in which they skirted every town or village they came across, but it didn't dampen their mood. Even Zhayra didn't seem to mind that Elinta rode with the boys instead of flying, something that had been a point of contention between them since they'd met. The dragon was just happy to finally be able to fly again and to be with Elinta. As for Elinta, she drank in the passing landscapes, her eyes snagging on familiar plants and medicinal herbs that made her think of home. The place she couldn't go back to.

As the day wore on though, Elinta's body grew more and more sore and she focused less on the scenery and more on the saddle pommel in front of her, or the back of Lorrin's head.

When they stopped to make camp, Elinta dismounted stiffly. A full day of riding had left her recovering body aching, unhelped by the medicine. But she didn't say anything to the boys. She didn't want them to worry since there was nothing to be done anyway but continue with their journey. So, she unsaddled Ash in silence, ignoring her droopy eyelids and the ache in her body.

Elinta sat down none too gracefully by the fire Lorrin was making. He shot her a worried look, but Elinta didn't acknowledge it. Talking to the Asali Council was much more important than her comfort as far as she was concerned. But the thought didn't ease the pain. Neither did an extra teaspoon of her medicine. If only she had access to Galen's hut, she could have made herself something from his stores that would ease the pain and speed along the healing. But what her body really needed was rest, something she couldn't give it.

If she thought a good night of sleep would help her, Elinta was wrong. She was just as sore as when she'd gone to sleep when she woke in the morning, and she felt her first real stab of concern. The wounds should have been healing, slowly sure, but not this slowly. While Lorrin and Niles bustled around the camp, Elinta, sitting against Zhayra's side, pulled back the covering across the cut on her hip. It came away speckled with dried blood. Elinta stared at the blood. *It's probably just the riding pulling on the wounds. That's all. Otherwise, it'd be sealed by now.*

There wasn't much she could do about it, though, other than to keep taking the medicine she'd been given. Maybe her thought last night about Galen's wasn't too far off. She could try to find something out here to put on the wound herself, to help speed the healing process along.

"How's it looking?" Lorrin asked, stopping in front of her as he carried his saddlebags toward Bentley. He'd already saddled her horse for her so she could check her wounds. A light smoke drifted through the air behind him from their extinguished fire.

Elinta smiled, though it felt somewhat forced. "It's all right." She replaced the covering, then stood, brushing dirt from her pants. "Are we ready to go?" Elinta kept her eyes firmly away from the bandage on her arm, though she wondered whether the cut there had been weeping too.

"Once I tie these up, we'll be ready." Lorrin smiled, lighting his blue eyes. "Are you in a hurry today?"

Elinta shrugged. "The sooner we get there, the better."

"You sound like Niles."

Elinta and Lorrin both looked over at Niles, already seated in his saddle and looking over his shoulder at them.

"What?" he said, noticing their glances.

⚑⚑⚑⚑

On their fourth full day of travel, the small peaks of the Benhurst Ranges drawing closer and closer, Elinta was at the back of their group, eyes closed to the drumming in her head as they cantered down a road used mostly only by locals to the area.

Why is my head pounding? Elinta thought. Her stomach sat uneasily within her, and even Zhayra's nerves seemed to have increased throughout the day. Elinta sighed, opening her eyes, and it was at that moment that Ash shied and Elinta lost her seat. She hit the ground with a grunt and a *whoosh* as the air left her lungs and lay sprawled in the dirt.

"El?"

Elinta groaned and closed her eyes to the bright light above her and the drumming, drumming in her head. *When was the last time I fell off a horse?* she thought blearily. Zhayra's keen echoed around her, but Elinta kept her eyes firmly closed.

The horses' hoofbeats drilled into her skull as the boys hurried back to her, and dust rose around her again. Their boots hit the ground with a crunch.

"El?" Lorrin said from beside her.

"I'm OK," she mumbled, rubbing her forehead.

"You don't look OK," Niles said from her other side.

She squinted up at them. "I don't feel OK," she admitted.

One of the horses squealed from further up the road and a moment later, a loud thump sounded and the ground trembled. Zhayra's head appeared above the boys, her amber eyes looking down at Elinta with clear concern. Sunlight glinted off the two horns on her head.

The boys looked up at Zhayra in shock, and glanced up and down the road but, luckily, there was no one within sight. Yet. Somehow, Elinta didn't think the dragon would care if someone did see her.

"You're bleeding," Lorrin said, turning back to her, worry tainting his voice as he peeled her shirt away from her hip.

Elinta struggled to raise her head and looked down at the blood seeping through the bandage. She groaned, and slowly pulled away the one on her forearm, already knowing what she would see.

Lorrin and Niles watched with worried, but curious, expressions as the bandage fell away to reveal the thin line of skin that had been stitched back together. It too wept blood.

Elinta let her aching head drop back to the ground, pressing her hand to her hip.

"Something's not right," she said.

The boys exchanged a glance, but Zhayra didn't look at them. She had eyes only for Elinta.

Zhayra growled low in her throat.

"Let's get you off the road," Lorrin said, carefully scooping her up before she could protest. Elinta felt her cheeks redden as he carried her to the side of the small road and gently lowered her to the ground so she sat against one of the few trees in the area. Low, tangled growth had surrounded them for the last hour, covering the edges of the dirt road.

"You really shouldn't be here," she said to Zhayra, who had followed them, her long tail covering the width of the road and disappearing on the other side. The dragon didn't respond though Elinta thought she seemed to be glaring at her. She could almost picture the dragon with furrowed eyebrows.

Elinta sighed and turned to Lorrin. "I've got some supplies in my backpack."

Lorrin called out to Niles, who was tying the horses to the trunk of a small yearling tree farther down the road, far enough that they weren't scared of Zhayra. They'd been left in the middle of the road when the boys had dismounted. Luckily, they were well trained and hadn't gone wandering. Niles untied Elinta's bag and hurried over, squatting in front of her.

"So, what's going on?" he said, looking at her bloodied shirt.

"I don't know," she mumbled, taking the bag from him and rifling inside. "They keep seeping blood," Elinta said, meaning the cuts in her hip and arm. Although this latest bleed was probably from falling. She sighed and rubbed her head. "And I have a headache. It shouldn't be like this."

"What are you looking for?" Lorrin said, gently taking the bag from her. He had a smudge of dust on his face, but it made his blue eyes stand out more. Elinta shook her head to dismiss the thought.

"There's some cotton pads in there," she said, letting her head drop back against the tree. Why was her head aching so much?

As Lorrin rifled inside the bag, Elinta tried to focus in on Zhayra, who seemed to grow more agitated by the minute. Elinta tried to steady her own emotions.

"I'm OK, Zhayra," she said, but her voice wobbled.

Zhayra's eyes were fixed on the bleeding wound at her hip. She shuffled on her large feet.

"Here." Lorrin pulled a few cotton pads from inside the bag and handed them to her while he pulled away the bloodied cloth with his free hand. His hand was covered in dirt and he was careful not to touch the wound. "Looks like you've torn a couple stitches," Lorrin said, frowning. "Do you have any thread in here?" He looked in the bag.

"In the front pocket," Elinta said, pressing one of the pads into the cut. "The medicine from the healer is in there as well."

Zhayra huffed.

"What's that mean?" Elinta said, but the dragon only huffed again.

Niles took one of the spare pads and covered the wound on her arm. "Zhayra's right."

Elinta's eyebrows rose and Zhayra tilted her head to look at Niles.

"You're falling apart," he said, but he watched her with concern.

The dragon snorted.

"I'll be fine," Elinta said, unsure which one she was talking to, as Lorrin found the needle, thread, and medicine. "You really shouldn't be down here," she said to Zhayra again, but the dragon didn't even acknowledge her words.

Elinta waited another five minutes before she pulled the pad away from her hip. After a few seconds, a small line of blood seeped from the wound, then it stopped.

Zhayra keened again. Lorrin and Niles exchanged looks.

"That shouldn't have been bleeding so much," Lorrin said.

"No," Elinta said, staring at the blood. In fact, if not for the remaining stitches, she was sure it would be bleeding nearly as much as the day she'd gotten the wound. She tried to summon an image of Mazen's weapon, wondering whether it had caused these strange effects in her wounds, but she couldn't push away her headache long enough to concentrate.

"Does *illayas* do this?" she asked, easily able to recall that much about the rare dagger Mazen had used.

Lorrin shook his head. "No. This is something else."

Niles pulled the pad away from her forearm. The bleeding had stopped there.

Elinta stared absently at Zhayra's face, not seeing the dragon as she struggled to think through the options for her hip. First, though, something to ease her head. Lorrin took over holding the pad in place, his rough hands brushing her skin as Elinta pulled the bag back to her. She fished out some flowers to chew on. Elinta was glad that she'd packed so many medicinal supplies for their trip, having packed them both for herself and for anything that might happen along the way. She hadn't forgotten the men that had tried to rob her and Lorrin near Lake Lusinata.

"Do we need to cauterise it?" Niles asked, rubbing his hands together excitedly.

Zhayra huffed a burst of hot air on his head.

"OK. Sorry. Just trying to lighten the mood," Niles said, putting a little more distance between him and the dragon.

Elinta smiled at the interaction. "No," she said, pulling the needle and thread toward her. "I'll have to stitch it back up." But she wasn't sure it would help if it hadn't before. Riding wasn't helping the wounds, but something else was going on. The wounds still looked fresh. All she knew was that if something was stopping her from healing properly, cauterising the wound could cause her more trouble by locking it inside her.

Her bond with Zhayra was also giving her some doubt, since the dragon's emotions were still as worried as before, even with the prospect of Elinta stitching the wound up. If the stitches would help, wouldn't Zhayra's emotions be happier? Surely Zhayra understood the concept ... could the dragon tell what was wrong with her? Elinta shook her head and refocused. Something was wrong, that much was clear.

"We'll give you some space," Lorrin said, stepping back as she finished getting everything ready. Niles gave her a grin and joined Lorrin off to the side. Zhayra even took a few steps back.

Elinta was infinitely grateful for the space. She loved them all, but right now, she didn't want them crowding over her, not when she had to concentrate. So, after cleaning the wound and chewing more flowers, Elinta redid the stitches that had torn. She'd never had to do them on herself before, and after a moment of trying to wrap her head around the different angle, she set the needle gliding through her skin. Although the flowers dulled some of the pain, it didn't seem to have eased as much as she'd thought it would and sweat beaded on her forehead as she worked. It only took a few minutes to replace the stitches though she had to start a new line due to the tear. When she finished, she covered the wound with the fresh cotton pads, sighing in relief. Thankfully, the weeping had stopped for now. But it was a small comfort when it'd bled so much from the tear.

Then she checked her arm again and changed the bandages.

When she was done, Elinta let her head drop back against the tree. Maybe ... maybe if Zhayra got out of sight and flew above them, she could have a rest here by the side of the road, just for a few minutes. Just until her head felt a little better.

"All done?" Lorrin said, crouching in front of her again.

Elinta nodded, the motion causing the bark to tug at her hair. "Can we just wait a couple of minutes?" Elinta asked, unable to keep the tiredness from her voice.

"Yeah." Lorrin pulled a cloth from her pack and dripped some water on it. He held it out to her. "You're a little dusty."

"Thank you." She smiled and rubbed the cloth over her face and gave it back to him, pointing to the smudge on his own face.

He packed up the supplies she'd left out and while he went to retie her pack to the mare, Zhayra approached her and settled into a crouch in front of her.

"I just want to rest a couple of minutes," Elinta said, not meeting the dragon's gaze. "Can you fly in circles for a little while?"

Zhayra didn't move.

"I don't want anyone to see you," Elinta said, groaning as she straightened herself. "We could be in a lot of trouble."

Zhayra blinked.

"Are you just going to ignore me?" Elinta said, both irritated and touched by the dragon's stubbornness.

Zhayra grunted and lowered her head to the ground.

"Huh," Elinta said, and rubbed the dragon's nose, which was just within her reach.

Elinta closed her eyes and tried not to focus on the pain or the stiffness settling into her back from her fall. She had a feeling Zhayra was thinking that wouldn't have happened if she'd been flying. She sighed and reopened her eyes, mustering her energy. They needed to get moving. It wasn't safe for Zhayra on the road.

"Oi, hang on," Niles called as soon as she started moving. The boys hurried to her side, took an arm each and gently helped her to her feet. Elinta didn't even object when they offered to help her onto the horse.

The rest of the day passed slowly to Elinta. She watched the landscape pass for a while, enjoying the way it changed from small, scraggly brush to grasses and trees. She caught Lorrin glance at her over his shoulder after only a few minutes in the saddle, and she smiled. If he was worried about her falling again, she was sure he'd hear the moment she hit the ground. There wasn't anything graceful about falling from a horse. It wasn't the last time Lorrin or Niles checked on her, and she knew Zhayra watched over her as well, but she didn't have the energy for conversation anymore. Hours before dusk, Lorrin led them off the road to an old campsite. It was earlier than they'd planned to stop, but Elinta was thankful. She unsaddled Ash in a daze, then stumbled away to rest. As soon as she sat down, leaning against Zhayra's chest, she was asleep.

CHAPTER TWO

E LINTA WOKE DRENCHED IN sweat. It was the middle of the night and, as usual, she'd fallen asleep pressed against Zhayra's side. They'd been on the road for five days and had finally reached the base of the Benhurst Ranges. The peaks loomed above her in the silver moonlight, a gentle mist hanging around them.

Elinta ran her hand across her sweaty forehead. It came away soaked. Her heart thundered in her chest and not just from worry. She sat up. A wave of dizziness and pain hit her, forcing her to lie down again. A high-pitched drone sounded in her ears.

"Zhayra," she groaned, but the sound came out little more than a whisper. She poked the dragon's side. "Zhayra."

The dragon grumbled and shifted. Elinta blinked her eyes hard, trying to dispel the dizziness, and prodded the dragon again.

Zhayra's emotions skyrocketed straight to panic as she woke. The dragon's head appeared above her, turned so that one of the amber eyes peered down at her, and grunted.

"Can you wake up the boys?"

The dragon roared. Elinta clapped her hands over her ears.

"What the he—" Niles yelled, and Lorrin loosed some kind of startled shout. She saw a leg fly up in the air from the corner of her eye and wasn't sure who it belonged to.

"Not quite what I had in mind," Elinta said weakly. Her hip and arm throbbed.

Zhayra grumbled, drawing the boys' attention.

"Zhayra?" Lorrin said, hurrying over. His brown hair stuck up at odd angles.

Niles appeared a second after Lorrin, white in the face and sending Zhayra furtive glances. Firelight flickered across their faces.

"What's going on and why did Zhayra just give me the fright of my life?" Niles said, but then he seemed to catch sight of the sweat on Elinta's face. "Oh."

Lorrin reached out and put a hand to her forehead. "You're really hot," he said and scrambled away, returning with a bottle of water.

"How are you feeling?" Lorrin asked, dabbing a wet cloth to her face, careful not to press on her bruised cheek.

"Dizzy," Elinta looked between them, "and it hurts."

Niles glanced at her hip. "Is it infected?"

"No. I don't think so. It doesn't look like it," Elinta said, trying to push herself up to sit against Zhayra, but another wave of dizziness hit her.

"Just lie down," Lorrin said. He put a hand behind her shoulder, helping her back to the ground.

"What's going on?" Elinta mumbled. It felt like an infection, but it couldn't be. Not when the wound looked so clean and *fresh*. She'd never seen anything like this in her time learning from Galen.

"Do you have something in your bag for a fever?" Niles asked.

"Um." Elinta shook her head, trying to think. "The medicine the healer gave me has something in it for infection. It should treat fevers as well." Her words sounded slurred to her ears. She hoped the boys didn't notice.

"But it's not working." Lorrin dabbed at her forehead again.

"No," Elinta agreed. The medicine hadn't been doing anything for the pain either, which was now getting worse rather than better.

Zhayra grumbled, and frustration tinged her worry.

"What can we do?" Lorrin said.

"I don't know." Elinta gasped as the pain increased, threading through her torso and along her arm. "It shouldn't be like this. I don't know how to fix it."

"It's still another two days to Liyarna, isn't it?" Niles asked Lorrin.

The prince dipped his head for a moment, his brow furrowed. Then he looked at her. "Maybe we should head off early. Get a few more hours in. They'd be able to help you there, El."

She nodded, thinking of the scar on her leg. The Asali could heal the cuts Mazen had given her just like they'd healed her in the White Mountains, and she'd feel better. But Elinta dreaded the idea of riding while dizzy and her body ached. Especially for the next two days.

Zhayra grumbled to get their attention, then looked from Elinta to her back.

"I don't think I could stay on, girl," Elinta said, not even thinking about her aversion to flying.

"Maybe you should ride with one of us from now on," Niles said. "You don't want to fall off again."

Elinta sighed and closed her eyes again to her headache. "Yeah, that's probably a good idea."

"Are you up for continuing on now?" Lorrin asked.

Elinta wanted to say no, but she nodded anyway. If the Asali could help her, then they needed to move.

"We'll get the horses ready," Lorrin said, and she heard the boys leave.

A soft rush of warm air played across Elinta's face, and she cracked open her eyes to find herself face-to-face with Zhayra.

"The Asali should be able to help, and if things don't get any worse, I can cope with two more days."

Zhayra wasn't fooled. Elinta knew the dragon felt the fear and helplessness settling in Elinta's stomach. Medicine had never failed her before. Not like this.

Zhayra blinked and gently nudged Elinta's shoulder.

"I'll be OK," she murmured, but she was saying it as much to herself as to the dragon. She stroked Zhayra's cheek.

Lorrin and Niles had to help her up, slipping her arms over their shoulders and grabbing her by the waist as she walked across to Bentley. A groan escaped her lips. They had to help her onto the horse, too. When Lorrin settled in the saddle behind her, she rested against him, unable to keep herself up as her head spun and sweat poured down her face.

"I've got you," Lorrin whispered and pushed Bentley into a trot.

By lunch time, the shivers had set in and Elinta could hardly keep any food down. She struggled to concentrate through the haze that was settling over her. The only thing that registered was the fear and helplessness she and Zhayra seemed to share, and the vague thought that Zhayra somehow understood what was happening to her. The dragon didn't argue when they were ready to set off again, but leapt back into the sky, waiting for them to mount the horses.

Lorrin had to carry Elinta to Niles's horse, and she spent the next few hours pressed against her friend's chest, shivering even as sweat trickled into her eyes and down her face.

"So, what do you think the city looks like?" Niles asked her, voice bouncing in time to Horse's gentle gait.

It took Elinta a moment to realize he'd spoken, and that he was talking about Liyarna. She tried to shake the fog from her mind, but only one thought broke through.

"Bright," she whispered back.

"Bright?" Niles said.

She thought of the way the Asali glowed. Their luminescent skin and shining eyes. *Yes,* she wanted to say, *bright.* But she closed her eyes and drifted off into nothingness.

"Elinta." She focused on the voice, wanting to ignore it but knowing she needed to wake. It was important.

"Elinta."

She groaned, the heaviness of sleep pressing against her.

"Elinta."

Something cold pressed against her face.

"Wake up. You need to drink something."

"Lorrin?" she whispered, fighting to open her eyes. The steady rush of running water sounded nearby. A gentle breeze caressed her face.

"It's me. Come on, have some water."

Cool water trickled over her lips, and she spluttered.

"It's OK," Lorrin said, pouring more into her mouth.

Elinta opened her eyes, squinting against the ache in her head and behind her eyes. Lorrin leaned over her, firelight reflecting in his eyes. *Firelight?* Elinta frowned.

"It's night," she mumbled. A shiver wracked up her spine.

"It's nearly dawn," he said. And it was true. The first streaks of colour lit the sky behind him, framing his face against the sky. "Have some more." He pressed the bottle to her lips again, supporting her head.

"Zhayra?" Elinta asked, after swallowing another mouthful. He lowered her back to the ground.

"She's down by the stream getting a drink."

Elinta smiled. "Did she go willingly?"

Lorrin's lips twitched, and he dabbed at her face again. "It took some convincing."

"I bet."

"We'll reach the Calaza Forest this morning." Lorrin sat back on his heels, looking into the distance as though he could see it in the dim light. "We should be in the city early tomorrow."

Niles appeared over Lorrin's shoulder. "I thought I heard someone talking over here. Why you hogging the lady all to yourself?" he said with a teasing grin and nudged the prince.

Lorrin chuckled. "I need to hoard every second with you around."

"Let it not be said that I got in the way." Niles winked. "But I thought you might like some food." He looked down at Elinta. The concern was clear across his face, but Elinta was thankful for his attempt to lighten the mood.

She shook her head weakly.

Niles's eyebrows rose. "OK, something is definitely wrong here. Lor, she's not hungry!"

Elinta chuckled, aggravating the ache in her head, and moaned.

"You need to eat something," Lorrin said, gently moving a piece of stray hair from her face before dabbing her forehead again. "Just a little bit, then we can get moving."

"OK," she whispered.

The boys propped her up against a saddle and while they packed up the camp, she ate a couple of small bites of bread. When Zhayra finally returned from the river, they were ready to go. The dragon gently nudged Elinta's body, then jumped into the sky.

When they passed under the tall trees of the Calaza, Elinta thought for a moment that she was delirious. Never before had she seen such trees. They stood tall, as if they were towers shooting into the sky. Their silver-white bark was stringy and hung from the trunks like ribbons. In contrast to these were the few trees of the lower canopy and underbrush, the tallest of which were barely two metres high. They had dark brown trunks, smooth and unblemished, the bark wrapped tightly around them. It was a completely different world to the wild forest by Kethmere, yet that one kept a special place in Elinta's heart. The air was cooler in the shade of the trees, but it did nothing to help her.

Zhayra followed above them, her shadow flitting along the ground, broken up by the large leaves of the canopy. Her feelings had shifted as soon as Elinta and the boys had entered the forest. Hope now mingled with her fear. And it gave Elinta hope, too.

The day passed in a confused blur. She shivered and sweated, hardly able to keep her head up for the dizziness assailing her while she rode. The boys continued to swap her between the horses, but always it was Lorrin who carried her and helped her mount.

When dark arrived, they built a small camp at the base of one of the large silver-white trees. Its roots formed a natural hollow that

Lorrin and Niles used for their own beds. Elinta, as usual, was laid beside Zhayra, who rested her head protectively beside her own. Elinta could hardly keep her eyes open as the boys discussed what to do in the morning. She found it hard to concentrate on their words even though they sat beside her to include Zhayra. All she knew was they would arrive in Liyarna tomorrow, and it couldn't come soon enough.

"Come on, let's get you up there," Lorrin grunted as he pushed Elinta onto Bentley before settling behind her. "We're nearly there. Just hold on a little longer," he whispered in her ear.

Elinta didn't have the strength to nod anymore.

"She's worse this morning," Niles said from beside them. He pushed Elinta's blonde hair back from her forehead and pressed his rough hand to her clammy skin.

"We need to get moving." Lorrin's voice reverberated through her back, pressed against his chest. She could feel the steady beat of his heart too. It was a nice sound.

"What was that?" Lorrin asked.

"What?" she rasped.

"You said something. Are you OK?"

Elinta frowned. Had she said something out loud about Lorrin? Or his heart? She blinked her eyes hard, trying to keep herself grounded. Now was not the time to think about Lorrin and how nice it felt to be in his arms.

Lorrin pushed Bentley into a trot and the silver trunks passed by in a blur to Elinta's tired eyes. The sight made her even more dizzy, and bile rose in her throat. With a groan, she closed her eyes to the sight and fought to calm her stomach, taking deep, even breaths.

"Where's Zhayra?" she croaked once her stomach had settled. There was both annoyance and nerves in the dragon. Had she seen her that morning? She couldn't remember.

"Above us. She's going to keep clear until we know Liyarna is safe for her."

Elinta didn't respond, and kept her eyes tightly shut. Her mind was swirling, a mess of confused thoughts and feelings, both her own and the dragon's. It made her head pound even harder. Bile rose in her stomach again and this time she couldn't keep it down.

"Stop," she gasped, just managing to lean in time to avoid vomiting on herself and Lorrin. If not for Lorrin's arms, she would have fallen straight off the horse. He held her up as she gagged, then rightened her in her seat.

"Are you OK?" Lorrin whispered.

Elinta leant heavily against him and didn't respond.

"Here." Niles held a bottle out to her, but she couldn't raise her arm to take it. She was just so tired. So tired. "I've got it." Niles guided Horse closer, then held the bottle to her lips.

Elinta only managed to swallow a mouthful before a shiver wracked her body and the water hit her raw throat, setting her coughing.

"We're not far," Lorrin whispered.

When they moved on, she closed her eyes again and focused on the steady beat of Lorrin's heart. It was the only thing that kept her from thinking of the pain in her body, the ache in her head, and the jolting of the horse that made it all worse. That and Zhayra, who was a constant presence within her.

Seconds seemed to pass in minutes, and hours passed in seconds, and soon she was swapped from Lorrin to Niles. Time continued on until Niles pulled Horse to a halt, and Elinta felt his heart quicken.

She cracked open her eyes, blinked away the sweat, and weakly raised her head enough from Niles's shoulder to see what had caused the boys to stop.

A young man leant against one of the silver-white trees, a piece of paper in one hand and a pencil in the other, but when his dark grey eyes looked up, he stopped writing. His skin glowed, even under the white shirt he wore, and his pants hung down to his ankles. Elinta's eyes landed on his feet, bare and luminous. A delirious giggle rose in her throat, and she swallowed heavily. A circlet of *illayas* wrapped around his right wrist. The man swept his shoulder-length hair from his face and pushed off from the tree.

"*Zruh nai ris?*"

CHAPTER THREE

E LINTA'S EYES IMMEDIATELY GREW heavy, but she could already hardly keep them open, and her head dropped back against Niles again. Zhayra's stomach tightened, but the dragon stayed out of view even as the Asali before them turned to face them front on.

"Lorrin?" Niles said quietly from behind her. Elinta's ears popped.

The prince cleared his throat. "*Ra ayn nai* Lorrin. *Rilan ayn nai* Niles *punnahs* Elinta." Lorrin paused and from the corner of her eyes, she caught him point at her. The desperation was clear in his voice as he said, "*Lira tai.*"

Dimly, Elinta recognised a few of the words from her lessons, but she couldn't force her mind to translate them. But she liked the way they sounded in his mouth.

The man looked between them, but when his eyes landed on her, something in his manner shifted. Another shiver wracked her body, and she closed her eyes, her breath stuttering.

"What's wrong with her?" the man said, using the common tongue.

"She was cut by an *illayas* blade. The wounds won't heal," Lorrin called, the loud sound sending a stab through Elinta's aching mind and causing her to flinch.

"It is not the *illayas* doing this to her," the man replied after a pause. "How old are the wounds?"

"Just over a week."

Horse shifted under them, Elinta's body swayed with the movements and Niles's arms tightened around her. There was a pause and then the man spoke again from beside her.

"Open your eyes."

Elinta forced her eyes to crack open. The Asali stood beside Horse, his glowing eyes fixed on her.

"I know your dragon uses your eyes, *Zearla lurai*. And no doubt your ears." He stepped closer, looking deep into Elinta's eyes. "There is a field in the city where you may land. We will not be long."

Elinta shivered again and watched as sweat dripped from her nose. *How can he tell? How does he know about Zhayra?* But more importantly, why did he think Zhayra could see and hear him through her? An image of Mazen appeared before her. He'd known about Zhayra too. Were these men in league together? They seemed about the same age, physically.

"Can you help her?" Niles said, his voice tight with worry.

Elinta wanted to tell him not to trust this man, but the words failed her.

"Not without my kin. But I can help you get her to them." The young man looked between the three of them before his eyes landed on her again. "I am Tamir Aylan."

The man settled his hand upon Elinta's knee, and the glow of his skin increased until it shone so brightly that it hurt her sensitive eyes. Niles jerked behind her at the sight, jostling her before steadying himself. Elinta closed her eyes to the brilliant shine, but the light shone through her lids. A gentle warmth, starting from under Tamir's hand, spread through Elinta's body, ebbing and flowing like a wave, and soothed the pain raging through her. The shivers died back. It wasn't by much, but the relief of even that unclenched her aching muscles. The warmth continued.

"We're still an hour from Liyarna. Hopefully, this will be enough."

"Thank you," Elinta breathed, eyes still closed. If this man was with Mazen, then she didn't care.

"Keep your eyes open," Tamir said. When Elinta frowned, he said, "I know it's bright, but keep them open."

Elinta peeled her eyes open again and turned her head, still against Niles's shoulder, away from the white light.

"I will lead you to the city," the Asali said, tucking his paper into the pocket of his pants. Niles and Lorrin urged the horses into a gentle walk, Tamir easily staying alongside her to maintain contact. The shine of his skin didn't fade or ebb as they walked on, and the warmth continued to pulse through her. But as the time passed, the pain grew again, and the warmth seemed to recede though Tamir's glow never faded.

Zhayra's worry returned full force to the forefront of Elinta's mind, even as the tremors began in her body once more. Elinta groaned as her whole body shook.

"She's getting worse. What's happening?" Lorrin asked, his voice tight with worry.

"My healing isn't enough," Tamir said from her other side. "As her condition progresses, my healing will do less for her."

Elinta shivered again and closed her eyes to the dizziness assailing her. Her mind continued to swirl.

"She'll make it though, right?" Niles said in her ear.

Tamir didn't respond, at least verbally, but Elinta hardly listened. Her thoughts were foggy, fading. Shivers ran up her spine again.

Tamir gently shook her leg. "Open your eyes, Elinta."

She tried. She did. But her eyes were too heavy. Her energy was gone. She couldn't.

"El?" The voice was faint.

Who's talking?

"We're nearly there."

She could no longer feel any warmth from the hand on her leg. She could no longer feel anything but the pain. There was a droning in her ears. She shivered and she sweated and that was all that was left. Then it was just the blackness, and it swallowed her.

CHAPTER FOUR

E LINTA'S HEAD ACHED. THAT was the first thing she noticed, but then she realised that nothing else hurt. Her hip
felt fine. So did her arm and her muscles. They all felt ... normal
though they'd been screaming just before. *Before?* Her memories
came rushing back. At the same time, Zhayra's stomach jumped
in excitement and an echoing roar carried through the air. Elinta's
eyes snapped open, and she bolted upright.

"Woah, that is so weird how she can do that!"

Elinta turned to find Niles and Lorrin standing beside her bed.
Two empty wooden chairs were behind them.

"Zhayra knew the second you woke up, didn't she?" Niles continued, sitting on the bed beside her.

"Are we in Liyarna?" Elinta asked, letting her eyes trail around the room they were in. It was beautiful. Constructed from the wood of the silver-white trees of the forest, the walls ran up to a curved ceiling, giving the room the feeling of a large pod. Delicate circular lanterns hung from hooks on the ceiling, casting them in a gentle glow. Hers was the only bed in the room, made from a brown wood that contrasted the light walls around her.

"It that a tree?" Elinta said as her eyes landed on a thick trunk that made up part of the wall to her left. The trunk ran up to the ceiling where it looked as though it continued through to the outside of the building. In fact, looking around again, Elinta saw another two trunks built into the walls. It was an odd look; the trunks were out of place with the design of the rest of the wall.

"How are you feeling?" Lorrin asked, drawing Elinta's attention back to the boys. They were in fresh clothes (Niles in his guard's uniform) though their hair was rumpled and their faces creased with concern. They both still had a light layer of stubble on their faces.

She didn't even need to consider his question. "Fine. My head's a little sore, but I feel fine otherwise."

Lorrin's shoulders physically slumped in relief and Niles grinned, pulling the scar on his lip tight.

"How great is this place?" Niles said, scanning the room.

"It's beautiful. How long have I been asleep?" Elinta asked, running a hand over the soft blanket still covering her legs. As she did, she spotted a new scar on her arm. The cut that Mazen had given her, now healed. Even though her leg had been healed by the Asali before, the sight of the new scar filled her with wonder.

"A couple of hours," a familiar voice said. The Asali from the forest, Tamir, appeared in the open door to the room. A larger room stretched away behind him.

"Hours?" Elinta frowned. She felt as though she'd been sleeping for days. The vague quality of her memories of the morning and the Asali did little to convince her otherwise. She almost felt like she needed to introduce herself to the man again. But he didn't seem to feel the same way.

"Yes," Tamir said, stepping into the room. His glow added to the light shining from the lanterns. "How is your head?"

"Sore," Elinta admitted. She looked curiously at the Asali, now able to see him properly. His brown hair was parted to the side and fell around his shoulders. Standing near the boys revealed Tamir to be shorter than them both ... and his feet were still bare. She hadn't imagined that. He did look to be in his mid-twenties though it likely wasn't his actual age.

Tamir nodded, unaware of her studying gaze. "That is to be expected. You will likely feel tired throughout the day. Dragon-blood poisoning is difficult to heal and takes a lot from the body."

"Wait." Elinta frowned. "Dragon-blood poisoning?"

Lorrin and Niles exchanged a glance, but Tamir spoke before either of them could. "It was only a small dose, but still, you are lucky to be alive."

It had been so much like an infection, yet not. But Elinta's mind was racing now. Dragon blood did this to her?

"But that doesn't make sense," Elinta said.

Tamir's eyebrows rose in question. Niles shifted on the edge of the bed, and Lorrin glanced curiously at her.

"I've had Zhayra's blood on my hands before," she said, recalling the day she'd found the dragon. She'd treated Zhayra's wings for wounds caused in her crash landing. "And I didn't see—" She cut herself off. The fight against Mazen had been a blur right from the second he'd drawn his weapon. It had been late at night and the corridors were dim, and Mazen had moved like lightning.

She wouldn't have known if there had been some blood on his weapon. Especially if it had only been a light layer.

Tamir waited for her to continue, but when it became clear she wasn't going to say anymore, he spoke. "The blood must enter your system. In this case, it was on the blade of your enemy. Did you have any cuts on your hands when they were covered with Zhayra's blood?" Tamir asked curiously.

Elinta tried to think back to that day. She didn't think she'd had any cuts on her hand at the time. But then, she'd cut her finger later when cutting up the fungi she'd fetched for Galen that day. How close had she come to poisoning herself without realising it?

Elinta finally shook her head.

Tamir nodded. "You must be careful when Zhayra bleeds, for your own life may be at risk. It took three of my people to heal you, even for such a small dose."

"But she's OK now?" Lorrin interrupted.

"Yes. Though she may want to rest for the remainder of the day."

"No," Elinta said. "We need to see the council."

"El," Niles said, "we can wait until tomorrow if you need to rest."

"No, I'm OK. Really. We came here to talk to the council, and we should." She had to ask them about Mazen. And where had he gotten dragon blood from? She paled at the very idea of him having more.

Lorrin watched her for a moment before nodding. "Could you take us to the council?" he said to Tamir. She just hoped the prince was ready too.

"I've already informed them that you wished to speak with them. Though they are expecting you tomorrow, I'm sure they will be happy to hear from you now," Tamir said, more to Elinta than to Lorrin.

"Thank you," she said as a rush of nerves hit her. Finally, they could speak to the Asali about all that had happened, and Lorrin could convince them to make another treaty.

"All right!" Niles said, jumping to his feet.

"I will wait for you." Tamir stepped out of the room.

But Elinta turned to Lorrin, distracted for the moment. "Is Zhayra OK?" she asked, still feeling the dragon's excitement. Was she at the field Tamir had mentioned earlier in the forest?

"She's been worried," Lorrin said, then, as though sensing what had crossed her mind, he continued. "You know she'll understand if we see the council first."

"Yeah." Zhayra would, though Elinta wished she'd thought to ask to see the dragon.

"We can wait—" Lorrin started, but Elinta was already climbing out of the bed. Admittedly, she had a different sense of privacy to others because of her time learning to be a healer. She had expected to be in the clothes she'd been wearing that morning though, but instead found herself in a fresh pair. Elinta smoothed out the wrinkles and ran her hand through her hair. Perhaps she should have asked for a few minutes to tidy up before going in front of the council. Her eyes landed on the mirror standing by the door.

"You look fine," Lorrin said, his eyes soft as he stared at her face. It was almost as though he was drinking in the sight of her. She looked away, feeling like she was intruding on something he didn't mean her to see, and fidgeted with her shirt.

"Well, except for that bit sticking out there," Niles said, pointing to a whisp by her ear. She batted his hand away and smoothed it out.

"Let's go," she said, grabbing her sword from beside her bed and strapping it to her hip as she followed after Tamir. He was waiting for them in the larger room that she'd seen from her bed. Three other doors led from it. The room had a similar design to the one she'd just left; but cushioned chairs decorated the same silver-white wood floor and curved ceiling instead of a bed. A table sat off to the side.

Tamir immediately set off as soon as the boys joined them. They walked through one of the three doors and emerged into the forest city. Elinta's jaw dropped.

The Green City. It really was the perfect description. The Asali had built the city around the forest, incorporating the trees into the architecture and the architecture into the trees. She twisted to look back at the building they'd left and counted a total of seven trees coming through different parts of the building and disappearing into the canopy above. The trunks in the wall of her room really were real trees. *How is that possible?*

Several small white and blue birds squawked at them from the tops of the trees even as they chewed on the bark of a branch.

"Come," Tamir said, shaking her from her reverie. She hadn't noticed she'd stopped walking.

"It's amazing," she said, hurrying after him. Lorrin and Niles seemed to agree, for they looked around with the same amazement as Elinta.

Tamir smiled. "I'm glad you like it."

Lorrin's eyes shone brightly as he took in the city. The more they walked, the more it all stunned Elinta, and her feet lagged again as she tried to see it all.

A small hut sat tucked between two trees to her right, the roots of the trees forming the lower half of the side walls. A platform with an elegant railing around it stretched between the two trunks several metres above the hut. From the ground, Elinta could just make out a small bed upon it. A cluster of silver and green butterflies had settled on the railing.

To her left was a large building with engravings she couldn't quite make out around the open entryway and beautifully designed to incorporate over a dozen of the massive, silver trees.

The leaves on their lower branches were like a decoration for the roof. Everywhere she looked was the same basic design. It was as though the Asali had never knocked down a tree for space. It made her wonder where the materials came from. How or where they sourced it. But the thought was gone within seconds, chased away by the wonder of the city and the wildlife and people that inhabited it.

There were Asali all around her. Some walked between buildings and along the pathways winding among the trees. Others were inside buildings, some of which had no doors, and turned curiously as her little group passed. A bird flew inside one of the homes, but the Asali didn't react at all to the intruder. Some of the Asali stared at Elinta's group, frowns creasing their brows. It struck her that, just like in the White Mountains, all the Asali around her had white, grey, or silver irises. None of them had any other colour. There certainly weren't any with maroon eyes. So how come Mazen was so different from the rest of his people?

"So where does a guy have to go to get a bite to eat?" Niles asked, hurrying forward to speak to Tamir.

"Niles!" Elinta hushed, but her stomach betrayed her with a grumble.

The Asali smiled. "I'll have some food brought to you once you've seen the council."

"What can you tell us about the council?" Lorrin asked, pulling Niles away from Tamir.

"It is better for you to see them for yourself." Tamir spoke to them over his shoulder. "Piran, Nakiah, and Aisla will hear whatever it is you wish to say but know that they have ruled since King Riah died. They seek to do what is best for our people."

Elinta didn't respond. The three council members had been in charge for a hundred and seventy years! What were they going to say to them? She'd thought about it during all those weeks of waiting at the palace in Nevira, but she hadn't rehearsed anything specific. Now she wished they'd had a whole speech written. Perhaps they would have planned something if she hadn't gotten ill on their trip. But Lorrin had to speak with the council too, so maybe she wouldn't have to say much. She hoped she wouldn't have to say much.

She ran over in her mind what they needed to tell the council. Luckily, it all boiled down to three things: Mazen, Zhayra, and a treaty. It was just that there was so much wrapped up in it all.

Lorrin reached out and squeezed her hand. "It'll be all right."

She smiled nervously and part of her wished that he wouldn't let go, but he gently dropped her hand.

Elinta's eyes grew heavy as they walked, and she frowned. The feeling tugged at a vague memory from their journey through the forest. *Is this what Tamir meant? What was it he said ... Zhayra can use my eyes? And my ears?* She focused in on what Zhayra was feeling, wondering if it would reveal that the dragon was seeing through her. The idea was strange, yet slightly comforting. Though they weren't together, Zhayra could still be involved and know what was happening. She wondered how many times the dragon had done it before. She was sure she'd felt this in her eyes several times, but she had never realised what it was. Or that it *was* something.

"It is just up ahead," Tamir said.

They rounded a large building wrapped around half a dozen trees, and the area naturally opened up, revealing a large, grey-stoned table with three stools seated along the length of it. Elinta hardly registered the people sitting at the table. Her eyes were drawn behind them, to what could only be described as netting. Vines and tree branches wove together like a screen, stretching across the space between three massive trunks of the silver white trees. White, pink, and yellow flowers grew along the green vines. The colours suited each other perfectly and only made the scene even more beautiful. Bees lazily flew between the flowers. Their soft buzzing floated through the air.

"Piran, Aisla, Nakiah," Tamir said, drawing Elinta's attention back to the three figures seated at the table. A jolt of nerves went through her stomach. "This is Elinta," he said, motioning for her to step forward. When she did, he continued, "With her are Prince Lorrin and Niles."

"*Layzun* Elinta, Prince Lorrin, and Niles. We welcome you to Liyarna," the man on the stool to the far right said in a deep booming voice. He had long, grey hair pulled back into a ponytail, but it looked long enough to reach his elbows when loose. The three members of the council looked at Elinta expectantly, and Lorrin gently nudged her.

Elinta hesitantly cleared her throat. "*Layzun*," she said, repeating the man's welcome, keeping the polite form.

"You've travelled a long way, *Zearla lurai*, and arrived near death. What is it you wish to discuss with the council?" the woman said. Her bright eyes were locked on Elinta with open curiosity and something like respect. Elinta shifted uncomfortably, unsure why the woman should look at her that way.

Elinta turned to Lorrin, nodding to signal her handover to him. Lorrin stepped forward, not a sign of nerves on him, Elinta noticed jealously. But as he opened his mouth, the woman raised her hand to stop him.

"Whilst you are welcome with the *Zearla lurai*, prince, we were told it was she who wished to speak with us. We will hear only from her."

Elinta blanched, shooting Lorrin a panicked glance. Lorrin recovered his composure first, only a hint of shock flickering across his face, before turning to Elinta. He squared his shoulders and nodded.

No, no, no. She stared at him with wide eyes, twisting, when he joined her, to put her back to the council.

"You can do this," he murmured.

Elinta didn't move. She wasn't supposed to be leading the whole meeting. Maybe she'd ask a question or two, but Lorrin was going to handle most of it. He probably would've even asked the things she would have.

Lorrin gently turned her around and pushed her in front of him, whispering in her ear as he did, "You *can* do this."

Elinta looked up at the council. All their eyes were on her. She swallowed nervously and cleared her throat. Then swallowed again. Sending mental daggers at the council woman for making her take over, she forced her brain to kick back into gear. This was their chance, and she couldn't let it go to waste.

"Well, there are a few things that need to be brought to the council's attention," Elinta said, wondering how to begin the tale she now had to tell. It seemed that all the Asali were somehow aware of her bond with Zhayra, something she'd have to ask about later, which meant she only needed to tell them about Mazen, and then bring up the subject of a new treaty. Although, she was sure they'd want to know how Zhayra had come to be in Eldras and how they'd met ... maybe she could avoid that. It would surely anger the council. She rubbed her sweaty palms on her pants.

The Asali on the far right nodded and gestured for her to continue. But before she could, a loud sound of the beating of large wings and rushing wind spilt through the air. A flock of birds rose squawking angrily from the trees behind them and disappeared over the city. The group looked up in time to see Zhayra appear in the opening in the canopy above them; the sun shining brightly off her scales. She flapped her wings twice to slow her descent and landed gracefully behind Lorrin and Niles. The netting behind the council table swayed.

The three council member's faces broke into large smiles that mirrored Elinta's, and it gave her hope. It was one less barrier than she had with the human royals.

"Welcome, dragon," the woman, Aisla, said, with a slight nod.

"This is Zhayra," Tamir said, a smile lighting up his already glowing face. Elinta wondered whether he had met the dragon while she'd been unconscious.

"We had not expected you to join us in the flesh since you may use Elinta's eyes," the man on the right said, "but you are welcome here."

Zhayra rumbled in response, and Elinta looked back at the dragon, wanting to cross the distance between them and hug her. But their reunion would have to wait.

"Please continue, *Zearla lurai*," Aisla said.

Elinta regathered her thoughts and picked up from where she'd been before Zhayra had arrived. "The first is the reason why I arrived in the condition I was in," Elinta said, shuddering at the memory of the fogginess that had captured her. "Just over a week ago, I was attacked in the Neviran Palace by an Asali of Liyarna named Mazen."

Tamir visibly jolted at the name and the colour drained from his face as he turned wide eyes on her.

"Impossible. Prince Mazen is dead," Aisla said, her eyes narrowing.

"Prince?" Elinta asked, sharing a shocked glance with Lorrin and Niles. Mazen was a *prince?*

The man on the far left—the youngest of the three—spoke for the first time. His brown hair fell over his forehead. His high voice seemed to float through the air. "Whoever attacked you must have been an imposter."

"Nevertheless, Nakiah, we should hear her tale," the other man, Piran she assumed, said. His eyes were even darker than Tamir's, and his grey hair swung behind him as he looked between her and the man.

Nakiah nodded and gestured for her to continue. When he did, Elinta saw an *illayas* bracelet on his wrist, similar to Tamir's.

What does that mean? she wondered absently, but her brain was stuck on the thought that Mazen might be royalty. They *were* thinking of the right person?

"Please continue, *Zearla lurai,*" Nakiah said.

Elinta launched into the story of her encounter with Mazen, repeating their conversation as best she could and including everything that she hadn't told Lorrin's parents and their advisors. Lorrin and Niles stood quietly beside her, prompting her whenever she forgot a detail. She was glad to have them with her. Even though they hadn't heard everything that Mazen had said to her the night of the Eggslaying, she had repeated it to them that same night. Except for the Asalin Mazen had spoken, which she couldn't remember anyway, she told them everything. As she spoke, the three council members' faces darkened, and Nakiah's brow deepened in confusion. When she finally reached the end of her tale, silence descended on the group.

"It is strange this imposter should have access to dragon blood," Nakiah said, looking at Elinta thoughtfully.

"He must have stolen it, just like the scales in his armour," Piran mused, rubbing at invisible stubble on his face.

With nothing more to add, Elinta watched the conversation curiously.

"But where from?" Nakiah said.

"Unless ..." Tamir spoke up, his voice sounding strained. The group turned their eyes to him as one.

"Go on, Tamir," Aisla said. "Though I know what you would say."

"Unless it really is Prince Mazen."

"Impossible," Nakiah said, his hands closing into fists on the smooth table. "The prince died over a hundred and fifty years ago."

Tamir shook his head. "So we thought."

"I'm sorry," Elinta interrupted, and the council members looked at her as though they'd forgotten she was there. Their renewed attention gave her pause, but she plunged ahead. "But I'm more concerned about what he's *doing* than who he is at the moment."

"Yes, very good," Nakiah said, straightening. "Whoever this man is, we do not support him or his actions."

The other council members nodded.

Seconds stretched by and the three looked at her expectantly. Niles broke the silence.

"That's it?"

"What else is there?" Aisla said slowly, as though drawing herself out of deep thought. "This 'Mazen' is not one of us, nor are we responsible for his actions."

"But he's Asali," Elinta said, frowning. This man was trying to kill her, Zhayra, and the human prince and they didn't care. "Shouldn't you be stopping him?"

"Eldras is a big country, *Zearla lurai*. We don't have the resources to track down a single Asali living in exile from his people," Piran said, then seeing her about to speak, he continued. "We condemn the attempt on your life and the prince's, but our people are not allied. We do not owe you our support or protection."

Elinta's frustration flared at the exact moment that a low growl escaped from Zhayra.

"He tried to kill us," Elinta said through gritted teeth. She took a deep breath, then continued. "This man is dangerous. The king and queen think that you are behind his actions. What he's doing is preventing all hope of a future treaty from being brokered."

"Hope?" Aisla frowned. "There is no hope."

"But—"

"Tell us, Elinta, does the prince's family know about Zhayra?" Nakiah said, his high voice turning harsh. A lock of his brown hair had fallen over his left eye, but he made no attempt to move it.

Elinta shook her head, her thoughts shooting back to Mazen and his similar question about Lorrin.

Nakiah nodded. "And why not? For the same reason we will not restore the treaty. Your people still wish to kill the dragons. A whole race of beings!"

"But that could change," Elinta said. She saw Lorrin step forward from the corner of her eye, but the council didn't let him speak.

"What guarantee is there that your people would not hurt the dragons again, *Zearla lurai?*" Piran said quietly. "There is none, and there will never be. After nearly two hundred years since driving them away, the humans' fervour hasn't decreased. You have not told us about the exact circumstances around your *ngaran* with Zhayra, but it is clear that your people have caused you pain."

"The Eggslaying would never happen again," Lorrin said in a low voice that seemed to surprise the council.

"Though your own change of conscious is a welcome surprise, you cannot guarantee the same changes in your people, prince." Aisla shook her head. "We are sorry, but there can be no friendship between our people."

"But—"

"No," Aisla said, cutting across him. "This is final."

Elinta's heart sunk. They'd wasted so much time in planning and getting to Liyarna, and it had all been for nothing. And what about Mazen? What would happen now? For a moment, she felt like she was floundering. All their goals, all their plans, had hinged on this.

"You and your friends are welcome to stay in Liyarna until you are well, *Zearla lurai,* though it is better that you do not go anywhere unattended," Aisla said in a placating tone as though this would ease their disappointment.

Elinta didn't look at Lorrin's or Niles's face, but she knew they would be as dejected as hers, if not more for Lorrin. He'd been trying to restore the treaty for longer than she had. And it was over.

"Everyone here will speak your tongue when addressing you," Piran was saying, "though there may be some that do not give the same courtesy to your companions."

"Why?" Elinta asked, exchanging a glance with Lorrin. He looked as though he was still ready to argue.

"You are *Zearla lurai*. They are not," Nakiah said as though this explained it, and cutting across Piran.

Piran glared warningly at Nakiah. "Your people bear the blame for the loss of the dragons, as would you if not for Zhayra."

"Oh."

"If it is alright with him, Tamir will continue to look after you whilst you are here," Piran said.

Tamir gave the council a shallow nod before turning. "Come, let's find you some food."

It seemed they'd been dismissed.

CHAPTER
FIVE

E LINTA TRUDGED OVER TO Zhayra. "I'll come to see you soon," she said, trying to hide the disappointment in her voice from the others. The dragon gently nudged her and shot back into the air to return to the field.

Their small group left the council behind them in silence. The beauty seemed to have left the clearing. The members' low voices drifted after them. Tamir seemed lost in thought as he led them away, and Niles and Lorrin spoke quietly to each other as they passed back out into the city. But despite the council's decision, Elinta had too many questions that still needed answering. She quickened her pace to catch up with the Asali.

"Tamir?" she asked hesitantly.

He looked up, his expression clearing as he saw it was her.

"Yes, *Zearla lurai?*"

She'd been going to ask him more about the council, but at the use of the term, she changed her mind. "What is *Zearla lurai?*"

Tamir smiled, tucking his hair behind his ear. "Do you understand any of our language?"

"A little," she said. "I know it translates to dragon friend. But where did it come from?"

Tamir nodded. "Dragon friend is the literal translation," he said, "but its meaning is closer to dragon kin."

"Dragon kin?" Elinta said.

"Yes. The bond allows for a relationship that is deeper than what you might have with another human or an Asali. It is closer to what the dragon's experience with each other, with their kin."

"And *ngaran?*" she asked, thinking of the word she and Lorrin had first seen in the scroll Ford had lent her some weeks ago.

"It means bond."

Elinta nodded, glad the man was giving her some clear answers. The last Asali she'd asked about the term had said it wasn't his place to tell her about the bond. Ciar had been a great help to her in the White Mountains, but he hadn't told her all she'd needed to know. He'd hardly told her anything.

"So, this bond was made by Zhayra?" she asked.

"Yes."

Elinta fell into silence, mulling over her bond with the dragon as they walked through the city. It was then, seeing so many Asali, that one of her earlier questions returned to her.

"Tamir," she said.

"Yes?" he said, without any hint of impatience.

"Why do all your people have white eyes? Irises, I mean."

"It is how we are. Why are yours coloured?" Tamir shrugged.

"No," she said, thinking back to the night of the Eggslaying festival. "I mean, everyone here and at the White Mountains has white, grey or silver, but Mazen's were maroon."

Tamir stopped dead in his tracks and Niles nearly walked into him, jolting to a stop only a hairsbreadth from his back.

"What?" Elinta asked, seeing the look of shock on his face.

"Maroon?" he whispered.

"Yes."

"Come with me," he said and without a backward glance, he turned and broke into a run.

Elinta exchanged a puzzled look with Lorrin and Niles before chasing after the Asali, having to sprint to keep up with him.

A moment later, they were back in front of the council's table and looking up into the confused faces of Piran, Nakiah, and Aisla. But when the three members saw Tamir's face, their expressions shifted to concern.

"What is it, Tamir?" Aisla said.

"It's him," he said, his voice surprisingly steady after the run back to the council. "The man that attacked Elinta *is* Prince Mazen. Beyond any doubt."

Piran's mouth opened slightly in surprise.

"How can you be sure?" Nakiah said, his voice full of scepticism.

"He had maroon eyes," Tamir said as though this explained everything, and apparently, it did, because Nakiah's doubt disappeared at once. The man ran a hand over his face.

"What has he been doing all this time?" Aisla said in wonder.

"Wait," Elinta said, so lost that for a moment she forgot she was interrupting the most important people in the city. "Why does it matter that his eyes were maroon? This man could be anyone, like you said."

The four Asali looked at her in surprise.

"Vaherin was maroon," Tamir said.

"Vaherin?"

"His dragon, child," Nakiah said.

Elinta heard two sharp intakes of breath from behind her.

"Dragon?" Elinta said, stunned. Mazen ... Mazen was *Zearla lurai*? "He ..." He couldn't be.

The council were talking but she cut across them again, vaguely wondering at how far she'd come that she could do so without cringing. "Why would a *prince*—a *Zearla lurai*—try to kill me and Zhayra?"

"That," Ailsa said, with a deep frown, "is a very good question. You are sure he wanted to kill Zhayra?"

Elinta's eyebrows rose, and she nodded. Silence descended over the clearing. The warmth of the sun seemed to have disappeared from the air, and she shivered. Even the bees seemed to have gone quiet.

"Why did he leave?" Elinta asked.

Tamir shook his head. "We thought he was dead."

"But ..." She thought back to the night she'd seen Mazen. How had he become like that? What had driven him, a prince and a fellow *Zearla lurai*, to hunt a dragon? And *where* was his dragon? She looked back at the council. "And Vaherin? What happened to him? I didn't see him in Nevira the night Mazen was there."

"We assumed he would have left with the rest of the dragons. After all, it was only days, the day," Piran corrected himself, "after the Eggslaying that Prince Mazen disappeared. But if Mazen is alive, and Vaherin is too, they will still be together." He stroked his chin.

"What does this mean for us now?" Lorrin said, finally stepping forward.

Nakiah frowned, but Piran spoke first, directing his response to Elinta. "You've given us a lot to think about. Please, why don't you give us some time to discuss this matter, and we will speak with you again tomorrow."

Nakiah and Aisla both nodded. Tamir didn't move.

"Tamir?" Aisla said, her voice soft.

He shook himself and looked at the council and then at Elinta. "My apologies. Let's go."

Once again, Tamir led the three of them away from the council and the clearing. But this time, Lorrin and Niles walked closely behind Elinta and Tamir.

Elinta was loath to ask Tamir more questions, especially as he seemed lost in thought and—Elinta looked a little closer at him—he seemed slightly pale. But she was desperate to know why Mazen's eye colour mattered so much. And why they matched Vaherin's scales.

"Tamir?" she asked.

"Hmm?" He focused on her. "Sorry, *Zearla lurai*, what is it?"

"Why are Mazen's eyes maroon? What does that have to do with Vaherin?"

"It is a part of the *ngaran*," Tamir said, pushing the hair back from his face. "The eyes of the Asali, or human, change to resemble the dragon they share the *ngaran* with. In Mazen's case, his irises are maroon, like Vaherin's scales. Perhaps you noticed that his pupils were not the usual ovular of the Asali as well? That they resembled a dragon's?"

Elinta gasped, remembering Mazen's strange eyes. He was right.

"Does that mean ... does that mean my eyes will be like that one day?"

Tamir nodded. "Though they will be white, like Zhayra."

"Wow," Niles said. It was the first thing he's said in quite some time.

Tamir frowned. "Didn't you know how I knew you were *Zearla lurai* earlier today in the forest?"

"No," Elinta said. "What do you mean?"

Tamir stopped and looked her full in the face. "Your eyes are already beginning to change."

"What?"

"They are?" Niles said, leaning in from her left and peering into her eyes. Lorrin pulled him away.

"Yes, though it is hard to see unless you know what you are looking for. The change is more apparent when Zhayra uses your eyes at the moment. But I doubt that a human would perceive any of these changes yet."

They continued walking in silence. Elinta hardly saw the city around her. Her eyes were going to change? Strangely, her first thoughts were of her brother and her father. What would they think? It was easy for her to guess her father's reaction, but Blaine? He'd seemed OK with her leaving Kethmere with Zhayra, but what would he think of her if her pupils changed to slits and her irises were white like an Asali's?

Elinta shook her head. She'd probably never know what Blaine would think. She'd probably never see him again. Her hope of fixing things for Zhayra and the dragons was evaporating fast and with it her hopes of being accepted at home. And even if she could go home, if she was being honest with herself, she wasn't sure she wanted to if it meant that Zhayra couldn't be with her.

"Here we are. I will have some food brought to you," Tamir said. Elinta looked up in surprise to find they'd already arrived at the building she'd woken in. "I have some work to attend to for the moment, but I will be back soon."

"Thank you," Elinta said. Lorrin and Niles ducked inside ahead of her, but Elinta still stood beside Tamir. "Where's Zhayra staying?"

Tamir pointed to their right. "The training field is down there. You'll see it after a hundred metres or so." He smiled. "Zhayra is welcome in the rest of the city. Wherever she can fit."

"I'll let her know," Elinta said, wondering whether the dragon would explore the city. Maybe they could do it together, but she was conscious of Aisla's advice not to go anywhere alone.

Seeing Tamir was ready to leave, Elinta hurried to finish. "Can I ask you more questions later, Tamir?"

"Of course, *Zearla lurai*," he said.

She felt his grey eyes watching her as she followed Lorrin and Niles inside, mind heavy with revelations.

CHAPTER
SIX

O VER THEIR LATE LUNCH, Elinta, Lorrin, and Niles discussed everything they'd seen and heard at the council's table. A man brought them some grain salad and meat belonging to a kind of bird to share and set it on the engraved table in the main room of their quarters. Surprisingly, Niles even contributed to the conversation, his love of food overshadowed by the need to process.

"I can't believe they won't help us stop Mazen!" Niles said, forcefully cutting into his meat.

"But they might now," Elinta said, looking between the boys. "Now that they think he's their prince."

"I can't believe he's royalty," Lorrin murmured. "I knew King Riah had a son ... but Mazen? That man was mad."

"Makes a guy wonder what else we don't know about," Niles said.

Elinta nodded, but at the mention of Mazen, her thoughts had turned to his eyes and then to her own. How had her eyes already changed? Had Tamir noticed her pupils weren't so circular anymore? Or were her irises lighter? How long before they turned from brown to white? She wanted to stand in front of a mirror and examine her eyes.

Elinta looked between Lorrin and Niles. Neither seemed concerned by the revelation that her eyes would change. In fact, compared to the knowledge that a dragon accompanied Mazen, the idea wasn't as much of a concern to her as she felt it should be. If anything, she felt more curious than worried.

Lorrin chewed thoughtfully at his food. "What about Vaherin? Did Mazen say anything that would have hinted at the dragon?"

Elinta shook her head. "No. He seemed alone."

She would have picked up on any hint of another dragon, especially if it meant it was with the man trying to kill her and the people she loved. She counted Zhayra as a person, of course.

"The dragon must have been with him, though," Lorrin said, frowning at his food. "How else did he get out of the palace so quickly?"

The idea of the other dragon being so close to her and Zhayra sent shivers down her spine, but Lorrin was right. Vaherin had to have been there. And if Vaherin was still with Mazen, he wasn't someone she ever wanted to meet. What would have happened if the dragon had found Zhayra? She shoved the thought away when Zhayra seemed to respond to the clenching in her gut.

Elinta sighed and spooned some more of the salad into her mouth. A sudden tiredness hit her, but it wasn't from her wounds. All this thinking, all the time in her own head, was exhausting. But there was so much to process.

"Are you feeling any better?" Lorrin asked, noticing her quietness. Niles looked up from his food to study her face.

"Yeah," Elinta said, "my head's a little sore still, but it's fine." In fact, the previous two hours had driven away all thought of her headache. Besides, it was nothing a good sleep or some camomile or mint tea couldn't fix. If she could find any here.

"Tamir said it should clear up soon," Lorrin said.

"Did you learn anything about him while I was sleeping?" Elinta asked, thinking of her first sight of the Asali. What had he been taking notes of out in the forest?

"Not really." Niles shrugged. "He's some kind of academic, I think."

Lorrin nodded thoughtfully. "The council seem to value his opinion."

"He looked really shocked when he heard Mazen's name," Elinta said.

"Wouldn't you be, though?" Niles said through a mouthful of food. "If I thought Lorrin was dead for nearly two hundred years, I'd be a bit surprised too."

"Only I *would* be dead after two hundred years."

"Technicality," Niles said, waving away the comment.

Elinta sat back in her chair and listened to the two boys discussing Mazen. Now that she'd processed everything, she found her thoughts turning more and more toward Zhayra, who grew increasingly more impatient with every passing second.

"I'm going to go see Zhayra," Elinta said, dropping her fork and jumping to her feet.

"Do you need someone to take you there?" Lorrin asked, leaning forward in his chair.

"I don't think so. Tamir gave me some directions."

"Say hi for us," Niles said, adding her plate of abandoned food to his own.

Elinta ducked out of the house and instantly headed in the direction of the field. Keeping out of the way of the Asali wandering the city, Elinta marvelled once again at the beautiful designs around her. Each and every building seemed to work with the trees and the surrounding environment. It looked like they hadn't even dug at the ground to level it out the way they did in Kethmere. And the birds and insects of the forest seemed at home within the city, too. She wouldn't have been surprised to see a herd of deer walking past. It was amazing. But it was a short walk and Elinta kept her pace up. She hadn't really spoken to Zhayra since they'd arrived, and she was desperate to be with the dragon.

The silver trees naturally opened into a clearing larger than where the council table was, at least sixty metres in diameter. Though there were Asali on the far end of the field, Elinta's eyes were only for Zhayra, who bounded toward her as soon as she stepped on the field.

"Hi." Elinta laughed as the dragon came to a stop in front of her. "I'm fine," she told Zhayra, hoping to abate the concern that still sat heavily in her stomach.

Zhayra lowered her head and looked her in the eyes for a long moment before she snorted hot air over her face and settled into a crouch. Elinta took that to mean the dragon was satisfied she was indeed fine and sat between the dragon's front feet.

She wasn't sure whether Zhayra had heard the conversation with the council about Vaherin or not. If her eyes grew heavy when Zhayra used them, then what happened when she used her ears? She didn't think her ears had felt any different during the meeting. Maybe Zhayra didn't know she wasn't the only dragon in Eldras.

"So," Elinta said, unsure where to start. "Mazen has a dragon with him."

Zhayra grumbled, but to Elinta's surprise, her stomach didn't jump, didn't clench. Her chest didn't tighten.

"Did you know about Vaherin?" Elinta said, looking up at the dragon.

Zhayra grunted.

"Do you think he's like Mazen?" Elinta asked. "Do you think he would have been happy to kill us?"

Zhayra cocked her head and looked down at Elinta, then grunted in affirmation again.

"What happened to make them like that?" she said, and they descended into silence.

After a while, Elinta found herself staring at Zhayra's white scales that were glinting in the afternoon sunlight. *My eyes will be that bright one day,* Elinta thought, watching the light dance off them.

Elinta still had so many questions. It was like she'd been building up a dam of them over the past several months and it had finally broken. If Vaherin and Mazen were still together, did that mean the *ngaran* was permanent? Or was it a choice? Not that she wanted to give Zhayra up, but she still knew so little about the bond they shared. If her eyes were going to change, was anything else going to?

And what was it that had made Mazen turn against the dragons? And the humans? Why would he try to kill Lorrin, a *Zearla lurai,* and a dragon? There had to be something bigger happening that she just wasn't aware of. And surely Vaherin wouldn't want to kill one of his own kind? Especially after the damage the Eggslaying would have had on their population?

"Do you think it would happen again?" Elinta said finally. "The Eggslaying?"

Zhayra remained quiet. Memories of the Eggslaying festival flooded Elinta's mind. The twisted dragon puppet running to its doom. Children with swords chasing after other puppets, excited to slay a dragon. And The Ballad of the Slain.

"Zhayra?" Elinta said, looking up at the dragon again.

Zhayra didn't respond, at least verbally. A lightness sat in her chest though it was coupled with a slight heaviness in her gut. It was like she was hopeful. Worried, but hopeful.

"Me too," Elinta whispered, thinking of Lorrin and the way he supported them. "I think things could change. If only there was a way to make them see it."

The sun was beginning to descend when Tamir came looking for her. Elinta still sat between Zhayra's feet, but her swirling thoughts had finally settled. Though, in the wake of this, the headache she'd had since waking had come to the forefront.

"Prince Lorrin and Niles were beginning to wonder where you were," Tamir said, coming to a stop in front of her and Zhayra.

"We had a lot to discuss," Elinta said, struggling to her feet.

"It is a pleasure to meet you properly, Zhayra," Tamir said with a small nod at the dragon.

Zhayra rumbled in response. Elinta had the distinct feeling that she was happy to see the Asali again, and the lightness in the dragon's chest confirmed it.

"The council have invited you and your companions to dinner. Your friends are waiting for you, *Zearla lurai*," Tamir said.

"You don't have to call me that."

"What does 'Elinta' mean in your language?"

Elinta shook her head. "I don't know."

"I will think of something else then," he said with a twinkle in his eye.

Elinta cocked her head but said nothing.

"We should go." He gestured over his shoulder.

Elinta said her goodbyes to Zhayra, then followed the Asali. As soon as they'd left the training field behind, Elinta's eyes grew heavy again, and she knew the dragon was watching through her. It was strange knowing that's what the feeling signified, but she was glad to finally know what was going on with her eyes.

With the sun going down in the sky and the shadows of the forest lengthening, Elinta's feeling that something else was different about the Asali returned to her. There'd been something in the White Mountains that she hadn't been able to put her finger on, but she hadn't thought of it since. And now, looking at Tamir's glowing form and the shadows from the trees and buildings stretching across the ground in the dim light, she realised what it was.

He didn't have a shadow. None of them did. Elinta looked for one from every Asali they passed, and not one of them had a shadow. A new sense of awe settled over her. She looked from her own shadow to the blank space on the leaf-strewn forest floor where Tamir's should have been.

"Ta—"

"We were starting to wonder if you'd gotten lost," Niles called from in front of their little building. Lorrin appeared a few seconds later from inside. The prince had attempted to clean up a little for their dinner with the council, and both boys had shaved. Though Niles's hair was its usual mess.

"No. Just a lot to discuss," she said, repeating what she'd told Tamir.

Lorrin smiled as she and the Asali drew alongside them. "How was Zhayra?"

"Good," Elinta said. "She seems happier now."

She reached up and tried to flatten Niles's hair, but he batted her away. "No point, El. It has a mind of its own."

Lorrin caught her eyes and nodded.

She laughed. If she was honest, she couldn't imagine Niles with neat hair, anyway. He must have given up a long time ago, though. He'd never tried to flatten it in the time she'd known him.

"If you're ready, we will go now."

Tamir lead them through the city again, toward the large building on their left that she'd seen earlier. When they reached the threshold, she looked up and saw the engravings she hadn't been able to make out before. They were dragons. Four of them spread across the beam in various stances. One had its wings open in flight, another walked, whilst another blew fire, and the last was simply a head, facing front and detailed down to the small scales at the tip of its muzzle. They were lined with *illayas*.

"This building serves us for important meetings. Our solstice celebrations also begin here," Tamir said, walking through the open entryway.

Lorrin gestured for Elinta to go through first and she followed the Asali. The building immediately widened into a large room with a long, silver wooden table set down the middle. It was a beautiful room with engravings along the walls. Elinta didn't look around properly as Piran, Nakiah, and Aisla were already seated with another man beside them. The four stood when they entered the room.

"*Layzun, Zearla lurai,*" Aisla said. Her long hair, more grey than blonde, was now piled on top of her head. "Please, take a seat."

Tamir, Elinta, Lorrin, and Niles all found seats at the long table together. Lorrin sat to Elinta's left, Niles directly across from her, and Tamir on her right. She found she was grateful for the Asali staying close to them. The council were not people she wanted to face alone.

Piran smiled, oblivious to her discomfort, and gestured to the other man seated at the table. He had short black hair, cut close to his scalp, and muscled arms. "This is Maaka, one of our finest fighters." Piran's eyes flickered briefly to Tamir as he said it.

"It is a pleasure to meet you, *Zearla lurai*," the man said, but Elinta noted his white eyes barely even glanced at Lorrin and Niles. Her heart sank as she realised what Piran had said earlier was true. Maaka only gave her the courtesy of the common tongue because she was *Zearla lurai*. Her friends were unimportant in his eyes.

Elinta plastered on a smile, hiding the revelation. "Thank you. It's a pleasure to be here."

Dinner with the Asali was an interesting affair. Elinta didn't broach the subject of Mazen again and was hesitant to ask many questions of the council. She felt comfortable speaking with Tamir due to his openness, but the council members, though they seemed to respect her because of Zhayra, were intimidating. It was due to a lot of things, but it all mostly came back to the same thing, their age.

Looking at Aisla and Piran, Elinta was sure they had to be at least double Tamir's physical age. Nakiah, too, was older than Tamir. What that made their actual age, she wasn't sure, but given Tamir could be around a thousand years old ... the council members had lived a long time. And she felt the difference like a wide gulf between them. She was little more than an infant when compared to their years of life.

Maaka seemed polite enough to Elinta, but whenever it was necessary to speak to Lorrin or Niles, he did so stiffly and often reverted to his native tongue. Luckily, Lorrin was able to translate his words and respond in kind. She didn't understand why the Asali should treat the two boys differently, especially the prince, but they handled it well.

"*How is your work fairing,* Tamir?" Maaka asked in Asalin, from opposite the man. Elinta was once again glad for her lessons from Lorrin, that allowed her to understand the question.

Tamir smiled. "Well," he said, in the common tongue. "I was working when Elinta and her friends arrived."

The stocky Asali nodded and continued in Asalin. "*It is good you were there. She would not have survived the peraka ayn myan.*"

Beside her, Lorrin translated the last of Maaka's words, knowing that he hadn't taught them to her. She knew *ayn* signified that verbs or some nouns were in present tense, but Lorrin confirmed her suspicions that *peraka myan* meant blood poison. Elinta paled. She wouldn't have survived the blood poisoning. She shivered at the memory of it running through her veins.

Maaka was then swept up in conversation with Nakiah, freeing Tamir.

"What work do you do, Tamir?" Lorrin asked, leaning around Elinta.

Elinta and Niles listened with interest as they ate their food, a delicate golden pastry packed with vegetables. Elinta grinned at Niles, thinking he was doing well to concentrate while eating such delicious food.

"I collect knowledge," Tamir said. "I suppose I'm closest to what you would call a historian, or perhaps a scientist."

Elinta smiled. "A researcher?" she suggested.

"Yes."

"Do you have any students?" Lorrin asked.

Tamir smiled. "None that are my own, but I help with the teaching of our children."

Elinta perked up at that. She hadn't actually seen any children since arriving. Where were they? Eiran and Laira had been beyond excited by the prospect of a dragon when they were in the White Mountains. Perhaps these children were busy with classes?

Or in another part of the city? But Elinta didn't say anything as Tamir continued talking about his work.

By the time she was halfway through the meal, Elinta's eyes were growing tired, and her headache had worsened. It had been a long day, and even though her wounds were healed, her body was still unwell. Elinta began to eat her meal a little faster though she noted Niles was gulping down his food at a speed she could never match. For a moment she considered sneaking some of hers onto his plate, but she didn't want to offend any of the Asali. Especially the council members.

When the meal finished and the awkward conversation continued, Elinta resorted to thinking of ways to catch Tamir's attention and tell him she needed to go to bed. She felt sure the man would help excuse them if he saw how uncomfortable she was. Elinta just didn't want to interrupt him.

Lorrin leaned in from her other side and whispered in her ear. "Are you OK? You look exhausted."

"I'm ready to go," she whispered back, shifting in her chair. "I'll try to let Tamir know."

"*Zearla lurai*," Maaka said, his tone causing Elinta to stiffen. She looked at the warrior. "You must tell us more about Zhayra and how you two met."

Elinta tried to hide her disappointment at being singled out and at the question. She'd so far avoided telling the Asali anything about her bond with Zhayra, including their meeting and flight from Kethmere.

"We met after a storm," Elinta hedged.

Tamir turned to look at her, possibly catching the tightness in her tone, and concern flitted across his face.

"Perhaps another time, Maaka. Elinta is still recovering from the poisoning and seems ready to return to her room now."

Elinta smiled and nodded, failing to hide her relief. It wasn't just that she was unwell. The proof to the council of how her people still hated dragons would only serve to further convince them an alliance between their peoples was pointless. Telling them about Kethmere was the last thing she wanted to do even if it was misleading.

Maaka smiled. "In that case, I look forward to our next meeting."

Elinta and the boys said their goodbyes to the council and Maaka before following Tamir from the building. Elinta had to stop herself from exhaling with relief as the night air hit her face.

"I'm sorry we didn't leave earlier," Tamir said to her. "Please do not hesitate to ask to leave next time. Or speak to me if you do not wish to talk to the others."

"Thank you," Elinta said, stifling a yawn.

They walked back through the city by the glow of Tamir's body and those they passed. Elinta's feet began to drag, at first from tiredness, and then from awe. Liyarna was even more beautiful at night, lit entirely by the glow of its inhabitants alone. She caught Lorrin's eye as they both gaped at the city and grinned. For a moment, it seemed as though they forgot their problems, and just enjoyed the otherworldliness of the city. She could have stayed out in the city all night if she hadn't been exhausted.

They stopped outside their quarters.

"I will come to see you in the morning. Sleep well." Tamir turned and disappeared into the city. His glow was soon swallowed up by the collective light of his people.

Elinta followed the boys inside, where they all stood in the small common area, at a loss for words after such an eventful day.

"Well," Niles said, "I'm going to bed."

"Goodnight," Elinta said.

"Night," Lorrin said to Niles's disappearing form.

Elinta and Lorrin stood awkwardly in the empty room.

"I'm glad you're feeling better," Lorrin said, his eyes scanning her face.

Elinta smiled. "Thank you."

She thought of the way he'd helped her on the road, how he'd carried her and held her, and felt her cheeks heat. So much had happened today. They'd hardly had a moment to process the trip to Liyarna.

"Goodnight, El," Lorrin said and, after pausing for a second, turned away and entered the room opposite hers.

CHAPTER SEVEN

E LINTA PAUSED IN THE doorway to her room.

"Hello," she said, voice lifting with surprise.

The young woman standing over her bed turned, pushing her wavy, long brown hair behind her shoulder.

"I'm sorry. I'd hoped to be done before you returned." The woman crossed the room and held out her hand. "I'm Serren. Tamir asked me to drop by and check on your rooms."

Tamir? Elinta shook the woman's hand. "I'm Elinta," she said, then cringed. Of course, the woman knew who she was. "Thank you. The place is great."

Serren smiled and returned to the bed, her willowy frame making her moves graceful. The two chairs that had been in the room earlier were now gone and one of the lanterns hanging from the ceiling had been lit. The ones in their building were the only ones she'd seen in the entire city. The woman finished straightening the blanket.

"How was dinner?"

"It was ..." Elinta searched for the right word. Dinner hadn't exactly been great, given the awkward company of the council members and Maaka's strange avoidance of the common tongue, but she didn't want to offend the Asali when her people had been so hospitable to her. "Great," she finally said.

Serren laughed. "I heard the company could have been better," she said with a wink.

Elinta, caught off guard, didn't respond. She supposed it was common knowledge who she'd had dinner with. Serren grabbed her pillow and gently fluffed it up before placing it back on the bed and turning to face her.

"Is there anything else I can do for you?"

"No. Thank you," Elinta said, stepping aside and eyeing her bed. But then her eyes landed on her shadow spread across the silver-white wooden floor. She glanced at Serren, who was walking the length of the bed toward the door. She looked back at her shadow. Would it be rude to ask about her shadow? Maybe Lorrin would know more. It would be awkward to ask this woman, whom she'd only just met.

Serren paused as she drew level with Elinta, her bright eyes studying her face. "What is it, Elinta?"

"Sorry?" Elinta said, refocusing on the woman.

"You look as though you want to ask me something."

"Oh." She cleared her throat. "Well, yes."

Serren's eyebrows rose.

"Why don't you have a shadow?" Elinta asked.

Serren frowned, tucking a strand of hair behind her ear, and for a moment Elinta thought she had offended the woman. "We are our own light."

Elinta let the sentence bounce around in her tired mind for a moment, testing it and turning it over. "What do you mean?" she finally asked.

"The sun has given us all the light it can give," Serren explained. When Elinta continued to frown, she continued, "If I were to face the sun, there would not be any more light on my face than on my back. We cannot cast a shadow just as a flame cannot."

Elinta stared at the woman in wonder, taking in the glow of her skin as though for the first time. "It's more like moonlight," she murmured.

"Even the moon's light is borrowed from the sun," Serren said, causing Elinta to jump. She hadn't realised she'd spoken aloud.

Serren tilted her head. "I heard about what happened with Mazen. I'm sorry for the pain he caused you."

"Did you know him?" Elinta asked, surprised by all the questions spilling out of herself.

"Not personally." Serren smiled sadly. "But my husband did. Goodnight, Elinta."

"Goodnight."

Elinta closed the door behind the Asali woman, then crossed to her bed where Serren had laid out a nightdress for her. She stared at it for a moment. How did Serren know she hadn't packed any nightclothes? But Elinta changed into the light garment gratefully, laying her sword against the wall by her bag.

She blew out the flame of the lantern and climbed into the bed, sinking into it. Her last thoughts as she drifted off to sleep were of Zhayra and the nights they'd spent together under the stars.

Elinta woke to the early morning light streaming across the ceiling of her room and for a moment, couldn't remember where she was. But as she took in the silver beams above her, it all came flooding back.

"Liyarna," she whispered. Elinta stretched out her arms and legs, revelling in her healed hip and arm.

Elinta sat up. She hadn't even looked at her hip wound since the Asali had healed her. She'd been so caught up in everything else. Elinta looked down and cautiously pulled up her nightdress. There was a thin white line across her right hip. She poked at it but didn't feel any pain. The skin around the scar was perfectly healthy, too. It wasn't even pink. A smile broke across her face.

Elinta jumped to her feet, letting her dress fall, and crossed to the mirror on the back of her door. The bruise that had formed on her cheek from Mazen's backfist was completely gone, too. She pulled her dress away from her thigh and compared the scar there from the mountain lion with the new ones on her hip and arm.

They were perfect scars. Not even a trace of the holes on the newer ones where the stitches had pierced her skin. She stared at them in wonder. What would it be like not to need healers? In the traditional, no, the human sense? She prodded at her healed cheek. Then leaned forward and stared at her eyes, studying them for the changes Tamir had mentioned, but they seemed normal to her.

Letting her dress drop back into place, Elinta ducked into a crouch to rifle through her backpack for a fresh pair of clothing. She emerged from her room a few minutes later in a loose green shirt and a pair of pants that stopped a few inches above her ankles. Her sword was back in its place at her hip.

"Ah, I was wondering when you were getting up," Niles said, straightening in one of the cushioned chairs in the centre of the room. There were three in all, one for each of the occupants of the three rooms. Brown and silver wood stretched between the chair legs in elegant patterns, twisting and rolling together.

She returned his greeting, even as he stretched out in the chair again.

Elinta's eyes drifted around the room.

"Nah," Niles said, giving her a knowing grin. "Lor's not up yet."

"Oh," Elinta said. "I wasn't ..." She let the sentence drop, then crossed the room and sat in the chair opposite Niles. There was no use arguing with Niles. Especially not after the way he'd asked about her 'intentions' with Lorrin, when they'd listened in on a secret council meeting not too long ago in Nevira.

"Good choice," he said with a wink.

"What do you think the council will decide?" Elinta asked quietly, her thoughts drifting back to everything they'd learnt the day before. Was Mazen really a prince? *The* prince?

Niles shrugged. "No use dwelling on it now. They'll tell us when they're ready."

"I suppose."

A surge of curiosity from Zhayra pulled her attention away from Niles. She frowned and focused in on the dragon. Zhayra seemed alert, focused. But she didn't seem scared. Elinta tried to glean what she could from Zhayra's emotions, but she was left confused. What was the dragon doing? Wasn't she at the training grounds?

Niles's face appeared in front of her. "Hello? Are you in there?"

Elinta blinked. "Sorry. I was just wondering what Zhayra was doing."

"What's she up to?"

Elinta shrugged. "I don't know."

"Hey." Niles dropped back into his chair. "Do you think you could look through her eyes? Like you heard the forest that time?"

Elinta slowly nodded, thinking about the time she'd heard crickets and the sound of a river while she'd been inside the White Palace of Nevira. If she could do that and Zhayra could use her eyes ... could she use Zhayra's?

"I guess I could," she said slowly, "but I don't know how I'd do it."

The other bedroom door opened and Lorrin strode into the common area. Elinta smiled.

"There he is!" Niles said as Lorrin sat in the remaining chair

"How are you feeling this morning?" Lorrin asked, right as Elinta was going to ask how he'd slept.

"Great," she said. "My headache's gone and I'm not tired anymore."

Lorrin smiled. "Has there been any word from the council?"

"Nope," Niles said, swinging a leg over the armrest of his chair.

Lorrin leant back and sighed. "They could be a while. We've given them a lot to discuss."

Elinta and Niles agreed.

"Any ideas on how to fill the time, then?" Niles asked. "This room is going to get boring real fast."

Lorrin started to shake his head, then paused, his eyes lighting up.

"What?" Niles asked, sitting up.

Lorrin looked at Elinta, who raised an eyebrow. "Would you feel up to some training?"

"Yes," she said, her hand naturally going to the hilt of her newly sharpened sword. She still hadn't had a chance to look at it since Lorrin had smoothed out the damage caused by Mazen. "We could use the field where Zhayra's staying."

Niles was already on his feet, his eyes alight. "Awesome! Who needs a guide? Let's go."

"Wait. Tamir said he'd be by this morning. We can check with him," Lorrin said. "I'm sure there's something we can do while we wait."

But they didn't need to find anything to fill their time with as Tamir appeared in the doorway.

"Good morning," Tamir said, walking over to where they sat. He was met with a chorus of 'mornings' in return. Elinta glanced at his feet, stifling a laugh at his lack of shoes. The Asali seemed quite professional until looking below his ankles. Did he ever wear shoes?

"I heard you had a training field here?" Lorrin asked Tamir. "Would we be allowed to practice there?"

Tamir's eyes flitted to Elinta's sword, then back to Lorrin. "Of course. I can accompany you there whenever you wish."

"Can we go now?" Elinta asked, itching to spar.

"Yes. Come."

Elinta, Niles, and Lorrin all jumped to their feet, each grabbing a piece of fruit from a bowl on their table and followed Tamir as he led them from the building. Elinta already knew the way to the training field and hurried to walk next to the Asali. The sight of him had brought back more of her questions from the previous day.

"Can you tell me more about the *zearla lurai ngaran?*" she asked, taking a bite of the sweet, green fruit.

"What do you already know?" Tamir asked, his hands clasped behind him.

Elinta swallowed and paused, considering all that she'd experienced. "Zhayra and I can share our emotions ... and apparently Zhayra can see through my eyes. I heard through her once too," she said, thinking back to her time at the palace. "And my hearing increased, so that I heard something I shouldn't have."

Tamir nodded. "What do these things have in common?"

Elinta frowned. Obviously, they were from Zhayra, but she didn't think that's what he meant. She wracked her brain. "Well, the sight and hearing are both senses?" she finally offered, unsure what other link there was.

"So are emotions," Tamir said, glancing at her as they walked. "A person may sense one's own emotions or sense someone else's. This is partially described by empathy."

Elinta paused in her steps. "So, you're saying we're sharing some of our senses?"

Tamir turned to her, shaking his head. "You may share all of your senses."

"Woah," Niles said from behind her.

"But ..." Elinta's mind boggled. *All* their senses? How was that even possible?

Tamir smiled. "As with everything, this takes time to learn." He resumed walking.

After sharing a glance with Lorrin and Niles, they hurried to catch up with him.

"How do I learn something like that?" Elinta asked.

"Practice," Tamir said, coming to a stop at the edge of the training field. Elinta's eyes landed on Zhayra, sitting in the middle of the field, her membrane wings tucked against her body and her tail snaking out behind her. She could share the dragon's senses? Her smell? Even her taste? OK, so that last one was something she didn't want to try, but the rest ...

"Right," Niles said, startling Elinta from her thoughts. "Let's get started."

Elinta strode out into the field, noticing as she did that they had the entire field to themselves except for a flock of birds scratching for food on the far side. It suited her just fine. She didn't like the idea of being watched by the Asali. Especially since she'd seen the way they could move and fight.

"Hi, girl," Elinta called to the dragon, who had risen to her feet and was following them.

Zhayra's tail twitched, and she hummed in greeting. She settled into a crouch as Elinta, Lorrin, and Niles halted in the middle of the field. Tamir sat at the edge, casually watching from a distance.

"My turn," Niles said, drawing his sword with a flourish. "You still owe me a match."

Elinta grinned. She and Niles were meant to have sparred the day after the Eggslaying, since she'd fought Lorrin in their training session the night of the celebrations. Instead, she'd gone on to fight with Mazen after the Eggslaying and spent the next day resting.

"Don't think I'll let you off easy," Elinta said.

"I don't know," Lorrin said, his face turning serious as he looked at her. "You might have to."

"What?" Niles said. "Why?"

"Well," Lorrin said, voice totally even. "You're the only one among us that hasn't fought an Asali now."

Niles's mouth dropped open and his eyes jumped between them. "Tamir!" he shouted, pivoting on the spot to face the Asali sitting on the edge of the field.

"No." Elinta laughed, grabbing his arm as he started walking toward him. Tamir's eyebrows rose in question. Elinta tugged on Niles's arm. "Niles."

"Fine," he said, facing her again. But Elinta was beyond glad that they could joke about what had happened to her. She didn't want that experience to hang over them. Though her wounds were now scars, it'd been barely two weeks since the fight.

"Contact?" she asked, stepping back from him and bouncing on her toes, feeling the compact earth beneath her feet.

"Flat of the blade only, please." He winked. "I'd like to keep these devilish good looks."

"Can't keep what you don't have," Lorrin said, causing Elinta to laugh.

"Oof." Niles placed a hand over his heart. "I've taught you well."

"Alright, let's start this training session," Lorrin said. "On three."

"One."

Elinta drew her blade and tried not to let her eyes flicker toward Tamir. She wished he didn't have to stay and watch them train.

"Two."

Niles winked and raised his sword.

"Three!"

Elinta pounced first, slashing out at his legs. Niles jumped back and Elinta followed, kicking out at his knee. Niles easily blocked her, then whipped his sword around and toward her side. Elinta danced out of the way, and she and Niles traded blows, each trying and failing to land a hit. But it was Elinta who managed to land the first blow, slapping the flat of her blade against Niles's back as she spun out of the way of his own blade.

"Good," Niles said, wiping his forehead. Elinta smiled, her eyes flicking toward Tamir, who still watched them. Niles took the opportunity to jump forward, aiming a strike at her leg.

Elinta whipped up her sword at the last second, and their blades met with a loud clang.

"You still with me, El? Don't think you've already won."

Elinta's response was to feign a strike at his chest, before landing a soft kick on his thigh. "Soon," she puffed.

Niles laughed and their swords clashed again. On it went. Back and forth. Niles hit her arm with his sword. Elinta punched his stomach. Niles grazed her shoulder with his fist. But Elinta ended the fight when she disarmed him with a flick of her wrist and left the tip of her sword an inch from his chest.

Niles sighed dramatically, an effect somewhat ruined by his heavy breathing. "That was just luck!" But his tone was teasing and proud.

Elinta grinned, lowering her sword. It was the first time she'd beaten Niles so definitively. She'd defeated him once before in their training at Nevira, but she was still convinced it was a fluke. No, today was her first proper win against her friend.

"I definitely need to fight Tamir," Niles mumbled.

Lorrin grinned. "You're getting good!" he said, fetching Niles's sword.

"Thanks," Elinta said, glowing at his praise.

Niles grabbed his sword from Lorrin and sat. "Unpack?" he said, looking up at them.

"Unpack," Elinta agreed, joining Niles.

Zhayra grumbled, rose to her feet, and trudged over to them, settling back into a crouch beside Elinta. She grinned at the dragon. "What do you think?"

Zhayra didn't verbally respond, but Elinta could feel the spark of pride sitting in the dragon's chest.

CHAPTER EIGHT

A FTER DISCUSSING THEIR TRAINING session, Elinta said goodbye to Zhayra, and she and the boys crossed the field to meet Tamir.

He stood as they approached.

"Are you ready for breakfast?"

"What kind of question is that?" Niles said. Elinta doubted the piece of fruit he'd eaten on the way to the field had done anything for his hunger.

Tamir glanced at Elinta, frowning.

"He means yes," Elinta translated.

Tamir nodded gratefully. "I will have something sent to your rooms."

They began the walk back through the city. "Do you normally train together?" Tamir asked.

"Yes," Elinta said. "Normally at night, though." The time of the training had originally started as a way to keep it secret, but then, once Lorrin had given her the sword, it had continued on out of convenience. Both Lorrin and Niles had busy days at the palace.

"Good," Tamir said. "Who taught you to wield a sword, *tarsi?*"

"Lor—" she paused, frowning. "What does *tarsi* mean?" She remembered his promise to find a new name to call her, other than *Zearla lurai.*

"It is a young female dragon," he said, a sparkle in his eyes.

"Oh."

"*Tarsi* were known for their fierceness and skill. Perhaps slightly hasty to fight at times, but they were also agile and smart."

Elinta smiled. It was better than *Zearla lurai.*

"You know, I taught her," Niles said proudly. Elinta heard the distinct sound of flesh on flesh and Niles yelped, adding a moment later, "And Lorrin helped."

Tamir smiled. "You've taught her well."

"I have," Niles agreed. Elinta waited for another yelp, but Lorrin allowed his friend to get away with the comment.

"If you wish to train again, I will be happy to take you back to the training field," Tamir said, stopping in front of their building. "You only need to ask."

"Maybe tomorrow, if we're still here," Lorrin said. "When can we expect to hear from the council?"

"It should not be long now," Tamir said. "I have some things to attend to this morning. I'll come back for you when they're ready to speak with you."

"Thank you," Lorrin said, Elinta and Niles echoing his words. While Tamir ducked away, Elinta and the boys went inside to wait for their breakfast. Niles went straight to the table, his eyes constantly flickering toward the door as he waited for the food. With a smile, Lorrin joined his friend.

Elinta took a moment to marvel at where they were. No matter what the council had decided about Mazen, she'd actually seen the Green City. But reality didn't stay away for too long and her concerns about Mazen returned.

"I wish they'd hurry up and make a decision," Elinta said, crossing the room and sitting in one of the chairs. She wished Zhayra could be with her too. The dragon's presence calmed her.

Niles tore his eyes away from the door. "Be careful what you wish for. We want them to help us too, not just make a decision."

Elinta hastily nodded. "But I don't understand why they need to talk about this. Mazen's their prince! Shouldn't they be doing something?" Elinta still couldn't believe that Mazen was royalty. Her stomach still dropped at the memory of him and his anger. And he had a claim to the Asali *throne*. What would he do if he were on it?

Lorrin sat forward in his chair. "Whatever their answer, it will at least let us know whether we need to be worried about them helping him out of duty. Mazen poses an even bigger threat to us now that we know he's royalty." His words echoed her own thoughts, but she couldn't believe he was so calm. But then, she supposed this was his job and he knew it well.

"How long do you think they'll be?" Niles asked, looking at the door again.

"The food or the council?" Lorrin asked.

"The food."

"Niles!" Elinta laughed. "Couldn't you pretend to worry about the council?"

Niles looked at her again, his brown eyes serious. "There's no use worrying about something we can't control. Besides—" his eyes flittered back to the door just as three Asali entered carrying a bowl each, "can't fix the country on an empty stomach."

Elinta was just about to start pacing when Tamir finally arrived to take them to the council, and Elinta felt Zhayra flood with relief. She wasn't sure, but she suspected her impatience had been driving the dragon crazy.

Elinta ground her teeth at Tamir's frustratingly slow pace as he led them back to the council's table. She hardly noticed the beautiful buildings surrounding her this time.

"El," Lorrin whispered, tugging at her hand.

"What?"

"Calm down," he said with a small shake of his head.

Elinta slowed her pace and took a deep breath. She didn't know why she'd worked herself up so much. Niles was right. There wasn't any use worrying about what she couldn't control, but it was hard not to. Elinta nodded, and Lorrin squeezed her hand before letting go.

"Prince Lorrin is right, *tarsi*," Tamir said. "Your haste cannot affect the council's decision."

Can't it? she thought, but she kept it to herself. She just wanted it over. The verdict handed down.

But when the clearing opened in front of them and the table came into view with the beautiful vines behind it, Elinta suddenly wanted to be anywhere but there. Zhayra landed a moment later and Elinta hurried to her side, finding comfort in the dragon.

"*Layzun*," Aisla said, nodding a greeting. "We're sorry to have kept you waiting, *Zearla lurai*. We had much to discuss." As before, the council hardly acknowledged Lorrin or Niles.

Piran smiled, his hair tied back into a bun today. "We trust your stay with us has been comfortable?"

Elinta fought to keep her impatience from entering her voice as she answered. "Yes. Thank you."

"Good. We would be honoured if you would join us for dinner again tonight."

"Of course," she said. She hoped her smile didn't appear as strained as it felt. Her own impatience was joined by a niggle growing inside Zhayra. She absently stroked the dragon's scales before letting her hand drop again.

Elinta studied Nakiah, who'd so far remained quiet, and tried to judge his mood. Of the council, she was sure he was the one who had the least interest in helping them. His face seemed less severe today, she thought, studying the younger council member. Her stomach began to sink, but she pushed at the thought that had begun to form in her mind. They couldn't have said no, could they?

Niles nudged Elinta, jolting her back to the present. Piran looked at her expectantly.

"I'm sorry." She blushed. "Could you repeat that?"

Piran smiled graciously and opened his mouth, but Nakiah spoke across him. "You appear to be distracted. Perhaps we should skip all the pleasantries and discuss the reason you are here."

Aisla frowned at the younger man. "Thank you, Nakiah." She smiled at their little group. "Perhaps he is right. We have come to a decision regarding Prince Mazen."

Elinta waited with bated breath, and she knew that Lorrin, Niles, and even Zhayra were hanging on the woman's every word as well. This was it.

"Prince Mazen Elliar has forfeited his right to the throne by leaving his people and going into exile. As such, we do not and will not support him or his actions."

Elinta waited for more, but Aisla seemed to have finished.

"That's all?" Lorrin said, surprise slipping into his voice.

Nakiah's eyes darkened. "We do not owe you anything, boy. Whatever Mazen's objective, it does not seem to concern us."

"We will not search for Mazen, nor will we actively oppose him, but you have our guarantee that as long as there is a council, he will receive no support," Piran said. His deep voice seemed to echo over them.

Elinta frowned, reigning in her emotions. "Does that stand for all the Liyarnan Asali?"

Aisla's bright eyes turned thoughtful. "A minority may support him should he return, which we believe is unlikely. And we have deemed that he no longer has a claim to the throne. You needn't worry, *Zearla lurai,*" she said. "Our people will uphold this council's verdict."

Elinta's mouth opened and closed, but she could think of nothing to say. She'd expected to be angry, to feel heat running through her veins. But she didn't. Her stomach sunk, but she had no desire to yell at the council. Their minds were set. There was nothing else she could say on the matter.

Zhayra grumbled beside her, voicing Elinta's disappointment as well as her own. Lorrin shifted on his feet, his face thoughtful.

Piran tilted his head, his eyes settling on Zhayra. "You are displeased that we won't help the humans, yet it is your people who have suffered the most at their hands. Curious."

Zhayra grunted, and despite everything, Elinta smiled. Zhayra did have every right to turn her back on them, yet she didn't. She let her gratitude wash through her, hoping the dragon would feel it and understand.

"And the treaty?" Lorrin asked, his voice steady now. No sign of the disappointment Elinta knew he must have been feeling.

"Nothing has changed," Nakiah said, coldly.

Lorrin stared at Nakiah. "I'm sorry to hear that. This treaty could have been something great for our people."

The council didn't respond. And Elinta's group said nothing more. She wasn't sure what else there was to say now. She wanted to learn more about Mazen, but she didn't think the council were the right people to ask. She didn't know who was, but it definitely wasn't these people.

"If that is all," Aisla said, shifting in her seat. Elinta glanced at Zhayra and placed a hand on the dragon's scales.

"Why would he want to kill Zhayra?" Elinta asked again. Why would a *Zearla lurai*, a kin of the dragons, want to kill a dragon?

"Mazen left the day after the Eggslaying," Piran said, repeating what he'd told her earlier. "The day his father died. Whoever he is now is not who we knew. We cannot speak for his motivations," he said softly.

"How old is he?" Elinta asked, picturing Mazen's striking face. He'd looked to be in his mid-twenties, but she knew the Asali didn't age like humans.

"Mazen would be about twelve-hundred years old now," Aisla said. "He is nearly mid-life."

"Huh," Niles said, "I hope I look that good when I'm mid-life." Elinta had to agree.

"Very well," Piran said, "if that is all, we can only leave you with the knowledge that we will be vigilant."

"You are welcome to stay with us again tonight," Aisla said, folding her hands on the table, "but we believe it would be best if you return to Nevira tomorrow."

Elinta nodded and tried to stop her shoulders from slumping. If she was honest, she would have preferred to leave now. But there were formalities they had to hold to even if things hadn't gone as they'd hoped.

Tamir finally broke his silence, speaking for the first time since they'd arrived before the council's table. "May I speak with Elinta and her friends for a moment?"

Aisla cocked her head. "Of course."

Tamir gestured for them to follow him a few steps away. Elinta followed curiously.

"If it is acceptable, I would like to come with you to Nevira. I believe I can help you with Mazen, and I can keep the council informed."

"Why?" Lorrin asked, his brow furrowed.

"I knew him," Tamir said simply.

Elinta's eyebrows rose and before she could consider it further, she was nodding. Tamir posed a valuable resource. He'd already told her so much about the bond she had with Zhayra and now he could tell her more about Mazen as well. Maybe their trip wouldn't be a complete waste. But it was little solace after their high hopes.

Lorrin was silent for a moment, his eyes thoughtful. She wondered what kind of position she'd put him in by accepting Tamir's offer.

"You're welcome to join us," Lorrin said. "My parents likely won't trust you, but they will understand that the council would wish to keep an eye on Mazen."

"Very well," Tamir said, and led them back to the council. "I would like to accompany Elinta back to Nevira where I can listen for any signs of Mazen. If anything arises, I will return to inform you immediately."

Aisla, Piran, and Nakiah exchanged glances before each nodded. "This is not the task we had intended to give should you have accepted our many offers to return to service, Tamir, but this is acceptable," Aisla said.

Return to service? Elinta glanced quizzically at Tamir, but his eyes were fixed on the council. His face was carefully neutral, but it seemed to her that he disapproved of the council's decision on Mazen.

Tamir bowed with a nod of his head, pivoted on the spot, and left the clearing.

Elinta looked after Tamir in surprise. *"Layzulla,"* she said, then hurried after him, Niles and Lorrin right behind her. Zhayra grunted, then a rush of air signalled she'd launched herself back into the sky.

"I'm sorry they won't help you, *tarsi*," Tamir said, crossing the room and taking a seat at their table. They were now back at their rooms, and Elinta, Lorrin, and Niles had invited the Asali in.

Elinta shrugged, trying to appear light-hearted though she felt anything but. "Thank you for offering to come with us."

A frown crinkled his brow. "Mazen is clearly planning something. It would be unwise of the council to ignore him completely."

Elinta cocked her head. It sounded like he was referring to something in particular, not just the attack at the palace.

"What do you mean?" Lorrin asked. He'd done well not to let his disappointment show, but what would he do now? What could they do now?

"Some of our people have disappeared recently. We don't know where they are going though we had suspected they were joining our people living elsewhere in Eldras. But if Mazen is alive, then they will be going to him. Despite what the council said, there are many who would still follow him despite his desertion."

"Didn't Raisa and Ciar say Asali were going missing too?" Elinta asked, turning to Lorrin.

"They did."

Tamir's frown deepened. "It seems he is recruiting."

"Recruiting? For what?" Elinta said.

"I do not know."

The four of them sat in silence, each lost in their own thoughts. A thrill of anticipation hit her from Zhayra, pulling her from her reverie.

Another tug. What was the dragon doing? Elinta stared at the table unseeingly, focusing on the dragon.

"You are not using the other senses," Tamir said, breaking into her thoughts. Elinta looked up. Tamir gestured at her with a nod of his head. "I noticed you don't seem to use any of your other senses with the dragon. I assume you use only her emotions, whilst the dragon also uses your eyes and ears?"

Elinta nodded.

Tamir paused. "I would be honoured to help you try to access them."

Elinta grinned. "Really?"

"Yes."

"Wicked," Niles said.

CHAPTER NINE

"THERE ARE MORE THAN just five senses," Tamir said, sitting cross-legged opposite her on the training field. They'd gone straight there. Lorrin and Niles were on either side of her so that they formed a small circle, but Zhayra was nowhere to be seen.

Elinta frowned. More than five? But then, she supposed if emotion was a sense ...

"We will just try sight for now," Tamir said, seeing her hesitation. "The others will come with time."

"OK." She rubbed her palms across her pants

"We'll do this in a series of steps," he said. "Close your eyes."

Niles closed his eyes and Elinta chuckled. She closed hers, too.

"Try to focus on Zhayra. Allow what she is feeling to fill you."

Elinta felt the tickle of excitement in Zhayra's stomach, the thrill of anticipation in her chest.

"Now, concentrate on how each emotion feels in her body. If she is sad, focus on the lump in her throat. If she is angry, the fire in her chest."

Elinta's lip quirked into a smile at the way Zhayra's stomach flipped and tightened. She shifted her focus up to the dragon's chest and the anticipation that was still building there. It was a strange feeling, but it intrigued her.

"Now," Tamir's voice said, "I want you to slowly narrow your focus to her eyes. Work your way up her body, feeling what she is feeling."

Elinta did as he said though she wasn't sure how exactly she would feel Zhayra's eyes. That didn't seem right. But she pictured the dragon's body and shifted her attention from her chest to her neck, then the spines running along it. She brushed over the dragon's ears and straight to her eyes. What was it the dragon was seeing? What was it that had her so excited?

She concentrated, digging deep and tuning out all the sounds around her until there were only Zhayra's eyes. A blurry image began to form in her mind as though she were looking through a dirty window.

Elinta gasped. There were vague colours shining through. She scrunched up her face and willed the image to become clearer in the way she might strain her eyes to see better. And slowly, ever so slowly, more details emerged.

She was flying. Treetops whizzed by underneath her, almost close enough to touch. Zhayra scanned the undergrowth as though searching for something.

"Do you see anything?" Lorrin's voice said.

"Yes." She grinned. The trees looked so different from above, like large fluffy green cushions sitting on silver poles.

"What do you see?" Tamir asked.

"I think she's hunting," Elinta said, watching the trees whip by underneath Zhayra, underneath *her*. "She's flying over the forest somewhere."

"Is the image clear?" Tamir asked, his voice betraying a hint of excitement.

"Yes," she said. In fact, it was beyond clear. It was *sharp*. The longer Elinta looked, the more she saw. It was amazing. Zhayra's eyes saw more than hers ever could. The colours were brighter, deeper than they ever were before, and there were fine details of the trees and the undergrowth that her human eyes would never have picked up at the speed the dragon was flying.

Elinta focused on the silver of the trunks Zhayra passed. She hadn't realised just how bright they were before. They were beautiful. She watched the green leaves, the brown-trunked undergrowth. When Zhayra glanced up, Elinta saw the deep blue of the sky and couldn't hold back a laugh. And the clouds! They looked like large, fluffy pillows in the sky! Pillows above her and cushions below her.

"Can she tell that I'm using her eyes?" Elinta asked.

"Yes, just as you can when she sees through you."

Elinta realised he was right. Zhayra's excitement had tripled so that she felt like the dragon's chest would burst at any moment. She let herself be immersed in the dragon, drinking in all that Zhayra saw. Is this what it was like when Zhayra looked through her? Did the dragon find her sight strange and new?

"Is she still flying?" Lorrin asked, his voice sounding from beside her.

Elinta jumped. She'd forgotten the others were there. She'd forgotten *she* was there.

"Yes," she said, her voice slightly raised, then after a moment longer she added, "How do I turn it off?"

"Pull back," Tamir said, "and open your eyes."

Elinta nodded and opened her eyes. Only nothing happened. Zhayra continued to fly. Elinta continued to see the trees whipping by underneath her. Her stomach jumped.

"Uh," she said. "Not working."

"You need to pull away from her, separate yourself from what she is seeing, what she is feeling. Focus on where you really are."

Elinta nodded, but she couldn't do it. She couldn't *see* where she really was. Zhayra's excitement dwindled, and worry rose in her. No, she wasn't supposed to be focusing on that. Elinta tried to shove the feelings away, but her own panic fought back. Zhayra's increased.

"I can't," she said, her voice cracking.

"Listen to my voice, *tarsi*," Tamir said.

Elinta's thoughts were spiralling, and her breath came quick in her ears. What if she couldn't stop it? What if she was stuck looking through the dragon forever?

"Elinta," Tamir said, "focus on my voice."

Zhayra's speed had begun to slow. The dragon glanced behind her, concern causing her to hesitate. Elinta's stomach rose at the quick movement, and she blinked fiercely, trying to return to herself.

"El?" Niles said.

"It won't stop," she said, chest heaving. "I can't stop it." She could feel tears on her cheeks, but her vision was crystal clear. Her panic doubled. Her own eyes weren't influencing what she saw at all. She screwed her eyes shut, hearing her breaths heaving in her ears, but the images continued. "It won't stop!"

"It's OK," Lorrin's voice suddenly sounded in her ear and his arms slipped around her from behind. "Elinta. It's OK," he shushed, pulling her backward to his chest. "It's OK."

"It won't stop," she sobbed.

"I know." His breath tickled her ear. "Listen to my voice. Can you feel my breathing?" He took a deep breath.

She nodded then because she wasn't sure if he saw because she certainly didn't, she said, "Yes."

"Focus on that," he said. "In." He took a deep breath. "And out." He exhaled. Elinta's body rose and fell with his. "In."

She gulped and forced herself to breathe in time with him. Forced herself to focus on his heartbeat.

"And out."

She exhaled.

"In ... and out."

The forest had lost its clarity. The colours weren't as sharp anymore.

"In."

Her vision began to blur.

"Out."

All she could see were faint colours.

"In."

And then there was nothing.

"And out."

Elinta waited. The images were gone. Zhayra's roiling emotions were still there though. But the forest was gone. She cracked open a watery, blurred eye. Tamir smiled gently from opposite her.

"There you are," he said.

"There you are," Lorrin's voice repeated softly in her ear.

Elinta allowed a watery smile and rubbed at the tears on her face. She also allowed herself another moment in Lorrin's arms before she pulled away to look at him.

"Thank you," she said.

He smiled. "Anytime." He relaxed his arms and Elinta shuffled to the side of him. Niles rubbed her shoulder.

"You did well," Tamir said, his face genuine.

Elinta shook her head. "I was terrible."

"Like all things, it takes practice."

"Will you ... will you help me?" Despite the panic she'd been feeling while trying to separate from Zhayra, using the dragon's eyes had been an amazing experience. And she did want to do it again. Just thinking about the clouds through Zhayra's eyes had her itching for another look. And she could see the benefits of it.

"Of course," Tamir said. "Eventually, when your concentration allows, you will be able to use the senses whilst completing other activities. You could see with the strength of Zhayra's eyes and fight with your sword at the same time."

"How do you know so much about this?" Elinta asked, wiping her eyes again. How could he know so much about the bond? She only just realised that she'd seen what he described in Mazen. Hadn't he known where Lorrin and Niles were and what they were doing while she'd been in an outer corridor of the palace with him? Hadn't he named them specifically in the process? Even Tamir's ears weren't that sensitive. No, Mazen had been using the—what was it Tamir had said?—strength of Vaherin's ears.

Tamir paused as he considered her question. "You are not the only *Zearla lurai* in my acquaintance."

"Someone other than Mazen?" she asked. Surely, he didn't mean the exiled prince? "Here?"

"Yes."

Elinta sat up straight, a movement reflected in Lorrin and Niles. "Can we meet them?"

"I will take you and Zhayra to them tomorrow. Before we leave."

Elinta's face fell.

"I need to speak with my *ngaparta, tarsi,*" Tamir said with a slight smile. "It is only one more day."

"You have a wife?" Elinta asked, the other *Zearla lurai* momentarily forgotten. "Will she be OK with you leaving? Who is she?"

Tamir frowned. "Serren," he said as though it were obvious.

"Oh," Niles said.

"That makes sense," Lorrin added. The Asali had been to their rooms several times since they'd arrived. She'd even mentioned a husband before.

"Are you sure about coming with us?" Elinta asked. She didn't want to tear him away from his wife, especially when Serren had been so kind to them.

"She will understand," Tamir said, rising to his feet. "I will leave you to return to your rooms. Please, don't wander."

After dinner, Elinta made her way back to the training field to see Zhayra. She hadn't had a chance to visit the dragon since her experience seeing through her eyes.

"Did you catch anything?" she asked the dragon, sitting opposite her.

Zhayra blinked. Elinta took that and her contentment to mean yes.

"We should find a way for you to say yes or no," Elinta said, the idea just occurring to her. "What if ... you blinked once for yes and twice for no?"

The dragon blinked.

Elinta grinned. "I can't believe I didn't think of this before." She wracked her mind, trying to think of all the questions she wanted to ask the dragon, but no simple 'yes or no' ones occurred to her. Finally, she said, "Have you ever listened through my ears?"

Zhayra blinked yes.

"What about any of the other senses?"

Yes again.

"Really? What other senses are there?" she mused.

Zhayra huffed and stared at her.

"Sorry." Elinta pivoted in place and shuffled backward to lean against the dragon. She stared up at the darkening sky. She could stay out here tonight with Zhayra. Lorrin and Niles wouldn't worry, and the Asali didn't need to know. She sighed. She wanted to speak to Serren though.

She still felt guilty about Tamir, not only in taking him away from her, but also because she hadn't even realised that they were married. Elinta looked up at Zhayra and the dragon tilted her head to look down at her.

"Can I come sleep with you tonight?"

Zhayra blinked once.

"I've just got to talk to Serren, then I'll be back."

Zhayra blinked again.

Elinta jumped to her feet, scratched Zhayra behind the spines on her cheek, and jogged back to the building they were staying in. The Asali woman had mentioned she'd drop by again after dinner with some supplies for their journey. If she hurried, she would catch the woman before she left.

"Is Serren still here?" Elinta asked, her eyes landing on Lorrin sitting in one of the chairs as she stopped inside the doorway. She tried not to think about his arms around her.

"She just ducked into Niles's room."

"Thanks." Elinta hurried to his room.

"Oi! It's not my mess, OK?" Niles called after her.

Elinta laughed. "No one else goes in there!"

She entered the room before he could respond.

"Serren," she greeted, closing the door behind her. Niles's room—decorated much like her own—wasn't as messy as she'd expected based on his comment. It wasn't as though they'd brought much with them to make a mess with.

The Asali woman turned to her in question, pausing in her work to fold Niles's clean clothes that had somehow become spread across the floor. She doubted General Sonnen would let him get away with even that small mess at home.

"Has Tamir spoken with you?" Elinta asked.

Serren's face cleared. "He has."

"Are you OK with him leaving? He doesn't have to come. He can stay. I didn't realise you were married."

Serren smiled and shook her head. "It is OK. This is something he needs to do."

Elinta frowned. "What do you mean?"

Serren sat on the edge of Niles's bed, which looked exactly like the one Elinta had been sleeping in. "Our people need to know what Mazen is doing, and Tamir is the best person for the task. Not only that, but he is the best person to help *you*."

"I don't want to cause trouble."

"You won't."

"I'll try not to keep him for too long."

Serren smiled. "That is not something you can promise. But it is appreciated."

"Thank you for all your help while we've been here."

"It is my pleasure," Serren said, returning to her feet.

"Please, don't worry about cleaning. He'll just make it messy again. Go be with your *ngapara*."

"Ah, you know some of our language!"

"Only a little," Elinta said as she opened the bedroom door and shooed Serren out.

"I will see you in the morning, Elinta," the woman said with a laugh as she ducked out of the building. Trailing Serren, Elinta caught a glint of *illayas* wrapped delicately around her left wrist as she went. She'd seen a few Asali with similar bracelets, a strange sight considering the rareness of the metal now. What could it be for?

"What was that about?" Niles said, sitting in one of the chairs, a leg slung over the side and bouncing in the air.

"Just a girl talk," Elinta said. Lorrin cocked an eyebrow, but Elinta didn't explain, only sitting in one of the other chairs. "How did you manage to spread all your clothes over the floor?"

"What do you mean *all* my clothes? I packed light!"

She smiled and shook her head. "I'm sorry you two can't visit the Asali *Zearla lurai* tomorrow," Elinta said. Tamir had promised to take her and Zhayra, not the boys.

"Seems like they're a bit secretive or something." Niles shrugged. "You'll tell us all about it though, yeah?"

"Yeah."

"Fine by me," Niles said. Lorrin nodded.

They didn't stay up for very long, knowing that they would rise early in the morning so Elinta could visit the *Zearla lurai* before they left. When Lorrin and Niles had gone to bed and their doors had shut behind them, Elinta ducked back out into the night and returned to the training field where Zhayra waited for her. She slept all night, tucked against the dragon's side.

CHAPTER

TEN

"E LINTA?"

Elinta opened her eyes and found herself facing a wall of white membrane.

"Is Elinta here?" Tamir's voice sounded from the other side, slightly muffled.

Zhayra tiredly grunted from behind her and Elinta grinned.

"I'm here!" she called, sitting up. Her head brushed the wing.

"Are you ready, *tarsi?*"

"I—" Elinta frowned and prodded at the dragon's wing, not wanting to shout.

With a groan, Zhayra's bulk shifted, and her wing slowly retracted to reveal Tamir standing on the other side.

"I'm ready."

"Good," he said.

Elinta jumped to her feet, running a hand through her hair. She hoped she didn't appear too ruffled for meeting the *Zearla lurai*, but she was willing to sacrifice her appearance for the good sleep she'd just had at Zhayra's side.

Tamir addressed Zhayra. "We will be going to the base of the closest of the *Illatin* Mountains," he said, using the Asali name for the Benhurst Ranges. "It will take us an hour or so to reach it. You are welcome to meet us there."

Zhayra blinked twice, shook herself, and took off into the air, circling high above them.

"She'll stay above us," Elinta said, glad for the new system she'd developed with the dragon.

"Very well. Shall we go?" he said, gesturing with his hand.

Tamir led her south through the city and out into the forest. Elinta studied the silver trunks as they passed, wishing to see them with the clarity she had through Zhayra the day before. They'd looked so beautiful then. They still were now, but it wasn't the same. She marvelled at how there had been no clear line between where the city had finished and the forest began. It all just felt like forest to her.

Though Tamir had said they'd be at the base, they actually climbed a small way up the mountain so that Elinta could look out over the forest below them. Soon the trees began to thin so they only dotted the landscape and small grey rocks jutted out of the earth. Droppings and scratches in the earth from small animals began to increase though she didn't see any of the creatures that had caused them. Then a small hut with the same pod-like shape as many of the buildings in Liyarna came into view.

It was made of the brown and silver trunks of the forest, but the two colours wove together and gave the hut an almost ethereal appearance. It was a strange look, but it drew Elinta to it. As soon as they stopped walking, Zhayra landed beside them, knocking down one of the few trees around the hut.

"I will see if she is—"

"*You didn't fly.*" An elderly woman appeared, glowing, in the doorway of the hut, her long, wispy hair pulled back. She was small and slightly bent over, but she seemed otherwise healthy.

"*Sa,*" Elinta responded.

The woman frowned and to Elinta's surprise, walked easily toward them. "Why not?"

"I don't like it," she said haltingly, matching the woman's change in language. Was this the *Zearla lurai?* She squinted at the tiny woman, trying to make out her eyes, but it wasn't until she was nearly opposite her that Elinta could make out the colour under their brightness and the reflection in them.

They were green. A deep, emerald green. Like the leaves on the trees outside Kethmere. She had the same white, slitted pupils of Mazen, but Elinta felt a pang of homesickness looking into those green eyes. Even if home didn't miss her.

How many other colours are there? She'd dreamt about the dragons once; the night she'd learnt Zhayra's name. But the memory had faded, and she couldn't remember what colours there'd been. Was green common? Was white?

"Where's your dragon?" Elinta asked, glancing around her.

Zhayra grunted in agreement, a twinge of excitement and nerves fluttering in her chest.

The woman shook her head. "Gone. A long time ago." She fixed Tamir with a long look. "I don't like visitors."

"I know, *ulla*. But I knew you would want to meet them, as they wanted to meet you."

"Humph," the woman grunted, but there was a shine in her eyes. She looked at Elinta. "Come with me. You too," she added, glancing at Zhayra. "Wait inside for us, Tamir."

Tamir bowed and walked over to the small hut, ducking inside.

"Come," the woman said, and led them further up the mountain in silence. Elinta watched the woman in shock as she easily navigated the rocky mountainside despite her bent appearance and small stature. She didn't stumble once, and nor did she speak. They passed through a wall of thin scraggily trees and came to an outcropping of rock. The older *Zearla lurai* stopped.

"How long have you had the *ngaran?*" she said, her back to Elinta and Zhayra.

"Four or five months," Elinta said. Had it really been that long already?

The woman turned in surprise. "And you are not flying with her? Not using her senses?"

"I—I've been in our capital," she stammered, feeling like she needed to defend herself to this woman.

"But you don't like it," the woman said, repeating her words from earlier.

"No."

"What is your name?"

"Elinta," she said.

"And the dragon?"

"Zhayra."

"Hmm." The woman's green eyes flitted over the both of them. "Why won't you fly?" she repeated.

"I don't like it," Elinta said, starting to feel frustrated. Why did the woman care so much? She'd hoped … she didn't know what she'd hoped. Maybe that the woman would help her understand the bond, not berate her on her dislike of flying.

"Why won't you fly?" the elderly woman repeated.

"I don't like it," Elinta said with a huff. "I don't want to fall off."

The woman smiled. "There," she said. "Why are you afraid of falling? Look at Zhayra."

Elinta frowned and did as the woman said. Zhayra held her eyes, feeling both confused and sad, but Elinta wasn't sure why.

"Do you think she would let you fall?"

Elinta's frown eased. She thought of the way Zhayra had saved her from the villagers at Kethmere, and the mountain cat in the Eggslaying cave. How they'd comforted each other after the Eggslaying festival, and the way Zhayra had been concerned for her safety as she'd walked back to the palace that night alone.

"No," she said quietly, realising why the dragon was sad. "She wouldn't let me fall." She knew if she did slip, the dragon would catch her. It didn't completely ease her worries, but it certainly lessened them.

Zhayra's stomach lightened, and she blinked twice. *No,* she was saying. *I wouldn't.*

"Good," the woman said, her tone losing some of its hardness. She sat on one of the large rocks jutting out from the ground and gestured for Elinta to do the same on one opposite. Zhayra settled into a crouch beside her.

"What's your name?" Elinta asked, sure that the word Tamir had used earlier was some kind of title rather than a name.

The woman laughed, a light sound at odds with her straight-forward nature. "To most I am '*Zearla lurai,*' or '*ulla,*'" she said. "To you, I am Aesira."

"Aesira," she said, feeling the name in her mouth. "What happened to your dragon?"

"Life," the woman said, her voice soft. "It's something you will never experience, but Zhayra will one day. I simply outlived him."

Elinta's eyes widened, and she glanced at Zhayra. She'd never thought of that. The dragons could live for hundreds of years, but she ... she only had another seventy. Eighty at most. What would happen to Zhayra when she was gone?

Zhayra's chest constricted.

"Have you been alone since then? What about your family?" Elinta asked, partly for herself, partly for Zhayra. Would Zhayra be alone? Or would she return to the dragons? She still didn't know why the dragon was in Eldras. She closed her eyes and hoped with all her being that the dragon wouldn't be alone.

"No," Aesira said. "My son and grandson died after the Eggslaying, but I didn't move out here until my foster son left Liyarna sixteen years ago."

Elinta remained quiet, not knowing what to say. She mulled over Aesira's words. She hadn't said it, but it was clear she'd been alone since she'd moved into the hut. Elinta shivered. She couldn't imagine what this woman had been through, to lose the dragon she was bonded to, then to lose the rest with the Eggslaying, and then her son and grandson—Elinta froze. Son and grandson. After the Eggslaying. The last king of the Asali had died after the Eggslaying, and his son was thought to have died too. King Riah and Prince *Mazen*. No, surely that couldn't be right ... but then how many fathers and sons could have died just after the Eggslaying? The Asali had long lives and were unaffected by sickness due to their healing. It was clear who Aesira meant. Only Mazen wasn't dead. Did this woman know that her grandson was still alive? What he was doing?

Zhayra grumbled and shifted closer to her. She absently rubbed the dragon's scales, aware that her emotions had just bounced around drastically within a very short period of time. But she couldn't believe the revelation she'd just had. She was looking at Mazen's grandmother.

Aesira was watching the thoughts play out across her face, but the woman didn't say anything. And neither did Elinta. She filed it away. The woman wouldn't be able to tell her much about

Mazen, Mazen as he was *now*. She had more pressing things to ask the woman. The bond was still so new to her, and this woman was the only one who fully understood it. Mazen would have to wait. She still intended to ask Tamir about him.

"Can you tell me about the *zearla lurai ngaran*?" Elinta said, impressed that her voice remained steady.

Aesira paused, as though acknowledging both the realisation and the decision Elinta had made. "There is much to learn, and most you must learn for yourself. There is no better way than to do," she said, "but I will tell you a story from among our people. Learn from it what you will."

Elinta frowned but nodded.

Aesira looked out over the trees below them, and the city that was somewhere among them, as though gathering her thoughts before she turned her eyes on Elinta and Zhayra and began.

"Thousands of years ago, there was an Asali man who shared the *ngaran* with a dragon. They lived together, spending time among the man's family in Liyarna and with the dragons in the Ash Mountains. They lived in this way for many years. Until the man's wife died. Distraught and unable to look upon his own kind for the grief he felt, he left his only son and the city behind. No one knew where he had gone.

"The man was gone for a long time. His son was an adult when he finally found his father. He'd been living among the dragons ever since the death of his wife and no longer recognised his mother-tongue. He spoke to his son, and the Asali that had accompanied him in the search, in the language of the dragons," Aesira finished, letting the silence stretch between them.

"But what happened to the man?" Elinta asked, realising the woman wasn't going to say any more. She recognised the tale. Though she'd never heard it in full, Ford had mentioned it to her and Lorrin the first day she'd met the historian.

"He stayed among the dragons." Aesira shrugged.

"But ... how did he forget his language? How did he speak to the others in the language of the dragons? Does that just mean with emotions? What happened to the son?"

Aesira shook her head. "It is a legend, Elinta. It is for learning. Nothing more."

Zhayra grumbled.

"Me too," she said to the dragon. What was she supposed to learn from that? That she might forget to speak the common tongue if she ever spent too much time with Zhayra? That it's bad to live alone? Don't leave your family? It was too late for the last one....

"Well ..." Elinta cast around for something else to ask, shifting to get more comfortable on the rock. "What about the Eggslaying? How do I convince the council it won't happen again?"

The older *Zearla lurai* shook her head. "I've said enough. You must learn for yourself. You must discover. I cannot do these things for you. Even if I wanted to, it has been many years since I've been in the world. I do not know it anymore."

Elinta opened her mouth to object.

"Uh," Aesira held up a hand to silence her, "I will say this; where there is misunderstanding or lack of communication, there will always be war."

"But we all speak different languages!" she said.

The dragons could hardly defend themselves against the allegations thrown their way, and no one else could defend them since they didn't know all the details. And it wasn't as though you could just ask the dragons, since no one could speak to them ... except for her, in a way. She sighed in frustration, and Zhayra echoed the response with a huff.

"You two are closer than I thought." Aesira's eyes twinkled. "We must return to Tamir now. He is still waiting, and I don't want any of my scrolls going missing."

Elinta managed to laugh and struggled to her feet. A flock of small green birds flew by overhead, moving toward the city. Elinta watched them for a moment before Aesira led her and Zhayra back down to the hut. All the while, Elinta turned over all she'd learnt and tried not to feel too frustrated at what she *hadn't* learnt, which seemed a great deal.

Aesira was Mazen's grandmother. She'd shared the *ngaran* with a dragon. And then there was the legend of the Asali man, a legend that seemed incomplete. What had really happened to the man?

Elinta's foot caught on a small rock, and she stumbled a few steps before rightening herself.

Aesira glanced over her shoulder and cast her a strange look. "You have much to learn. No wonder you worry about falling."

Elinta stared at the back of the woman's head, then shot Zhayra a confused look. What did that mean?

Zhayra grunted, and Elinta's frown deepened. What did *that* mean?

When they reached the hut, Aesira walked through the open door and returned a moment later, shooing a grinning Tamir out.

"Do I need to check your pockets?" Aesira said in a strict tone, but Elinta thought she saw a sparkle in the woman's peculiar eyes.

"No, *ulla*."

"Good," she said. "Elinta and Zhayra will be flying on part of your journey back to Nevira."

Elinta's mouth dropped in shock. How did she know Tamir was coming? How did she know that was where they were going?

Tamir nodded.

"You should go. It is getting late. *Layzulla,*" Aesira said, twisted on her heel and disappeared inside her hut before Elinta could say anything.

Elinta and Zhayra stared after the woman.

"She is right," Tamir said. "It is getting late, and the council will want to see you before we leave as well."

"Right," Elinta said, turning away from the closed door of the hut and following Tamir back down the mountain. Zhayra flew lazily above them.

After a few minutes of walking in silence, Elinta turned to Tamir. "How did she know we were leaving?"

Tamir cocked his head. "I told her."

"You hardly spoke to her." Elinta frowned.

Tamir's face cleared, and he laughed. "I spoke to her as she led you away. You forget she is *Zearla lurai*."

"What do you—" She paused. "Oh. She can still access the dragon's senses even though he's dead?"

"Only as her own. She cannot access him anymore, but she can hear with the strength of his ears."

Elinta remained silent, trying to wrap her mind around that. She wasn't sure how that worked, but then, there was a lot about the *ngaran* that she didn't know.

An hour later, Elinta, Lorrin, Niles, and Tamir stood before the council on the outskirts of the city. The Asali had seen to it that they had enough food to see them back to Nevira, and all their gear now hung from the saddles of their four horses. Tamir had already said goodbye to Serren in private, and the woman now stood away from their small group, watching.

"*Layzulla. Zetayn nalliyan ayn palla kli ayn karn mai ris,*" Piran said, looking over their group.

Elinta bit back the angry retort that rose to her lips about Mazen trying not to let that happen and repeated the phrase back to him in the common tongue. "May the sun continue to shine on you."

Her mind flashed back to her conversation with Serren, how the woman had said they believe their light came from the sun. *Huh,* she thought, *so that's where the blessing came from.*

Aisla, in turn, wished them well, and Nakiah managed to say goodbye though he didn't acknowledge any of the others except Tamir. And finally, they were on their way back to Nevira, but Elinta couldn't help feeling they hadn't really accomplished anything at all.

CHAPTER
ELEVEN

T HE DAY PASSED SLOWLY. Elinta, Lorrin, Niles, and Tamir kept the horses at a steady trot while Zhayra flew above them, her shadow slipping through the canopy and flitting across the ground with them. Elinta mulled over Aesira's words, her eyes unconsciously drifting up toward Zhayra even when she couldn't see her white form. Zhayra would never let her fall, or, more precisely, if she did slip, the dragon would catch her. It eased her mind, only a little, but maybe it was enough.

She thought back to her first, and only, time riding the dragon. It had been a terrible journey. They'd been fleeing for their lives, and she'd been cold and uncomfortable. But then she remembered the fun she and Zhayra had swimming in Lake Lusinata. What was she missing out on by keeping her feet firmly on the ground?

Aesira had been surprised by her aversion to flying. Maybe the woman was right. Maybe it was time for her to fly again. She felt her resolve solidifying and, with it, a flutter of nerves. Tomorrow, once they were out of the Calaza, she'd fly.

In the morning, the air already heavy with heat, Elinta was finishing her breakfast in silence when Zhayra walked over to her, knocking a sapling down in the process. The dragon stopped in front of her and lowered her head to look her in the eye.

"I'm fine," Elinta said, knowing Zhayra could feel the ball of nerves sitting in her stomach.

Zhayra cocked her head.

"We're going to fly today," she said quietly, not wanting the boys to know yet. She was sitting away from their group, sorting through her backpack as she ate a loaf of bread. It was a poor attempt to psyche herself up—by ignoring it all together.

Zhayra pulled back her head and roared. A wave of the smell of burnt meat swept over her. Elinta rocked backward, her ears ringing. She coughed.

"What? What's going on?" Niles jumped to his feet, looking around their small campsite for any sign of danger.

Lorrin, his hand on the hilt of his sword, frowned. "I think that was a happy roar."

Tamir smiled. "They are going to fly."

"We're going to fly today," Elinta confirmed, wishing all the while that she hadn't said anything. Maybe there was a way to tie herself to the dragon? That way, she definitely wouldn't fall.

Niles grinned, rubbing his hands together. "This I have to see."

Elinta sighed and shot a look at Zhayra. "Thanks," she mumbled, but it didn't hold any real bitterness.

Zhayra just grunted and lowered her bulk into a crouch, waiting patiently for them to pack up camp.

All too soon, they were ready to move on, and Elinta stood hesitantly in front of Zhayra. Lorrin bumped her shoulder. "You'll be fine," he said, unable to hide the excitement in his voice. He hadn't seen her ride Zhayra either, she reminded herself.

She straightened her spine and crossed the remaining distance between her and the dragon, stopping in front of her bent front leg. *How did I do this last time?* she thought, staring at the distance between her and Zhayra's back.

With a sigh, she clambered onto the dragon's leg. Then, with a slight jump, she pulled herself up, landing with her belly on Zhayra's back. She fought for a grip on her scales, then slung one leg over. Elinta waited a moment, flat against the dragon, and evened her breathing, then sat up and looked down at Lorrin, Niles, and Tamir.

"Easy," she said.

Niles shook his head, a smile on his face. She fully expected a comment about her lack of finesse from one of the boys, but they were too excited. Niles looked ready to bounce on his toes.

A light breeze played across Elinta's bare arms, prompting the memory of her last ride. "Can someone throw me up a jumper?"

Lorrin grinned and trotted across to her horse, rifling inside her bag. He returned with a cotton jumper Kalla, the palace tailor, had made her, and tossed it up to her. Though the air was thick down here on the ground, it was likely to be cold up in the sky.

"You'll have to find an easier way to mount, or practice until it becomes effortless," Tamir said, rubbing his chin as she pulled on her jumper. Sweat beaded on her forehead within seconds.

"Maybe I could stick to that today?" she said half-heartedly.

Zhayra grumbled, her wings shifting against her body.

"I was joking. Well, let's go then, girl."

"We'll see you at our next break," Lorrin said.

"Alright."

"Elinta?" he said, drawing her attention again. His blue eyes were sparkling.

"Yes?"

"Don't forget to breathe."

She nodded and smiled, taking a deep breath as Zhayra spread out her wings. It was a much nicer take-off than the one Elinta had experienced in Kethmere. Zhayra had shot into the air then, leaving the lake behind them in seconds. But this time she gently flapped at the air, and they slowly rose in place. Lorrin beamed from under them.

Elinta smiled with relief, but something shifted in Zhayra that made her stomach drop and her face fall. Mischief.

"No, please," she said, flattening against the dragon and digging her fingers into her scales. But it was too late, Zhayra's huge wings beat at the air in rapid succession, and they shot upwards, the wind pushing down on her. Elinta's blonde hair pulled loose from her hair tie and fell into her face. She spluttered but didn't dare remove one of her hands to move the hair whipping across her eyes and mouth. She closed her eyes and gritted her teeth.

Then, all of a sudden, the pressure of the wind stopped. Zhayra's wing beats slowed and a soft breeze played over her, but a gentle warmth from the sun hit her at the same time. Cautiously, Elinta lifted her head and looked around. The ground was far below them though not as far as she'd expected. She could still make the boys out, now on their horses and moving along the ground at a snail's pace.

Zhayra's wings no longer moved, but remained spread out, smoothly riding the air. The dragon twisted her neck around and looked at her, a twinkle in her eye.

"That was mean," Elinta said, but she couldn't stop a smile from playing through.

Zhayra snorted, blinked once, and turned to look ahead of them once more.

Digging her fingers in again, Elinta twisted to look behind her and saw the vast expanse of the Calaza stretching away. To her right were the Benhurst Ranges, where she'd been only yesterday, talking with Mazen's grandmother. Ahead of them was an endless landscape of different colours and textures. Trees dotted the ground, which was a patchwork of yellow and green. She rested herself against Zhayra's neck again and looked down, fighting a moment of vertigo to watch the tiny figures below.

They were circling the boys, she realised, so that they didn't leave them far behind. Zhayra could probably have her back in Nevira by tomorrow if she wanted.

Looking down at Lorrin, Niles, and Tamir, she wondered how Zhayra saw them, but after her experience on the training field, she was too frightened to try accessing the dragon's vision while they were in the air. While Zhayra would catch her, she didn't want to tempt fate with a fall.

Maybe she could try it again another time, though, while her own feet were firmly on the ground.

"Zhayra?" she called hesitantly.

The dragon grunted.

"You can—you can go a little faster."

Zhayra's stomach jumped, and the dragon's wings began to beat again. The wind tugged and pulled at Elinta's hair. She shoved at the nerves clenching her gut. She wanted to enjoy this. She really did. But her fingers dug deeper, tearing her nails, and her legs clenched even tighter. But the dragon didn't seem to notice. Or if she did, she ignored it. Her own feelings were a deep contrast to Elinta's. Excitement bubbled in her chest and contentment sat in her stomach. So Elinta focused on those, pushing her own fear away, and slowly, her grip relaxed. Then the muscles in her legs. And it was then that she realised she was smiling.

With a laugh, Elinta closed her eyes and let the feeling of effortlessly soaring wash over her.

"How was it?" Niles said as soon as Zhayra's feet touched the ground.

Elinta, still flat on the dragon's back, grinned.

"That's promising," Lorrin said, joining his friend and shielding his eyes as he looked up at her. The horses were tied up some distance behind them.

"It wasn't too bad," she admitted, sliding one leg over Zhayra's back and slipping to the ground. Her legs wobbled, and she caught herself against the dragon. "I still wish there was a way to hold on, though."

Zhayra had been flying at the same level and at quite a gentle pace the entire time they'd been in the air. And she was sure that was the only reason she'd stayed on. She couldn't imagine trying to hold on when the dragon was moving around more, or even just going at a faster pace. As it was, her fingers were throbbing, and her nails were a mess.

"Thirsty?" Lorrin asked.

With a nod, Elinta pushed off from Zhayra and accepted the bottle Lorrin offered her. His eyes lingered on her as she took a sip, and she ignored the warmth it brought to her cheeks. She couldn't imagine what a mess she looked, but Lorrin didn't seem to care.

"You seemed quite comfortable," Tamir said.

Elinta flexed her aching fingers and shook her head. "Not at first, but it wasn't as bad as I remember."

Zhayra hummed, lowering her chest to the ground, and watching the four of them talk. Elinta tried her best to flatten her hair before pulling it back up with another hair tie, but the wind had made it a tangled mess.

When she'd finished, Niles handed Elinta a strip of dried meat, and the four sat where they were. Elinta peeled off her jumper, sweat beading on her forehead again. She'd almost forgotten how warm it was on the ground while she'd been in the air. Summer wasn't over yet, and the days were still heavy with heat.

"What do you call 'lunch'?" Elinta asked Tamir, glancing curiously at the food in her hand.

"We call the mid-day meal *sallar*," he said, before taking another bite of his food.

"*Sallar*," Elinta repeated. She watched Tamir in silence, and wondered, not for the first time, how Mazen had come to be the way he was.

After lunch, Elinta mounted the palace mare, and they rode until late afternoon. When they made camp, Elinta, Lorrin, and Niles seemed to naturally drift toward the space where they'd have the most room, their hands already inching toward their swords.

Tamir sat by the fire, Zhayra to his left, and watched with interest. Lorrin drew his sword before Niles could free his own, and Elinta and the prince danced until dinner.

The next day, during another mindless hour of riding through the same unchanging landscape, Elinta stared at a tree on the horizon. She'd been trying to 'see with the strength of Zhayra's eyes,' as Tamir put it, for the last half hour. Aesira's rebuke of her lack of use of the senses, as well as flying, had been echoing around her mind ever since she'd heard the words. The challenge had been set, and she'd meet it.

Elinta followed the steps Tamir had taken her through when she'd accessed Zhayra's sight, and started wide, slowly narrowing her field of view until all she saw was the tree. Then she tried to see its branches, whether they were moving in a light breeze or perfectly still. She tried to make out other details, straining her eyes as hard as she could, and fighting her rising frustration, when something clicked and there it was.

It was a gum tree, with a light brown trunk and faint green leaves. The branches were twisted. Spread out on either side of the trunk, they dipped and turned and there was no way she could make out those details with her own eyes.

"Woah," Elinta said.

"What?" Niles asked from beside her. Her eyes flickered to him, and she startled. He was so ... so *clear*. His eyes somehow seemed browner. If that was possible. And they were lighter closer to his pupils. She studied the rest of his face. The scar on his bottom lip seemed clearer, too. She'd always thought it was white, but it was actually silver. Elinta looked down at Horse. Tiny particles of dirt had collected on the fine bristles of his hair, glinting in the light.

"Er ... Elinta? You're freaking me out here."

"Oh," she said, looking back at Niles's face. "Sorry."

"What are you doing?" he asked, his brow furrowed. She watched the muscles under his skin move in fascination.

Excitement made her words gush. "I accessed Zhayra's eyes."

"But you can see me," he said.

"Yes," she said, "I'm using her sight as my own."

Niles's face cleared. "That explains why you're looking at me like you've never seen me before. You're experiencing my good looks like never before."

Elinta laughed and twisted in her seat to look at Lorrin. He raised an eyebrow. Her breath caught in her chest. The prince really was handsome.

"She's using dragon eyes," Niles called back.

"Dragonsight," she corrected.

"I like that," Niles said.

"You're using her sight as your own?" Lorrin asked.

She nodded, and tearing her eyes from Lorrin, looked at Tamir. "Your light is softer in her eyes," Elinta said curiously. She'd expected his glow to hurt her eyes, but it didn't. He wasn't fainter either, the light just seemed gentler.

Tamir cocked his head. "Interesting."

She glanced once more at Lorrin, soaking up this view of him, before facing the front again. Now all she had to do was turn it off. *Right,* she thought, *distance myself.*

Elinta looked again at the tree in the distance with its twisting branches and pulled herself away. Where before she'd tried to bring the tree into focus, now she tried to do the complete opposite. She let her vision blur, squinting her eyes to warp the image even further.

Almost instinctively, she knew when her eyes were back to their usual strength and allowed her vision to clear. And there the tree was. Distant. Blurred. She couldn't even tell it was a gum anymore.

She sighed in relief.

"You did it?" Lorrin said.

"Yes," Elinta replied. She'd done it. Now all she had to do was learn to withdraw when she was looking through the dragon's eyes, but a small part of her had to admit the idea of Lorrin helping her again had its appeal.

Elinta spent the rest of the day thinking of all the things she still had to learn and loving it. She'd always thrived on learning, and now she faced a lot more. She went through a mental list; she had to learn to use the senses she shared with Zhayra, she had to learn just *what* they were, then there was Mazen, flying with Zhayra, Asalin, and her usual combat training with the boys. And rather than be overwhelmed, she grinned.

That night, as Tamir built the fire and Elinta and the boys unpacked their gear, she stared at the Asali, questions running through her mind. He'd said he'd known Mazen, and she needed to know more about him. Her stomach twisted at the idea, but she forced her feet to carry her to Tamir and sat hesitantly beside him. She glanced at Zhayra, who was several metres away and twisted around a large tree trunk. There wasn't a lot of room for the dragon in their latest campsite. She caught the dragon's eye and gestured to her ears, hoping she'd understand. She knew Zhayra would be able to hear their conversation from where she was, but she also wanted to know what it felt like to have her listening through her, and to be sure the dragon didn't miss anything. A moment later, her ears popped.

"What is it, *tarsi?*" Tamir asked, stacking some branches onto the pile of tinder and kindling.

"Can you tell me about Mazen and Vaherin?" she asked.

Tamir paused, drawing a flint and steel from his pocket. "They were bonded in thirty-five seventy-six. Ninety-one years before the Eggslaying," he said, reciting the facts in an even tone and striking the flint. Sparks flew. "Mazen was nine hundred and thirty-nine."

Elinta didn't interrupt though part of her was aware she'd have to repeat it all to the boys later. She wasn't sure whether he'd have been comfortable with a larger audience, so she hadn't wanted to risk it or to put him in a situation where he felt he couldn't refuse. Besides, Niles wouldn't have been able to resist commenting on whatever it was Tamir had to say. And ... she was worried that if he mentioned Aesira, since he was obviously close to her, she'd have to explain who she was to the boys, something she'd ultimately decided against for now. The boys wouldn't trust the woman if they knew who she was and, well, it also felt like encroaching on Aesira's personal life. She hadn't even told Tamir that she knew who the woman was.

"We drifted apart after that," Tamir continued, drawing Elinta's attention back, and striking the flint again. The spark took, and the flames consumed the tinder, quickly moving onto the kindling. Tamir sat back, his eyes switching to hers. "We grew up together," he said by way of explanation. "But then he began to spend all his time with Vaherin. They were inseparable. He seemed to lose interest in everything else: his friends, his family, even his duties as prince."

"What happened the day he left?" Elinta asked, scarcely above a whisper. Had the two of them been close friends? There was a trace of pain on his face, and she couldn't shake the way he'd reacted to hearing that Mazen was alive. Like someone who'd grieved a loss, only to learn it was a lie.

"I don't know." Tamir shook his head. "I wasn't with him. It was the day after the Eggslaying and King Riah had died. It all must have been too much for him. I thought he'd died too."

"How did King Riah die?"

"We don't know," Tamir said, looking into the flames. "There wasn't a mark on his body. He was just ... dead."

Elinta sat in silence. Why had Mazen left then? If his father was dead, then he would have been set to inherit the throne. Why would he abandon his people? And what had happened between then and now to make him the way he was? And Vaherin? Was he going along with whatever it was Mazen was doing?

She sighed. Mazen remained a mystery for now, but one she intended to solve. One she *had* to solve.

CHAPTER
TWELVE

T HE NIGHT BEFORE THEY would arrive in Nevira, Lorrin found Elinta on the banks of the Afonlin, her feet dangling in the water. She'd been thinking about Mazen and Vaherin again. Her hand was tracing the scar at her hip.

"Hey," he said, slipping off his boots and sitting beside her.

"Hi." She pulled herself from her thoughts, letting her hand fall away from her side. Silence descended. Elinta watched as a little bug skimmed across the surface of the river.

"Elinta," Lorrin said, hesitation in his voice.

She turned toward him at the unusual tone and found him studying her face. His own was strangely closed off.

"Where will you go when this is all over?"

Elinta's eyebrows rose in surprise, and she blew out a long breath. "I don't know," she said. Then, looking at Lorrin and the disappointment he was trying to hide, thought she'd better explain further. "Zhayra and I ... we belong together. But I don't belong with the dragons, and she doesn't belong here or in the city."

Lorrin didn't say anything.

"And we still don't know what 'this' is," Elinta added. "Or why Zhayra is here." Though, she thought, it seemed to have something to do with Mazen. Hadn't he said he'd been following her?

Lorrin remained silent for a moment. "You'll always be welcome at the palace," he said quietly, "and maybe Zhayra will be too."

Elinta didn't want to acknowledge how that made her feel, so she focused on the problems with what he was saying. Even though it put distance between them. "Thank you. But how can we guarantee the Eggslaying won't happen again?" She thought of all the children she'd seen at the festival. How their faces had shone with glee as the puppet dragon had died in 'The Ballad of the Slain.' They were just raising another generation to continue Cenric's legacy of death.

Lorrin shook his head. "We won't let it happen again. We know so much more now. We'll make sure everyone knows the truth about the dragons."

Starting with your parents, she wanted to say, but instead she said, "*We* don't even know the truth about what happened with Tristan."

"It doesn't matter."

"Maybe it does!" A tinge of anger in her voice surprised her. "Where there's misunderstanding, there will always be war," Elinta repeated Aesira's words, feeling the truth of them in her bones. Hadn't her life since meeting Zhayra been a reflection of that? Her family, her village, the human royals, and the Asali council had all fallen to that trap. She wished this conversation could have gone differently. But it couldn't. Not while there was so much wrong in Eldras. And not when so few people were willing to make a change.

"What are we going to do when we get back?" Elinta whispered.

"We'll make them see."

It was meant to make her feel better. But it didn't. Because she couldn't see how they would.

The two of them fell into silence, their words hanging in the air between them as Zhayra flew by overhead, a dark silhouette against the night sky. There was an idea stirring in Elinta's mind, something to do with the bond, but whenever she tried to look at it, it scuttled away. So, she let the silence stretch and wondered what she would do if she couldn't stay with Lorrin when she couldn't go home either.

"I'll come see you soon," Elinta said, rubbing her hand down Zhayra's smooth muzzle. The dragon nudged her, then slipped under the trees of the wood. Elinta watched until the tip of her tail disappeared then, as a group, they turned nervously toward the capital.

Elinta didn't feel Zhayra's absence as keenly this time, knowing that she and the dragon could easily check on each other through their ears and eyes whenever they wished. Her attention was focused now on what lay before them; explaining to King Aldon and Queen Mira where they'd been, what they were doing, and why they had returned with an Asali. Not to mention why she hadn't started her history lessons with Ford.

She felt strange now, no longer having that cover story to hide behind. Now all she had was her friendship with Lorrin. He'd been quiet since their conversation last night, and she knew his mind was working, trying to solve the problems they faced.

Before they reached the outskirts of the city, Lorrin drew a dark cloak from his bag and handed it to Tamir. "Just until we reach the palace," he said apologetically. "It's best if my parents meet you before the whole city knows you're here."

Tamir slung the cloak around his shoulders, drawing the hood up and over his head. It would have cast his face into shadow if his skin didn't glow. The Asali turned his eyes down to the ground, hiding their strange colour. Like that, Tamir almost seemed human. Almost.

"Would you wear some socks?" Elinta asked, staring at his glowing feet.

Tamir's eyes flicked up. "Of course, *tarsi*," he said though he sounded reluctant.

Niles threw him a pair of socks, then shrugged into his grey guard's jacket.

Ready, they finally made their way into the city, the White Palace looming over them. The late afternoon sun bounced off the white road and into their eyes. The reflection bit at Elinta's face. People turned as they passed, their faces clearing in recognition as they saw the prince. Elinta glanced around in mild surprise. The city seemed exactly the same as when they'd left. For some reason, she'd expected it to be different. To have changed in their absence. In the way she now felt different.

Her eyes ran over the familiar cobbled streets, the closest watch tower, the cafés and shops lining the street. They followed the very road that the Eggslaying festival had taken the day of Mazen's attack, but the march was the ghost of a memory. There were no dragon puppets littering the road, no children screaming in mock terror of the blue dragon, no fake king leading the charge. People just went about their business.

"General Nash is going to be so mad," Niles whispered, drawing her attention. His eyes widened. "My dad!"

Lorrin laughed, but the sound wasn't quite genuine. "Yeah, they will be."

Elinta shook her head, glad for a distraction from her own fear of advisor Shae sneaking in. The woman had suspected her of murder, as well as stealing the dragon scales, for months. "General Nash won't be."

The boys turned in their saddles to look at her in surprise. She'd just been thinking about the first day she'd arrived in Nevira and when she'd met Niles and General Nash, Lorrin's aunt.

"Do you remember what she said when we arrived from the White Mountains?" she said to Lorrin.

"'Where have you been?'"

Elinta shook her head. "'Take Niles with you next time,'" she said, paraphrasing.

Lorrin's eyes widened, and then he laughed. "You're right."

"Great," Niles said. "Just my dad and your parents, then."

"Yeah," Lorrin said, but they both seemed less nervous now.

When they crossed through the gate and into the inner courtyard of the palace, the stableboy, Jae, darted out and took the reins from Lorrin and Niles. His master, a tall, lean man who Elinta had never seen before, followed close behind the boy and took Elinta's and Tamir's horses.

"Thank you, Darien," Lorrin said. "Have our guest's bags sent to my room as well."

The man bowed and led the horses away.

Looking up the steps at the open palace doors, Elinta half expected General Nash to appear, like she had so many months ago.

"You alright?" Niles asked.

"Yeah," Elinta said with a smile. "I was just remembering the last time this happened."

Niles grinned. "You were as pale as a sheet, you know."

"I was not!"

"You were. Until you saw me." He winked.

Elinta slapped his arm.

"Let's go," Lorrin said.

Elinta and Tamir fell into place behind Lorrin and Niles as they led the way inside. It made sense for the two of them to lead the way since no one knew just how important Elinta's part in the trip had been, and no one knew about Tamir yet. She was more than happy to hand the important jobs back to Lorrin and fade into the background where it was safe. She just wished she knew how this meeting was going to go. They hadn't made any plans for after this moment, as it all hinged on what the monarchy would say.

Elinta grew more and more nervous the closer they drew to the throne room, marking their progress with each turn or painting. That's where they'd decided to go when they arrived. Either the king and queen would already be there, or they would receive word that their son had returned and would meet them there. Elinta was experiencing a strange sense of déjà vu as they moved through the palace. The cornices were just as beautiful as she remembered, and even the pale grey of the stone beneath them was beautiful. Only this time Elinta's eyes were heavy, and she knew it was Zhayra watching through her.

She wished she could run her hand over the dragon's scales, but instead she tried to look at as much of the palace as possible so Zhayra could experience it all.

Their small group received several interested glances as they passed the busier rooms of the palace. Tamir kept his head tucked down the entire way, but his cloaked figure drew the most notice. It impressed Elinta that he didn't trip once as they walked.

When they arrived at the large double doors to the throne room with two guards stationed on either side, Lorrin took a deep breath and knocked. Elinta smoothed out a crease in her shirt. Her stomach jumped as a voice called out.

"Enter."

With one last glance around their group, Lorrin pushed the doors open, and they entered the throne room.

"Lorrin!" Queen Mira's voice hit them before they'd even passed through the doors.

King Aldon's eyes widened as they landed on his son. "Where have you been?" His voice was even and controlled, but Elinta sensed an undercurrent of anger in his words. "Three weeks, Lorrin. It's been nearly three weeks and not a word."

Just like the first time Elinta had entered the room, General Nash stood at the base of the steps leading up to the two thrones. Her blue eyes were fixed on her nephew though her expression betrayed none of her thoughts. But Elinta had straightened at the king's words as a thought struck her. She did a quick mental calculation. Her birthday had happened sometime within the last few days. She'd turned seventeen without even realising.

"Everything's OK," Lorrin said, drawing her attention back to the present. "But there's a lot we need to discuss."

Beside Elinta, Tamir kept his eyes down, but it didn't stop the king from noticing him.

"Who is this?" He gestured to Tamir.

Lorrin turned. "Tamir?"

Elinta knew Lorrin had hoped to explain things before introducing Tamir, but his cloaked figure posed too big a question. But as Tamir stepped forward, the door to the throne room opened and Shae walked in.

Elinta's stomach dropped as Shae's eyes settled on her. *No,* she thought angrily, squaring her shoulders. *I'm not afraid of her. Not after everything.*

"Shae," King Aldon said. "This is good timing. Is General Sonnen around?"

"Reynard had some business to attend to," the small woman said, stopping next to General Nash. "We're glad to see you, Prince Lorrin. You've been gone for some time."

Lorrin nodded but his eyes flickered toward Elinta, and she knew Shae's words didn't fool him. Suspicion seemed to hang behind them.

"We were just speaking about their new companion," King Aldon said, prompting them to continue.

Elinta was never so glad to not be the centre of attention. Shae's beady eyes for the moment moved from her to Tamir, who raised his head and calmly dropped the hood of his cloak.

"An Asali?" Queen Mira asked, a light frown crinkling her brow.

"What is this?" King Aldon's voice hardened. "Why would you bring one of them into the palace?"

Lorrin replied evenly, "Tamir's here to report to the council on Mazen's movements."

"Did it occur to you that he might report on *our* movements?" the king said, his hand twitching as though it wanted to clench.

Elinta fought to keep her face blank. Why would the council care what the human monarchy was doing? They hadn't cared for nearly two hundred years. Why would they start now?

Lorrin was apparently thinking along the same lines. "Why would he? If they were going to spy on us, they would have started a long time ago. Tamir may also be able to share some information on Mazen."

The king opened his mouth to respond, but Queen Mira touched his arm and cut across him. "Start from the beginning, Lorrin."

Lorrin told them the story of their trip to Liyarna, of Elinta's dragon-blood poisoning though it was quickly agreed to keep the nature of the poison secret. He detailed their first meeting with Tamir and all that had occurred with the council. General Nash didn't say a word the entire time, but Elinta secretly thought the woman looked impressed with what they'd accomplished. Shae's face was like steel.

"Mazen is different from his people in more ways than one," Lorrin said, coming to the biggest revelation of their trip. Elinta was already watching the faces of everyone in the room, wanting to catch their reactions. "Mazen is *Zearla lurai*. He rides a dragon."

The royals and advisors were stunned into silence, but Elinta could tell right away that the only word they heard and understood was dragon. *Zearla lurai* meant nothing to them, and they didn't give Lorrin a chance to explain. With pale faces, the king and queen spoke to each other in low voices that didn't seem to even carry to General Nash or Shae.

Elinta took the time to glance around the room. As she'd suspected, there was no one else in the room to hear all that had been said. No guards against the pillars or the walls. The royals were probably glad for it now. Word would have spread quickly about Vaherin, no matter what secrecy was asked.

"None of you are to share this with anyone," King Aldon said after pulling away from his wife. "The news of a confirmed dragon in Eldras is not something we wish to spread. There have been rumours for months, but they will become nothing more."

They all nodded though Elinta couldn't see how the king could hope to keep word of Vaherin from the people. If Mazen acted again soon, the odds were the dragon would be nearby and easily spotted.

"What if Liyarna had been in on it with Mazen?" King Aldon continued, looking at Lorrin, though his voice had lost some of its edge. "He was here to kill you."

Lorrin shook his head. "Mazen is an oddity. He might have been the prince, but he doesn't represent his people."

King Aldon turned his eyes to Tamir. "You're a historian?"

Tamir nodded. Elinta watched the interaction cautiously.

"And something close to what your people would call a scientist. A researcher. I am here only to report on Mazen. Nothing more," Tamir said.

"You volunteered to come?"

"Yes."

"Why?"

"Mazen poses a threat to my people as well as yours, Your Majesty."

King Aldon cocked his head and silence descended upon the room. The king stared long at Tamir, his eyes hard. "Though I'm not happy with this turn of events," he said, an edge returning to his tone, "my son has vouched for you. You are welcome to stay in the palace, but you may not venture into the city."

Tamir merely nodded.

"I will not hear anything you have to say about your people," the king continued. "Nor am I interested in any kind of treaty despite what my son may have suggested." He glanced at Lorrin as he spoke. Queen Mira said nothing, but her calm expression suggested she agreed with her husband.

Elinta's jaw dropped before she knew it. She hurried to close her mouth, glad that all eyes had been on Tamir, but she continued to stare at the king in shock. Did that mean he wouldn't hear what Tamir had to say about Mazen? Elinta had never been terribly familiar with the king, but in that moment ... she wondered whether she had ever known him more than any of the people walking the streets of Nevira. This was—this was absurd! She bit hard on her tongue.

"And what about you, Elinta?" Mira asked. Shae perked up at the question. "You were meant to be studying with Ford?"

Elinta saw something flicker across Tamir's face, but when she looked, whatever it was had gone. She resisted the urge to hide, wondering if her thoughts about the king had lingered on her face as everyone had turned to look at her. They certainly lingered in her mind. "Some things are more important, Your Majesty," she said.

"And now?"

She shook her head. "I'll speak with him." Though she had no intention of pretending she was going to study with him anymore. That lie was done.

Lorrin spoke up. "I'd like for her to stay here, whether Ford agrees to take her or not. She doesn't have anywhere else to go."

King Aldon and Queen Mira exchanged a long look, and in it Elinta saw all the teas she and Mira had shared, all the afternoons sketching by the gardens. The queen finally nodded.

"Don't expect to be going anywhere anytime soon though, Lorrin," General Nash said. "You'll find you won't be able to sneak out for a second time."

"I wouldn't dream of it, Aunt Jaida."

Niles, who had remained silent the entire time, butted in. "That's alright, I can get into enough mischief for the both of us."

General Nash smiled. "Oh no, you can't. Your father has made sure you are under the same conditions as Lorrin."

Niles's face fell.

"You three are dismissed," King Aldon said, his eyes not leaving Lorrin. "We'd like a moment with our son."

Elinta, Niles, and Tamir exited the room. As the door closed behind her, Elinta cast one last look back at Lorrin. He caught her eye and gave her a nervous smile. They hadn't had a chance to properly talk with his parents about the Asali or the treaty. Despite what King Aldon had said, she knew Lorrin would try to convince them.

Once out in the hall, Tamir swung the cloak from his shoulders and slung it over his arm. One of the guards started in surprise at the sight of an Asali in the palace, but quickly collected himself. His eyes kept flitting between the wall and Tamir, as though he couldn't quite believe what he saw. It was a good thing they'd just come out of the throne room, or the guard might have tried to arrest them.

"Do you think they'll be long?" Elinta asked Niles right as the door opened behind them and General Nash appeared.

Elinta watched the door for any sign of someone following but exhaled in relief as the door closed behind her.

Then it opened again, and Shae strode out, her mouth set into a grim line. When she looked at Elinta, the hate and suspicion that had been put to rest when it was revealed Mazen had stolen the scales that had gone missing last year was shining anew in her green eyes. But she didn't speak a word and passed their small group.

Tamir watched on with interest, but no one spoke until she disappeared up the corridor.

"I didn't expect him to go running off again so soon," General Nash said, looking at Niles, "but at least you went this time."

Niles saluted. "I'm told you wanted me along, General."

"I won't be confirming that," General Nash said, her eyebrows rising. "Your quarters will be on the third floor," she told Tamir.

"Thank you," he said. General Nash didn't seem at all nervous or uncomfortable around Tamir even though he had to be the first Asali she'd met. And if she noticed his lack of shoes, General

Nash didn't say anything, but Elinta thought she saw a smile tug at the woman's lips. Tamir didn't look comfortable in the socks at all.

"I'd suggest you keep your heads down for a couple of days," she said, looking between Niles and Elinta. Elinta couldn't agree more after witnessing Shae's attitude. Maybe the woman wasn't as bad as Mazen, but she could cause them a lot of trouble.

"Of course," Niles said.

"Has there been any word about Mazen?" Elinta asked. She hadn't wanted to draw too much attention to herself while in front of the king and queen. It wasn't her place to ask them questions, but she felt comfortable enough with General Nash.

"No," the general said. "It's like he was never here."

Elinta nodded. She wasn't sure what she'd expected, but no news was good news, right? Maybe Mazen wouldn't try breaking into the palace again ... but then, he'd gone through all that trouble. He might be planning something right now.

"I'm glad to see you're feeling better, Elinta," General Nash said, pulling Elinta from her thoughts, then disappeared up the hallway. Her boots echoed on the stone floor.

"She is the king's sister?" Tamir asked, watching the general go.

Elinta glanced at Tamir. His brow was furrowed thoughtfully. She supposed it was a good question. Given how different the two were.

"Yes," Elinta said.

The engraved doors to the throne room opened again before Tamir could respond and Lorrin joined them in the corridor.

"So ..." Niles said, dropping a hand on Lorrin's shoulder, "how bad is it?"

"Not as bad as it could have been. I don't think my ears will stop ringing for a few days," Lorrin said. "They still won't talk to the council."

"Why not?" Elinta asked, frustration tainting her voice. Why couldn't everyone just get along?

Lorrin shrugged. "It doesn't matter. The council won't speak to them either. Let's go find Tamir a room."

"And an afternoon snack," Niles added.

Elinta followed the boys through the palace, her mind racing. If the council wouldn't speak to the royals, and the royals wouldn't speak with the council ... then it was up to them to find a way to bring their races together. It was up to them to fix things. But how?

CHAPTER
THIRTEEN

E LINTA'S ROOM LOOKED THE same as she'd left it—aside
from a tidy—when she entered it hours later. She closed the
door behind her with a sigh and stood with her back against it.
Despite her separation from Zhayra, it felt good to be back in the
palace. Once again, the feeling that she could be perfectly at home
there crept up on her. If only Zhayra wasn't so far away. If only
their plans with the council and the royals had worked. At least
Tamir was still happy to help her learn more about being a *Zearla
lurai*, even if there was nothing else for him to do here.

She trudged to where her backpack sat on her large bed, pushing the curtains aside, and rummaged for some night clothes to

wear. Then she remembered that she'd left her nightdress in the tall wardrobe before going to Liyarna. She chuckled at herself and fetched the dress before going to the bathroom and running the bath.

Elinta turned to the mirror as steam began to rise in the air. It'd been just over a week since she'd last seen her reflection properly. Her blonde hair was messy after a full day's riding, and there was a smudge of dirt on her face, but it was her eyes that held her attention. They felt normal with Zhayra no longer looking through them. She leant in as close as possible to the mirror and stared hard at them.

What was it that Tamir and the other Asali could see? That Mazen had seen that night in the outer corridor by the training rooms? That she hadn't in the mirror in Liyarna? She stared at her irises, but the colour was exactly the same as it had always been. Brown. A dark, deep brown, devoid of any other colour. So, she studied her pupils, looking for any changes in the shape of them, but they were still perfectly rounded.

With a shrug, she turned back to the bath. "Oh!" she said, hurrying forwards and turning the water off. It was a little high, so after she'd undressed, she slipped carefully into the water.

She scrubbed the dirt from her tanned skin and the dust from her hair, enjoying the sweet perfume of the soap, then settled back, leaning her head against the top of the tub.

Her thoughts were back on Zhayra. It had been weeks now since the last time they'd been separated and if it felt strange for her, she was sure it felt strange to the dragon. As soon as she focused, she realised she was right. The dragon's emotions were flat. Zhayra was bored.

What was she doing now, out in the woods by herself? Curiosity bubbled away at her, and a hesitant idea began to form. Zhayra's emotions mirrored hers. But the dragon would know what she was thinking in a moment if she managed to pull it off. She shifted to get more comfortable.

But if she was going to look through the dragon, she needed something to help her return to herself. Lorrin wasn't here to help her again. Though it was tempting to go see him, she wanted to do this now. She wanted to be able to do it by herself even if her stomach clenched at the idea. Looking around for something, anything, that might help, her eyes landed on the hair tie at her wrist. Maybe that would do.

Closing her eyes and taking a deep breath, Elinta pictured Zhayra just as she had before. She zoomed in on the dragon's face, her muzzle, then her eyes. She focused on them, drawing to mind their amber colour and the black slits of her pupils.

"Yes," she whispered as an image began to form. Large tree trunks in the gloom. She was sure that to her own eyes they would have been nothing more than a darker shadow against a dark background, but Elinta could make them out through the dragon. Not well, and not clearly. But as though there were a little more light than there actually was. Almost like it was dusk. She felt sure that she would have been able to walk through the woods without crashing into anything.

Zhayra's stomach jumped, and the dragon's eyes slowly began to scan the area as though showing off the landscape to her. Elinta felt herself grin as she studied the woods through Zhayra's eyes. A flicker of movement caught her attention, and the dragon froze, focusing. It was an owl, up in the tallest branches of a tree to the dragon's right. Its feathers were ruffled, and it shook itself as it looked down at Zhayra. The dragon let her eyes travel upwards over the owl and to the sky. Elinta's breath caught in her chest. The stars. Oh, the stars! She didn't know there could be so many stars in the sky. And they were so sharp. And now she could tell they had slightly different colours to them. Some were white, some were silver. Some seemed to have a yellowish tinge to them. She could have sworn one was red.

It was only her awareness of the bath and the sweet perfumes rising from the water that stopped her from getting caught up in Zhayra's eyes. Her skin would go shrivelled soon, and the water was no longer hot.

"OK," she whispered, even though the dragon couldn't hear her. "Time to finish up."

She ran her hand down her damp arm where it rested on the edge of the bath, until she found the hair tie at her wrist. A spout of nerves rose in her, the memory of her last experience looking through Zhayra's eyes threatening to distract her, but she held onto the hair tie. She focused on it, twisting and rolling the band in her hand, until it was all she could think about. The stars began to fade, and then they disappeared. All was dark.

With a start, Elinta realised her eyes were still closed. She cracked them open and found herself looking at the white ceiling of her steam-filled bathroom. She'd done it! She'd actually done it! Zhayra's emotions soared with hers.

Grinning, Elinta climbed out of the bath, dried off, and pulled on her nightdress. She looked at the hair tie. From now on, that's where it would stay. As long as it was there, she could return to herself.

She turned to the mirror again. "Happy birthday," Elinta said to her reflection, her face alight with excitement.

She was still smiling when she left the bathroom, and nearly jumped out of her skin at the sight of someone in her room, straightening the already impeccable covers on her bed.

"Neva?" Elinta said, recognising the familiar figure. Her heart took a moment to settle.

"Oh!" The young woman squealed and rushed to her side, sending her dark hair bouncing. "You're really back!"

"Yes, I—"

But Neva had just gotten started. "Oh, there was such a to-do when everyone realised you were gone. And the prince and Niles as well! You should have seen it. And no one knew where you'd gone." Neva hurried over to the bed and started fluffing the pillow as though her hands needed something to do, still talking. "The king and queen were so worried! And Ford came when he'd heard you were gone."

Elinta stiffened at the mention of the mysterious history teacher, but Neva didn't notice.

"He had no idea you were going, let alone *where* you'd gone!"

Elinta relaxed. Ford had played his part well then. He hadn't known where they were going—though she was sure he'd suspected—but they had told him that they *were* going. To give him time to prepare for whatever questions would come his way once they'd left. And it seemed the time had worked.

Elinta brushed her hair as she listened to the maid get all the chatter out of her system. Though the night was now drawing on, and though she wanted some time to herself, it was good to see Neva again. Even if the woman talked without stopping for breath. She could afford to stay up a little later for the sake of the maid.

As it turned out, the king and queen weren't the only ones terribly worried about their disappearance. It seemed Shae had made quite a fuss over Lorrin ... and her.

"You should have seen her. She was so angry you'd all vanished. And she kept asking about you. Don't ask me what she meant by it all. I guess she just really cares about you three. But once Ford had come in, she stopped asking about it all."

"Really?" Elinta said, playing the part of surprise. So, Shae's interest in her had been renewed right from the moment they'd left. No wonder the woman seemed so cold toward her. Not that she'd ever stopped. But it had been nice not to worry about her.

It was at least thirty minutes later when Elinta finally sat on her bed alone with a long exhale. What a day!

She shook herself, pulled back the covers from her bed, and climbed in. She almost sunk into the mattress. It had only been a week since they'd left Liyarna and their beds behind, but the road had been long and the ground uncomfortable. Not to mention the pace they'd set. The only thing she'd miss about those nights was being pressed up against Zhayra's side.

It was early in the morning when she woke. A life of rising early to help her father with the horses before helping Galen had made it almost impossible for Elinta to sleep in. Though the curtains around the bed might have helped her sleep longer, she didn't like to pull them closed. The light of morning was the perfect wake up for her. She lay staring at the ceiling for a moment, waiting for the heaviness in her mind and limbs to abate. Stretching out her arms and legs with a groan, Elinta focused on the beams of light above her … it was morning! Elinta threw back the covers and crossed to the wardrobe.

She pulled out a pair of light pants and a loose shirt and slipped into them. It was so nice to have fresh clothes, ones that hadn't been rolled up inside her bag for three weeks. Her sword was at her hip, now a familiar weight. She'd have been lost without it now. Elinta pulled on her shoes and glanced out the window, gauging the light. It was still early though the staff would already be roaming the halls. Normally, she and Lorrin would be running in the gardens soon…. She cocked her head. It was as good a morning as any. Though she hadn't arranged anything with Lorrin, she would go down there for a run even if it meant she ran by herself. It would be good to get back into their old routine.

Elinta slipped from her room and wove through the palace halls, making her way down to the first floor, past the queen's tea rooms, and out into the gardens. The sweet perfume of the many flowers reached her and she took in a deep breath through her nose, turning her face up toward the hot sun.

"I didn't expect to see you here!"

Elinta opened her eyes just as the sound of heavy footfalls reached her and smiled. It was Lorrin. He was already running, tracing their usual route around the gardens. With every passing second, he was drawing closer to her. Her heart warmed a little at the way they'd both fallen into their old routine.

"I didn't expect to see *you*," she said with a laugh, "but I missed our runs."

When he drew alongside her, she took off, keeping pace with him. She waited for him to say something about what had happened yesterday with his parents. They could still regroup and work out a new plan. If things couldn't be solved between their people and the Asali, then what hope did the dragons have? It was up to them. They had to fix it.

"Did you want to train tonight, then?" Lorrin asked, surprising Elinta from her thoughts. Maybe he needed more time before he wanted to talk.

"Yes." She paused. "I was thinking of inviting Tamir?"

"That sounds like a good idea," Lorrin said, voice bouncing in time with his footfalls. "You two could get started on the senses. Why don't we start earlier so you can have more time? That's at least one thing we can do without my parents being involved." He sounded only a little bit bitter as he said it, but Elinta understood what he meant.

"Yeah, thanks," Elinta said, willing for the moment to let go of her worries about Liyarna. She'd give him a little more time to collect his thoughts and plan around his father. They fell into the easy rhythm of a familiar activity, enjoying one another's company as they ran.

✦✦✦✦

After breakfast, Elinta hurried up the steps to the third floor, head tucked down. She needed to change her clothes after her run with Lorrin, then she'd check in on Tamir to make sure he was—Elinta ran straight into something and fell on her bottom at the top of the steps.

"I'm so sorry," she said, jumping to her feet and straightening her shirt. "I wasn't looking where I—" She looked up. "Ford?"

"Elinta," the historian greeted, looking as firm on his feet as though she hadn't just run into him. Ford had allowed a light stubble to grow on his face, which suited him quite well, but she doubted it would be there for long. He'd always been cleanshaven whenever she saw him.

"I wasn't expecting to see you," she said, staring at the man. She still wasn't sure what to think of him. He'd been key in maintaining her excuse for being in the palace, and he'd even offered her information on the dragons, but she didn't know much about him. She shifted under his gaze, suddenly missing the openness being among the Asali had offered her.

Ford's lips twitched. "So I gathered."

"I'm sorry for running into you."

Ford waved her apology aside. "You seem well."

"Yes," Elinta said, her hand trailing to her hip. Did he know about the wounds Mazen had given her? He couldn't know about the poison. "I saw a good healer," she said, going out on a limb.

"Good."

Elinta stared at the man, debating with herself. She was sure he knew they'd gone to Liyarna, and that he knew, at least in part, why they had gone there. More importantly, *she* wanted to hear his thoughts on the council's decision and what they'd learnt about Mazen. He was an untapped resource to them.

"I was just heading to my room," she said finally. "Would you come with me?"

Ford cocked his head. "Of course."

"So, Tamir came back with you?" Ford asked. They were sitting in her room, her on the edge of her bed and Ford in the chair by the cold fireplace, and she'd just finished detailing their trip to Liyarna, carefully leaving out any mention of Zhayra or Aesira.

"Yes," she said.

"Interesting," he said, his dark eyes thoughtful and a slight frown crinkling his brow.

"He wanted to keep track of Mazen," she repeated. Despite the king's orders not to tell anyone about Vaherin, Elinta had told Ford. She needed any help she could get with working out what to do about the pair.

"Then he's sure it's the prince," Ford murmured. He didn't say anything more, but Elinta didn't speak for a moment. He'd been shocked to learn who'd attacked her ... or as shocked as the normally guarded man would show. And she suspected he'd already known that a dragon would be with Mazen. *What does he know of the self-exiled prince of Liyarna?*

"I can't believe the council won't help," Elinta said, slumping a little. She'd been counting on them. Even more after learning who Mazen was.

"They aren't known to care for our people," he said quietly.

Elinta thought about the scroll he'd given her on the dragons so long ago, and the information she'd learnt about the *zearla lurai ngaran*. He already knew a lot about the dragons, more than anyone other than the Asali seemed to. And he was a historian. Time to return the favour. Besides, maybe he could offer her some more insight.

She cleared her throat, glancing at her door to make sure it was still closed. Ford raised an eyebrow.

"I, uh, learnt something about the dragons while we were there too," she said, "and the *zearla lurai ngaran*."

"Really?"

She nodded, bracing herself. "They could access each other's senses. All of them."

"Interesting." Ford's face betrayed nothing.

"Aren't there meant to be more than five, though?" she said, trying to glean something from him.

"Yes," he said, "and there would be some that the dragon had that the Asali or human would not."

Elinta's eyes widened. She hadn't thought of that. "What do you mean?"

"Well, for example, we know birds seem to have a strong innate sense of direction based on magnetic fields. Something that we don't have."

"So," Elinta chose her words very carefully, "if his dragon had this sense, then Mazen could use it?"

"Yes, he would be able to use such a sense. There are also lesser-known senses. Ones that are often debated among certain fields."

Elinta leant forward in her seat, her eyebrows rising.

"I would think … that a *Zearla lurai* would be able to access a dragon's memories. After all, these contribute to one's sense of self."

"Sense of self," Elinta repeated in a whisper, forgetting all about Mazen. An image of dragons flying around a group of islands appeared before her eyes. Of the moment a name had been burned into her mind. That dream. *Her* dream. The one that she'd had in the White Mountains, pressed against Zhayra's side. She'd seen how Zhayra had seen herself. The gasp was through her lips before she could stop it.

Ford was watching her carefully, and she fought to control her face.

"What are your plans now?" he asked, breaking the silence. "I can't pretend to teach you."

"No," Elinta said, her mind only half present. "Lorrin spoke to his parents. I can stay here for now."

"Good," he said. "Mazen will emerge again. It's best that you're here. I must go." He stood and was gone before Elinta had even processed what he'd said. The door clicked shut behind him.

Why did he think she needed to stay at the palace? If he knew the same story as everyone else, that Mazen had been after Lorrin, why did he think she could be at risk? This game of dancing around the truth they had going left her with swirling thoughts. What did Ford know, and what did she just think he knew? She sat on her bed in silence, wondering at the man.

CHAPTER
FOURTEEN

"I SPOKE WITH FORD this morning and you'll never guess what he said." Elinta sat at the long table Lorrin, Niles, and Tamir had settled at in the dining hall. Tamir looked at her in surprise.

"You spoke with the historian? Here?"

"Yes," she said. He must have heard them talking about Ford once. She didn't think she'd detailed her original excuse for being in Nevira to him. Elinta had thought the throne room was the first time they'd talked about Ford with the Asali there, but apparently not. But that didn't matter right now. "The senses, do you think that would include sense of self?"

Tamir hesitated, and then nodded.

"Ford said that memories contribute to our sense of self," she said, her words coming out in a rush, "and I think he's right."

Lorrin glanced around to make sure no one was close enough to hear them, then leaned forward eagerly. "You could access Zhayra's memories?"

Elinta shook her head. "I *have* accessed Zhayra's memories."

"What?" Niles said, spluttering as he took a sip of water. "When?"

"The night you found us in the White Mountains," Elinta said to Lorrin. "I was dreaming about dragons. And when I woke up, I knew Zhayra's name."

Tamir shook his head in wonder. "I've not heard of this before."

"I wondered how you knew her name," Lorrin whispered.

"It seems logical," Tamir said.

"I think they'd only be important memories, though," Elinta said. "If they're a part of her sense of self, they wouldn't just be any memory."

"Do you remember what you saw?" Tamir asked, sitting straighter on the bench seat.

"It was mostly just a jumble of pictures," Elinta said after a moment. "I only really remember the islands."

"*Their* islands?" Niles asked, his eyes widening. It was a comical look on him, given the mess of his blond hair.

Elinta nodded. "There were dragons flying over them. It was amazing."

Tamir stared at her wide-eyed.

"Imagine what we could learn!" Lorrin said. "Are you going to try it again?"

"I—maybe. Yeah."

Elinta grabbed some toast and put it on the plate in front of her, spreading some jam on it. She wanted to. But part of her didn't want them to know … or to be a part of it until she knew what she'd see. What if Zhayra's memories were deeply personal? Or embarrassing? Or she wasn't even able to access the memories at all?

"You should," Lorrin said.

Elinta frowned but pushed her agitation away. Lorrin didn't mean to be pushy, he was just excited. And she couldn't blame him.

"Tamir," Elinta said, changing the topic. "We're going to train tonight. Do you want to come?"

"I will be there."

"Are we going to keep training at night?" Niles asked around a mouthful of food.

"I think so." Lorrin shrugged. "Our days are going to be pretty busy now, with all the work my parents and the generals have assigned. It might be the only time we can meet for so long without being interrupted."

"But can we have a shorter session tonight? I want to go see Zhayra." *And try accessing her memories properly*, she mentally added. A thrill ran through her veins. Her earlier plans to train her senses with Tamir were forgotten. What she'd experienced in the White Mountains had been a jumble of feelings and images, but if she could access just the memories … she could finally learn more about Zhayra, learn the things the dragon couldn't tell her. Maybe she'd even find out why the dragon was in Eldras.

"Sure." Lorrin exchanged a look with Niles. "When were you planning on telling us about your birthday?"

"Huh?" Elinta stopped the glass she'd been raising to her lips.

"Yeah!" Niles said. "We had to find out from Neva! She said she heard you talking to yourself last night."

"When was your birthday, *tarsi?*"

Elinta glanced between them in surprise, feeling just a little harassed by their questions and indignation. "I only realised yesterday that I'd had it sometime on our trip back from Liyarna," Elinta said, lowering her glass back to the table. "It's not a big deal." To be honest, she didn't know how she felt about her birthday. It was the first one she'd had since leaving home. It felt strange not to have celebrated with Blaine and her father. But even more, it seemed insignificant in comparison to all that was happening to her and her friends now.

"And you didn't tell us?" Niles said.

"It wasn't an important birthday," Elinta said quietly.

"But it's your first since leaving Kethmere and your family," Lorrin said.

"That settles it." Niles stood up. "We need to get you a present."

"Now?"

Niles sat back down. "I need some time to think about it. But we're going to see Merton tomorrow for cake."

Lorrin and Tamir nodded. Elinta glanced in surprise at the Asali, but a warmth spread through her. Friends like these were hard to come by.

⚔⚔⚔

"So, you going to try it?" Niles said, slamming Elinta's sword aside and aiming a kick at her abdomen.

She spun away, slashing out at his leg. "Maybe," she said.

He leapt back. "What kind of answer—" their swords met with a loud clang, "—is that?"

"Well—" Elinta said, shoving Niles's sword to distract him before stepping forward and stopping a kick an inch from her target between his legs.

Niles's eyes widened. "That's a low move."

She shrugged and was back on the attack. Not finishing her earlier sentence.

"So, are you?" Niles asked a moment later.

"Yes," she said. She was going to try to access Zhayra's memories. Her stomach jumped at the thought.

"Tonight?"

"Yes," she said, trying not to sound too irritated.

"Good."

Niles's sword tapped her shoulder. Elinta returned with a tap on his thigh, wiping the grin from his face. The fight finally ended when Lorrin called it. According to him, they had both died from blood loss, and so they'd both lost.

"But who died first?" Niles asked, wiping his brow.

Elinta rolled her eyes and turned expectantly to Lorrin.

"Oh, no. You both died."

Niles looked at him in disbelief.

"At the same time," Lorrin added.

"At the same time?" Niles asked with a loud sigh. He turned to Tamir, who sat against a wall near where Lorrin stood. "What do you think?"

Tamir shook his head. "You are both dead."

"You're not very helpful."

Tamir shrugged.

"Says the dead man," Elinta said.

Niles's mouth dropped. "Says the dead *girl!*"

Laughing, Elinta returned her sword to its scabbard and gulped down a drink of water.

"I should get going," she said. "I don't want to get stuck outside the gates." She paused. She hadn't given Lorrin long, but maybe a nudge would be good. "We should find a time to meet up and work out what we're going to do now about the treaty and the dragons."

The boys all nodded.

"See you at breakfast," Lorrin said.

Elinta waved goodbye as she hurried from the training room.

As the door closed behind her, she caught a snippet of conversation from Niles, "You know, we could do this for real. We have Tamir's healing ..."

Elinta shook her head. Trust Niles to think of that. If he brought it up tomorrow, she'd put her foot down on that one. But she couldn't imagine Lorrin agreeing to it even if his friend was a bad influence.

She took Ash, the mare she'd ridden to Liyarna. The road to the woods was familiar, and memories flooded her of all the times she'd gone to visit Zhayra during their first stay in Nevira.

It seemed as though no time had passed when she ducked under the trees, dismounted Ash, and continued forward on foot.

Zhayra was waiting for her, her bulk just a shadow in the darkness. Elinta adjusted the light of her lantern as she drew closer, placed it on the ground, and hugged the dragon's chest.

"I wondered if I could try something?" she said, her face pressed against Zhayra's white scales.

The dragon grunted, and Elinta pulled back to look her in the eyes.

"I heard I can access your sense of self," she said. "Your memories."

Zhayra blinked yes.

"Could I—" She cleared her throat. "Could I try?"

Zhayra's emotions lifted, and there was a change in her chest. It was like relief. Zhayra blinked once again.

"OK," Elinta said. Leaves crunched under her as she sat. She stared at the dragon, the dim light of the lamp only reaching halfway down her back. "I ... I just don't know how to do it."

Zhayra grunted and shifted in place, apparently getting more comfortable.

Elinta frowned. "OK ..." she drew the word out. She could start by thinking about Zhayra?

What did she know about the dragon?

She summoned the memories of the times Zhayra had helped her, protected her, cared for her: helping her leave Kethmere; protecting her from the mountain lion; keeping her warm in the snow; waking the boys up when she'd been sick from dragon-blood poisoning. She thought of the times she'd shown a more playful side: their swim in Lake Lusinata and her playful flying on their way back from Liyarna. She allowed memories to flash through her mind; Zhayra meeting Niles; Zhayra knocking saplings down with her tail; sleeping in odd positions when the sun landed on her; her grunts and keens and hums as she tried to talk and interact with Elinta. Finally, she remembered the sadness and grief that had weighed on the dragon when they'd found the remains of the eggs destroyed in the Eggslaying.

Elinta let the memory linger, but as it dissipated, her attention was drawn away from the dragon and to the heavy silence that was sitting over them. A cricket chirped in the distance.

She sighed and cracked open her eyes. Zhayra was watching her intently, her head now resting on the ground.

"It didn't work."

Zhayra grumbled, but she only felt a flicker of annoyance. If anything, the sinking in her stomach seemed more like disappointment.

"I'll try again," she said, shifting to a more comfortable position so that she leant against the dragon's leg.

She ran through the memories again. Nothing happened. She tried to remember the dream, but it had been so many months ago. It was only the dragon islands that stuck in her mind. And she hadn't seen much of the islands themselves, just a glimpse of land and dragons flying through the air.

Elinta laid down, her back against the ground, her right arm resting against Zhayra's leg.

But she hadn't been thinking of Zhayra that night, had she? She'd just been attacked. She'd only left home a couple of days before. Wouldn't she have been thinking of those things? Elinta sighed again, shifting to remove a stick digging into her back.

Zhayra's head appeared next to her, her long neck stretched around to allow her to look at Elinta and rested her chin on the ground.

"Could you tell when I used dragonsight on the way back from Liyarna?" she asked. If they could tell when looking through each other's eyes, might Zhayra be able to tell when she used the strength of her eyes?

Zhayra paused, then blinked twice.

"Really?" Elinta said, staring at the stars above them. "That's strange."

Zhayra's tail flicked around, and the tip landed on Elinta's stomach.

Elinta laughed in surprise, her hands going automatically to it. "What are you doing?"

Zhayra hummed, and twisted, so that one of her eyes faced upwards, looking at the stars too.

"They're beautiful, aren't they?" she said.

Zhayra grunted.

They watched the stars together for a long time, and Elinta fell asleep like that, Zhayra's tail resting across her and her arm pressed against the dragon.

She was standing on a rocky ledge, looking out over the island, looking out over her home. Her claws clutched at the rock, but a spring of anticipation was in her stomach. A shadow fell across her and she turned to see a large yellow dragon beside her. Familiar.

Safe. The dragon, who towered over her small frame, nudged her gently with her snout, pushing her closer to the edge.

She spread her wings. The air tugged at the membrane. Her wings wobbled, her body shifted, but it didn't rise. In a blur of movement, the dragon beside her took off and a yearning consumed her: to be with her, and to be with her in the sky. She kept her eyes locked on that figure and jumped. She plummeted. The wind tugged, tore at her small wings in a vicious prompt to use them. She beat them furiously, watching as the ground drew nearer, and she beat all the harder. Then something happened. She stopped falling. Then she began to rise. A small roar escaped her, more of a croak really, but she was proud. Another rush of pride hit her that wasn't her own and she raised her head, searching for the source. There! There she was, as bright as the sun. Mother.

She beat her wings harder and harder, pushing herself upwards until she drew level with the ledge. She hovered there, feeling the current of the wind running over her. Shifting her wings as she beat them, she was pushed sideways. With a startled grunt, she shifted her wings the other way, and was pushed left. Her mother flew down, hovering beside her, watching with sparkling red eyes as she worked out how to move her wings. Then she had it! She flew forwards, then angled down, then back up! The yellow dragon roared. Everything faded to black.

When the image cleared again, she was flying over the sea. Her wings were larger now, and beat at the air in stronger, harder strokes, pushing her forwards with a practiced ease. The sun was shining off the water, but it couldn't hide what was beneath. At the first sign of movement, she shot down, ducking into the water and snatching up a fish in her jaws.

She flew up, up, up above the clouds, their moisture beading on her scales. She ducked in and out of them. Over and under. It never failed to amuse her. Flying. She'd never understand how the two-legs in Mother's memories could stand to be stuck on the ground. As she ducked below the clouds again, something caught her eye in the distance.

She stopped, beating her wings to hover in place. Glancing behind her, she knew that whatever it was, it was further away than she was supposed to go. Home was already a distant smudge on the horizon. The mainland wasn't far. But what was it that rode upon the waves?

With another backward glance, she shut off her link with Mother and pushed forward. She'd already been closed to the others for this flight. Now there was an emptiness within her where her mother usually was. But she wanted to see. Wanted to know what was riding the sea like it belonged there as surely as she belonged in the air. The others couldn't shut off from her mother, not like her.

There were things moving on it. She was too far away to tell what they were, but they were like ants, scurrying all over the thing's back. Almost instinctively, her wings began to beat harder, and she drew closer, ever closer. What was it? She squinted. It was too far away to see its heat. If she just got a little closer, she might be able to make out the little ants, though.

She pushed herself further. Until the ants came into view. Her eyes widened and her stomach dropped. They were the things her mother had shown her. The ones that had killed. Driven them from their home. The wind tore at her wings as she came to a grinding halt in mid-air. She cocked her head, studying their small forms. Yes, that was them. But beside the fear in her was a curiosity she couldn't suppress. What were they doing out on the water, so far from their territory? They hadn't noticed her so far away and up near the clouds. Her scales blended in well. Maybe she could get closer still.

Even as the idea occurred to her, a blur of movement came from her left and something shoved into her from in front. She grunted, *shaking her head to clear her vision, but a loud grumble answered her unasked question. Mother.*

Cautiously, she reopened the bond between her and the yellow figure in front of her. Emotions bombarded her, each telling their own story. Fear, anger, disappointment. Her mother growled again, low in her chest, and she couldn't stop the quiet keen from escaping her. Mother pushed at her again, and with one last look at the humans, she turned and followed her back to the islands.

When the blackness cleared, she was on the ledge again, just as she'd been when she'd first learnt to fly. Months had passed since she'd seen the humans, and she hadn't strayed far enough to see them since. She was standing next to her mother, whose scales shone brightly in the afternoon sun, looking out over the islands. Beams of sunlight shot from the sky, striking the ground and making the grass fields and rocks vivid with colour. The islands were at their most beautiful today. It was fitting.

Her mother was calling to the others, summoning them all for the ceremony. They did it once a year. They all came together to remember. Her mother would project the memory into each of them, and they would remember the loss and the suffering. But they would be thankful there hadn't been more. They would be thankful for their new home where they were safe, happy. She turned her eyes to her mother, watching her as she spread the message. A silent urge to come. One day, that would be her.

He was in front of her, blocking her view of the way to Mother with his large bulk. His mind was closed off to her, and it puzzled her. The maroon dragon had returned with his bonded only days ago. Mother didn't stop them from going to the mainland though it was no secret that she disapproved. She wanted to leave the others to themselves. It was better that way.

Vaherin had been closed off from her the second he'd arrived, and she'd sensed her mother's uncertainty at whatever she could feel there. Looking at him, she wished she could sense him despite his withdrawal, the same way her mother could. But even his eyes were carefully blank. Vaherin twisted, his head snapping to look behind him at the exact moment her mother felt ... her mother felt fear. A stab of fear and sadness so raw that it shook her to the core. And pain unimaginable. She bounded forwards, her heart skipping every second beat even as sparks rose in her throat unbidden. She didn't know how she'd gotten past Vaherin. Only that his distraction had given her the chance she'd needed, and she slipped through the gap in the rock to where Mother was. Where Mother was with the two-legged. Vaherin's bonded, the glowing one, stood over her mother. She was on her back. The hilt of his blue sword protruded from her yellow chest. Her lifeless red eyes reflected the cloudless sky above her.

Mazen's eyes were like her mother's when he looked at her.

"Vaherin!" he called.

The sound of scales scraping rock told her he was coming, that he was right behind her, and she shot into the air. She was smaller than him, and though his wings were more powerful than hers, she knew the islands better than he did. She'd lived and breathed them her whole life.

The mournful cries of her kin echoed around her, but she had no time to stop, no time to tell them what happened. She pushed her wings harder than she'd ever pushed them before and shot into the clouds. Not daring to look back, she angled toward the mainland, trusting in the memories of her mother.

The sky was dark over the land of her ancestors, and the wind grew fierce and wild. It was stronger than she'd ever known it to be, but she kept going. She couldn't stop. He was out there. He was after her. Her throat was thick, and she longed to loose the roar that was building, building in her chest, but she couldn't. He might hear her.

He might find her. The land was under her before she knew it, but she kept going. Mother's memories were in the north, ever north. So, she kept going. The wind grew stronger. Rain battered at her scales. The sky rumbled, echoing the roar of her kin.

A current whipped up, smacking into her side, pushing her left wing up while another burst hit her from above and she was tumbling, tumbling down and down and down.

There was a girl. That's what they were called, wasn't it? Her legs were shaking, but otherwise she was stock-still.

"You must have come down in the storm," the girl whispered. It didn't seem dangerous.

She lowered her head to the ground. They stared at each other from across the lake. When the girl started to move, she keened, wanting the girl to stay. Not wanting to be alone. Even if it meant her death, too. Just days ago, she'd spent her hatch day surrounded by her kin, now she was alone. She'd never been alone.

The girl kept moving, muttering to herself. "That is a dragon. Not some soft-hearted mare ... "

None of the humans in her mother's memories had talked to themselves. The girl's bright brown eyes were locked on her, but as she kept mumbling to herself, she raised one of her feet and stepped forward. What was it doing? She flicked her tail. The human continued forward. It crept toward her, inch by inch, never moving its eyes from her. It reeked of fear, yet it continued toward her. It was nothing like those humans. The ones that had attacked them. It didn't even have a sword.

The girl stopped in front of her. Licked her lips. "Hello there."

She'd done it when the girl returned. There was a gulf inside her. Though she could still feel the others, even out here on the mainland, she'd turned them off. Their pain and sorrow were too much. It didn't matter that she could have shown them what had happened now that she could claim her birthright. She couldn't go back while Vaherin and his bonded were there. But looking at the girl, the girl who defied her mother's final memories of her race, she yearned to know what it was feeling. Beyond the fear that made its heart hammer. She wanted to know what it was truly feeling. Who it really was.

She'd done it while the girl had been crouched by the water, her back to her. When the girl pressed the plants into her wing and she felt the fear knotted in her stomach, she knew she'd done it. She stared at the girl, at her kin, and didn't feel so alone.

CHAPTER
FIFTEEN

E LINTA WOKE WITH A start and bolted upright. Sweat had beaded on her brow in the warm air. It was morning already. A light breeze pushed through the trees, fresh against her skin, but Elinta didn't notice. She burst into tears. Zhayra grunted in surprise beside her.

"He killed your mum?" she sobbed, feeling the echo of Zhayra's memory in her body. The moment she'd realized Mazen had killed her mother and the moments that followed. It was met with present-day Zhayra's sadness too, the tightening and sinking of her chest. Her sobs redoubled.

Zhayra nudged her softly, a flicker of amusement lighting in her. Elinta wrapped her arms around the dragon's head in long overdue comfort.

"I'm sorry," she whispered. And it had been her birthday, too, sometime just before. What a birthday present.

Zhayra uttered a low keen, nudging her again.

Elinta pulled back and sniffed, rubbing at her face. "I think I kind of overreacted," she said with a small laugh, but her heart was still aching for the dragon. Zhayra had lost her mother, the queen of the dragons, just days before they'd met. And it had been Mazen who'd killed her.

"You knew who he was all along," Elinta said, sniffing again and looking at the dragon. "That night he attacked me, and I came to see you the next day, you knew who he was." She stroked Zhayra's cheek. "No wonder you were worried."

Zhayra blinked.

Elinta sighed, shifting closer to lean against Zhayra's side. Sunlight shined down through the trees in thin beams, almost like in Zhayra's memory of the Eggslaying service on the islands. Had Zhayra already experienced Eldras from the islands she'd been born to purely through memory? Was there any part that she hadn't seen? She leant her head back.

"Zhayra," she said, turning to look at her face, realization striking her. "You're the queen!"

Zhayra paused, then blinked twice.

"What do you mean? Your mother was the queen, wasn't she?" Elinta said, thinking back to all of Zhayra's interactions with her mother.

Zhayra blinked.

"But you're the heir!" Elinta stared at the dragon in wonder. She blinked again.

"But you're not queen yet?"

Two blinks.

Elinta frowned. "Do you have siblings?"

Two blinks.

Her frown deepened, but she didn't know what else to ask. How did the throne work in the dragon's society? How did the heir become queen?

She thought through the dreams again, mulling over all the details she could remember, focusing particularly on the one with Mazen and Vaherin.

"Vaherin," she murmured.

Zhayra's stomach squeezed.

"In the drea—memory," she corrected, "he closed himself off to you. Is that normal?"

Zhayra blinked once. Elinta smiled unconsciously at their system. It was working well.

"But he couldn't to your mother? To the queen?"

She blinked twice.

So, the queen could access senses even if the others didn't want her to ... except in Zhayra, the heir, who'd closed off to her when investigating the ship. Elinta kept shifting through the memories and settled on the last one. The one of her.

"Mazen and Tamir were right," she said, glancing at Zhayra's amber eyes. "They said you made the bond."

Zhayra sighed. Elinta moved with the dragon's chest as it expanded and contracted.

"I don't mind," Elinta said, having long accepted the bond. "I couldn't imagine not having you there anymore."

Yes, she'd lost her family and her home, and maybe that wound would never heal. But Zhayra hadn't done that. She had done it herself, and so had her family. Even if she could, or wanted to, giving up the bond wouldn't change things.

The last part of Zhayra's worry and fear seemed to leak from her. Elinta knew everything now.

Elinta looked out at the trees around them in a new light. The woods seemed almost otherworldly in the morning light. Not in the way the Calaza had, but in a fresh and young way. Like everything was new. But it was just her, seeing things so differently.

Zhayra nudged her and grunted, looking up at the sun.

"What?" Elinta said, following her gaze. "Oh. How late is it?"

Zhayra grunted again and nudged her.

"It's fine. I should be with you."

But Zhayra just grunted again.

Guilt began to nibble at her. She knew what Zhayra was thinking. She'd been out all night, and the boys didn't know. They were probably looking for her. Just as they had when she'd disappeared at the Eggslaying festival. And Lorrin—her heart warmed at the thought of him—he was probably worried. Zhayra nudged her again.

"OK, OK!" She laughed.

Clambering to her feet, she twisted and gave Zhayra another hug. "I'm sorry," she said again. "I'll come back soon."

Then she hurried from the clearing, knowing that if she lingered, she'd never want to leave.

It was mid-morning by the time she got back to the palace and probably too late to go to breakfast, but she stopped by the dining hall anyway to make sure none of the boys were there. The hall was empty apart from a couple of soldiers sitting at the end of one of the tables and locked in conversation. She'd have to try Lorrin's room.

Elinta hurried up the steps to the third floor and along the corridor, past her own room, and stood in front of Lorrin's door. She reached out a hesitant hand and knocked. There was no answer. She knocked again. Harder. Her mind raced. They couldn't have gone looking for her. She hadn't passed Lorrin or Niles on her way back from the woods. Where were they?

She pivoted, looking back down the hall toward her room. Had they ducked in there looking for her?

"Elinta?"

She was halfway down the hall and whipped around in surprise.

"Where have you been?" Lorrin jogged toward her, relief etched across his face. He glanced down at her clothes. "Weren't you wearing that last night?"

"I was," she said, feeling slightly guilty at the worry she knew he must have felt. "I was out with Zhayra."

"But Bentley is here," Lorrin said, frowning.

"I took Ash."

"Oh." His face cleared. "What happened?"

Elinta shook her head. "Where are Niles and Tamir?"

"Ah." Lorrin glanced over his shoulder. "Looking for you."

"Maybe we should find them first?" She didn't want to have to repeat the story of what had happened. She still felt raw from what she'd seen.

"OK." He looked at her eyes, his own bright with worry. "But are you alright?"

"Yeah," she said, wondering if he could tell she'd been crying.

He stared at her a moment longer, then nodded.

"OK," he said, and led her back up the hall in search of the others.

As it turned out, Niles and Tamir were only around the corner, ducking into each of the public training rooms to make sure she wasn't in any of them.

"Where have you been?" Niles practically shouted when she tapped him on the shoulder and he pulled his head from an empty room.

"It is good to see you, *tarsi*," Tamir said, closing a door opposite the room Niles had been peering in.

Niles cleared his throat.

"With a friend," she said, answering Niles's question.

"But ..." Niles frowned. "But Bentley?"

"She took a different horse," Lorrin said.

"Oh," Niles's frown deepened. "I didn't think of that."

"Some guard." Elinta laughed, poking him in the chest.

"Hey!" he said, but his face cleared.

"Perhaps there is somewhere else we can talk?" Tamir asked. He'd pulled his dark shoulder-length hair back into a loose bun though some had fallen out at the back. The more relaxed look suited him. It was good he was becoming more comfortable around them.

"My office," Lorrin said, nodding.

Niles spun her in place and marched her down the hall. "I can't believe you missed breakfast," he muttered as they went into Lorrin's office. Elinta laughed. Lorrin's arm brushed hers as he passed.

"What happened?" the prince asked as they all sat. Niles perched on the edge of Lorrin's desk, which nearly overflowed with paperwork. "Why were you out for so long?"

"It worked."

"You saw Zhayra's memories?" Tamir asked, sitting forward.

"Yes."

"What did you see?" Lorrin said.

Elinta paused. She wasn't sure whether to mention that Zhayra's mother had been queen, and that therefore meant Zhayra could be. That was something to consider for another time once things with Mazen had settled down. She didn't know what it would mean for her and Zhayra, but it would mean *something*, and she wasn't ready to discuss it with them.

"I know why Zhayra is in Eldras," she finally said. "Mazen killed her mother."

"What?" Lorrin and Niles said.

"*Inna*?" Tamir echoed, so surprised that he reverted to his native tongue.

"She saw him. His blade was in her mother's chest," Elinta said, her voice sounding hollow to her own ears. "He called Vaherin and she fled. She followed her mother's memories of Eldras but came down in the storm over Kethmere."

Tamir's face paled. "He killed a dragon," he said, shock dripping from his voice.

Lorrin ran a hand through his hair. "But why? Why would he kill her?"

"I don't know. They looked like they'd been meeting in private, but Zhayra didn't know what it was about."

"This guy is crazy," Niles mumbled, then frowned. "Was the sword *illayas*?"

"Yes," she said.

"He only had a dagger with him the night of the Eggslaying," Lorrin said, brow furrowing.

Tamir sat back in his chair. "He didn't have his sword when you met?"

"No," Elinta said, remembering the *illayas* dagger with a shudder.

"What happened to it, then?" Niles said to the room. He pushed up the sleeves of his jacket.

"I didn't see."

"Is Zhayra alright?" Lorrin asked, concern flitting across his face again. Elinta felt a small, appreciative smile cross her face.

"Yes. I think she's relieved I finally know." They descended into silence, each thinking over what they'd learnt, though Elinta might have snuck a glance at Lorrin once or twice. She loved the way he thought of Zhayra, the most out of the boys.

"How did you access her memories?" Tamir finally asked.

"I'm not sure," she said, pulling her gaze from the prince and leaning back in her chair. "I tried for ages, and nothing was working. I guess I fell asleep and the next thing I knew, I was reliving her memories."

"Wow," Niles said.

"You said you were asleep the first time it happened too," Tamir said, cocking his head.

"Yeah, that's right."

"Perhaps this sense can only be accessed in sleep. To accommodate for the memories."

"Maybe," Elinta said. It made sense. She turned to Lorrin. "What's being done here about Mazen?"

"I don't think anything's changed since we left. There are more guards around and they've all been told what he looks like, but we can't go looking for him. We wouldn't know where to start."

Elinta sighed. "I don't suppose you're all free today to work out a plan then?"

Lorrin shook his head. "I have a lot of paperwork to go through," he said gesturing at the piles on his desk. "But ... I could try to shuffle it around. Make some time."

A smile of relief began to cross her features, but it was soon wiped away.

"No can do. I'm on duty in fifteen minutes," Niles said. Then, almost as an afterthought, he added, "I was beginning to wonder if I'd see you before I started. We'll have to go for birthday cake another time."

"I'm sorry," Elinta said. "I didn't wake up until really late." And that was the end of her plans. A wriggle of frustration ate at her. They needed to work this out, but how could they when no one would help, and the boys were busy with their other responsibilities?

"We will find time, *tarsi*."

"I'm sorry," Lorrin said. "Is there anything you can do today?"

"I can go to the library." She shrugged. "I want to see what other senses there are that I don't know about."

Lorrin smiled. "Good idea. I think the more you learn about them, the better."

"Would you mind if I joined you?" Tamir asked. "I'd love to see the palace collection and learn some more about your people. Perhaps it will help when we speak with the king again."

"Of course," Elinta said though she couldn't help feeling a stab of frustration. Speak with the king again. Whenever that would be. "I'll have to meet you there. I need to change." *And maybe have a bath,* she thought.

Elinta sat in her old spot in the library (in a comfortable chair by a window) surrounded by books. She'd pulled half a dozen down from the shelves and flicked through the pages, searching for any information on the human senses. Even though Ford had suggested that Zhayra would have some that she didn't, there was no way for her to find them through the books in the library. Her time searching the books during her last stay in the palace had taught her there was little to no information to be found on the dragons.

As it was, Elinta's mind was swimming with what she had found. Tamir had been right when he'd said there were more than five senses, but now she realised just how right he'd been.

There was a person's sense of balance, something she knew about from her training as a healer, but never made the connection that it was an actual sense, in the way sight was. Proprioception was a sense of where your body was at any given moment, while chronoception was to do with the passing of time. There were others that, now it had been pointed out to her, seemed obvious: pressure sensors in the skin, tension sensors, and thirst or hunger sensors. There were so many. And she could access them all through Zhayra?

Elinta poured over the books, drinking in as many details as possible, but in the back of her mind the disbelief and doubt ate at her. *How am I supposed to access these?* she wondered. And why would she? What use were pressure sensors and the passing of time? Using Zhayra's eyes had been hard and seeing her core memories had been even harder. How was she supposed to use tension sensors?

She sat back in her chair, closed her eyes, and ran a hand through her hair. She sighed. Maybe she'd bitten off more than she could chew. It was true; she loved to learn. But staring in the face of all this ... Well, it was a bit overwhelming.

For now, maybe she didn't need to worry about kinaesthesia and chemoreception. Sight, hearing, memories, they were enough to keep her busy. Not to mention fighting and Asalin.

Elinta closed the books and set about returning them to their places, mindful of the librarian's gaze as she searched for their spots among the maze of shelves. Tamir was in the history section, sitting cross-legged on the floor, and didn't look up when she approached. She cocked her head to read the title on the blue cover. It was an account of their more recent history, after the death of King Cenric.

"Anything interesting?" she asked.

Tamir jolted in surprise, turning round eyes on her. "I did not hear you."

Elinta chuckled. "That answers my question, then."

"Yes." Tamir smiled, rising to his feet. "I am unfamiliar with many of the events among your people following the Eggslaying."

"We don't have much on the Eggslaying itself," Elinta said, once again wondering what really happened.

Tamir seemed to notice the longing in her voice. "We do not know what happened either. It was between Prince Tristan and the dragons."

"Hm," Elinta said. *The dragons* ... She stilled. "Tamir?" she said hesitantly. "What happened to the dragon that killed Tristan?"

She couldn't believe she'd never thought of it before. The blue dragon killed in the Eggslaying hadn't been the one to kill Tristan. She'd just been in the wrong place at the wrong time when Cenric had carried out his revenge. So, what had happened to the dragon who'd killed Tristan?

Tamir shook his head, his silver eyes growing thoughtful. "We've long wondered the same thing. We do not even know who it was."

Elinta's shoulders slumped. Why was there so little information? She glanced out at the sky. "Dinner will be ready soon. Do you want to head down now?"

Tamir glanced back at the book he held. "I doubt Niles will wait for us?"

"No." Elinta smiled. "He won't."

He closed the book and slipped it back onto the shelf, and the two went down to dinner.

"Perhaps you might practice two skills tonight?" Tamir said, standing against the wall in their usual training room. His glow lit up the wall around him, fighting off the shadows their lanterns couldn't reach.

Elinta was standing opposite Lorrin, her sword drawn. "What do you mean?"

"Fight while using dragonsight," Tamir said, simply.

"Oh," she said, her sword dropping. "I—I'll try."

Lorrin gave her an encouraging smile, and she looked around the room, searching for something to focus on. Geoffrey, their training dummy, was in the corner. He'd do. She stared at the eyes Niles had drawn on him, willing the blackness into a sharper clarity. Elinta tried to count the number of lines in the fabric underneath those beady eyes. There was a box-like formula, with solid horizontal lines and the occasional solid vertical. But was it one or two thin verticals and then the solid line?

Just like when she'd been staring at the tree in the distance, something within her clicked. There were actually three thin verticals in those small boxes. She grinned.

"Got it?" Lorrin asked.

She nodded, and raised her sword again, trying to resist the urge to study his face with her keener eyesight.

Lorrin lunged. Half a second. That's what dragonsight gave her. She saw his muscles rippling beneath his skin, half a second before her usual sight would have, and stopped his blade in mid-air. The prince grinned. He whipped his sword out and around, aiming for her legs, but Elinta saw his muscles brace and harden, then ripple again in another direction. His sword followed the movement, stopping briefly, before flicking up to her side. Elinta's sword met his there.

And it was on. Half a second. It wasn't much. It was a mere blink, and it was over. But it gave her an edge that she didn't have before. She landed the first hit—on Lorrin's arm—spun away from his return attack, then danced forward and slapped him on the leg with her blade.

That half a second didn't stop him from returning the blows. But there were less. She couldn't help a laugh from slipping through her lips, and she and Lorrin fought like never before. Lorrin's face was a mirror of her own. She found herself wishing this dance would never end.

When they pulled apart, puffing, Elinta could feel three new bruises forming. Lorrin, she knew, had at least four.

"Good!" Tamir and Lorrin said at the same time. A surge of pride raced through Zhayra, who'd been watching the fight through Elinta's eyes. The door opened and the three of them jumped.

"Sorry I'm late!" Niles said, closing the door behind him. He shot Lorrin a look of exasperation. "I think the generals are punishing me. I had a double shift." He was still in his uniform but had unbuttoned the grey jacket.

Lorrin nodded, sympathy etched across his sweaty face. "You should see the amount of paperwork dropped off for me this afternoon."

"So, how's it going?" he said, looking between the three of them. "Has she destroyed Lorrin yet?"

Elinta raised her eyebrows, glanced at Lorrin, then slowly nodded.

Lorrin laughed and Niles grinned.

"Good," he said.

Elinta hurried across the room to grab a drink as they talked, but her toe caught on the spongy flooring, and she stumbled before awkwardly straightening.

Lorrin's laugh reached her. "Of course, now I'm wondering how she managed it."

She shot him a playful glare as she gulped down some water.

Tamir stepped forward. "Would you be willing to try something else?" he said, mainly addressing Elinta, but including the boys.

The three nodded, Elinta, still with dragonsight, somewhat hesitantly. She lowered her empty glass. Tamir pulled a piece of cloth from his pocket.

"You read about the senses today?"

"Yes," she said, frowning at the cloth.

He stepped forward, gesturing at her face with the fabric. Still frowning, Elinta nodded.

Tamir slipped behind her and tied the cloth around her enhanced eyes. He grabbed her shoulders and steered her to a different place in the room. His hands left her. "You are in the centre of the room," he said. His footsteps retreated. She couldn't see a thing.

Tamir spoke to the boys in a low voice, his words no more than a soft whisper that she couldn't understand.

"I want you to tell me where we are" came Tamir's voice from her left.

"… How?" Elinta turned toward his voice. But no reply came. "Tamir?" Nothing.

She frowned. How was she supposed to know where the boys were without seeing them? Would her hearing do that? She strained her ears, listening for any sign of them, but the floor was padded and Lorrin and Tamir, at least, were barefoot.

Zhayra watched and listened, curiosity bubbling in her stomach. Elinta strained, trying to force her ears to pick up the sound of their feet, but nothing happened. Her shoulders slumped. What other senses had she read about earlier? Hunger and thirst weren't going to help her. Or time. She wracked her brain.

A finger prodded her in the back, and she slapped out at the hand but missed. Niles chuckled from her right.

"Well, that's easy," she said dryly, pointing to where she'd heard his laughter coming from.

"Keep trying, *tarsi*" came Tamir's reply.

Sighing, she tried to summon a picture of the room. Imagining herself in the centre, Geoffrey off to her left, the door behind her, and the three boys somewhere near her. She watched their outlines moving around her. She imagined Niles weaving around her, always close, Lorrin moving evenly around the room, and Tamir—Tamir stood in the corner, next to … Geoffrey? It was hard to tell, hard to distinguish Geoffrey from his surroundings. But Tamir, Niles, and Lorrin … she gasped. Her hand flew to her mouth.

"What?" Niles asked.

"I can ... I can see you," she stammered around her fingers. Niles stopped in front of her, and she slowly reached out and poked him in the chest.

"No way!"

Lorrin's figure joined him a moment later. She prodded his shoulder. "Tamir's in the corner."

Niles made a noise of shock.

"You can see us?" Tamir asked.

"Kind of," she said, looking at him. She couldn't make out all the details of their faces, or anything much about them other than their outlines. No, that wasn't right. It was as though she were looking at a rainbow silhouette of them, but with a small amount of detail included. Lorrin and Niles were a mess of red, orange, and yellow, even a little bit of green, against a backdrop of blue and black.

"You look different though," she said, pressing at the cloth on her face to be sure it was still there.

Tamir's figure tilted its head. "How so?"

"Lorrin and Niles are a mess of colours. Red in their chests, orange faces and legs. But you're completely red. And all the same shade."

"Their chests are the darkest?"

"Yes."

"Are their fingers lightest?"

Elinta looked. "Yes."

"You're seeing our heat!" Tamir's voice rose in excitement.

"What?"

Niles's and Lorrin's figures twisted, looking toward the Asali.

"A human's core is their warmest, while their extremities are cooler. My people are different," Tamir said, his words growing faster.

"Because of your light," Elinta said, catching on.

Niles waved his hand in front of her face. She batted it away. "So … so I'm looking at your body heat?" she asked, more for herself than out of any real doubt.

"Yes."

An image came to her mind, of Zhayra's face and the three pits running just above her upper lip on either side, like a snake. *Like a snake.* People said that snakes could see body heat. That was how they hunted in the dark.

"Wow," she whispered. She raised a hand in front of her face and waved it back and forth.

"Can you see this?" Lorrin raised his hand, the one holding his sword, and swung it around.

"Yes," she said, dropping her own hand and watching the blade. Its outline was easily distinguishable from the deep blue wall behind it though the image was awkward to her mind.

Tamir pushed off from the wall and crossed to her, untying the cloth from her face.

She opened her eyes and gasped. "That's impossible." She waved a hand in front of her face again. She didn't know how to describe it. It was like she was seeing two images at the same time. What her eyes were seeing, which were still tuned into her dragonsight, and what the other sense she'd accessed was seeing. There were two images in her mind, not overlapping in any way.

"You don't look any different," Niles said, peering into her face. There were two of him.

A wave of dizziness hit her, and she reached out, grabbing Lorrin's arm and closing her eyes.

"Are you OK?" he said, touching her shoulder. She could still see him, the heat version of him, but with her eyes closed, the dizziness eased.

"I could see you," she said, struggling to explain. "Normal you and the heat version of you. At the same time."

"How?"

"The sense you are using is not from your eyes, but the image it creates must be connected to the same part of your mind as the image formed by your vision," Tamir said, leaning in to look at her. "Perhaps they share a nerve in the dragon, and so they do in you as well when you use it."

Elinta's mind boggled. "I ... I need to turn this off."

"OK," Lorrin said, squeezing her shoulder. "You can do it."

She turned her head to the hair tie on her wrist, seeing its blue form on her orange skin. She opened her eyes and pushed aside the coloured image and the dizziness accompanying it. The dragonsight allowed her to study the details of the band, details she couldn't see with the other vision. The colours of the heat image began to fade. She squinted, forcing her eyes to work harder, her mind to forget about the other sense that wasn't hers, and the image disappeared.

Then she turned off the dragonsight, following the same steps she had the first time she'd accessed it. Looking at the hair tie and realising the texture of the band seemed mundane and boring now, she sighed with relief.

"That was unbelievable," she said, looking from Lorrin to Niles, and finally to Tamir.

"You have heat vision," Tamir said. Niles's mouth dropped open.

CHAPTER
SIXTEEN

"**M**ISS!" NEVA BURST THROUGH the bedroom door.

Elinta jumped, turning from her wardrobe, where she'd been searching for a dress to wear. She'd been daydreaming about Zhayra, and the mystery of how she could be the heir but not queen. "Neva?"

"Queen Mira's invited you to tea this morning! Isn't that exciting?" the maid said, waving a piece of paper clutched in her hand.

Elinta felt her face drain of colour. Her hands trailed to wrap themselves in her nightgown.

"What is it?" Neva asked, hurrying to her side. "Are you sick today?"

"No," Elinta said, taking the invitation from Neva and staring at it. "I haven't really spoken to her since before I left." And ... had Mira somehow heard of her son's plans to meet to discuss the treaty today? To decide what to do from here?

"Oh," Neva said, but Elinta knew she didn't understand what she'd said. She didn't know the full story of where she'd been though rumours had been spreading through the palace since they'd returned with Tamir. The king and queen were playing it close to their chests. But Elinta and the queen had gotten along well before she'd left with Lorrin and Niles to go to Liyarna. Something the king and queen didn't approve of. And now, she wanted to meet on the day, at the exact *time,* she and the boys had finally carved out to meet uninterrupted. And she couldn't refuse. Not without causing more trouble. Not without drawing more attention to herself.

She tried to remember how the queen had supported her staying in the palace whether she was Ford's student or not. Maybe the woman wasn't angry. She was just doing what she felt was right. Though she was making things worse.

Elinta forced herself to smile as she looked at the maid. "It'll be nice to see her again." She tried to make herself believe it. Maybe nothing had changed between them. Maybe nothing would.

Neva smiled. "That's the spirit, miss. You'd better get dressed."

Elinta stood in front of the small door to the tearooms and exhaled nervously. Mira had always been kind to her. Why should things have changed? The queen didn't know the whole story of the reason for their visit to Liyarna. To her, she'd just gone along with the prince out of friendship. Maybe calling her here really was just a way to disrupt Lorrin. The prince had certainly been frustrated when he'd heard of his mother's invitation. Elinta knocked on the door.

It swung open and a maid ushered her inside. The small room was much the same as Elinta remembered it with its mix of soft and bold colours against the white stone. Just like her previous visits with the queen, Mira was sitting at the small table by the windows looking over the palace gardens. When she smiled, Elinta felt herself relax. Mostly. The coincidence of their meeting time was still a little too much for her.

"Good morning," the queen said, gesturing for Elinta to sit with her. Crossing the room, Elinta took her usual seat at the table, positioned so they could both look out of the large windows. The maid poured them some tea and then left them alone.

Mira's dark hair was mostly down today, with an intricate braid pulling it back from her face. Her green eyes searched Elinta's brown ones. "I've missed our teas."

"Me too," Elinta stuttered, straightening out a crinkle in her shirt. Mira graciously didn't draw attention to her nerves.

"Have you spoken with Ford?" Mira asked, taking a sip from her cup.

"Yes," Elinta said, cupping her tea in her hands, and going along with the innocent conversation. "We've decided not to continue with my teaching."

Mira's green eyes turned sympathetic. "I'm sorry to hear it."

"Thank you," Elinta said, then hesitantly added, "It was worth it."

Mira's head cocked. "You support Lorrin's attempt to make a treaty?"

"Yes," she said tentatively. She'd never discussed anything like this with the queen, always careful to keep herself out of scrutiny. But now, it didn't matter so much. The royals knew she'd been to see the Asali this time. And Mira had called her here for a reason. Maybe she could help make a difference.

"Yet it seems my husband and the Asali don't." Mira looked out over the gardens.

"... What about you?"

The queen smiled. "Things are never simple, Elinta. I'm proud of my son's efforts whether they were misguided or not, but I support my husband."

They fell into silence, and Elinta mulled over the queen's words. Did that mean she would be open to a treaty if the king was? Or did she dislike the idea just as much as him? Why did she have to intervene with their plans!

"Mira," Elinta said, drawing the queen's attention. Before she could scare herself out of asking, she let the question that had plagued her for months slip through her lips. "Do you know what happened between Prince Tristan and the dragon?"

"What do the Asali say?"

"They don't know."

Mira nodded, and Elinta saw some of the openness disappear from her face. "The dragon killed him," she said. "Yet our peoples have come to very different conclusions on how we should have reacted."

"But," Elinta said, "what *happened?* No one seems to know."

"Why does a dog attack its owner? No one knows. But now it will never happen again."

Elinta felt her eyes widen in surprise, but just managed to stop the full extent of her shock from showing on her face. For a moment, for one small but infinite moment, she'd forgotten the queen, and every human other than her, Niles, Lorrin, and Ford, believed the dragons were beasts. She knew she should respond to what Mira had said, but she couldn't.

At the same time, the need to ask her if she'd known about her son's plans for the day nearly burst out of her. Of course, the queen knew somehow, but why couldn't she just come out and say it?

A spike of curiosity and worry came from Zhayra.

"Have you drawn recently?" Elinta finally managed to say in a desperate attempt to change the subject. She'd said enough today. Mira accepted the change and smiled—perhaps thinking Elinta agreed with her response—oblivious to her internal struggle.

"Yes," Mira said, and their conversation drifted for the next hour. They spoke of drawing, Mira's niece and nephew Cassia and Aiden, the upcoming visit of the king's cousins, but they never turned back to the Asali or the dragons. When Elinta left, her heart was heavy. She'd let the past few days of settling into the palace distract her from the problems she faced, but the queen had brought reality crashing back. How could she stop the Eggslaying from happening again if people believed dragons were nothing more than gigantic, vicious dogs? That idea continued to dance on the edge of her mind, dodging her every attempt to grab it. Things needed to change, but how?

🔥🔥🔥

Elinta knocked on the door to Lorrin's rooms. Her meeting with the queen had been bouncing around her head for hours. The idea lurking at the edges of her mind had continued to elude her, but her conversation with the queen about the dragons and the Asali plagued her. How could she show the people dragons weren't evil, but another race? *And after that,* she thought with a mental sigh, *we've got to find a way to communicate.*

Her first instinct had been to go to the library, but she knew there wouldn't be anything there to help her. Her second was to see Lorrin.

The door opened, and the prince grinned. "Elinta."

"Hi," she said, entering when he stepped aside. It was mid-afternoon now, and Lorrin had lit a lantern at his desk, the light from the window in the back wall too dim to work by. She'd already gone to see him after her meeting with the queen, to reassure him that nothing had happened. He'd been relieved, but strangely quiet. A delivery of urgent papers had arrived for him to sort through by the afternoon. He hadn't been able to salvage a talk with Niles and Tamir at all.

"What's going on?" he said, leaning against his desk. Papers still covered every inch of it.

"I ... I wondered," she started, then tried again, "Those books in the secret room that Alexander guarded were there any about the Asali? When we first met them?" She'd been thinking of her visit to that room for hours. She'd been too caught up in the dragon scales at the time to appreciate the rest of the contents of the room, but she remembered there'd been books. And they had to have been very important to be in a room with dragon scales, kingly armour, and ancient jewels.

Lorrin cocked his head. "There were diaries from some of the old kings," he said. "Yeah, I think there would be!"

"Could I see them?"

Lorrin nodded slowly. "I could get you one."

Elinta finally let herself smile. "Thank you!"

Lorrin went quiet. "I'm sorry things didn't work out today." His face fell, but there was a tint of anger in his voice as he continued, "I think my parents are hoping I'll forget about it if my schedule is full. They even added more hours to Niles's guard duty."

"It's OK," Elinta said, taking in his demeanour and berating herself. She'd begun to forget that the treaty had been his idea, his project since before she'd even met him. It had to mean as much to him as to her, even if they'd originally had different reasons for wanting it. Lorrin would still be trying to think of ways to fix things, even if they hadn't all been able to talk yet, just as she was doing the same. They'd come so close today.

"I'll keep doing what I can," she said. But it was the wrong thing to say.

"You shouldn't have to," he said, his hand coming down hard on the desk under him.

Staring at the prince, Elinta didn't say anything for a moment. She'd heard him frustrated once or twice before ... but not angry like this. Even if it wasn't really directed at her, it shocked her.

"I'm sorry," he said to the silence. Lorrin ran a hand through his hair. "I just—I just meant that I wish I could help. We've been trying to do this for so long and we're not getting anywhere."

"I know," she whispered. "We're doing what we can. Things will clear up soon."

A smile tugged at his lips and his eyes softened. "I hope the book helps."

"Me too," she said. Elinta stared at him a moment longer before she crossed the distance and tentatively hugged him. Lorrin's arms slowly rose to return the embrace, and she felt what tension remained drain from him.

Blushing, she pulled back, thanked him again and excused herself so he could return to his work. She could feel his eyes on her as she left.

"Here you go," Lorrin said, placing a book in Elinta's hands the next day at breakfast.

"A book?" Niles said around a mouthful of food. Tamir looked on with interest.

She stared down at the book. "It's so ... new." The diary Lorrin had retrieved for her was a small red book, no more than half a centimetre thick. But the diary looked to be in near perfect condition, with only a small crinkle on the front cover and along the spine. There was a name printed on the front cover. E. Coombs.

She gasped. Edwin Coombs was the first human ever recorded to meet with the Asali and their king.

"The original was damaged beyond repair a long time ago. Even if it wasn't, it's been over three thousand years," Lorrin said.

"Good point," Elinta said. He seemed in better spirits today, she thought, looking him over. She just hoped he didn't let his parent's attempts to distract him get to him so much again.

Lorrin smiled. "So … why did you want to see it?"

"I had an idea," Elinta said. *Or more like a vague inkling of an idea,* she thought, but she didn't say any more about it. She wasn't even sure what she'd find inside the diary. "But I need to look at this first."

Lorrin nodded. "Well, I guess you're set for the day then?"

"Yes." She glanced at the book again. "I think I'll get started now. See you all later."

She jumped to her feet, tucking the little book into a pocket, and hurried from the hall, her footsteps echoing on the stone floor.

Immersed in her thoughts, Elinta didn't notice a door opening to the left of the dining hall until a hand had reached out and yanked her inside. Elinta blindly shoved at the person, stumbling away and rubbing at the spot where their iron grip had been. Her hand instinctively trailed for her sword.

"I know who you are."

Elinta stiffened and looked at the figure that now blocked the door.

"Shae?" The small woman's eyes were hard as she watched Elinta. She forced her hand to move away from her weapon. "What—what are you talking about?" Elinta said, her throat suddenly dry. Shae couldn't know who she was. She couldn't. Elinta had been so careful. So, so very careful.

Shae laughed bitterly, shaking her head. "The king and queen can't see it, but I'm no fool," she said, her beady eyes scanning Elinta.

Elinta hung onto her every word, dimly aware that Zhayra was now listening through her ears.

"Prince Lorrin would never act so recklessly as to go to Liyarna without an escort. You," she said, pointing a finger at her, "you convinced him, didn't you? You've got him wrapped around your finger."

Relief began to crack through Elinta's panic. The advisor didn't know about Zhayra. She thought she was just a trouble-maker. Elinta stared at the woman in disbelief.

"Lorrin was planning to go a long time ago," she said, thinking of their time in the White Mountains when they'd first met. He'd been talking about going to the council even then. "If he snuck off to the White Mountains by himself, why wouldn't he go to Liyarna?"

Shae's eyes darkened, but Elinta didn't care what she'd revealed to the woman. No one had known Elinta knew about that side-trip the prince had made on his way back from Tremass in the west. But Elinta reasoned that if she had been with him on the trip to Liyarna, the king and queen would assume she knew about the White Mountains as well. She hadn't really revealed anything.

Shae seemed to be thinking along the same lines. "You and Niles are no good, *corrupting*—" she practically spat "—the prince."

Now it was Elinta's turn to laugh. As all her worry about having been found out dissipated, anger took its place. Anger mimicked by Zhayra.

"Lorrin didn't need corrupting," she said, hardly hearing herself. "He's quite capable of making his own decisions. Now, if you'll excuse me, I'm late for something important."

Shae stared at her in open-mouthed shock, but Elinta was too angry to think about the way she'd just spoken to the advisor. She'd had enough. Enough of people interfering and enough of Shae. She crossed the room and grabbed the doorhandle, fully expecting to shove the woman aside if she had to. Shae slowly stepped away, her eyes on fire.

"I'll be keeping an eye on you," she said. "The king and queen may believe you're here just for the prince's attentions, but I have their ear."

Elinta's cheeks heated at the woman's words. "Attentions?" she stammered.

Shae grinned, but it didn't reach her eyes. "Weren't you late for something important?"

Elinta stumbled from the room as Shae slammed the door shut behind her. She stared at the door, her brain struggling. Everyone thought she was only there to win Lorrin's heart? *That's ridiculous! I don't even—we haven't—*"Argh!" She threw her hands up into the air and trudged down the hall.

Zhayra's stomach tickled. Elinta frowned.

"Are you laughing at me?" she mumbled, glancing around to make sure no one was nearby to hear her. The tickle grew stronger.

"Hmph!" She turned down another corridor, stomping the last of the way to the library. A maid scuttled out of her way. This was one encounter she wasn't about to pass on to Lorrin *or* Niles. They'd never let her hear the end of it. *His attentions!*

Elinta flopped into her favourite seat by one of the windows and pulled out Edwin's diary, glad Shae hadn't noticed the little book tucked inside one of her pockets. The woman didn't need another reason to think she was a bad influence on Lorrin. Huffing, she cracked open the book, flipping through the pages until she found what she was looking for. Edwin's entries looked small, but their importance could be enormous. She could find out how their races had communicated with each other at their very first meeting. And maybe it would help the idea hiding at the edges of her mind to form.

> *'They're meant to be just stories, yeah? The people of light. But I saw one, I saw one of them today. Stunning, she was. Deep, black hair and eyes the colour of the purest silver. It was like she was the sun, the way she glowed. I'm going back out tomorrow. I have to see her again.'*

Elinta flipped to the next page.

> *'She was there again. Moving through the trees like a wraith. Can't believe how fast she moves. Gave me a heart attack that first day, popping out of nowhere with that spear. I don't speak a lick of whatever it is she speaks, but at least she can say my name. It sounds beautiful from her mouth. Anything would. Reckon she could insult me, and I'd thank her. She told me her name. At least I think it's a name. Lila. She looks like a Lila.'*

Elinta turned to the next page, then flicked back. There had to be a day or two missing. The next page detailed Lila taking him to King Asa. But how had Edwin convinced her to take him there? But there was nothing there, no attempt at talking recorded for her to learn from. Resigned, she moved on to the meeting with the king ... who, somehow, spoke the common tongue.

"What?" Elinta whispered, staring at the king's recorded words. Was it possible Edwin had later translated the conversation? No ... by Edwin's description, he was just as stunned as she was at the king's use of his language. It was amazing, but also not what she had been hoping to find. No matter, there was still Lila. Elinta skimmed the meeting with the king, looking for Lila's next entrance. Edwin seemed somewhat taken with her, surely, they would meet again?

"Oi," a voice whispered in Elinta's ear. Jumping, Elinta twisted to find Niles, Lorrin, and Tamir all standing behind her.

"Niles!" she said, then frowned as she looked at the three boys. "What's going on?" For a second, she wondered if they'd all somehow heard about Shae. But Tamir wouldn't tease her about that.

"Cake," Niles said. "Lorrin managed to grab some spare time, and I swapped my shift. We're under strict instructions not to scheme though."

Elinta glanced down at the diary, then back up at the boys and the huge grins lighting their faces. Edwin and Lila could wait. Besides, she could do with some cake after *that* little discussion this morning. Which she most definitely wasn't still thinking about. Closing the book, they hurried to her room, where she tucked it under her pillow and turned back to the boys, crowded in her doorway.

"Let's go!" But she paused, looking at Tamir. "Are you ... are you allowed to come?"

"No," Tamir said, "but I will see you off, and Niles has promised to bring me a piece of cake. He says Merton's food is worth dying for."

Elinta grinned. "Maybe I should be the one to carry the cake back. You might not get it if Niles has it."

"True," Niles said thoughtfully.

"I will see you tonight for more training. We'll work on your heat sense again."

"And eat cake," Niles said.

"And eat cake," Tamir repeated.

Niles and Lorrin took her to their favourite café. Merton Alvey's.

"Your Highness!" Merton said, coming out from behind the long counter to greet them. He had flour smeared over his left cheek and in part of his thin moustache. It was rare to see him without flour on his face somewhere.

"Merton," Lorrin said, a tired grin on his face. "It's just Lorrin."

"Of course, Your Highness," Merton said with a laugh. "What can I do for you?"

"Ah," Niles said, "it's not so much you, but Mrs. Alvey."

"Cake?" Merton said.

"Birthday cake," Niles corrected.

Merton looked between the two boys before settling his gaze on Elinta. "I know it's not either of these two—" He jerked his head at them. "I have their birthdays marked down so we can bake extra cake! Happy birthday!"

"Thank you," Elinta said, completely unsurprised by the revelation the Alveys had to bake extra cake because of the boys. Niles would try to eat a whole one on his own if he was allowed.

"Well, grab a seat, and I'll see what the missus has out back."

"Thanks, Merton," Lorrin said. "Could you bring out an extra piece for us to take back?"

With a nod, Merton hurried off.

The three crossed the room to a wooden table in the corner, carefully weaving their way around the other tables and customers. Elinta took in a deep breath, inhaling the scent of fresh bread, pies, and sweet cakes that filled the shop. It had been too long since they'd been to Merton's.

Sitting at their little table, Elinta listened casually to the boys' conversation, just enjoying the moment. They wouldn't be able to talk about the Asali out here, something she was sure had factored into Lorrin and Niles both getting time off, so she let herself forget about that for now.

"She has me on another double shift tonight!" Niles said, shaking his head at Lorrin. "I won't be able to train." At this, Niles glanced apologetically at her as well, but Elinta had straightened in her seat for a different reason. Niles had given her an idea. One that could help get Shae off her back.

"Lorrin," she said.

Both boys gave her their full attention.

"Is there something I can do around the palace?" she asked. It seemed like the perfect way to distract Shae. If she appeared to be busy, to be doing something other than spending all her time with Lorrin, Niles, and Tamir—not that she'd been able to do that lately—or researching in the library, maybe the woman would back off on her suspicions. Or at the very least, it might discredit some of her concerns. Besides, now that people didn't think she was only there until she began lessons with Ford, it seemed like the right thing to do.

"What do you mean?" Lorrin asked.

"Well, I want to help out."

Lorrin frowned.

"I don't have a reason to be in the palace anymore. A reason that everyone knows, anyway," she added, seeing both of them about to argue. "I should be doing something. People are probably wondering why I'm even there."

"You're worried about getting kicked out?" Niles asked.

"No," she said, "I just ... like I said, I don't have a reason to be here."

"You have me," Lorrin said.

Elinta's cheeks heated at that. But she knew he was just referring to how he'd asked his parents to let her stay. That's what she told herself, anyway. And she definitely didn't think about what Shae had said.

"But I see what you mean," he said.

Niles nodded. "You could be a guard!" he said.

Elinta raised her eyebrows.

"No, I know ..." Niles waved his hand.

"Here we are!" Merton said, arriving at their table with three plates and a paper bag. He placed a piece in front of each of them, gave Tamir's to Lorrin, wished Elinta another happy birthday, and disappeared back behind the counter.

Momentarily distracted, Elinta looked down at the cake. Merton had sourced their favourite cake. Chocolate. It had two layers, with a thick sliver of chocolate cream to separate them. The slice was topped with chocolate icing, covered with chocolate chips. She was going to feel sick after eating it, but it would be worth it.

"That woman is the best," Niles said, reaching for his slice. "Happy birthday, El."

"Happy birthday," Lorrin said, and they all dug into their cake.

"You could work in the kitchen?" Niles said around a mouthful of cake.

Elinta shook her head. "I can't cook."

"You've cooked for us," Lorrin said, referencing their trip to Liyarna, and even the first time she'd travelled with him from the White Mountains. But it was possible he'd forgotten the taste of those meals. Even Blaine had always teased her that it was a good thing she only cooked for them and no one important.

"I can't cook well," she amended.

"What about the library? Connor could always do with some help, and he's seen you there enough to know you could."

Elinta thought about it as she took another bite of her cake.

"OK," she said, finally. Maybe she'd have to be a little more careful with visiting Zhayra for the next few days too, while Shae continued to look closely at her.

"Only," Lorrin said, "he's meant to be on leave. I don't think you'll be able to talk to him for another week."

"That's OK." Elinta shrugged. What was another few days? She'd still be here.

CHAPTER
SEVENTEEN

D AYS LATER, ELINTA FOUND herself walking the halls on the third floor, searching the paintings for Prince Tristan. She'd been on her way to finish reading through Edwin's diary, since the librarian still hadn't returned, when it occurred to her. There were images, paintings, and even statues of King Cenric throughout both the palace and the city, but there were hardly any of Tristan. There had to be some. In fact, she was sure she'd seen one before. She just couldn't remember where. But the third floor seemed like the place to start looking, since it was where the royals lived and paintings covered the walls. So, she'd left the diary under her pillow and ventured out into the halls.

Elinta wanted to look at him, the man for whom all this had happened. If Tristan hadn't died, Cenric wouldn't have killed the dragon and the eggs, the Asali wouldn't have cut them off, and Zhayra would have been living in the White Mountains, which would have still been called the Ash Mountains. Of course, that would mean they'd never have met. But it was hard not to be curious about the prince. To wonder what he'd been like.

Besides, tonight was the night she and the boys were finally going to talk about their plans for the treaty though it had taken much manoeuvring and secrecy, and she wanted to have as much information as possible.

It was late afternoon, and she'd wandered all the way to the council chambers and even into a part of the palace she'd never been to before. There was a painting of King Cenric's brother, who'd taken the throne once he'd died. King Bada. He looked like his brother. The same strong jaw and heavyset eyes. His eyes were blue, though, where Cenric's had been green. But still, Prince Tristan was nowhere to be seen. Her boots echoed around the hall as she moved to the next painting.

A door cracked open several metres in front of her and an older man stepped out. Elinta stared at the familiar man's back, her mind struggling to comprehend what she was seeing. It was as though, because the man wasn't where he belonged, she couldn't recognise him. Her eyes darted from his speckled grey hair, over his stocky form, and to the sword at his hip. Oddly enough, it wasn't the sword that made the stuttering cogs in her brain start up again. It was something in the way he carried himself. She couldn't put her finger on what it was, but a name jumped into her mind at the sight of him walking from the room. Jareth. It was Jareth. The man who had led her village against her and Zhayra by the lake. And General Nash was following him out of the room.

Elinta clamped a hand down hard over her mouth to stop the strangled cry building in her chest from escaping and dived into the corridor to her immediate right, the one she'd just come from. Suddenly, she was back in the forest. Fear eating her innards. Her heart hammering in her chest so hard she thought it would jump out of her ribcage. Zhayra was looking through her eyes in an instant.

No, no, no, no! What was Jareth doing here? What was he doing with General Nash? Bile rose in her mouth. What if he'd told Lorrin's aunt about her? What if she now knew? Elinta's back was pressed against the cold stone of the corridor, and it was only that feeling that kept her from complete panic. She squeezed her eyes shut. Voices drifted up the hall, too low for her to hear. If only she could use the strength of Zhayra's ears! Then she could hear what was being said. She tried to focus on the soft murmur of their voices, but her raging emotions were too much.

Elinta waited for their voices to fade with bated breath. She needed to get to Lorrin. She had to tell him what was happening. And then—and then ... what? Elinta would have to leave the palace. It wouldn't be safe for her here anymore. Where would she go? Zhayra's large stomach was clenched and Elinta spared a moment to think of her, unable to see or know what had scared Elinta so much that her chest was constricting. But if she peered around the corner and Zhayra saw Jareth, assuming that Jareth didn't see Elinta, what would Zhayra do? No. It was better if the dragon didn't know yet.

A door closed in the hall, and the footsteps began to fade. Had General Nash gone back into her office, or was she now accompanying Jareth down the hall? The steps moved away from where Elinta hid. Just to be sure, she waited another minute after all had fallen silent before she pushed off from the wall and bolted back the way she'd come. She had to get to Lorrin.

When she rounded a corner, Elinta fought to slow her pace, fought to control her legs, to stop the mad sprint and walk like nothing was wrong. If she ran now, people would want to know what had happened to make her run like death was on her heels. Despite her best intentions, she wasn't able to keep to a slow walk and her brisk pace drew a couple raised eyebrows from a maid and solider she passed. But she ignored them, her mind so far ahead of her body she hardly knew what was happening around her.

Elinta's breath was coming in gasps when the door to Lorrin's office came into view. She didn't bother knocking, couldn't stop her body long enough to allow it, and burst into the room.

Lorrin glanced up from some paperwork, surprise on his face. She doubted anyone ever burst into his office. Other than Niles.

"Elinta?" Lorrin's face paled as he took in her agitated appearance. "What is it?"

She hurried into the room, running a hand through her hair as she closed the door. Her eyes were still heavy, but she wasn't sure if Zhayra was listening. Her heart was still too loud to tell. She dropped her arm. "Jareth is here."

Lorrin stared at her—when had he stood up?—not comprehending, but Zhayra's stomach jumped and fire burned in her chest.

"Jareth," she said again, desperation in her voice, "the man who led Kethmere against us."

Lorrin's face drained. He was beside her in a heartbeat. "Where? When?"

"Just now. Lorrin, he was talking to General Nash."

"Come with me," he said, diving from the room and not waiting for her to follow. Elinta ran after him, slamming the door behind her in her haste.

"Lorrin?"

"I've got to talk to her," he said, slowing his long strides enough for her to draw alongside him. Neither of them was running, but the urgency in their walk was clear.

The soldier and the maid Elinta had passed on her way to Lorrin's rooms were now gone, and the way to Jaida's office was clear. Elinta wasn't sure whether that made her feel better or not. She didn't know what Lorrin was planning, but if the woman knew about her now, she wasn't sure she wanted to be near her. She should be in her room, packing her things.

Before they reached the hall, Elinta grabbed Lorrin's shoulder to hold him back and peered around the corner, making sure that Jareth hadn't returned. The hall was clear.

"Lorrin ..." she whispered, standing so close to him that she inhaled his scent. Old books and leather mixed with the scent of perfumed soap.

He squeezed her hand, then strode down the hall, Elinta half a step behind him. They stopped in front of the door.

"Lorrin?" she whispered again.

"Wait here," he said. "I'll talk to her."

"Lorrin," she said again, placing her hand on his arm.

He turned, his features softening when he looked at her, and he pulled her in for a quick hug. "It'll be OK."

He pulled away and knocked on the door. Elinta retreated a few steps so General Nash wouldn't see her when the door opened.

"Come in," came her muffled response. With one last look her way, Lorrin pushed open the door and went inside.

When the door closed with a soft click, Elinta fell against the wall and ran a hand over her face. Zhayra was still watching through her, but was she listening? "If anything happens, stay there," Elinta whispered to the empty hall. "I'll come to you."

The knot in Zhayra's stomach loosened for a moment, then tightened again. "Please, Zhayra." She couldn't have the dragon coming into the city even if it meant Elinta had to find her own way out. But that wasn't entirely true. Lorrin and Niles would help her if they could. Lorrin and Niles. She couldn't bear the thought of losing them too.

Her mind continued to jump ahead. Maybe she and Zhayra could return to the White Mountains. Ciar had said they were always welcome, hadn't he? But then what would happen with Mazen? Or the Asali? And what about Zhayra? She should be the queen of the dragons. She couldn't stay in hiding forever.

The door opened wide enough for Lorrin's head to appear.

"Come on in," he said. His face gave nothing away.

Elinta swallowed heavily, nodded, and forced herself over to the door, her legs like jelly. He opened the door wider for her to duck inside, then closed it behind her.

General Nash's office was nothing like she'd expected. Much like Lorrin's, there was a desk piled with paperwork, bookshelves filled to overflowing, and chairs for any visitors. But that's where the similarities stopped. General Nash collected weapons. Swords hung displayed along the wall behind her desk as well as on the right wall. Some were long, some were short, one was a long sword with a two-handed grip. Elinta's eyes landed on a sword of half illayas-half steel, a somewhat rare blade though not nearly as rare as its pure cousin. Next to a map of Eldras hung a painting of Nash's family on the left wall, Cassia and Aiden no more than babies in her arms. The map hung from a horizontal piece that looked remarkably like a sword in its sheath.

"Elinta?" General Nash stood behind her desk, a puzzled frown playing across her face. Lorrin led her over to the desk and gestured for her to sit. Elinta perched on the edge of a hard chair. She stared at the woman, who seemed at a loss for why Elinta would be there. If General Nash didn't know who she really was, what had Jareth been to see her about?

"Would you please repeat what you just told me, Aunt Jaida?"

General Nash's eyes flickered to her nephew's. "There have been reports of an Asali seen in a village to the south."

"Mazen?" Elinta said.

"I believe so."

"What village?" Lorrin prompted, even though they all knew.

"Kethmere," General Nash said. After a pause, she added, "Apparently, there were sightings of a dragon there some months ago, too."

"Was there anything else?" Elinta asked, not daring to believe she had gotten away clean.

General Nash glanced at Lorrin. "Actually, there was."

Lorrin stood up straighter. "What?"

"There are two villagers missing. They've probably just moved without telling anyone. It sounds like they had some family trouble a few months back. Except it looks like they didn't take anything." She shrugged. "Normally we wouldn't be involved in something so small, but there seems to be a lot happening in the area."

"Who?" Elinta breathed, not hearing the last of Nash's words. Her heart had stopped. It no longer thundered in her ears. It had stopped now, as though it already knew what General Nash was going to say. "Who was taken?"

"The local horse trainer and his son," General Nash said, frowning at Elinta's word use. She could read the thoughts playing across the general's face. Why would someone take a horse expert? But Elinta knew.

She felt the blood run from her face and stared wide-eyed at Lorrin. Realisation dawned on his face.

"You're sure?" he said, turning to his aunt.

"Yes."

A strangled sound left Elinta's throat.

"When was this?" Lorrin asked, his voice urgent.

"At least a week ago."

"Was there anything else?" Lorrin said. "Anything at all?"

"No, the man couldn't tell me anything more." General Nash studied Elinta's face. What she saw there, Elinta wasn't sure, but she could guess. A lie. She saw a lie come undone. Why would

Elinta, supposedly from Donlee, a village in the far north, care about two villagers from the far south?

"What's going on, Lorrin? I was going to bring this up tonight at the council meeting, but ..." she trailed off, gesturing to Elinta, who hadn't been able to form any words. She was still trying to process what she'd heard.

Lorrin ran a hand through his dark hair and dropped into the seat beside Elinta. He cast an anxious glance her way, then turned back to his aunt.

"Don't tell anyone," he said. That drew Elinta's attention.

Nash frowned.

"Please, Aunt Jaida. Leave this with me. There's more to this than you know."

The general looked long at Lorrin, her eyes studying him. The seconds trickled by, during which Elinta was planning what she'd do. She had to find her father and Blaine. Oh, Blaine. Zhayra's heart tugged in her large chest. Elinta felt tears sting at her eyes, but she viciously shoved them away and focused on General Nash. The woman had turned her blue eyes on her, a thoughtful expression playing across her face.

Finally, the woman nodded at her nephew. "I hope you'll tell me what's happening."

"As soon as I can," Lorrin promised.

"I hope you find them," General Nash said to Elinta.

"Thank you," she choked out, surprised her vocal cords still worked.

"We should go," Lorrin said. "Thank you, Aunt Jaida."

Nash nodded and walked them to the door. "Be careful, Lorrin. Your parents won't let you sneak away for a third time."

Lorrin nodded. "Don't worry."

"I wish I couldn't," the general muttered, closing the door behind them.

Elinta turned wide eyes on Lorrin. "What are we going to do?"

"We're going to go find Niles and Tamir," he said. "Then we're going to figure out a way to find your family."

He took her hand, gave it a gentle squeeze, and they walked back down the hall to find their friends, hand in hand.

Half an hour later, the four of them were piled in the sitting room of Niles's home. Elinta and Tamir were shoulder to shoulder on the couch while Lorrin and Niles were on chairs stolen from the kitchen. General Sonnen was working at the palace, and they had the house to themselves. Elinta vaguely felt that she should be more interested in her surroundings and the glimpse it offered into Niles and his father, but her thoughts were solely on her own family. Zhayra was watching and listening to their every word, and though she felt guilty that they couldn't have the conversation in her presence, Elinta knew that every second mattered. Every moment counted if she was going to find her family.

"What are we going to do?" Niles asked the silence that had descended over their group after Lorrin had finished explaining all they'd learnt from General Nash.

"We have to go get them!" Elinta said. Fear had long since disappeared. Fire ran through her veins now, just as it ran in Zhayra's.

"We will," Lorrin said. "But we need to plan this. We don't even know where they are."

"So, we'll go to Kethmere," Elinta said though the thought threatened to cool the fire in her. "Mazen would have left a sign for me." She was sure. Why else would he take them if it wasn't to get to her? He had to know that the poison hadn't killed her. Maybe he wanted another shot at killing her and Zhayra. The *Zearla lurai* and the heir to the dead dragon queen. She was willing to give it to him if it meant saving her father and Blaine. But she was going to come out the other side.

Tamir spoke for the first time since hearing Lorrin's report. "That is a good idea. If he means to bait you, he will have left a clue to where they are."

Elinta was glad that no one had voiced the fear that was hiding on the edges of her thoughts. That Mazen had no reason to hold them and had just killed them and moved on.

Lorrin nodded, unaware of Elinta's thoughts. "Kethmere would be the best place to start, only ..."

"What?" Niles asked.

"I'm going to have trouble leaving the city."

"Why?" Elinta asked, remembering what his aunt had said.

"I've already snuck away twice." Lorrin sighed. "I've got a follower."

"I'm sure we could lose them," Niles said with a shrug. He gave Elinta a confident smile, one she didn't return.

Lorrin cocked his head, his eyes going thoughtful.

"No," Elinta said though it hurt her to say it. "We can't risk it."

"Why not?" Niles asked.

"If we can't give them the slip, they'll see Zhayra. They'll know everything," Lorrin said reluctantly, looking into her eyes and voicing her thoughts. She nodded. Or, if someone stopped them from leaving the city, her chance would be gone. It was a pity Nash couldn't just call them off, but she was under orders from the king and queen.

"I'll go with you," Niles said to her.

Lorrin shook his head. "You're in the same position as me."

"Really?" Niles asked. "I've got a stalker?"

"Yes."

Elinta felt her shoulders slump. It would be hard, but she'd be OK without Lorrin. But without both of them? How was she supposed to face Mazen alone?

"What are we going to do?" Elinta said, knowing in her bones that she would go anyway.

"I will go with you," Tamir said. Everyone turned to look at him in surprise. "I am not held by the same constraints as Lorrin and Niles and will not be missed. Besides, I told the council I would report on Mazen. I will still be following my duty even if your king doesn't know it."

"Thank you," Elinta said, looking at his cloaked form. They'd had to sneak him out of the palace in the same way they'd snuck him in so that word wouldn't reach King Aldon that they'd broken his command. The king had been true to his word and hadn't shown any interest in Tamir or the Asali since their arrival.

Niles looked doubtfully at Tamir. "But there'd be only the two of you."

"It is enough for the village," Tamir said. "And if we find where they are being held, we don't have to come face-to-face with Mazen."

"I don't like this," Niles said.

Lorrin caught Elinta's eye. "Please don't go up against Mazen again."

"I won't," she said, but deep down, she knew that if it came to it, she would. Lorrin seemed to sense it but said nothing more.

Niles sat forward, nearly tipping the chair he was perched on, and looked Tamir in the eye. "You better make sure she makes it back."

"I will," Tamir said, voice perfectly even. Elinta studied his calm exterior. What was he thinking? He'd known Mazen when they were younger. What did he think of the man his friend had become?

"Will you be OK?" she whispered.

Tamir's glowing eyes caught hers. "Yes."

"In that case," Lorrin said, exchanging a glance with Niles, "we have something for you."

"For me?" Elinta asked.

Niles nodded and hurried from the room. "It's a late birthday present," he shouted. There were several loud thumps and clangs from the other room. A pained grunt echoed in. A moment later, he returned weighed down by a large package. Zhayra felt a tickle of anticipation when Elinta looked at it.

"What is that?" Elinta asked.

"We spoke to Tamir about it," Niles said, "and ... we might have snuck out to see Zhayra."

Elinta's frown deepened. "Zhayra?"

Lorrin nodded.

"I hope it will serve your needs," Tamir said.

Elinta cast him a puzzled glance.

Niles handed her the package. She looked curiously between the three boys, but they gave nothing away. Elinta tore the wrapping paper away and opened the box underneath, revealing ... Well, she wasn't sure what it was. A pile of leather straps sat inside, dotted with clips and buckles.

"What is it?" she repeated.

"A harness," Lorrin said with a grin.

"What?" Elinta looked back at the box and pulled out the straps. Her stomach jumped in excitement. "A harness?" she whispered, trying to make sense of the loops and buckles. "For Zhayra?"

"Tamir will have to show you how it sits," Lorrin said. "But you clip yourself into it from your belt and strap your legs in."

Elinta's mouth dropped. "Thank you!"

"Tamir will just have to hold on tight," Niles said with a grin.

Elinta glanced at him.

"I will be fine," he said, his eyes sparkling.

"How did you get this?" she said to the room.

"Threatened someone," Niles said.

Elinta's eyes widened. Niles waved away her worry with a laugh.

"Nah. I made him think it was for a prank and had the guy make it in parts. He had no idea what he was making."

She slapped his knee, earning herself a grin in return, then she looked back at Tamir. "When will we go then?"

"As soon as you are ready."

"We could go from here?" she said. She didn't have anything with her, but that didn't matter. All she needed was her sword and the clothes on her back. There'd be food in Kethmere.

Lorrin shook his head. "We need to go back to the palace like nothing has changed. Niles and I still have our followers, and they'll probably report to my parents if they see you leaving."

Elinta opened her mouth to object, then stopped. He was right. If they went now, while the spies could see, it would negate the point of leaving Lorrin and Niles behind.

"We'll go tonight," Elinta said.

"I don't like it," Niles said again.

"Me neither," Lorrin said. But he helped them work out the finer details of how they would slip away from the palace, anyway. His eyes kept locking on hers as he talked, concern written clearly in them.

Lorrin reasoned that Elinta and Tamir would easily leave the palace after dinner. They'd only left the palace in the middle of the night when they'd departed for Liyarna due to the nature of their trip. If they'd gone out during the day, their bags would have given them away before they'd even gotten through the gate. But Elinta and Tamir would be travelling light. All they needed was their swords and themselves. Elinta would take her backpack to carry the new harness in, but she often took the bag with her into the city. No one would give it a second glance.

"You can't take a horse," Niles said. "It would draw too much attention."

Lorrin nodded. "You can't look like you're leaving. If they're watching us, they might be keeping an eye out for you at the gate."

"Alright." Elinta shrugged. She'd walked the distance to the woods where Zhayra was before. It didn't bother her. Just as long as she got there.

"We'll try to think of an excuse for the two of you leaving. It'll have to be good," Lorrin said thoughtfully. Elinta couldn't agree more. As soon as Shae realised she was missing, the woman would either celebrate or try to send the whole palace guard after her. "We should finish up. It'll be dinner soon."

Niles, who was still looking unimpressed at the idea of not joining Elinta and Tamir on their trip, perked up. "Yes," he said, "we can't be late for that."

Elinta started packing the harness back into its box, folding some of the straps, but shoving others. Lorrin watched on with a grin, but it quickly disappeared when he glanced at Tamir and then outside.

"I'll take Tamir back up to the palace. He's been gone too long."

"OK," Elinta said, still shoving at the straps. "We'll clean up here and head on up."

Tamir readjusted the cloak to hide his features, and the two ducked out into the city. Done with the harness, Elinta helped Niles rearrange the furniture and pack up any mess they'd made, able to take the time now to look around the house. It was sparsely decorated, yet comfortable. Functional, just as she'd supposed General Sonnen would want it. Finally ready to go, the large box weighing her down, Elinta turned to walk out into the hall near the entrance when her gaze landed on a portrait of a woman.

"Is this your mother?" Elinta asked softly, crossing to look closely at the painting. She was a beautiful woman. Her face was soft, with a light splattering of freckles under bright green eyes.

Niles had inherited his messy hair from her, though hers was brown and curled where his was blond and straight.

"Yes," Niles said from beside her.

"She's beautiful," Elinta said. Why did he never talk about her?

"She was."

"Do you remember her?" Elinta asked quietly.

Niles smiled. "A little. Dad doesn't talk much about her. He means to, but he never manages it."

Elinta nodded, thinking of how her own father had reacted when her mother died. He'd become hard and quiet, more than he had been before anyway, and he never ever spoke about her. But she'd had Blaine to tell her stories about their mother.

Elinta studied Niles's face. She'd always wondered how he'd become so different from his father, a kind but serious man. Maybe it had been a choice, she thought, looking at the spark in his eye, to be so full of humour and mischief. He loved making people smile; she could tell from the way his own face lit up. Maybe this was why. He was trying to make things easier for people, and he'd started with his own father and maybe even himself until it had become who he was. He was being a light for whoever needed it in whatever darkness they were facing.

"What?" Niles said, shifting under her gaze.

"I just realised something about you," she said.

"What?"

She shook her head. "I'll tell you another time. We should get going."

CHAPTER
EIGHTEEN

L ORRIN AND NILES WALKED Elinta to her room after dinner. They'd already dropped Tamir off at his room, and
the mood was solemn among them. Niles wasn't even making
any jokes. They hadn't said anything to her, but she suspected
they had spoken to Tamir before dinner about their concerns for
her. It would be the first time they'd been apart since they'd met.
Pausing outside her door, she looked up and down the hall. It was
empty. She dived forwards and wrapped her arms around Lorrin.
After a pause of surprise, he returned the embrace.

"Be careful," he whispered in her ear. Something else was in his
voice, but he left it unsaid.

Nodding, she pulled away, not looking into his eyes, and grabbed Niles for a hug as well.

"We'll see you when you get back," he said and pulled away. She twisted and opened her door.

"Oi," Niles said. She turned. "Don't be too long."

"You won't even know I was gone," she said, making her voice as light as she could.

Niles grinned. "That's what I like to hear. Come on, Lor," he said, slapping Lorrin's shoulder. The prince held her eyes for a second longer, nodded, and followed their friend up the hall.

"Hello miss," Neva said as Elinta slipped inside. The maid was standing by her bed, sorting through her clothes. "I was just tidying up before you got back. I didn't expect you so soon!"

"I know," Elinta said, trying not to sound as though she'd just said goodbye to her friends. "Don't worry about finishing this tonight."

Neva glanced between her and the pile of clothes. "Are you sure? I shouldn't leave them here," she said, continuing to fold them.

"Really," Elinta said, casting the bed a cautious glance. She'd slipped the box containing the harness underneath the foot. The blankets hanging down the sides seemed undisturbed.

Neva dropped her hands, letting the shirt she was holding crumple. "Would you like me to bring up some coffee? Or some tea? Maybe some chocolate?"

"No, it's fine, Neva." Elinta laughed.

"Well, if you're sure." She cast the clothes a doubtful look. In truth, it looked as though there were only a few shirts out, and they wouldn't take long to pack up. Neva gave her a smile as she passed. "It's so good to have you back."

Elinta smiled and nodded. Once Neva had closed the door behind her, Elinta let the smile drop and hurried to the bed. She reached underneath, slid the box out, and dropped it on her bed. Then she crossed to the wardrobe and pulled her backpack out from inside. She tipped the contents onto her bed. Her Asali clothes sprawled across the covers, which she'd put back inside the bag when they'd returned from Liyarna. She gathered them up, intending to shove them back into her wardrobe, but hesitated when the jumper caught her eye. The fabric had kept her toasty warm when she'd been in the snowy landscape of the White Mountains, perhaps it would do the same as she flew on Zhayra. Making her decision, she pulled it free of the pile, throwing it onto the bed, then shoved the rest of the clothes in the wardrobe. She threw the shirts Neva had left on her bed on top of them.

Elinta turned to the harness with curiosity. Right now, it looked more like a pile of junk than anything she could use. She tried to imagine it on Zhayra but all she could picture was a giant saddle, which looked nothing like what was before her. Elinta carefully stuffed the harness into her bag, then shoved her Asali jumper on top. It took her a few minutes of shoving, pushing, and reorganising to be able to close the bag but, eventually, she had it. Then she noticed the water bottle beside her bed. With a sigh, she snatched it up and unzipped the bag.

It was another five minutes before she finally had the bag closed again, this time with the bottle inside, and she stood surveying the room. This was it. It was time to go. She drank in this last sight of her room, wondering whether she would ever see it again. Whether, depending on how things went in the coming days, she would be welcome in the palace again. She thought of Queen Mira, General Nash's children Cassia and Aiden, Neva and even Ford. The people she'd come to know during her stay. Hopefully, one day soon, she'd see them all again. She didn't worry about Lorrin and Niles. They'd find a way to see one another. And her family would be safe, and Mazen ... well, maybe he'd give up on

Zhayra. It was a bit much to ask, but she wanted to believe it anyway, despite the memory of him killing Zhayra's mother.

Elinta slung the bag over her shoulder, turned her back on the room, and left. She walked down the hall at an even pace. Tamir's room was only four doors down from hers, and she knocked gently on it when she arrived.

Tamir opened the door. She wouldn't have recognised him, or that he was Asali, if she hadn't known it was him. She amended the thought. Perhaps if she'd leant forward and peered under his hood, she might have noticed his strange, glowing eyes and shining skin. But the cloak covered his entire form, and he'd hidden his usually bare feet inside a pair of Niles's shoes. They were too big for him.

He looked up from under the hood, catching her eye. "Is it suitable?"

She nodded. "I'll lead you out of the city. Just stay close behind me."

Tamir stepped from his room, his cloak swirling with his movements as he closed the door.

The third floor was almost empty since dinner was still being served in the dining hall. Even though they weren't doing anything suspicious, Elinta's stomach clenched as they set off. And so did Zhayra's. Elinta felt stiff, awkward, walking down the stairs with Tamir close behind her, but she made her legs move. Her shoes echoed on the stone floor though Tamir was silent as ever. They made it down the first flight of stairs without being stopped. Not that there was any reason to be. Not any reason that anyone knew of, anyway. It could be anyone walking with her, and no one expected it to be Tamir, who'd agreed so readily to staying within the palace walls.

A burst of laughter rang from the dining hall right as they passed the open archway, and Elinta nearly jumped from her skin.

"Relax," Tamir whispered. "You will draw attention if you appear nervous."

"I know," Elinta said, shaking her head at herself. "I can't help it."

She forced herself to continue walking at an even pace, Tamir on her heels. A sigh of relief escaped her when they'd passed the hall. They continued through the corridors and halls to the next flight of steps and down to the first floor.

They turned onto the final corridor with the front doors in sight. Elinta hitched up her bag and stepped forward. And a short woman with beady, green eyes almost walked straight into her from one of the side rooms.

"Shae," Elinta said, coming to a dead stop. The woman had seen Tamir in the very same disguise that he wore now when they'd arrived at the palace nearly two weeks ago. "How—how are you?"

Shae's eyebrows rose. "Well," she said. Shae stepped to the side to walk around Elinta, who felt a moment of relief, until the woman's eyes landed on Tamir. Her eyebrows rose even higher. "Who's this?" Her voice was dripping with suspicion. Elinta remembered her promise to keep an eye on her.

Elinta's mouth opened and closed, but Shae was still watching Tamir, who hadn't moved an inch. She began leaning forward as though to look under the cloak.

"Niles!" Elinta shouted, making Shae jump. "You know what he's like," she said, leaning in conspiratorially, forcing a smile. She actually saw the interest leave Shae's eyes at the mention of Niles. Elinta smiled to herself. The woman hadn't even noticed that the figure behind her was too short to be him. "He saw Tamir wearing the cloak that day we arrived, and he's been bugging him about it ever since."

"I see," Shae said, pulling back.

"I think he's planning on scaring someone." Elinta shrugged. "We're going into the city for some … dessert and he insisted on the cloak."

Shae's attention had already left her, and she was looking down the hall.

"Great," she said with a wave of her hand, then continued on her way without another word.

Elinta grinned at the woman's disappearing form.

"Niles?" Tamir asked, lifting his head slightly to look at her.

"She can't stand him."

"Interesting." He paused. "Good thinking. We should move on."

"Right," she said.

Elinta held her breath as they closed the last few metres and emerged into the fresh air. Long shadows played across the court-yard in the evening light. Jae ran from the stables shouting over his shoulder and disappeared through the open gates.

Elinta and Tamir descended the steps, crossed the courtyard, and approached the gate, looking like anyone else heading into the city. The guard turned to face them.

"Make sure you're back before midnight," the guard said. She recognised him as Aaric, the guard who'd let her in late on the night Niles had first met Zhayra.

"We will," she said, not letting her steps slow. And then they were through. From there, it was an easy trip through Nevira. They followed the main road out, jostling amongst people head-ing to and from the various shops, looking for both wares and food. Tamir pulled his cloak tighter around him and stayed on Elinta's heels. She spotted Merton Alvey and shifted to the side, putting a group of people between them, and held her breath until they'd passed. Soon the crowd began to thin, and they were out of the city.

It was a long walk to Zhayra, but the path was clear and there was still enough light to guide their way. Once they'd put the city well behind them, Tamir raised his head and drew alongside her, no longer needing her guidance. Elinta hardly noticed him. Her thoughts were glued to her family.

What had Mazen done to them? What was he *doing* to them? Images of them injured and scared rose in her mind. Blaine bruised and bleeding. Her father unrecognisable.

"We will find them," Tamir said.

"What?" Elinta said, pulling herself from her thoughts long enough to look at him.

"We will find your family."

Elinta didn't answer. How could he be sure? What if Mazen had already finished with them?

"Do not give up hope yet, *tarsi*."

Zhayra was at the edge of the woods when they drew near, her amber eyes glinting in the dimming light. She was tense, physically and emotionally, but she grumbled a soft greeting when she saw them.

"Hello, girl," Elinta said, lowering her backpack to the ground. She was glad the dragon had been listening to their earlier conversation about what Mazen had done. She wasn't sure she had it in her to explain it all again.

"How do you feel about a harness?" she said instead. Zhayra knew about the harness, but it didn't hurt to ask.

Zhayra lowered her head and sniffed at the bag, then snorted. Elinta frowned.

"I'm not sure what that means," she said. Zhayra's emotions hadn't shifted in response to her question, and it was likely she was feeling the way she was because of Mazen and not the harness. "Can we use it?" she asked, choosing her words carefully so that Zhayra could answer.

She blinked once.

"Great." She turned to Tamir, who'd lowered his hood. His glow was even more noticeable now in the low light of dusk. "Lorrin said you'd be able to show me how to put it on her?"

Tamir nodded and stepped forward. "Here." He grabbed the mess of leather straps and set to work.

Elinta and Tamir stepped back to admire their handywork. The harness reminded her of the breastplate sometimes used for horses pulling loads. A band looped over Zhayra's neck, resting down below her larger scales and near where Elinta would sit. At the centre of Zhayra's chest, a strap dropped down from the harness and passed between the dragon's front legs. There, it connected with another strap that hooked, from behind the leg, up to join with the neck strap. There was one on either side. From these dangled another piece that would tie Elinta's legs in place. All the straps could be adjusted to tighten or release.

"This is also for you." Tamir held out the final strap. It was a leather belt with a small metal ring that would clip onto a piece hanging from Zhayra's neck strap.

"Thank you," she said. She took the belt, swapping it with the one already at her hips, moving her sword across too. Then she pulled her jumper from her bag and pulled that on as well. Now she felt ready to fly. "Are you sure you'll be alright?"

"Yes," Tamir said. "As long as she flies smoothly."

Elinta didn't tell him that Zhayra's emotions turned to something suspiciously like mischief.

"We should get going," she said instead.

Zhayra lowered herself so that her white stomach pressed against the ground, and Elinta clambered up her leg and onto her back. Tamir watched as she strapped her legs in place and clipped into the harness. Then, with her backpack on over his cloak, he pulled himself effortlessly onto Zhayra's back, settling into place behind her.

"How do you make that look so easy?" she grumbled, holding onto Zhayra's neck strap so she could sit upright.

"You will be able to do it too ... if you practice," he said, a hint of amusement in his voice. Elinta shook her head. She didn't have the Asali's level of grace or balance despite what he seemed to think.

"Hold on," she said and his hands slipped into place at her hips.

Zhayra stood, walking out from under the trees and into the open, before spreading her wings and shooting into the air. Tamir's grip on her tightened.

"Zhayra!" Elinta shouted, her own grip on the dragon like iron. Wind buffeted her, sending her blonde hair shooting back into Tamir.

Zhayra's stomach lightened, but she eased back on the speed and the angle of their rise into the sky. When the trees below them were nothing more than a large smudge on the ground, the dragon evened out.

Tamir's grip on her slackened and he laughed. Elinta's own mouth twisted, and Zhayra's chest was light. They were flying and it was ... alright. The ground whipped by under them, a testament to Zhayra's speed, but it was OK. And the wind was cold on Elinta's bare skin, but the Asali jumper was doing its job. She felt comfortably warm. She was OK. For just a moment she let herself forget her worries, and smiled.

The sun had dipped below the horizon, and deep blues and long shadows played across the landscape. The stars slowly blinked into existence above them. Tamir's glow had become more and more noticeable, and now Elinta could see it from the corner of her eye.

"It is a good time to practice accessing Zhayra's senses," Tamir said. "We have many hours ahead of us."

Elinta nodded. She still had the hairband on her wrist, so she felt comfortable to try some of the senses … just not looking through Zhayra's eyes. She'd wait until her feet were on solid ground for that one.

They whittled away the time with Tamir asking her to describe things through her dragonsight. Then she tried the heat vision, but with her eyes closed and her grip on Zhayra the tightest it had ever been. Even as they were plunged into darkness, Tamir had her describe everything she could see with the dragon's vision.

"We're nearly there," Elinta said, shifting to ease the ache in her backside. The forest outside her village had appeared in the distance as a dark smudge even in dragonsight, but it was growing closer with every second and becoming clearer and clearer.

"We'll need to land by the lake," Elinta called to Zhayra, her stomach tightening at the idea of returning to that place. But it was the only location Zhayra could land near Kethmere without being seen. Tamir's grip tightened once more on Elinta as Zhayra descended and landed lightly by the lake. Elinta was still tapped into the senses and could easily see their surroundings. The smooth surface of the lake and the tall trees at the borders of the shore. Her breath caught in her throat as the memories assailed her and even Zhayra grumbled.

"This is the place?" Tamir asked quietly. She'd told him the full story of what happened in her village as they'd travelled to Nevira. It hadn't been a story she'd wanted to share completely with the council.

"Yes." Elinta cleared her throat. While she unclipped from Zhayra and freed her legs, Tamir slipped from the dragon's back.

Elinta joined him on the ground a moment later. Her knees didn't buckle this time, but her legs still shook. One day she'd be used to flying, just as she'd grown used to riding the horses. But for now, it seemed that day was still in the distant future.

Elinta trailed ahead of Tamir, her eyes flitting around the clearing. Ghostly memories clung to the trees, and she tore her eyes from them. Squaring her shoulders, she turned to face Tamir and Zhayra.

"You two will need to stay here while I go into the village."

Tamir opened his mouth to object and Zhayra grunted. The water gently lapped at the shore beside them.

"Both of you would draw attention," Elinta said pointedly. Tamir's cloak couldn't hide his glow in the darkness, and nothing could hide Zhayra's bulk, which would still appear as a gigantic shadowy form if there were no lights. But at the moment, a soft glimmer was reflecting off her scales.

Tamir exchanged a glance with Zhayra. Zhayra grumbled again.

"My family isn't here," Elinta said, her voice tight, "and neither is Mazen. The only danger is the villagers, who won't even know I'm there if I go alone."

"Very well," Tamir said, "but if you fail to come back, we will both come for you."

Zhayra blinked once, grunting even as she did.

Elinta nodded. There was no use arguing with the two of them. "Give me two hours."

She didn't hang around to give them an opportunity to change her mind. Her stomach was clenched in her gut and her hands were sweaty. But she had to go. She had to see for herself.

Her eyes grew heavy as she plunged into the shadows of the trees, relying on dragonsight to help her keep the balance between safety and speed. Her hand was glued to the hilt of her sword, finding comfort in the weapon even if it were likely there'd be no cause to use it.

The walk through the forest was strange. She'd never passed through it in the dark and, though she knew it well, it made the trees seem alien and unfamiliar. Nevertheless, when she reached the border of the forest and found herself staring across the grassland at her old home, she wanted to retreat back into its depths.

There was Galen's home, unlit and quiet in the night. And his herb garden. She'd spent hours every day looking after it. Perhaps Tully, the young girl running errands for the village's other healer, had now taken her place tending it. Elinta couldn't stop a stab of bitterness rising in her at the memory of Galen's betrayal as she stared at his home. But just as quickly as the feeling had risen, it dissipated. He'd only done what he thought was right. Maybe even she would have done it in his place.

Her house was on the northern edge of the village. She wouldn't have to pass through it to get there. It was this thought and the fact that already twenty minutes must have passed that pushed her into action again. She kept her distance and walked in a crouch, careful lest anyone was awake and staring from their windows should see her. It was unlikely, being now past midnight, but a figure skirting the village would raise suspicion, especially after all that had happened to Kethmere.

The familiar outline of her family home and the stables soon appeared, and her breath stuttered in her chest. Longing hit her like a wave, and Zhayra, whose interest had been piqued upon seeing the village, felt a pang of sadness. Elinta wanted to tell her she was OK. To reassure her that she didn't regret leaving. But the dragon wasn't using her ears and she had no way of signalling to the dragon that she wanted to talk. She'd have to find a way to do that.

Crossing the remaining distance to the house, another thought struck her, and she looked out across the paddocks. The horses had all been put in the stables, presumably for the night. Someone had been looking after them. Elinta turned to the house. What if someone was in there? What if whoever was looking after their animals had moved in? She stared at the dark building. There was nothing for it but to check. Ducking low, she crept inch by inch toward the house, grateful beyond anything that the building was between her and the rest of the village. Though she was in the open, no one could see her unless they were inside her home.

She reached the window to Blaine's room, took a deep breath, and peered inside. It was empty. Elinta crossed to the kitchen window. Nothing. Sighing, she opened the front door and stood in the doorway. It was then that she remembered Zhayra's heat sense and how she would have been able to see if anyone was inside without risking giving herself away. She shrugged. It was too late now.

Eyes scanning the room, Elinta was struck by how hollow the place felt. How empty. She stepped inside. Blaine's coat still hung beside the door. Grabbing it, she brought it up to her face and inhaled the scent of him. Tears pricked at her eyes. She placed the coat back on the hook, letting her hand trail down it. Old coals sat in the fireplace, dishes were still in the kitchen sink and even on the table. Though someone was looking after the horses, no one had been inside since Blaine and her father were taken. It was clear beyond any doubt that her family hadn't left Kethmere on their own accord. Standing alone in the house, Elinta wished Lorrin could have been beside her.

She searched every inch of the place by the light of the moon and the strength of Zhayra's eyes, checking for anything, *anything* that might hint at where her family had been taken. But there was nothing. It was as though her family had just vanished one morning without a trace. She checked her father's room, rifling through the chest of drawers there, then hurried down to Blaine's. Still nothing. Blaine's clothes were even still lying on the floor. His sword on a hook by his wardrobe. Finally, with nowhere else to check, Elinta turned to the closed door of her own room.

What would she find? Had her father cleared it out? Erased all trace of her? She stumbled the last few steps and pushed open the door, an eerie creak echoing in the house. She gasped.

It was ... it was exactly the same as when she'd left it. There was her old jacket, slung over the end of her bed. Her wardrobe, pushed into the corner, was still bursting at the seams from when she'd shoved her clothes inside. Lurching into the room, she drank it in. This echo of her old life. But as she looked closer, she realised there were actually two things out of place. The first was her satchel. Elinta scooped it up from her bed and stared at it in shock. She'd left it on the shore of the lake the day she'd fled with Zhayra, hadn't she? She was sure of it. What was it doing here? She held it close, partly from surprise and partly for its familiarity. It was still full of her gear and smelt of yarrow and evening vine. As she stood, holding the proof that her old life had existed, her eyes landed on her pillow and the other thing that was out of place. A piece of paper. She stumbled over to it, still gripping her satchel, and snatched it up. Orange sand fell from the paper onto the floor.

Frowning, she looked at the paper. As her eyes settled on it, Zhayra's feelings darkened. It was a note. And her eyes widened as she read it.

> 'We'll be waiting for you. Don't disappoint me, Elinta Ferran. I can't wait to see you two.'

She became all too aware of the thump of her heart in the seconds that followed. It was the only sound in the room. She read the note again. He was waiting for her where? Elinta flipped the note over. The back was blank. Grinding her teeth, she read the words on the front again, blindly moving to sit down as she did. But as she moved, her feet crunched on something on the ground. The sand! Crouching, she picked up a pinch of the grains and stared at them. Had he left her a clue to find them? But why not just tell her?

Shaking her head, she studied the sand grains. They were dark. Darker than the white sand she knew covered the beaches on the east coast, at least around Culmar. She'd never seen the west coast, but why would Mazen take her family there? It was too populated, not to mention his own people lived in the west. Presumably, he wanted to stay away from them like he had for nearly the last two hundred years.

So where were the grains from? *I can't wait to see you two.* They'd need somewhere big, open, and isolated. Where there wouldn't be anyone to see her kidnapped family, the Asali, Zhayra or Vaherin. And there had to be sand.

"Bradfin," she whispered. They were in the desert.

A floorboard creaked behind her. Elinta stiffened. Had she been wrong in thinking no one was waiting for her? She reached for her sword.

The flat of a blade tapped her on the shoulder.

"Don't move," a crisp voice said.

Elinta's mind was racing. It wasn't an Asali. There was no accent, neither gentle like Tamir's or strong like Mazen's. This was one of her own people. If she told this person who she was, would they raise the alarm? She was still a traitor. Wanted for arrest. But if she didn't say who she was, that this was her house … her hand crept closer to her sword. It was dark, and the sword was on her left side, furthest away from the man. Maybe he hadn't noticed it. Maybe he thought he'd caught a thief.

"Who are you?" the voice said again. She knew that voice. It was one of the villagers. Likely one from the defending force, but who? She couldn't place it. Part of her was sad she couldn't recognise the person. There was a time she would have. There was a time they'd have known her too.

Her hand grabbed the hilt of her sword. Closing her eyes, she answered his question, "Family."

"Elin—"

Ducking under the sword at her shoulder, Elinta whipped around, bringing her own sword out to slam into his near the hilt. His sword clattered to the ground. She caught the white of his eyes in the darkness, before leaping forwards, straightening as she did, and bringing the pommel of her sword into the side of his head. He crumpled to the ground, unconscious.

"Sorry, Warin," she said, finally recognising the older man. It seemed Kethmere *was* being more careful now, after all that had happened. She smiled humourlessly in the dark. She'd just given them another reason to up patrols. Again.

Half an hour later, Elinta was crashing through the last of the trees, branches whipping her face, and emerging by the lake. Zhayra and Tamir rose to their feet as she arrived.

"I know where they are," she said, handing Tamir one of the apples she'd collected from the kitchen on her way out. She'd carried them in her satchel.

"Where?" he asked.

"Bradfin." Too afraid that he might say it was time to go back to Nevira for help, she didn't let him speak. "We need to go."

Tamir didn't move. "Is that wise?"

Elinta pulled herself up onto Zhayra. "It's been over a week since he took them, Tamir. They can't wait any longer."

Tamir cocked his head. "They will have to." She opened her mouth to object, but he cut across her. "I promised Lorrin and Niles I would look after you. It will be daylight when we arrive in the desert, and Mazen will see you coming if you make your move then. We will have to wait until nightfall to rescue them."

Elinta, still about to object, faltered when Zhayra grunted in agreement. Zhayra, who understood more than anyone what it was like for a loved one's life to be in Mazen's hands. Zhayra, who had lost someone to him. If she agreed, then so did Elinta.

"OK," she said. Then hurried to strap herself in. Tamir, satisfied, jumped up behind her. "Thank you, Tamir."

It was a long flight to Bradfin, and Elinta clutched her satchel almost as tightly as she clutched Zhayra's harness while the sun slowly rose. What did Mazen have planned for her family? She knew they were probably flying into a trap, but there was nothing else she could do. She had to get to them. She had to save them. If they were even still alive.

They landed on the outskirts of the desert, where the air was heavy with heat, but small trees and bushes still covered most of the ground. Elinta slid stiffly from Zhayra's back, staring out over the desert that hid her family. Tamir, usually graceful, dropped tenderly to the ground beside her. They'd landed beside a river, one that eventually became the Afonlin in the south, down by the woods that Zhayra hid in outside Nevira. Here, they camped for the day, drinking their fill and bathing in turns.

As the day dragged on, they sat in the shade of Zhayra's bulk. Elinta pressed her back against Zhayra's scales and Tamir sat beside her, but not touching the dragon. This held her curiosity, driving her worry to the background of her mind.

"Have you flown on a dragon before?" Elinta asked, thinking of Vaherin.

"No," he said, to Elinta's surprise. He'd seemed comfortable on the dragon, although now he kept a respectful gap between them.

"You're only the second to ride Zhayra," she said. Would Lorrin one day ride with her, too? She'd love to share a flight with him, even if it was just once.

"I am honoured."

"Tamir ..." Elinta said, her fear returning. His dark grey eyes studied hers.

"Yes?"

"Do you think there'll be anyone else there? Other than Mazen?" Asali had been disappearing from Liyarna and the White Mountains ... if they were going to Mazen, did that mean some were waiting for them?

"I believe so."

"If—when," she corrected, "we find my family if we have to fight ... I don't want to kill anyone."

Tamir sighed, pulling his hair back into a half bun. "I do not wish to kill anyone either. They are angry, but they're not seeing clearly. We'll rescue your family, and no one will die."

Elinta nodded, but she couldn't see how they would manage it. Mazen wouldn't be the only one there, there'd be others, and she'd have to fight them.

"You don't have to face him," Elinta said quietly. She could find a way to keep them apart. She could try.

Tamir dropped his eyes. When he spoke, his voice was low, "I will have to one day, *tarsi*."

"How close were you?" she asked. Hadn't he said they'd grown up together? But she wanted to hear it.

"As children we were like brothers."

"I'm sorry," she whispered, "for what he's become." She just wished she knew why he was doing this. Why he'd targeted her.

Tamir swallowed. "Me too."

They fell into silence, each lost in their memories of Mazen Elliar.

"Time to go," Elinta said as soon as darkness fell. She slung her satchel over her shoulder again. The satchel was somewhat pointless with Tamir around, since he was able to heal with a touch, but it felt nice to have it there again. Natural, even.

Tamir rose, his cloak already in place. This time, Elinta wouldn't go alone. They were all going to go, and they were all going to save her family. Once they found them, they would work out the finer details. Elinta cast a curious glance Tamir's way, but his face betrayed nothing. He had to be nervous about facing his old friend, but there was no time to ask him. They had to get moving.

Once they were in place again on Zhayra's back, she took off into the air, keeping low this time so they could search for any sign of Mazen. The desert was big. But he wouldn't have made it too hard to find him. The wind buffeted them, making Elinta's nose ice cold within seconds.

An hour later, in the centre of the desert, they found what they were looking for. It was a large building of dark, crumbling stone looming in the darkness. It seemed like the perfect place.

"Land," she called to Zhayra, her breath coming as a cloud on the air. The dragon dropped from the sky, her two passengers holding on tighter than they ever had before. At the last second, she pulled up and landed lightly on the ground. Elinta spat the sand from her mouth that Zhayra's wings had kicked up.

"OK," Elinta said, her ears feeling strange with the sudden stop of wind rushing against them. "I want to sneak a little closer and see how many are inside." She didn't say it, but she'd tried to use Zhayra's heat sense while they'd been in the air, but they'd been too far away. But all she needed to do was get close enough to confirm that the building was at least inhabited.

"I will come with you," Tamir said, pulling the hood on his cloak up. Though his glow was easy to see now, the cloak would hide it well as they crawled along the sand dunes.

Elinta didn't argue but turned to Zhayra instead while Tamir tied the backpack to Zhayra's harness. "Wait here and watch. If we get into trouble, you'll have to come."

Zhayra blinked once, then nudged her gently.

"I'll be OK," Elinta whispered. Then she and Tamir hurried into the cold night.

CHAPTER NINETEEN

T HE MOON LIT THEIR way across the dunes, but even so, Elinta was tuned into her dragonsight. It was too early to use the heat sense, and she didn't want to use it for long. She might get dizzy again. The sand dunes shielded their approach on the building, but they also kept them from knowing whether they'd been spotted. She wished she could tune into the strength of Zhayra's ears though it might be too much for her coupled with the senses she already used. The thought didn't stop her ears from straining to hear even a whisper of sound coming from the large, crumbling building, but all that reached her was the soft crunch of the sand under their feet. When they crested another sand dune, ducking low so as not to stick out, Elinta studied the structure.

It had to have been empty before Mazen claimed it. The left wall had almost completely fallen down with large blocks of grey stone sprawled across the ground. At the front, the roof had caved, and a scraggly vine ran up the front of the building. It didn't seem like the kind of place he would have set up to live in permanently.

Barely forty feet away from the building, Elinta drew Tamir to a halt as they summited another dune, her breath coming as a cloud in the cool night air. Dropping to her belly, she inched forwards. When the building came into view again, she closed her eyes and tried to see it without her sight. First, she imagined the building in front of her, painting it by memory, and then she willed herself to see it, and she did.

A blue-black image appeared.

"I see it," she whispered, her voice just louder than her breath.

"How many?" Tamir murmured.

There were two figures on the roof, all a uniform red. As she watched, another moved past the front entryway but disappeared when it walked behind the wall.

"No!" she said. "I can't see through the stone." She shook her head. How were they supposed to know what was happening inside? "There's at least three. Two on the roof and one near the front opening."

Tamir didn't say anything, his silence stretching so long that she shifted to look at him. "They'll be in there, *tarsi.*"

They inched closer. Elinta didn't shut the sense off. She couldn't risk not being able to access it again. She shoved at the sinking feeling in her chest. There was no time to worry about what they were walking into now. They'd suspected Mazen wouldn't be alone, now it'd been confirmed. She wouldn't turn back now.

Elinta and Tamir crawled down the other side of the dune on their bellies, and the building dropped out of sight. Sand had slipped inside her clothing and, with every inch they moved, more joined it, rubbing and chafing her skin, but she ignored it. At the top of the next dune, Elinta studied the building again.

After several long minutes, she shook her head. "I can't see any more," she whispered. An inkling of doubt wriggled into her mind again, but she pushed it aside. It didn't matter how many there were. It *didn't.* "We can do this," she said, turning to Tamir and focusing on what her eyes were seeing.

"Can you get us to them?" he asked, matching her low tone.

"Yes." She didn't mention that she didn't know where they were. But Tamir knew that. What mattered was that she would try. It was too late to go back. Her family needed her.

"Can you see Vaherin?"

"No." She frowned. The dragon wasn't anywhere out in the open and, in his case, it didn't matter if she couldn't see inside the building. "He wouldn't fit in there, though."

Tamir frowned, but eventually nodded. There was no way to hide the dragon's heat out here. If she couldn't see him, he wasn't there.

"We're going in, Zhayra," she whispered, knowing the dragon was listening.

Her only response was a tightening in her large chest.

Elinta turned and said as confidently as she could, "Follow me."

She crawled forward, down the slope, fighting the nausea rising in her stomach. It was the heat vision. She couldn't keep it up much longer. The dual image in her mind was making her dizzy, making her stomach churn. But she had to keep it on if they were going to rescue Blaine and her father. The building would be dark. She might not see them with her eyes, even with dragonsight.

Closing her eyes, she led Tamir the last of the way purely by the heat signatures. Despite the cold temperature of the air, the sand dunes still glowed a soft green from the heat they'd absorbed during the day from the sun. It made it easier for her to discern where she was going. The coloured world was hard to navigate, but the differences in the shades at least offered her a way to continue on. It seemed impossible that Zhayra saw like this, with two images, every day and didn't struggle in the least.

With only a few metres to go, Elinta stopped. Tamir drew level with her. They were too close to the building to talk now, even in whispers, but she hoped Tamir would trust her. She hoped she appeared more confident than she felt.

The two red figures on the roof were approaching the edge, looking out over the desert. If they remained still, and Tamir kept his face downcast, they would seem nothing more than two shadows among countless others to them. She waited with bated breath, her heart the only sound in the still night. A second passed. Then another. Finally, the Asali turned and marched down the side of the roof.

Elinta inched forward again, placing her hands carefully, aware of every minute sound the sand made beneath her palms. The Asali on the roof wouldn't hear it, but to her the sound seemed to tear the night apart. Tamir followed. She opened her eyes again as the ground levelled out, and the door came into view. It was an open entryway. Whatever door there had been was long since gone. Gesturing for Tamir to follow, she rose and sprinted across the remaining two metres, pressing her back into the cold stone. Half a second later, Tamir had flattened against the wall on the other side of the entrance.

She peered at the building, debating within herself. Her dragonsight would allow her to see better than her normal eyes. But the heat sense would reveal people as soon as they appeared. Even an inch of their body and she would see them and know whether they were Asali or human. But then, her head was spinning from the effort of using the two images in her mind. She wouldn't be of any use in this state, and she couldn't even see through the stone. She shut the extra sense off.

Nodding at Tamir, she silently drew her sword, gripping the hilt tight in her sweaty, sandy hand. Tamir copied her movement. She'd seen one Asali near the entryway, and she signalled to remind him; raising one finger in the cool air, then pointing through the door. He nodded. They were ready. With a final nod, they pushed off the wall and ducked inside.

There was no one there. They looked up and down the dark, stone corridor, but there was no sign of him. Elinta hardly stopped a rush of air from escaping her in relief. The tip of her sword lowered as the silence stretched around them.

The Asali had been moving to her right so, purely to avoid him, Elinta led them left. Flickering light from lanterns hung every ten metres prodded at the darkness. Elinta longed to douse their light, so she might hide in the shadows. With each one they passed, Elinta half expected to find Mazen standing under it, just as he had been at their first meeting. She shivered.

They crept on, walking as lightly as they could. Sand covered the stone floor, and small, scraggily plants had wriggled out of the grooves between the stones. She did her best to avoid stepping on them. Elinta glanced down at Tamir's feet, wondering at how quiet he was despite wearing shoes too big for him. That's when she noticed that he'd taken off Niles's shoes. Her eyebrows rose. But his idea seemed to be working. In the socks that still hid his glow, he didn't make a sound on the cold stone floor. But Elinta's boots, though she tried to be quiet, seemed deafening to her ears, even if their soft padding couldn't have carried even to Tamir.

She turned right, leading them further into the building, and walked straight into a cobweb. Fighting the urge to spit at the web on her mouth, and carefully pulling it aside, Elinta continued on.

There was no time to care about comfort and minor dislikes. She scanned the hall as they walked, looking for any signs of her family or Asali. Cracks spread up the walls on both sides of them, but the building, despite its outward appearance, seemed relatively intact inside.

At the next corridor, she turned, taking them deeper again. It would make sense that they'd hidden her family in the very centre of this deserted building, luring her further and further from safety and deeper into whatever trap they'd set. Mazen thought she would be alone in here, separated from Zhayra due to the dragon's size. But he didn't know about Tamir. Would he freeze when he saw the familiar figure of the researcher? Would he care that his old friend was here?

They pushed on, deeper and deeper. Elinta's breath was shallow and quiet. Her palms and face were sweaty, and her heart thundered in her chest, but they didn't come across anyone. All was silent. She exchanged a confused glance with Tamir.

Where was Mazen? Where was the Asali she'd seen before? She found herself almost wishing that someone would appear to try to stop them. It was too easy. Tamir seemed to be thinking along the same lines. They had to be near the centre of the building, and he pulled her to a halt. She locked eyes with him, and he raised an eyebrow. She shrugged. They were nearly there. Things might be wrong, but they were too close to back out now. He let her pull away from him and followed her, sword still ready, as she turned down the next hall.

An Asali was there. She jumped back, stumbling into Tamir, but it was too late. He'd seen her. The man, standing in front of a door, turned to her, a grin on his face. His mouth opened to speak, but the words died on his lips as Tamir stepped forward, raised his hands and lowered his hood. The guard's grin faded.

"Zruh nai ri?" the man called, drawing his sword. "She was meant to be alone or with the prince."

"I'm a friend," Tamir replied. "Get your family, *tarsi*. I will deal with him."

Elinta didn't object, mostly because Tamir had run forward, crossing the distance to the other Asali in less than a second. His sword whipped up and clashed with the other man's in a blur of motion. The loud sound of it shoved Elinta into action. If there was anyone else nearby, they would hear the sound of their fight and come running.

"Stay there, Zhayra," she called, racing forwards. The man tried to block her path, but Tamir forced him to abandon the door with a string of lightning attacks. He'd have to fight if he wanted to live, and that meant ignoring Elinta. Not sparing a glance for Tamir, trusting that he was as capable as he and the council had hinted, she dived through the door the Asali had been guarding.

"Lin?" a weak voice croaked from her left. Pivoting, and feeling the world slow to half its usual speed, Elinta's eyes landed on the dim form of her brother.

"Blaine."

A thin rope bound his wrists in place, the other end tying him to a rusted metal rung hanging from the wall. He was seated, his legs sprawled out in front of him, but his hands were in the air, the rope preventing him from resting his arms.

She ran to him. "It's OK. I'm going to get you out." She glanced around the musty room and gasped. Her father was on the other side, similarly tied under a lantern and opposite her brother. He was filthy. His beard had become wild and stained with dirt and blood, hiding the natural grey. But his eyes were open, and he was staring at her in disbelief.

"Hi," she stuttered. Then turned back to Blaine, not wanting to give her father's face the opportunity to turn stony. In a distant part of her mind, she registered that her father's hair had gone completely grey in the months since she'd last seen him.

"Are you OK?" she asked Blaine, cutting through the rope restraining him.

He nodded, not looking away from her face. It was like he couldn't believe she was there. Like he was afraid she'd disappear if he blinked.

His arms came free, but she caught them, stopping them from dropping. Instead, she lowered them slowly, knowing his shoulders would be stiff from lack of movement. Outside, the clash of steel on steel continued to ring.

"Blaine?" she said, crouching in front of him. His face was streaked with blood, one of his eyes swollen shut and his blond hair a bloodied mess. She pushed the hair back from his face to study the damage better.

"I'm OK," he said. Her brother jerkily raised a hand and pressed it to her face, his healthy eye wide in shock.

She paused, allowing herself a moment, then nodded, racing across to her father and setting to work. Now that she was here in front of him, she didn't know what to say. And it seemed neither did he. But his face said a thousand words. It was bloody, like Blaine's, with a long cut across his cheek, and dirt had settled into the lines of his face, but his green eyes were hard, mirroring the coldness of the last time she'd seen him.

"Why are you here?" he finally grunted.

"I couldn't leave you," she said, fighting to keep her voice calm. Had he actually thought she wouldn't come? She cut his hands free and stood back to survey him. "Can you stand?"

He shook his head and gestured to his leg. "Broke my ankle."

The blood left Elinta's face. A cut she could dress. A burn she could cover. But a broken bone? There was nothing she could do right now. There was nothing to splint it with, and Tamir was too busy to heal it.

"I can help him," Blaine said, grunting as he stopped beside her. There was no time to question him. If he could stand by himself, that was good enough for her. She'd have to fight if they wanted to get out.

The clanging of steel abruptly stopped. The silence felt unnatural in its absence.

"Wait here," she said, darting to the door and not daring to let her fear surface.

Tamir met her at the door. "We must go."

Her father gasped at the sight of him. "Elinta," he said. But she ignored him. Whatever he had to say about Tamir, it could wait. In fact, she'd be happy not to hear it at all.

"Let's go," she said, locking eyes with her brother. He glanced uncertainly at Tamir, then back at her. He nodded, pulling their father to his feet and gripping him around the waist.

Elinta led the way from the room. "Take the rear," she said to Tamir. He fell in behind her family, sword still at the ready. Her father grunted with every step they took, and Elinta flinched with every sound. But it didn't matter. Mazen would know she was here now. Wherever he was, he'd be coming for her.

They hurried past the unconscious bodies of the guard and another Asali that had come to his aid, checking the next hall before turning down it. They crisscrossed their way back through the building, moving ever toward the front entrance. Running feet echoed around them, but it was impossible to tell where they came from. Elinta's muscles ached from being constantly tense. Her father cried out in pain, but they kept going.

An Asali dove from a room to Elinta's right, tackling her to the ground in a tangle of limbs. Blaine shouted as they fell. Elinta shoved at the luminescent body and scrambled away, slipping on the sand-covered stone as the figure tried to collect itself. They both stood at the same time, and Elinta just managed to raise her sword in time to meet the blow that swiftly followed. The clash of their steel echoed in the corridor.

When they pulled back, Elinta stared in surprise at her attacker. It was a woman with short blonde hair and stunning silver eyes. She hadn't expected another woman. The brief pause passed, and the Asali was on her again. Elinta couldn't retreat—her brother and father were right behind her—but she couldn't match this woman blow for blow. So, she ducked, twirled, and dodged, keeping as close as she could to the woman even brushing her skin or her clothing as she moved. Tamir darted forwards, his sword glinting in his own light as he waited for an opening. Elinta, puffing, tried to give him one as she continued her rapid dance around the woman. As the Asali struck out for her shoulder, Elinta twisted, ducking the blow and coming up behind the woman. The move left the Asali off balance and Tamir struck, his sword darting into the woman's hip.

She cried out and Elinta slammed her sword into the woman's. The weapon bounced off the wall and fell to the ground. Then Elinta sent the woman after it, ramming the hilt of her sword into her head. She would be OK if any of her friends found her and healed her soon.

"Thanks," she said to Tamir. Now she knew why Mazen had led her into the centre of the building. With even only a couple of Asali, Elinta might not have made it out if she hadn't had one on her side as well.

Blaine stared at her, open mouthed, but she ignored him, leading them on instead. Tamir fell to the back of their line again. They hadn't even left the corridor when another Asali appeared, this time behind them.

"Keep going," Tamir shouted while he steadily retreated, dodging and blocking the man's attacks so he could keep up with their group.

Blaine tripped, sending him and their father careening into a wall.

"Blaine!" Elinta grabbed him by his shirt and tugged as hard as she could, putting him back on his feet.

"I'm alright," he said, dragging their father along. Pain twisted both their faces.

Elinta hurried ahead. When the entryway came into sight, she sighed with relief and ran into the fresh air.

An arrow slammed into the sand in front of her. Before she could even react, a burning in her shoulder ignited, and another arrow landed in the sand. Elinta dove back into cover, stumbling into her brother and forcing him back. A dark patch steadily spread across her torn jumper, heavy and warm.

"Lin!" Blaine gasped.

"I'm fine," she grunted. Fire flared in Zhayra's chest. Tamir continued to fight the Asali at their rear. They had to get out of there. But how?

"Zhayra," Elinta said frantically. Blaine and her father stared at her like she was mad. "There are two on the roof. We can't get out. Can you deal with them?" She'd never seen the dragon attack anyone before, but if they stayed much longer, they'd be finished. "They have bows," she added.

The legends said that only *illayas* could damage a dragon. She desperately hoped that was true. Because a long roar echoing across the sands was Zhayra's answer.

Blaine paled and her father's eyes bulged. Elinta pushed past them to help Tamir, but with a final flick of his wrist, his opponent was down, unconscious. She lowered her sword, wincing as she did.

"Are you alright?" Tamir said, his eyes landing on her shoulder.

"I'll be fine until we're out of here."

Then there came a rushing of wind, and the sound of something large moving through the air. Elinta scurried back to the entryway, peering into the sky with her enhanced vision. Zhayra, who would be all but a dark shadow moving through the air to the others, was shooting toward them.

"She's here," Elinta said, more to herself than the others. Her eyes were glued to the dragon, fear making her chest tight. Zhayra disappeared above them in a blur of movement. Terrified screams sounded from the roof. Then two bodies fell through the air, landing with a heavy thud on the ground in front of the entrance. One still had his bow clamped in his hand. Neither moved.

Zhayra landed heavily on the ground behind the Asali. Relief spread through them both.

"Hurry," Elinta said over her shoulder. She spared the two Asali a glance, noting that their chests rose laboriously. Then she raced out to Zhayra's side. "Can you carry four?" she asked.

Zhayra paused, then blinked once, tension back in her chest.

"Just far enough away to be safe," she said.

Zhayra blinked once, more readily this time.

"Great." She turned to her family. There was no time for introductions now.

"Tamir, help me get my father up."

Her father jerked at her words. "I'm not riding that beast."

Elinta heard her voice harden. "Either you ride *her* or you stay here."

"Father," Blaine said in a low voice.

"Fine," he grunted. After much manoeuvring, they finally had him in place.

"You're next," she said, turning to Blaine.

"You've got a lot to tell me," he said, a small smile on his lips. "I've missed you."

"Me too," she said. Her brother climbed up Zhayra, settling in behind her father. His face was pale, but a smile of wonder tugged at his lips as he looked at the white scales under him. Elinta looked uncertainly at the dragon's back. She wasn't sure two more would fit in the space in front of Zhayra's wings. And it would be near impossible to stay on behind them. She sent Tamir up next, then looked at their squished bodies again.

"There is room," Tamir called down. With a doubtful look, Elinta climbed onto Zhayra's leg, careful not to use her injured arm. Tamir offered her his hand and helped her swing into place behind him. It was an awkward position with Zhayra's wings on either side of her. Elinta's legs rubbed against the joints of Zhayra's wings, and she was pressed hard against Tamir, but she fit.

"Let's go," she called, unsure how long this was going to last. But Zhayra had spread her wings as soon as Elinta had settled.

CHAPTER
TWENTY

Z HAYRA BEAT AT THE air, large, strong beats that should have sent them shooting into the night sky. She rose slowly. It was agonising, watching the ground below draw further away only metre by metre, rather than in one large movement. But they were rising. Asali began to emerge from the ruined fortress, their swords hanging uselessly by their sides. Elinta held tightly to Tamir from her awkward seat, her calves rubbing against Zhayra's wings. When they'd risen higher than the building, the dragon swung back around toward it.

"What's she doing?" Elinta shouted. "Zhayra?"

The night in front of them tore open in a burst of bright orange flame. The sound of it was dampened by the wind, but to Elinta it sounded just as she imagined a hurricane would. She watched the orange stream in fascination, even as beams lying haphazardly across the roof caught fire. The flames licked at the roof, turning the stone black. The stream died, and Zhayra turned around in a wide arc, taking them away from the building once more. A deep satisfaction in her belly.

Two more figures stumbled out of the fortress. The small group grew more distant, but Zhayra rose no more than an arrow's height before levelling out.

The fortress burned behind them, sending smoke into the air. It wouldn't do much. Once the wood was burnt out, the fire would die rather than spread into the stone, but Elinta grinned as the burning building disappeared behind them.

Elinta's heart throbbed in her shoulder, but her satchel was pressed between her and Tamir, and even if she could reach it, she wasn't sure she would have been able to do anything with the cool night air whipping around them. Zhayra struggled on, but there was a determination in her. Elinta wasn't sure how to describe it, but she was sure that it was what pushed the dragon on. That and the thought of her fire still lighting up the sky.

Unable to stop herself, Elinta glanced behind them every few minutes, checking to see how far they'd travelled. Checking to see when it would be safe for Zhayra to land. But soon, the movement jostled her arm too much and she stopped turning. Blood was still seeping from the wound, but it had slowed significantly. If she was lucky, it would stop before they even landed.

As the brush-speckled borders of the Bradfin came into view, Zhayra's height started to drop. She hadn't been as high as she usually flew to begin with, but now, the features of the lightly vegetated landscape were clear to her enhanced eyes.

"Tell Blaine to yell for Zhayra to land," Elinta called. Tamir passed on the message, and Zhayra's descent quickened. When the dragon landed heavily, Elinta slid down first, jostling her shoulder. The backs of her calves felt raw from the rubbing of Zhayra's wing joints, but she had to ignore it for now. Tamir landed beside her a few seconds later, and when he turned to help Blaine and then her father, she saw the blood she'd left on his cloak.

Elinta stumbled around to Zhayra's head and stroked her cheek. "Good job," she mumbled, allowing herself a moment to feel tired. She turned off her dragonsight, shocked at how dark the night really was. The memory of Zhayra's fire flared in her eyes, and she grabbed onto the pride and wonder filling her, hoping the dragon would feel it. Then she steeled herself, tucking away her pain and tiredness for later, and turned back to the others. Her father was hobbling away from Zhayra as quickly as he could, mumbling under his breath. Tamir crossed to her side, his windswept hair sticking out at odd angles.

"Let me heal this," he said, looking at her shoulder.

"No. Help them." She gestured toward her family. "I've got this." She didn't know how far Tamir's healing ability stretched, but she wanted Blaine and her father well before he helped her. Tamir himself seemed unhurt though she wasn't sure if that meant he'd healed himself or hadn't been injured in the first place.

"I do not think your father will let me," he said, his dark grey eyes landing on her father's figure.

He had lowered himself to the ground, with his back up against a rock, his legs stretched out before him. Blaine stood near him. He seemed dead on his feet.

"It might help if he sees you heal Blaine," she said.

Tamir nodded. "You did well tonight," he said, then crossed to Blaine.

"I am Tamir," he said. "Please, let me heal you."

Blaine frowned. "Heal me?"

"Yes." Tamir didn't say any more. Blaine's eyes flicked to her again, seeking reassurance. Elinta, marvelling and somewhat uncomfortable with the idea of her brother looking to her, nodded.

Blaine looked again at Tamir and hesitantly agreed, ignoring their father's glare. Tamir took Blaine's wrists in his hands and his healing power shined brightly, rising up in the dark between their figures. Elinta watched curiously. She'd never see it done to someone else and, well, she'd hardly seen it done to herself. The torn skin at Blaine's wrists slowly knit itself back together before her eyes, and the bruises began to retreat and fade. Blaine's eyes widened, and soon his right eye was open just as far as his left.

Satisfied, Elinta turned her back on them and stiffly dropped to sit on one of Zhayra's feet. She stifled a groan as she stretched out her legs and opened her satchel.

The dragon huffed, sending hot air over her.

"I know," Elinta said, then returned her attention to her satchel. Inside, just visible in the dim light of the moon, were all her old supplies.

Though some water to wash the wound at her shoulder would have been good, it wasn't necessary with everything else she had. She unzipped her jumper, wincing as she pulled it away from her shoulder. Then tugged at her bloodied shirt to bare the wound. If she craned her neck, she could just see it though the movement pulled her skin tight and sent pain up her neck and down her arm. It was a deep gash down the front of her shoulder, about three inches long from where the arrow had slid before slamming into the ground. She shuddered. She was lucky it hadn't embedded in the muscle or bone there. Her arm would have been useless after such an injury.

Pulling some cloth from her satchel, Elinta watched as Tamir ministered over her father. He was glaring at the Asali, but he let the man heal his ankle as well as his other wounds. She'd thank Tamir for her father's sake later since she knew he wouldn't say it.

She pressed the cloth to her shoulder and grunted. It came away covered in old, crusted blood. The wound had stopped bleeding. She fetched some jars from her bag and set to work, relishing in the familiarity of the task. While others would have been daunted by the prospect of treating their own wound, Elinta felt at home in that moment. She was doing something she knew and knew well. As her hands worked, her mind turned to Lorrin and Niles. If only she could tell them they'd successfully rescued her family. That she'd see them again soon. She could have done with some friendly banter right now, too. Or even just their silent company.

When Tamir had finished healing their father, Blaine turned to stare at her, his eyes shifting between her and Zhayra. She smiled, a strained smile as she was still tending to her own wound, and it seemed enough to help him come to a decision. He crossed the space between them.

"Let me," he said, reaching out to take the cloth, now covered in a herbal mix, from her. Zhayra's head shifted to better see him. Blaine jolted at the movement, but he still took the cloth.

"Is this Zhayra?" he asked, dabbing at her shoulder with a surprisingly steady hand.

"Yes," Elinta said, hesitantly. Now that she was with him, Elinta didn't know what to say. Didn't know how to act. What did he really think of them?

"I'm Blaine," he said, looking the dragon in the eye. Elinta's mouth dropped. She managed to recover before he returned his gaze to her. "I thought I'd never see you again."

She searched his eyes and there wasn't a hint of anger there. "I thought about writing," she said, "but it was too dangerous."

"Where have you been?" he asked, glancing back at Tamir.

Elinta grinned. How she must seem to her brother now, returning armed and with an Asali in her company! "I'll tell you later," she said, taking the cloth back from him and tying it to her shoulder. She rolled up her pants, taking a quick look at her calves, and finding them much as she'd expected. They were rubbed a deep red, even speckled with blood in places where the skin had torn. Sighing, she rubbed a salve into them.

"Tamir," she called once she was done. He strode forward, his bare feet gleaming in the night, and she fought to suppress a grin. She glanced at her backpack, retrieved from where he'd tied it to Zhayra, and slung over his shoulder again. It seemed too much to hope that he'd put Niles's shoes in there before they'd set out to find her family, rather than leaving them in the desert. "We should get back to Kethmere. We'll have to go in twos."

Zhayra couldn't carry the four of them that far, but she'd try if she asked.

The dragon grumbled at her words, proving her thoughts.

"Don't argue," she said to the dragon. She didn't mean to be so stern, but with her family relying on her, Elinta had to step up. There was no time to sit around discussing what to do. Decisions had to be made. Mazen might be on his way to them even now. Her stomach was sitting uneasily within her at the very thought of him. Why hadn't they seen him? She shoved the thought away, concentrating instead on the more imminent problem. "We'll head back there, get some supplies and horses, and then ride back to Nevira."

Tamir nodded.

"Nevira?" Blaine asked, but Elinta didn't have time to explain yet. She knew he'd probably expected her to say Liyarna, since she was travelling with Tamir. It had been a long time since the Asali were in Nevira.

"My father should go first," she said, thinking out loud and watching her father's shadowed figure. He caught her gaze and his green eyes hardened once again. Elinta didn't say what she was thinking, but Tamir seemed to realise what was going through her mind. Her father wouldn't go if he had to fly with her *and* the dragon. But Elinta didn't want to send an unarmed Blaine with him.

"I will go with him," Tamir said.

"Thank you," she said. "Blaine and I will find somewhere to hide in the meantime."

Zhayra grumbled again.

"Do you think you'll be OK?" she asked the dragon. She had a long journey ahead of her, after already completing one. Zhayra would be exhausted when they all finally arrived in Kethmere. At least she'd be able to rest on the return trip to Nevira; the dragon could fly ahead of them and sleep while they caught up.

Zhayra blinked once.

"Oh!" she said. "If I need you to listen through me ... I'll blink twice if you're already looking."

Blaine stared in puzzlement at them.

It didn't solve the issue of signalling Zhayra when she wasn't using her eyes, but they could work that out later, and she had a feeling the dragon would be checking in on her regularly, anyway.

Elinta stood, ignoring the throbbing in her shoulder, but Tamir frowned.

"There's no time," she said, cutting across him. She didn't comment on the circles under his eyes or the way he was no longer holding himself in his usual perfect posture. He didn't know, but Elinta had seen the way his feet had struggled to work after finishing with her family. Her wound was clean and had stopped bleeding for the moment. It could wait until they were all safe and Tamir was rested.

Fully healed, her father climbed onto Zhayra, his strong muscles making it easy to scale the dragon. Blaine strapped his legs into the harness while Tamir climbed up, missing his usual grace. Elinta stood in front of Zhayra.

"I'll see you soon," she said, resting her head against the dragon's muzzle. The faint smell of smoke came from the dragon's mouth.

Zhayra hummed, and Elinta stepped back.

"Go," she whispered. With her passengers in place, Zhayra shot into the air and disappeared into the night.

"So, uh, what's been happening?" Blaine said, stepping up beside her.

Though it was still dark, Elinta and Blaine crawled under some light brush. It wouldn't stop Vaherin from seeing them with his heat sense if he was close, but it would be enough to hide them from a fly-over. Elinta propped her head on her hand, carefully positioning her injured arm across her body, and smiled nervously at her brother. She hadn't answered his questions about the last several months, insisting they needed to hide first, but now, now she was ready to talk. Or as ready as she'd ever be.

"What would you like to know?" she asked.

"Everything."

Elinta summarised as much as possible though it still took her over an hour to tell it all to him. She left out some things and toned-down others, but she thought it was an honest account.

"The prince taught you to fight?" Blaine said, eyes wide, when she'd finished.

"Yes, and Niles."

"And you're living in the palace?"

"Well, I was …" Elinta trailed off. What would she do now? Even assuming she would be welcomed back to the palace, she had her father and Blaine now. But even as she thought of her family, she knew they wouldn't play a part in where she would go once they were all back in Nevira. Her father still didn't want her around. Though she wanted to stay with Blaine, she couldn't if he stayed with their father. And he had his own dreams to follow, dreams she didn't want to hold him back from.

Blaine shook his head in wonder, but Elinta was now looking at him cautiously.

"Are you still going to Culmar?" she asked quietly. She hadn't forgotten his dream to go to the port city and start a horse training and farrier business there. Had he?

"Lin," he said, taking in her expression. She'd forgotten how well he'd always been able to read her. She couldn't hide her worries from him. "You didn't stop me from going." He laughed. "I think you've helped push me toward it. Although, Father will have to come now."

Elinta frowned. "Blaine."

"No! I'm thankful." He smiled, a genuine grin that lit his hazel eyes. She shook her head. He couldn't go home because of her, and he was happy.

"I didn't just mean this thing with Mazen," he said after a few seconds. "Watching you go with the dragon ... I don't know. It made me think about my dream and how much I wanted it. I didn't feel so guilty since I wouldn't be leaving you alone with Father ... and I thought I might see you there one day."

Elinta smiled. "I would have gone looking for you. You would have been easy to find, too."

Blaine cocked his head.

"You'd be the best trainer in Culmar."

She expected him to deny it, but instead, his eyes lit with mischief. "I will be. When this is over, I'm going."

Elinta grinned, studying his face. Whatever had happened while he'd been captive hadn't changed him. He was the same person she remembered ... if a little more confident.

"Blaine," she started, realising there was still one more thing she had to ask him.

But Blaine shook his head. "I know what you're going to ask, but he was never there. Not that I knew, anyway. The Asali just watched over us and made sure we were uncomfortable. They never even said why we were there."

"Mazen was never in the desert?" She'd been going to ask him to recount everything that Mazen had said and done, but …

Blaine shook his head again, and Elinta felt her frown deepen. Where was Mazen?

CHAPTER
TWENTY-ONE

I T WASN'T UNTIL THE next night that Elinta, Blaine, and their father crept into Kethmere. It had taken a lot of convincing, but their father had finally agreed that it wasn't safe for them to stay in the village while Mazen was after her. He'd agreed, but bitterly. Elinta gazed around her room. Now that she wasn't panicking about where her family was, she could drink it all in. Crossing to her wardrobe, Elinta ran her hands along her old clothes. Her work apron was hanging on the outside of the door, still covered in dirt. A pair of ragged boots sat at the end of her bed.

A knock sounded on her bedroom door. Spinning around, Elinta found Blaine in the doorway. He'd taken the opportunity to change into some fresh clothes and wash the dirt and blood from his face. He almost looked as though he'd never been taken.

"Are you alright, Lin?"

Elinta smiled again at the use of his nickname for her. How she'd missed it.

"Yeah," she said, her hand resting on the strap of her satchel. Blaine had told her he'd found it in the aftermath of Elinta's flight from the lake all those months ago and taken it home. While Tamir had healed her shoulder and legs when they'd arrived in the forest, Elinta wasn't about to let it go again. "I didn't think I'd ever see any of this again."

He glanced around her room. "I wouldn't let him touch it."

"Thank you," she said, as their father clattered around in the kitchen.

"Are you taking anything with you?" he asked.

"Just Mum's old necklace." She touched it where it now hung at her neck. It was all Elinta had of her mother. It and her looks. The necklace was a simple golden chain. It used to have a pendant hanging from it, but they'd lost it years ago. She could hardly remember what it looked like now.

Blaine's eyes studied hers. "You made the right choice, Elinta. She'd still be proud."

Tears tugged at her eyes, and she managed a small smile. "I—"

"Aren't we meant to be in a hurry?" their father growled from behind Blaine.

Elinta jolted, wiping her eyes. "Yes."

"Then let's get going."

Elinta cast one last look around her room and followed her family down to the stables.

When Elinta and her family emerged through the trees at the lake nearly an hour later, they were leading four horses. They couldn't take any of the others with them. A shuttered lantern lit their way. Tamir and Zhayra were waiting for them where Elinta had first seen the dragon. Across the lake, the trees that had been damaged in her rough landing were now surrounded by new growth. It was difficult to see the ruined trees, with even the fallen trunks covered in bracken. Her feet stopped, and she stared at that crash site. So much had changed since then, all because of a storm. A smile twitched at her lips. Without the storm, she'd never have met Zhayra, or Lorrin and Niles.

Tamir rose from a crouch in front of Zhayra and waited for Elinta to draw level with them. Blaine and her father waited by the forest's edge with the horses.

"Ready to go?" Elinta asked, feeling excited at the idea of finally getting back to Nevira and the boys even if she didn't know what was waiting for them in the palace.

Tamir gave Zhayra a significant glance, and the dragon's stomach sank.

"What is it?" Elinta asked.

"I need to return to Liyarna before I join you on the road to Nevira."

"Oh," Elinta said, not quite understanding Zhayra's reaction.

"I've spoken with Zhayra," Tamir said, glancing at the dragon again. "I'll need her to take me if I'm to rejoin you soon."

"Oh," Elinta said again. Zhayra pushed out her neck and lowered her head to be level with hers, staring into her eyes. Elinta looked away. "That makes sense."

Zhayra grunted, drawing Elinta's gaze again and gently nudged her.

"Don't be too long, OK?" Elinta said, rubbing Zhayra's muzzle. An ache had already settled in her heart at the idea of being parted from her again. It didn't matter that they would be parted again once they reached Nevira. That was still several days away. This was now.

Zhayra keened quietly, slipped her head over Elinta's shoulder and pushed her so that Elinta stumbled forwards to her chest. Chuckling, Elinta hugged her, ignoring the thickness rising in her throat.

"I'll see you soon." Zhayra released her and Elinta turned to Tamir. "How long will you be?"

"A day and a half, two at most."

Elinta nodded. They'd be nearly at the capital by then. "We'll be on the main road."

"I won't keep her from you for long," Tamir said seeing through Elinta's attempt to seem nonchalant.

"Take as long as you need," Elinta said even though she hoped he'd be quick. "Say hello to Serren for me."

Tamir's face lit up at the mention of his wife. "I will." He turned, then paused, looking at the *illayas* circlet on his wrist.

"Are you certain Mazen had only the *illayas* dagger? And no sword?" he said.

Elinta cocked her head. "Just the dagger." An image flashed through her mind, a memory of the Asali prince standing over the body of a yellow dragon, a sword protruding from her. He'd once had an *illayas* sword, but not anymore. Perhaps that had been the last time he'd used it.

Tamir seemed puzzled. "He made the dagger in the early days of his bond with Vaherin, but he always favoured the sword. I wouldn't expect him to lose it."

"How many pure swords are there?" Elinta asked.

"We destroyed all but three after the Eggslaying. Our royal family had one, which we presumed lost with Mazen, the council has another, and the human royal family has the last. We asked them to destroy it, after what it had done, but they refused."

Elinta didn't comment on this last sword. She'd heard about it from Mazen himself. "Can't he just make another one?"

Tamir shook his head. "When the secret of forging the pure swords was discovered, the swordsmith kept it to himself. He was scared of what too many swords could mean for the dragons even as people argued for more. Even though Mazen was involved in making his dagger, he never learnt the full technique. The secret died with the swordsmith."

Elinta nodded, happy at the idea that there would never be more than the three swords in existence, and maybe there were only two now. But she wasn't sure why Tamir was asking her about it.

"I should go," Tamir said, climbing onto Zhayra's back.

"*Zetayn nalliyan ayn palla kli ayn karn mai ris,*" Elinta called.

"And you," he said.

Zhayra nudged Elinta one last time, then shot into the air, buffeting her with wind.

"Good," her father said, not bothering to lower his voice. Watching them go, Elinta pretended she didn't hear his comment.

Zhayra's shadowy form quickly vanished into the darkness, and Elinta turned back to her family, her heart sinking at the sight of her father's stony face glowing in the light of the lantern he held. It would be a long trip back to Nevira.

🔥🔥🔥

They stopped at dawn in a copse of trees off the road for a small meal and a rest in the cool morning air. Elinta had tried to remain friendly with her father, but now she'd put some distance between them. His constant glares and short replies, if he gave any at all, were beginning to be too much.

Blaine rose from his seat against a saddle and sat beside her. "You miss her, don't you?"

Elinta turned to him in surprise. "Who?"

"The dragon," he said. "Zhayra."

"Yes."

Blaine shook his head. "So much has happened to you since you left. You speak Asalin?"

Elinta laughed. "Only a little."

"And you can fight," he said, looking at her sword. Blaine had his own strapped at his waist now. She wondered whether she'd beat him in a sparring contest. "The prince and his friend taught you well."

"They did," Elinta said. She'd told him all about her lessons with Lorrin and Niles, and even her fight with Mazen though she'd neglected some of the details so he didn't worry. "I can't wait for you to meet them." She pictured Blaine, Lorrin, and Niles all in a room together, laughing at a joke one of them had told. Then she pictured Lorrin and Niles roping Blaine into a prank. "On second thought," she said, "maybe I can wait."

"What's that supposed to mean?" he said, slinging an arm around her shoulders and pulling her into his chest.

"You might get into trouble," she said, laughing and shoving him. Their father cleared his throat, but Blaine ignored his quiet objection.

"When have I ever gotten into trouble?"

Elinta cocked an eyebrow. "I'm not going to answer that." It was true. Blaine wasn't nearly as mischievous as Niles, but she wondered what her friends would bring out in him. It would be worth it though, just to see all her favourite people, or humans, in one place.

Blaine sobered. "You've changed," he said. "You're more confident in yourself. You're not the quiet healer girl anymore."

"I haven't been in a while."

"No, I suppose not." He paused. "Are you going to tell me more about Prince Lorrin?"

"Why?" Elinta asked, glancing at her brother.

He tilted his head, raising his eyebrows as though she were hiding something. "I heard the way you talked about him while we were waiting for Zhayra to return, Lin."

"What?" Elinta straightened. "If you use the word 'attentions,' I might just kill you."

He laughed, lifting his hands in a gesture of surrender. "OK. I won't say a thing."

Silence settled between them, but Elinta found it comfortable, friendly. Even if he had tried to discuss her feelings for Lorrin, feelings she hadn't shared with anyone ... not even herself.

Blaine groaned and shifted to lean against the tree they sat under and closed his eyes. They weren't moving on for another hour or so and even her father was looking like settling in for a nap as well.

Elinta took the opportunity to check in on Zhayra, making sure her extra hair tie was still on her wrist before she tried accessing the dragon's eyes. She turned her back on her father, knowing her sightless eyes would unnerve him, and focused on the dragon.

A minute later, an image appeared in her mind of a wide, open field with large silver trees bordering it. Zhayra's stomach lightened as soon as Elinta tapped into her eyes. Elinta, wishing she could tell the dragon to listen to her, whispered, "Hello, girl."

Tamir was nowhere to be seen within Zhayra's view. Presumably, he was talking to the council about Mazen or catching up with Serren, his *ngaparta*. Elinta watched just a moment longer before pulling back with a sigh. If only she were with the dragon or, really, the dragon was with her and her family.

Shuffling so that her back was pressed against the same tree as Blaine, she leant back her head, and closed her eyes, finally letting sleep overpower her.

"Elinta, time to go." Blaine's voice pierced through her sleep and slowly drew her back. Even though they'd managed to catch up on some sleep as they'd waited for night to fall upon their return to Kethmere, Elinta still felt tired after the rescue.

She cracked her eyes open and stared up at the cloudy sky through the leaves of the tree. When she'd mustered some energy, Elinta pushed herself up from the tree and found that Blaine had already saddled the horses. They were ready to go. She smiled her gratitude to her brother and swung up into the saddle of her horse.

The day passed slowly to Elinta. When she and Blaine lapsed into silence, Elinta would check in on Zhayra, but she couldn't tell what the dragon was doing. As soon as the image would sharpen, Zhayra's eyes would be pointed at the open sky or the Liyarnan canopy. Elinta puzzled over this as they rode. Why would the dragon be looking at the sky? And where was Tamir? But Zhayra's emotions never flickered to fear or anger, so even if she had no idea what was happening, Elinta knew she was safe. But she couldn't help feeling a stab of confusion and hurt as realisation dawned after the third time this happened. The dragon was trying to stop her from seeing something. But what? And why? But no answers occurred to her.

So, her thoughts turned again to Mazen. Why hadn't he pursued them? She'd been sure he would be in the fortress. He'd invited her there. But Vaherin hadn't been there and if Blaine was right, Mazen had never even been there. But why? What was the point of luring her there if he wasn't waiting for her?

Not that she wasn't thankful. Mazen was still too strong for her, too skilled. If she'd fought him again, she'd have needed help. But it didn't make any sense. Things had been too easy. Unease began to grow in her, spreading through her body and sitting heavily in her stomach.

That night as Elinta lay under the stars, her thoughts were still on Mazen. Questions swirled in her mind in a never-ending cycle. Why had he killed Zhayra's mother? Why was he now trying to kill her and Zhayra? What had driven him to this? She thought back to the memories she'd seen of Zhayra's life. Maybe she'd missed something, some clue that would help explain what he'd become. Elinta shifted under her blanket. She needed to watch them again. She needed to know. So, she tried to replicate all that she'd done that night under the stars, pressed against Zhayra.

She thought of all she knew of the dragon, everything she'd learnt, summoned the memories she'd seen, and fell asleep with one word echoing in her mind: Zhayra.

The bonded one was in front of her, stopping her from seeing her mother as he talked with the Zearla lurai. *He was closed off to her, and it only heightened her confusion about him. She was still studying Vaherin when something caught his attention at the exact moment that her heart plummeted. Her mother! A terrible pain was in her chest, in her heart, and vanished a second later. Something was wrong. She dove forwards, slipping past the other dragon, through the rock, and coming to a skittering halt at the nightmare that awaited her. Mazen turned his cold eyes on her. Murder stared at her from his eyes and from the ground at his feet. Mother.*

Elinta woke gasping, sweat pouring from her forehead. Colour streaked across the cloudy sky above her.

"Lin!" Blaine leaned over her. "Are you OK? I couldn't wake you up. What's hap—" Blaine froze, his features clear in the dim light of dawn. "Your eyes," he said, pulling back and leaning on his heels. His brow was furrowed.

"What about them?" Elinta sat up, wiping the sweat from her face, and hanging on to her brother's words, the memory momentarily forgotten.

"They're ... different."

"How?" Elinta asked, frustrated. Tamir had said her eyes would change like Mazen's had. Were they white now? Slits?

"Your pupils. They're ovular," Blaine said, a question in his voice as though he couldn't quite believe it. "Like an Asali."

Elinta sighed in relief. Ovular. She nearly laughed. If Blaine was surprised by that, wait until her eyes really changed.

"It's normal," she said, but curiosity tugged at her. What did they look like?

"Really?" Blaine asked.

Elinta nodded and gathered her things, reality driving away her curiosity. "We should get moving," she said. Despite her efforts to avoid looking at her father, she still saw the look of horror and disgust he gave her when he saw her eyes as he saddled the horses.

Blaine glanced once at their father, then joined Elinta in packing up their campsite, nothing but open curiosity and wonder playing across his face.

Back on the road, Elinta's father was quieter than ever and not once did he look at her. But Elinta was grateful for it. It gave her time to think, not just about her eyes, but also about the memory she'd seen during the night. Nothing had changed in the dream. It hadn't revealed anything new to her, but even so, there was one image that haunted her more than the rest: Mazen's cold, lifeless eyes. A shiver ran down her spine just thinking about them.

She thought back to the last time she'd seen him. His eyes, so strange in colour and shape, had been hard then too, cold even, but not as they were in the moment he'd stood over the body of the dragon's queen. There wasn't a drop of regret in them. Elinta didn't know why she was so hung up over Mazen, but she just needed to understand.

It wasn't long before all thought of Mazen was driven from her mind, and it all came down to one thing. A jump in anticipation from Zhayra. Elinta searched the skies, a smile spreading across her face. There! To the west, in the distance, was a large form in the sky. From here, it could almost have been an eagle, but Elinta knew it was only the height playing with her eyes. Because the figure was too big to be an eagle, but not too small to be a dragon.

As she watched, it grew larger and larger until Elinta could make out Zhayra's membrane wings and long tail. But Zhayra didn't fly any lower, in fact she rose, and Elinta's heart sank just as Zhayra's did.

It was still broad daylight, and they were on the main road to Nevira. They couldn't risk her being seen. But excitement quickly replaced Elinta's disappointment and with Zhayra so close, she felt she could face the rest of the day with her father's silence in relative ease.

She nudged the horse into a trot, and they rode on, the fourth horse trailing behind Blaine.

🔥🔥🔥🔥

"Zhayra!" Elinta flung her arms around one of the dragon's front legs.

Zhayra made a strange grunting in her chest and settled into a crouch so Elinta could reach her face.

Tamir laughed, sliding from the dragon's back. He had a large bag slung across his back.

"I think she wanted to land as soon as we found you."

Elinta laughed. She'd wanted them to as well.

It was night now, and they'd found a place well off the road where Zhayra could land without being spotted.

"How was your trip?" Elinta asked, raising an eyebrow at Tamir's bag. She kept a hand on Zhayra's muzzle.

"It went well," Tamir said, ignoring her unspoken question. "The council are happy for me to stay with you."

"Great!" She enjoyed Tamir's company, and the help he'd provided was invaluable. "They didn't change their minds about Mazen?"

Tamir frowned and shook his head.

Elinta tried not to show her disappointment though she hadn't thought they would; it was hard not to hope, especially now that it was clear Mazen wasn't going to leave her alone. Elinta turned to Zhayra.

"Notice anything different?"

The dragon lowered her head to look her in the eye and hummed deep in her throat. Her tail swung from side to side behind her.

Elinta laughed at the tickling sensation in the dragon's chest.

Tamir smiled. "I wasn't sure you had noticed, *tarsi*."

"I didn't," she said, looking over her shoulder at Blaine rubbing down the horses.

"He took it well?"

"Yes." Her eyes flickered to her father and then back to Tamir. Her father had barely spoken a word to her all day and had kept as much distance between them as possible. She wondered what the boys would think when she got back. What Lorrin would think.

Tamir gripped her shoulder and walked into the campsite. He dropped the large bag at the edge and sat by the fire. Blaine brought him some food and sat with the Asali as he ate. Elinta smiled at the sight. No matter what her father was like, she always had Blaine.

Elinta and her family had already eaten, and the night was drawing on, so she settled in against Zhayra and closed her eyes. For the moment, her thoughts were quiet. She didn't worry about Mazen or her father. She didn't even worry about what would happen when they reached Nevira tomorrow. She just enjoyed being with Zhayra again.

Elinta and Zhayra spent the rest of the journey flying together. They were mere hours from reaching Nevira, and Elinta wanted every last second that she could have with Zhayra before they'd be parted again. And flying didn't seem so bad now that she was literally strapped to the dragon.

The sun was shining, and the wind had dropped back to a whisper on the ground, but she still wore her Asali jumper up here in the sky, which she'd done her best to clean and repair. Zhayra flew lazily through the air. At first, they'd explored the surrounding area, flying too high to be seen from the ground, but not too high for Zhayra's vision. Now, so close to the capital, they just savoured being together.

Elinta had just finished telling Zhayra about their uneventful days of riding while she and Tamir had been gone when she sat up straighter, the harness tugging at her belt.

"Do you see that?" she asked, looking straight ahead. The main road was taking them directly to Nevira, following a north-easterly course. Far in the distance was a plume of dark smoke.

Zhayra's emotions jumped in curiosity at the same time, underlined by a spike of alarm.

Elinta stared at it, then double-checked the position of the sun and of the road far beneath them. "That's from the city!"

Zhayra's stomach clenched. It was too much smoke to be a simple house fire. A deep sense of foreboding settled over Elinta.

"We should land," she said, stroking the dragon's neck more to comfort herself than Zhayra. Tamir wouldn't be able to see it from the ground. It was too far away.

Zhayra grunted and immediately began to descend. Elinta watched the smoke as they lowered. When they landed in a rush of air, Elinta realised she'd been right; the smoke wasn't visible from the ground.

"What is it?" Tamir asked, taking one look at her face and knowing something was wrong.

"There's smoke coming from the city."

CHAPTER
TWENTY-TWO

T AMIR FROWNED. "WE'RE STILL a couple of hours from
Nevira. You shouldn't be able to see anything small."

"I know," Elinta said, urgency sneaking into her voice as she
looked down at the Asali. Lorrin and Niles were there. What if
something had happened to them while she'd been gone?

Blaine glanced between them, not understanding. "What's
happening?"

Tamir seemed to come to a decision. He swung down from his
saddle and lowered his bag to the ground. "Come here, *tarsi*."

Puzzled, Elinta unclipped herself from the harness and climbed down from Zhayra's back. Elinta's father hung back from the group, but Blaine joined them.

"Speaking to the council was not my only reason for going to Liyarna," Tamir said. "Zhayra and I made this for you."

Elinta had just a moment to wonder if this was why Zhayra had always been looking at the sky when she checked in. When Tamir opened the bag, blue metal glinted in the light. Elinta stared at the metal pieces in confusion, unable to work out their shapes. Blaine understood before she did.

"Armour?" he said, bending to touch the *illayas*.

"Yes."

Elinta stared at him in shock. "This is … this is made of *illayas*?"

Tamir nodded. "It was not easy to find the material, but I had some help."

Elinta wondered at that though she thought she knew who had helped but didn't have a chance to answer.

"You should wear this, *tarsi*. I suspect all is not well in the city."

She looked down at the armour. It was beautiful, but she couldn't wear that into the capital city. Zhayra grunted her disapproval at the thoughts Elinta's feelings must have betrayed.

"I—" she stuttered. "What if it's nothing?"

"What if it is Mazen?" Tamir returned. "For you to see smoke from here, the city must be on fire, *tarsi*."

Elinta shook her head. He was right. She was just afraid. Afraid of revealing herself, her real self, to the palace. But if Mazen was there, her secret wouldn't last for much longer. For the city to be on fire, Vaherin had to be there too. Her heart jumped as her thoughts returned to Lorrin and Niles.

"OK," she said. "How do I put it on?"

Tamir smiled. "I will help you."

He pulled each piece out from inside the bag and ordered them on the ground in front of her. Elinta gasped as her eyes landed on the final piece. In the centre of the breastplate, just below where her collarbones would meet, was a single white scale.

"Is that the one?" Blaine asked.

Elinta frowned, glancing between her brother and Tamir.

"It is."

"Is it what one?" Elinta asked.

Blaine smiled. "Remember when I said I wouldn't let Father throw anything out?" He spoke as though their father wasn't there. Though he was too far away to hear their conversation, and he showed no interest in them, Elinta had a feeling Blaine wouldn't have cared if he could hear them.

Elinta nodded.

"Well, I tidied up a little so he wouldn't have an excuse to go in there, and I found something in the pocket of one of your dresses."

Elinta still didn't understand. Blaine nodded toward the scale in the armour.

"The scale?" she said, then gasped. She remembered! The day she'd turned up to check on Zhayra by the lake, she'd found scales littered across the ground. The dragon had been shedding, and Elinta took one to remember her by. She'd forgotten all about it!

"I kept it. I've had it with me since I found it, actually," Blaine said, "but I asked Tamir if he could have something made for you with it sometime. I thought maybe a pendant for mum's necklace or something...." He stared down at the armour. "This is much better."

Elinta hugged her brother, then hugged Tamir. "Thank you."

"Let's get you into it," Blaine said.

Tamir picked up the first piece. It was something akin to a jerkin. Made from a thick material like leather, it looked like it would hang down past her waist where it split down the middle to allow better movement. The last seven to eight inches were lined with *illayas*.

"Put this on," Tamir said, gesturing for her to step behind Zhayra. "You will need something thin underneath it." She took it, expecting it to weigh her down, but it was no heavier than a shirt or a jumper.

When she re-emerged, she tossed her shirt and Asali jumper to the ground. She handed her sword to Blaine. Her mother's necklace was still around her neck.

Tamir was already holding the next piece, the breastplate. It had a small collar, twisted up to protect her neck. He slipped it over her head, and once again, Elinta was shocked as the solid metal fell into place. It weighed ... nothing. Or next to nothing. It was like she wasn't even wearing it. She could have still been in her shirt and jumper for all the difference in weight.

Tamir smiled at her surprise. "*Illayas* is known as the strongest metal in this world, but it is also the lightest."

As he dressed her, with Blaine's occasional help, Tamir explained the armour to her. "It will match Mazen's dragonscale armour in every way, except one. It is not fireproof." Elinta ignored the memory of the damage Zhayra's fire had caused in Bradfin and focused on Tamir.

"*Illayas* is invulnerable to every metal except itself," Tamir said, helping slip the greaves into place over her pants. They started just below her knees, covering her entire shin, and stopped just above her ankle. "You will be safe from any attack other than from Mazen's dagger."

Elinta nodded.

Tamir stepped back. "That's it. I didn't want to restrict your movement, especially with trying to ride Zhayra."

Elinta looked down at herself. Though her arms were bare from a few inches below her shoulders, and there was a gap from her knees to half-way up her thighs, she felt beyond protected. They'd moved her belt to the outside of her armour and over the long jerkin, so she could strap her sword to it and have the clip exposed. She ran a finger over the scale at her chest.

"Thank you." She thought back over his words. "What about the other swords? The ones that are half *illayas* and half steel? Will they damage this?"

Tamir waved aside her concerns. "The steel removes most of the effect of the *illayas*. They act more like a normal blade. You need not worry."

"Tamir ..." she said, her voice dropping as she caught sight of the scar on her arm. He'd said nothing about dragon blood, which she knew would coat Mazen's weapon. What would she do if he poisoned her again?

Zhayra shifted at the change in her mood, drawing her attention. The armour couldn't protect her from everything, but Liyarna wasn't so far away when Zhayra was flying. She could make that trip again if she had to.

"So, what now?" she asked, shaking off her fear. Though she couldn't see it, she looked in the direction of the smoke.

Tamir gestured at Zhayra. "We will fly over the city and see what is happening."

Elinta nodded, then looked at Blaine and her father. "Stay here. We'll come back for you."

Blaine shook his head. "I'm coming with you."

"Blaine!" their father grunted, having moved closer as Elinta put on the armour.

Her brother ignored him and locked eyes with Elinta. "I'm not leaving you. If something's happening there, I want to be with you."

Despite herself, Elinta smiled.

Blaine grinned in return, seeing the acceptance in her eyes, and turned to their father. "We'll leave the bags for you. Stay here off the road. We'll come back for you after."

He stared at Blaine through hard eyes, but his face was softer than it was whenever he looked at Elinta. Looking at him, Elinta thought he'd never looked older.

Their father nodded. "Be safe," he said.

Elinta swallowed. "We won't be long," she said, unsure what else to say. She opened her mouth to say more, to tell him she loved him, but he cut across her.

"You can't promise that," he said and walked away.

Elinta shook herself, trying to ignore the hurt in her chest. She'd been getting used to it ever since the rescue. She looked between Tamir and Blaine. It was time to go. They climbed onto Zhayra, Tamir, ever graceful, at the back. When she was clipped in, Blaine slipped his arms tightly around her. Elinta tapped his arms.

"Just a little lighter," she strained.

"Right," he said, loosening his grip.

"We're ready," Elinta called. Zhayra rose back into the air, slightly laboured. Blaine's breath caught in her ear, and Elinta spared a moment to be thankful he didn't yell.

As they rose, Elinta's eyes were on the spot where she knew the smoke would be, hoping it would have gone out while she'd been on the ground. That it wasn't as serious as it had looked. But the plume of smoke came into view again. And it had grown, turning the horizon hazy.

Elinta felt split in two. Part of her mind was asking what could have caused this. The other part was whispering back: a dragon. But she couldn't fully believe that second voice. Not yet. The idea that Vaherin and Mazen were waiting for her ...

Zhayra sped toward the city, low to the ground and nearly silent. Elinta, Blaine, and Tamir all leant forward in their seats, lending their angle to Zhayra's speed.

Elinta felt like they couldn't get there soon enough while she also wished they'd never arrive. What would they find when they did? Images of Lorrin and Niles rose in her, and she fought to keep her fear in check. They'd be OK. They had to be. Lorrin lingered before her eyes. She didn't know if she could take losing him, losing her new home.

Zhayra closed the distance to the city in barely a quarter of an hour, but it was the longest fifteen minutes of Elinta's life. The open land seemed to stretch on forever, then the Afonlin flashed by, and they were over the endless woods. Time snapped back and there was the city.

Thick black smoke billowed from its centre, and Elinta's breath caught in her throat. There were figures in the white-stone streets, some running, some fighting, some not moving at all. But it was what was in the air that caused her mind to stutter in fear.

"No," Blaine whispered.

Dragons. Elinta only caught a brief glimpse of their figures soaring through the air, before Zhayra, impossibly, sped up and swooped down into the city, right in front of the White Palace.

CHAPTER
TWENTY-THREE

C HAOS. THAT'S WHAT FOUND them in front of the palace. Fire raged all around them, but the bulk of it seemed to be coming from the western side of the palace itself. Thick smoke poured into the sky. From her place at the palace gates and looking out over Nevira, Elinta could see flames billowing from the closest of the northern watch towers. Civilians and soldiers alike, many of whom had run away upon seeing Zhayra, sprinted through the city. But dotted among the people surrounding her were Asali. Elinta shook her head in disbelief but snapped back to herself when a soldier was cut down barely twenty metres away.

"Get down," she called back to Tamir and Blaine. Dropping to the ground, she joined them in a crouch in the shadow of Zhayra's near-impenetrable form.

Elinta forced her mind to work, to not give in to the fear churning in her gut. "There's an armoury in the palace," she said to her brother, unable to stomach the idea of him in the city without some form of protection. She told him where to find it, hoping that no one would stop him from taking any armour, assuming there was still some there. She'd never been inside herself, so she couldn't tell him what he'd find there.

He nodded, accepting her directions as he'd so quickly accepted the situation, and moved to leave, but Elinta gripped his arm and turned to Tamir.

"Please, stay with him."

Tamir nodded. "*Zetayn nalliyan ayn palla kli ayn karn mai ti,*" he said, then grabbed Blaine and the two hurried through the now abandoned gate to the palace.

She watched them go, told herself they'd be OK, and turned back to the city. Elinta scanned the sky. Two of the dragons, deep blue in colour, were hovering high in place above them. They were looking down upon her and Zhayra, not moving from their position though occasionally they seemed to glance away over the city. It was like ... like they were unsure. What were they waiting for? Elinta couldn't see Vaherin, but she was sure this was where he was. He'd never been in Bradfin. He'd been on his way to Nevira with Mazen, finally ready to step out of the shadows.

A detached part of her hardly believed what was happening. Mazen had only ever been a threat to her, Zhayra, and Lorrin, but it had to be him behind this.

But Mazen and Vaherin weren't the only ones on Elinta's mind. She stepped away from Zhayra, scanning the area around them for Lorrin and Niles. They wouldn't be in the palace. She knew that much about them. So where were they?

"Can you see them?" she asked Zhayra. Her eyes widened as they locked onto a man fighting an Asali in a street to her left. Ford Mayes.

She watched in disbelief as the historian whirled around the Asali man, twin daggers in his hands and a sword at his hip. His mouth and nose were covered with a cloth to filter out the smoke. Ford stuck in close to the Asali, just as Elinta had tried to in the fortress at Bradfin, but he didn't need any help. His daggers locked onto the man's sword, and with a twist, the blade flew from his hands and disappeared.

Undaunted, the Asali continued to fight, but Ford had the upper hand now. He twisted behind the Asali and slashed his blades across the back of his enemy's knees, crippling him in one seamless motion.

Ford stepped back, pushing his cloak away from his form, and glanced up, locking eyes with Elinta. The historian, completely unsurprised to see her standing beside a dragon and dressed in *illayas* armour, nodded. "Good," he called. "You're back." Then he darted down another road.

Elinta gaped after him. But there was no time to wonder at the man. Asali were still roaming the streets, and the dragons were still somewhere over the city. Heart pounding in her chest, Elinta returned to her search for Lorrin and Niles, but she was unwilling to leave Zhayra alone in the city that was too small for her. Desperate, Elinta centred herself, and tuned into her dragonsight. Opening her eyes, she searched what she could see of the city again.

Screams assailed her ears, and she could practically taste the fear in the burning air, some of it hers. But her sight made the horrors even clearer. Was blood really such a deep red? She'd worked around blood for years but seeing it with strengthened eyes was something different. The smoke seemed thicker to her now, but it didn't stop her from seeing everything. She turned, following a billowing trail of it to its source at the palace. There was so much of it.

A woman, closely followed by a man, darted out of the front doors of the palace and down the stairs, heads down, blue-tinged swords in their grips. When they looked up from the gate, they screeched to a halt.

General Nash's expression was unreadable as she looked between Elinta and Zhayra, her blonde hair a frizzed mess. Right behind her, Niles's father seemed to do a double take. Ignoring the fear tightening in her chest, Elinta cleared her throat and called out to them.

"Have you seen Lorrin and Niles?" She was impressed with how steady her voice sounded.

General Nash only hesitated for half a second before she responded, pulling her blue eyes away from the dragon.

"Not since it began. They were fighting in the courtyard."

Elinta exchanged a worried glance with Zhayra. Whose blood was it smeared across the stones of the very same courtyard?

"They were OK," Nash added.

Elinta nodded.

"Mazen?" she called, not even sure what she was asking.

General Nash shook her head. "I haven't seen anyone with the eyes you described."

"What about Vaherin?"

Nash frowned, but General Sonnen spoke up. "Maroon, wasn't he?"

Elinta nodded.

"Saw him earlier." General Sonnen looked up, seemingly just noticing that at least two of the dragons had pulled back. "What's happening, kid?"

"He wants revenge," Elinta said. That much was clear to her even if she didn't understand anything else about Mazen or his actions. He hated humans for the Eggslaying. But she didn't mention his desire to kill her or Zhayra.

A glowing figure darted out from behind a building and ran up the white cobbled road toward them, but one growl from Zhayra sent the woman scurrying away.

"Useful," General Sonnen grunted though his face had paled.

"I need to find Lorrin and Niles," she said, trying to keep the desperation from her voice.

General Nash frowned. "I told them not to stray far, but they could be anywhere."

A woman ran screaming from a house a hundred metres down the main road, and an Asali followed her out. General Nash and General Sonnen exchanged a glance, then moved to charge after them.

But there were two other figures running after the Asali and the woman, and Elinta felt tears of relief prickle at her eyes. Lorrin and Niles seemed unharmed as they sprinted after the Asali man, their swords raised and ready.

General Sonnen laughed gruffly as the boys incapacitated the Asali. "Knew they'd be fighting somewhere."

"They've lost Lorrin's guard, though." General Nash smiled and turned back to Elinta, who was scanning the city for Mazen and Vaherin again. "Lorrin said something about the kidnapping being a diversion. That Mazen wanted you out of the city."

Elinta frowned. "Why?"

Mazen had nothing real to fear from her, not with Vaherin and several other dragons on his side. One of the blues looked larger than Zhayra, while the other was smaller. Zhayra couldn't fight even the three of them, let alone the others they'd seen as they'd flown in.

"I don't know. I assume it's to do with your dragon." General Nash gestured toward Zhayra.

Elinta frowned, then absently remembered she hadn't introduced Zhayra to the generals. But she didn't get a chance because Lorrin and Niles were getting ready to move on and the generals straightened.

"We need to go," General Nash said and darted down the road after her nephew. General Sonnen followed, the old scar on his neck standing out. The boys were yet to see Elinta and were too far away to call out to, but she was happy simply knowing they were OK and soon to be with the generals.

Her eyes drifted back up to the blue dragons hovering over the city. Why weren't they attacking? She glanced at Zhayra, then back up to the two dragons. Mazen hadn't wanted them around ... and as soon as Zhayra had arrived, these two dragons, at least, had pulled back. Because they'd seen her. They'd seen the heir.

"Lin!"

Elinta spun as Blaine and Tamir ran down the steps from the palace, stopping where General Nash and General Sonnen had been only seconds earlier.

Blaine was in a light steel armour, similar in design to hers but without the greaves. His sword was in his hand, and his eyes darted around the city.

"Have you heard anything?" Tamir asked.

"Mazen's been here," she said. "General Nash said Lorrin seems to think Bradfin was some kind of diversion."

"Diversion?" Tamir asked.

Elinta nodded, but she didn't tell him why she agreed. Not even Lorrin knew.

"Have you found your friends?" Blaine asked.

Elinta pointed through the smoke down to where Lorrin and Niles stood, now with the generals. Blaine's face lightened.

"I expect to be introduced when this is over," he said.

She grinned. "Of course."

The fighting was beginning to draw closer to them again, with more and more people abandoning their fear of Zhayra in favour of their fear of the Asali. Soon, people were running past within metres of the dragon, only sending her a terrified glance as they sped by. A mother carrying her child stumbled as she ran but pulled herself together and hurried on. Elinta knew that Zhayra watched all this with a tight stomach. The skies weren't safe for her, but the streets were too narrow for her to fight. She couldn't help. She could hardly move.

Elinta didn't know what to do, but soon a decision would be made for her. A soldier tumbled out of a side street, an Asali hot on his heels, and Tamir darted over to help. Maybe Elinta wouldn't have to leave Zhayra to fight. The Asali would come to her.

Even as she had the thought, another two Asali emerged from down the main road, between her and Lorrin's group, and sprinted toward the prince. "Lorrin!" she screamed, but her voice was drowned under the screams, clangs of steel, and the roar of countless fires echoing over the city. She watched helplessly.

But Lorrin saw the Asali coming and ducked a blow before slashing his sword toward his opponent's shoulder. General Nash joined her nephew while General Sonnen and Niles fought the other Asali side-by-side. Elinta sighed in relief as she watched the group. Lorrin and his aunt took turns stabbing and striking, sometimes attacking at the same time but never in the way of each other. Elinta wished for a moment that she was there to take the general's place.

Elinta kept scanning the skies. Why weren't the dragons attacking anymore? Was it really because of Zhayra? Mazen was still nowhere to be seen. Her back was on the flaming palace now as she searched, still unwilling to leave Zhayra. No Asali had made a move toward her or Zhayra yet. What could she do to help without leaving the dragon? She huffed in frustration. She had to do *something*. But what?

A loud clang drew her attention, and Tamir's sword darted under his opponent's guard and struck deep into his thigh. The man fell. The soldier Tamir had defended scrambled to his feet and ran away without a single word of thanks.

No sooner had Tamir finished with one enemy did another appear, and he was sent back into a furious dance of blades. Her normal eyes would have struggled to keep track of their movements, but the dragonsight allowed her to watch in wonder at the speed with which they moved. Their swords glinted as a stray beam of light pierced the smoke over the city.

Blaine was still beside Elinta, exactly where she wanted him. If he tried to take on an Asali by himself, he wouldn't survive. Even as she had the thought, an Asali with greying hair sprinted toward him. Elinta, stomach in her throat, jumped in front of her brother and met the man's blade in the air with her own. His face darkened and his eyes flicked to Zhayra, but the dragon didn't move. Her own eyes were fixed on the dragons above them. Elinta advanced on the man, her fight with Mazen hanging over her even as she sent her sword darting toward the man with a stomp of her foot.

He jumped sideways, letting her sword pass through thin air. They surveyed each other. Elinta's eyes scanning his every move. It was strange. This man didn't move in the way that Mazen did … but then, neither had the Asali in Bradfin that she'd fought.

The Asali feigned a strike at Elinta's thigh, but she jumped back, her thoughts still whirling even as she tried to concentrate. She thought of all the research she'd done on the senses only weeks ago. Mazen. Mazen, who moved with superior grace and speed to all the other Asali she'd met and fought, was using more dragon senses than she'd thought.

Elinta ducked a swipe from the Asali's blade, forcing her mind back to herself and thankful for her dragonsight giving her that precious extra half a second. She struck out with her own sword as she came back up. The man whirled away and Elinta forced herself forward, putting distance between them and her brother. This man might not be Mazen, but he was still a very skilled fighter. But as she twisted aside, Elinta caught a glimpse of Blaine following them, looking for an opening to help.

"Stay back, Blaine," she called. Elinta leapt forward, knowing her best chance was to get in close to the man, just as she'd seen Ford do earlier.

But as a large shadow drifted over them, the Asali pulled back and darted into a side alley before she'd even processed what had happened. Elinta's sword lowered in surprise, and she glanced up to see what was blocking the sun. And saw a maroon dragon with a small, luminous figure on his back. Smoke drifted over them.

"Vaherin," Elinta whispered. Though it was her first time seeing the dragon with her own eyes, his large bulk was familiar to her. He had an extra ten or so feet on him than Zhayra, and the spines on his head and cheekbones were longer, their tips glinting in the mid-day sun. He looked exactly as he had the day Mazen had killed the dragon queen.

Zhayra's stomach plummeted, but fire rose in her chest. Beside her, Blaine's eyes widened at the sight and his face paled, but Elinta's brother moved closer to her rather than moving away.

Mazen's lean body was clad in his scale armour, the three stolen blue dragon scales in an arc across his chest standing out against the maroon surrounding them. Elinta concentrated on Mazen's face, using the dragonsight to bring it into focus. She'd forgotten how unnerving his maroon eyes were, coupled with his white dragon-like pupils. His mouth was moving.

She narrowed her field of view so that all she saw was his mouth, his lips moving in soundless speech, and pulled the words into focus.

"Elinta Ferran," he said, his voice as beautiful and cold as she remembered. "Can you hear me?"

"Yes," she said, dimly aware she'd just accessed the strength of Zhayra's ears for the first time.

"What?" Blaine said, but she held out a hand to quiet him.

"I didn't expect you so soon, but I'm glad you're here."

"Why are you doing this?" she asked, looking both at him and at Vaherin. Mazen's black hair was unusually messy, windswept from flying through the air and from the wind Vaherin's large wings kicked up.

Zhayra grunted from beside her.

"Ah, yes," Mazen sneered, "Zhayra. Did you really think you could hide from me, *tarsi*?"

Elinta flinched at the familiar word though now it was being used in the proper context. Zhayra growled deep in her throat, but Elinta felt the fear clogging it. This was the man who'd killed her mother, who'd attacked her bonded.

Elinta fought the urge to cross to her and comfort her. Instead, she drew Mazen's focus back to her. Vaherin's amber eyes were boring into her.

"It *was* a diversion?"

Mazen laughed, the sound raising goosebumps on her skin. His maroon eyes shined. "Yes," he said simply. "Though I'd been hopeful you wouldn't survive. But then, this isn't the first time you've survived something you shouldn't have, is it?"

Elinta's hand trailed to the scar at her hip, remembering the poison that had spread through her body.

Mazen smirked, then looked off to his side, finding Tamir. "I should thank you for bringing my old friend too," he said, amusement in his voice. "This is quite the reunion."

"Leave him alone," Elinta growled. How could he be so candid? So uncaring? Tamir hadn't shared any of his memories of Mazen, but she knew they'd been close once.

A smile twisted Mazen's lips and without another word, Vaherin pulled away.

"Why are you doing this?" she shouted after them.

Mazen's reply was a dark chuckle. "Love the armour by the way, Elinta, but it won't save you."

The two rose back through the air and joined the two dragons hovering above the city.

"That's the man who tried to kill you?" Blaine's voice was rough with anger.

"Yes."

It was as though Elinta's body thawed as Mazen and Vaherin moved away, then froze again as she watched another dragon, and another, and then two more join them. Two green, a yellow, and a maroon, they all joined Vaherin, Mazen, and the two blues hovering over the city. Seven dragons. There were seven dragons over Nevira. Her stomach plummeted.

"Impossible," Blaine whispered, snapping Elinta back to herself.

She spun around, panic building in her chest.

"You should go to Tamir," she said. Nowhere in the city would be safe with so many dragons flying over it, but anywhere would be safer than with her.

"Or Lorrin," she said, looking down to where he and Niles fought another group of Asali, the generals still helping. "You'd be safer with them. Just tell them who you are. They won't turn you away."

"No," Blaine said, "I'm not leaving you. I didn't do anything for you by the lake. I won't do that again."

"Blaine," she began, but stopped. Her brother's face was determined. He wasn't going to leave her. "Stay close," she said. She switched off her dragonhearing.

He gave a small smile and nodded, pushing his sweaty blond hair back from his face. But another breath of the smoky air sent him coughing.

Whatever reprieve Mazen's presence had given them was over now, and the Asali Elinta had been fighting before re-emerged, another hot on his heels.

"Stay close to Zhayra," she amended, sprinting forward to meet the Asali before Blaine could argue. She didn't think he moved, but as long as he didn't follow her, he'd be OK. Mazen had been pushed from her thoughts. As her weapon clashed with the older of the two Asali, she spun out to block the path of the other. Blaine was all there was in her mind now. She had to protect him.

Elinta fought like she'd never fought before, abandoning her earlier tactic of sticking close. She ducked, whirled, stabbed, and kicked, always stopping the Asali from moving forward but never gaining ground herself. A cut opened on her forearm, a gash on her thigh, but still she fought. Their blades scraped across the armour protecting her body, but it held.

Her breaths came in deep gasps. The smoke was thickening at ground level now, cutting at her throat and making her eyes water, but she couldn't stop. Zhayra would try to protect Blaine, but she had limited space. She wouldn't be able to move. She'd have to rely on her deadly fire rather than tooth and claw, and that would destroy even more of the city. And maybe it wouldn't be enough to match the Asali's speed.

"Some of the dragons are moving away!" Blaine called.

Elinta ducked a wicked slash from the older Asali and spun away, letting her own blade slice through the air as she did.

"What?" Elinta puffed, not daring to take her eyes from her opponents.

"Three of them are leaving," Blaine called, but then he made a strangled sound. Elinta didn't need to ask him why as the rush of several large wings sounded through the air, close to the city. The others weren't just staying, they were returning. The roar of fire slammed into her ears, and the screams within the city doubled. A gust of wind pushed smoke down on them, sending Elinta into a coughing fit.

A flash of pain across her thigh, just above her knee, forced Elinta to focus on the fight in front of her and not the one above and the feeling of helplessness it raised in her. She blinked the water from her eyes and sucked in a gulp of fresh air as the smoke cleared for a moment. She dove back into the fight.

Grunting, Elinta feigned a strike at the younger Asali's chest, before sidestepping and bringing the weapon down across the other one's back. He cried out in pain but whipped around, his weapon coming down upon her. Elinta jumped forward within his reach and plunged her weapon into his abdomen. Her breath caught in her throat as he fell to the ground, but a strange sense of relief hit her when she heard his moans of pain. He was still alive.

The swing of a blade came from behind her and the beat of wings upon the air above her. As she twisted toward the sword, Elinta felt a surge of panic from Zhayra, echoed in the roar she gave. Blaine cried out in warning, moving in the corner of her eye. Irritation rose in her at his desire to help putting him in danger from her own blade. Then her sword met that of the remaining Asali with a mighty clash. She shoved the man away and then advanced, twisting and ducking, stabbing and striking, desperately trying to end the fight before all her energy was gone. Before Blaine got in the way. When the man tried circling her, Elinta followed and glimpsed a figure lying still on the ground.

"Blaine?" she choked, her sword dropping an inch. A flash of steel flew past within a centimetre of her eye. Fire soared in her chest, and she slammed her sword into the Asali's. His eyes widened in surprise. Elinta advanced, seeing nothing but red and her brother lying on the cold stone beside her. She had to get to him. Help him. Her body felt alive. It was like she was feeling it, experiencing it, for the first time. She didn't even need to look to know where every part of her was. She didn't worry about her balance. She didn't even think. The Asali retreated, but Elinta followed, her weapon nothing more than a blur to her eyes, until she brought it down with enough force to cleave the sword of her enemy, whipped her blade up and drove the hilt into his temple. Elinta didn't see his body crumple to the ground.

Her knees slammed into the stone road as she skidded to a halt beside her brother. "Blaine!"

The hilt of a knife protruded from his chest, straight through his armour, and she couldn't work out how it had gotten there, what it was doing in her brother. He'd been behind her. Away from the Asali she'd fought. The feeling drained from her body.

"Blaine?" She pressed her hand to his cheek, searching his hazel eyes. Blood poured from his mouth. Tears blurred her vision and ran down her cheeks.

"Blaine," she repeated. Elinta's other hand trailed to the knife, but her eyes were fixed on his face. "Something's wrong. Something's wrong." She didn't realise she was mumbling the words out loud. She couldn't hear anything above the pounding of her heart and her ragged breaths in her ears. The smoke was growing thick in the air around her again. Dimly, she knew she was coughing.

"Tamir!" Elinta screamed, her tears dripping onto her brother's face. She fumbled for her satchel, but her hands grasped at empty air.

"No," she gasped. Her satchel … she'd left it hanging from the saddle of her horse. The one still hours away with her father. She cried out in frustration, but it was OK because she could use something else, she could. If she could get her armour off, she could use the shirt under her jerkin ... or she could—she could use some of the clothing from the Asali she'd knocked out! Just until Tamir could get to them. Just until he could heal Blaine.

"Tamir!" she screamed again, her voice tearing her raw throat. Where was he? When had she last seen him? "Tam—" the word died in her throat. Because it was in looking back down at her brother that Elinta finally noticed. His chest wasn't moving. Her hand went numbly to his face.

"No, no! Blaine." She slapped his cheek in time with the words. "Blaine! No, no, no, no."

His eyes stared unseeingly at the sky.

CHAPTER TWENTY-FOUR

E LINTA'S HAND STILL CLASPED the hilt of the blade in Blaine's chest. The blade in his heart. A sob rose from deep in her chest, but her lungs constricted against the smoke-laden air. She couldn't breathe properly, taking deep gasps around the sobs, desperately trying to force some oxygen into her body. But all it did was send her coughing again. Zhayra's low keen echoed through the air, a testament to their bond.

"Touching," a cold voice said from above her. The shakes wracking Elinta's body stopped. She slowly looked up.

"Mazen," she choked. Realisation hit her, and she looked down at the blade still gripped in her hand. A familiar hilt, belonging to a dagger made of *illayas*. Her body began to shake again, but not with sorrow. In the back of her mind, she noticed he was speaking as though he stood beside her, not even raising his voice. She'd unconsciously turned on her dragonhearing again.

Mazen smiled, looking down on her and the body of her only brother. "It wasn't meant for him," he said, a tinge of disappointment in his smooth voice.

Vaherin grunted.

"It was the perfect throw. You had no idea it was coming, but he did." Mazen's beautiful face darkened. "His death is in vain, be assured of that."

Wind assaulted her as Vaherin rose back into the sky. Red clouded Elinta's vision. She grabbed her blade, which had lain discarded beside her, and sprinted to Zhayra.

"Elinta!" Lorrin's voice rose above the clamour, but she ignored it. She ignored them all.

"Let's go!" she yelled, bounding up onto Zhayra's back and clipping herself in. She shoved her sword into its scabbard.

With a furious roar, Zhayra shot into the sky. Wind pummelled her. The yells of their friends echoed after them, but Elinta refused to look down at Lorrin and Niles who she knew, instinctively, had been moving, fighting, toward her as she'd cradled her dead brother.

Elinta pressed herself flat against Zhayra's scales, letting the air rush over the dragon unimpeded, helping her move faster than she ever had before with a passenger.

They were hot on Vaherin's heels. The resentment and anger in Elinta and Zhayra were perfectly matched. They'd both lost someone to Mazen. And they were both going to stop it from happening to anyone ever again. Mazen had to be stopped.

They rose higher and higher into the sky, and away from the city. The air was thick with smoke, and it caught in Elinta's throat and lungs, but still they flew on.

Finally, when the air had cleared. Vaherin and Mazen swung around to face them. Mazen easily pushed his feet under him, balancing perfectly, impossibly, on the dragon's back.

Zhayra continued. In her anger, Elinta drew her sword.

Mazen laughed. "Come, Elinta," he said, not drawing his own weapon but spreading his arms open wide. "We both know ordinary weapons are no use to us now."

Zhayra didn't stop and Mazen sighed in the second before they met in the air. They slammed into Vaherin, and Elinta struck blindly and viciously at Mazen, but he deflected her weapon with an almost careless flick of his own steel sword. She hadn't even seen him draw it, or the moment he'd sat down again.

"You can't hurt me, Elinta."

"I'm prepared to test the limits of steel," she spat.

Zhayra grumbled her agreement. Elinta's weapon may have been useless against Mazen's armour, but Zhayra's claws were not.

Vaherin pulled back so his head was level with Zhayra's and bared his teeth, a vicious growl slipping through, but he didn't attack.

"No doubt," Mazen said, ignoring the dragons, his eyes growing unfocused. "Yet, I think your friends would prefer to see you one last time before you die. They're scared for you, especially your prince."

Elinta frowned. "Don't lie," she said. Even if what he said was true, there was no way he could see or hear her friends now. The distance between them was too great.

"Tamir fights the same as he always did," Mazen said, his eyes still unfocused. "I'm surprised he came, but then he was always interested in humans. Even that one my grandmother apparently took in."

Elinta looked back at the city. Sure enough, she couldn't see Lorrin, Niles, or Tamir. Miniscule figures ran through the city, but they were unknown, no more than a vague shape in a toy city.

"How do you—" she said, then stopped as her eyes landed on a green dragon hovering over the city. Scanning the city. *No,* she thought, *that's not possible.*

He laughed. "They're planning something stupid, so I'll make this quick." Mazen's strange eyes cleared, and he smirked at her. "I'm ready to call it a day. You may have noticed some of our friends have left." He gestured in the direction the three dragons had gone, then fixed his eyes on Zhayra. "A mere stumbling block, something that will soon be corrected, but they are right. The fighting is done for today. "So," Mazen said, looking back at Elinta, "as we've already discussed, there is no use to us fighting now, not with my dragon armour and your *illayas*. A gift from Tamir, no doubt," he added. "So, I'll make this easy for you, Elinta Ferran. You can make all this stop. No one else has to die. We can leave it at your dear brother. All you have to do is give yourself up."

"What?"

Zhayra growled.

"I want you to pass this on to your king so he sees how merciful I can be, and so you can see how little he will care for your life now he knows what you are. I know you need some time to work out how valuable your friends really are to you, so you have until the sun falls tomorrow to hand yourselves over. Both of you. If you don't, I promise everyone you love will die. If only one of you comes, everyone will die."

Elinta growled and Zhayra's maw shot toward Mazen.

With more speed than Elinta would have thought possible for the large dragon, Vaherin dodged above them, clipping Elinta's armour with a claw as they passed under him. Elinta's body rocked backward and to the side, her seat slipping. She hadn't strapped in her legs in her haste to chase Mazen. The ground seemed to open up under her. Gasping, she grabbed the harness at her belt.

"Enough!" Mazen called over Vaherin's low growl.

Elinta struggled to righten her seat, dragging her body back into place as she hauled on the harness.

Zhayra stopped, worry piercing her anger. Elinta patted the dragon's neck to let her know she was OK. But Vaherin's attack had gotten through to her. She couldn't fight the dragon or Mazen with her steel sword, and she couldn't leave Zhayra to face the dragon alone. Mazen was right. The battle was done for the day.

"Why are you doing this?" she asked through gritted teeth.

"Surely you know." Mazen cocked his head, brow furrowed. "I'm going to save them." He gestured at the dragons below them, one still hovering over the city while the others swooped in low, breathing their fire down into the streets. "The Eggslaying will never happen again. Not when I'm done with your people. Make sure you tell them that. But *how* this happens is up to you."

"This is wrong!" Elinta shook her head. What was he going to do to her people? "But what about Zhayra? You're not keeping her safe, either."

Mazen's cold maroon eyes studied her, making his handsome features seem harsh. She didn't think he was going to respond but, finally, he did. "She's in my way."

The words hung in the air between them.

"My offer still stands, as does my mercy," Mazen said. "See you tomorrow, Elinta."

Vaherin sent a burst of hot smoke over them, blurring Elinta's eyes and sending her into another coughing fit. When the smoke cleared, they were nothing but a speck in the north-west. It was Mazen's last message to her. She was to meet him at the fortress in Bradfin.

Elinta held Zhayra's harness with a white-knuckle grip, staring after Mazen, warring within herself. Despite knowing she couldn't hurt him, the urge to chase him was overwhelming.

Zhayra keened. And her worry grew. And it was only this that drew Elinta back to herself.

"I know," she said. Turning in her seat, she looked back at the smoking city.

The three remaining dragons were pulling away. If Mazen held true to his word, any lingering Asali were sure to be vacating the city as well, scurrying to gain distance between themselves and the Neviran soldiers before they realised what was happening. *Mercy,* Mazen had said. This had all been a show of power, nothing more.

A gust of wind played across Elinta's face, caressing the long dry tears on her cheeks. No more were falling now. A strange numbness was settling over her as her anger drained away.

She didn't know how long they hung in the sky before enough of her mind came back to her. "We should go back to the city," she said, her voice sounding dead to her own ears.

Zhayra grunted, and began the descent back to Nevira, moving much slower than she had when they'd left.

Zhayra landed where they had earlier that day—right in front of the palace—where Lorrin and Niles were waiting for them. General Sonnen and General Nash were also there.

Elinta's eyes were only for her brother. They'd covered him while she'd been chasing Mazen, but it didn't stop her from remembering his sightless eyes and the dagger in his chest. And the blood. His blood had now seeped across the ground, visible even beyond the spread of his covering. She was coated in it too, her blue armour stained red.

"Elinta," Lorrin stumbled forward, his eyes heavy. His arms pulled her into him, but the warmth of his body couldn't pierce the coldness in hers. In some detached part of her mind, she was glad to see him, but that part couldn't be reconciled with the rest of her. When he leant back, his hand went to her cheek.

"Your eyes …" he whispered.

"They're ovular," she said tonelessly, remembering how they'd changed two nights ago.

"No," Lorrin said. "They're white."

CHAPTER
TWENTY-FIVE

T HE WHITE PALACE WAS almost unrecognisable. Smoke continued billowing from within, out of the windows and through the front door. Large pieces of scorched white stone littered the courtyard.

Around her, people moved to collect the bodies of the fallen and injured. Vaguely, Elinta recognised Ford helping a man bleeding from his head. But the relief she felt at the sight of him seemed inconsequential. She stumbled away from Lorrin, who'd opened his mouth to ask her something, and Niles, dropping to her knees beside the body of her brother.

It was then that a thought did manage to penetrate her mind. What was she going to tell her father? Her throat clogged, and she had to look away from Blaine's covered face.

"Tamir!" She jumped to her feet and hurried over as the Asali stumbled onto the main road. Blood trickled from a gash on his forehead and his hand was pressed to a wound at his side.

"I am fine, *tarsi*," he said, but his eyes were unfocused.

Elinta shoved her body under his arm.

"Can't you heal yourself?" she asked, thinking of another reason why it was pointless to fight Mazen.

Tamir shook his head, wincing at the movement.

"What?" Elinta gasped, helping him sit with his back against a wall. She shoved the loose hair back from her face.

"We can't heal ourselves, only others."

"You—you can't heal," she stuttered. *Mazen* couldn't heal.

"I'll get a healer," Niles called.

Elinta pulled Tamir's hand away from his side, and blood trickled from the wound. She pushed his hand back into place.

"You'll be OK," she said.

Tamir's eyes locked with hers. "Help me to him, *tarsi*."

Elinta stared at him. Could he ... could he still help her brother?

Tamir's eyes softened, and he shook his head at the thought that must have so clearly played across her face. Swallowing the lump in her throat, and unsure what he planned to do, she pushed her shoulder under Tamir's arm again and helped him stumble toward her brother.

Tamir slipped to the ground beside him and placed his hand where Blaine's forehead would be under the covering. "*Zetayn eyan pepyan eka ayn air kli nalliyan.*"

The words echoed within her head, drawing to her the last, and first, time she'd heard them. When Mazen had gloated that he'd won their fight after poisoning her and disappeared into the night, he'd said them to her. She knew what those words meant now, and their significance seemed clear. *May your light return to the sun.* It was a death blessing.

"Thank you," Elinta said, her voice wobbling.

The same healer who had treated Elinta after that very fight with Mazen the night of the Eggslaying dropped into a crouch beside her.

"Let me see," he said to Tamir, pushing his glasses further up his nose.

Elinta stood back, giving them some space.

Lorrin touched her arm. "Let's get you seen to."

"No," she said. Not even feeling the cuts littered across her arms and legs. "Help those who need it."

"You need it."

"So do you," she said, noticing the blood on his thigh for the first time. Had he been limping? She looked at him properly. His armour protected his torso and neck, but his lower arms and his legs were exposed. But there didn't seem to be any major wounds.

"I'll get seen to once you do." He glanced behind him. "Wait here. I need to speak with the generals quickly." He hesitated, reaching out to touch her cheek again before hurrying away.

Elinta numbly watched him go. Niles, a purple bruise forming around his left eye, was already talking with his father and Lorrin's aunt, but he sent her worried glances every few seconds. She couldn't summon even a ghost of a smile to tell him she was OK. Because it would have been a lie. Blaine was lying dead beside her. She wondered at what point the boys had realised who he was. Who he'd *been.*

Arms hanging limply by her side, Elinta slowly became aware of the stares of countless eyes. Everywhere she turned were people peering at her from doorways, between buildings or even in the open streets. Soldiers and civilians alike fixed her with their gazes, some curious, some full of hatred. She shifted uncomfortably and turned to Zhayra, who had eyes only for her.

She turned as footsteps sounded behind her.

"Elinta? There's going to be a meeting at Ford's," Lorrin said, his gaze sweeping over the palace. "It starts in an hour."

She nodded but seized with an overwhelming desire to leave, she turned away, seeing nothing but Zhayra, but still feeling the eyes of the city on her.

"El?" Lorrin followed her to Zhayra's side.

Elinta didn't respond, the numbness overtaking her again.

"Elinta?"

She clambered onto Zhayra, who nudged Lorrin affectionately.

Lorrin stroked her muzzle. "I'm glad you're OK too," he said to the dragon. "Where are you going?"

Elinta shrugged, feeling a tinge of guilt at the way she was treating him as she tied down her legs. But she couldn't stand to be in the city anymore.

"I'll be back for the meeting," she said. And Zhayra shot into the air.

They floated through the air currents for most of that hour. Elinta cried, her face buried into Zhayra's neck, her tears falling onto the dragon's scales and drying in the wind.

She didn't speak, but she knew Zhayra understood, she understood in more ways than one, and in ways that no one else could. The dragon keened softly, a long mournful sound that drifted down over the ruined city, before she took them further away.

Elinta cried until her throat hurt and the tears dried up. Then she stared out over the landscape stretching away below them. Smoke from the city continued to rise into the sky from her left, but the rest of the world seemed oblivious to all that had happened. It didn't know about Blaine.

She looked at her bloodied hands and thought of her brother, of his insistence on joining her in the city and in the battle. And mostly, she thought of his dream to set up a horse business in Culmar. She'd once wondered whether he'd had to give up that dream because of her when she'd fled Kethmere with a dragon. Now she knew for certain he would never see that dream. He would never dream again.

A small sob escaped her tight throat.

Her brother. Her *brother* was gone.

Their words echoed in her ears. *You'd be the best trainer in Culmar.*

I will be. When this is over, I'm going, came her brother's response.

"Blaine," she whispered. An ache settled in her chest, a longing like she'd never had before, to have just been able to hold him as he'd died. To have spoken to him one last time. But if meaning he hadn't suffered meant she didn't get closure, then she would live with it.

Wiping her face, she pushed herself upright. It was nearly time to head back to the city and face Lorrin's parents, but there was one more thing she needed to do.

"Zhayra," she called, "take me to him."

They landed in her father's campsite, startling him to his feet. Her father took one look at her face and knew.

"You disgust me," he said, his face crumpling.

Elinta kept her own blank. He was talking about her eyes, she knew, lashing out in his pain. And she deserved it.

He stood, grabbing the reins of the horses he must have saddled in the hope of his son returning to him. "I'm going to Culmar," he said. "Don't come looking for me. I have no children now."

He threw her satchel and bag to the ground at her feet, swung up into the saddle of a bay mare, and pushed her straight into a canter. Elinta and Zhayra were left in the dust of his pain. But Elinta had no more tears to shed.

Zhayra had to drop her by the palace since there was no room for the dragon to land anywhere closer to Ford's. The sight of her sent people scurrying away again.

"I'll see you after," she told the dragon after tying her bag to the harness. Zhayra grunted, and as she flew away, Elinta's eyes grew heavy, and her ears popped.

She lingered a moment in front of the palace, but her eyes were unable to look at the place where her brother had fallen. The area was clear of bodies now. Dimly, Elinta realised that there had been no bodies from the Asali she'd fought earlier. They must have lived and escaped when Mazen called them off, because there'd been no sign of them when she'd returned. She filed the knowledge away for later. It would have cheered her to know she hadn't taken any lives if she could have felt anything.

The walk to Ford's only took her ten minutes, but each one weighed on her and seemed to stretch into eternity. Her body was stiff from the fight. Her skin and the material clothes under her armour taut with dried blood. It made the walk even harder. But she was grateful that her body hadn't caught up to the pain of her wounds yet. Why the royals had chosen to meet at the historian's place, Elinta had no idea, but she was glad to be walking somewhere at least partially familiar to her.

If being with Zhayra hadn't already marked her as different, as a traitor, her eyes did that all by themselves. All around her, people gave Elinta a wide berth. Though they didn't know about the *Zearla lurai,* they understood enough. She glimpsed her reflection in the window of a small bakery and found slitted pupils and white irises staring back at her from a dirty and bloodied face.

Elinta wiped at her cheeks, trying to smudge the tracks that ran along them from her long-dried tears as her feet carried her ever closer to Ford's.

She'd only been there once, but it was enough for her feet to remember the way even if she wasn't consciously thinking about it. She couldn't concentrate with the smoke clogging the air and the stares, the ever-present stares, of those around her. The city had never seemed so busy and yet so lonely. The damage in this part of the city wasn't as severe as by the palace, and maybe that was why the royals had chosen to meet at Ford's. Most of the buildings were intact though the cobbled streets were scorched with fire in places. It would be easier to defend than an area surrounded by rubble.

The presence of soldiers told Elinta that she was drawing close to the historian's place. They were stationed along the street she walked on and on several of the side streets. When Ford's place came into view, soldiers surrounded it, the red lapels at their shoulders marking them as palace guards.

A stab of guilt hit her. Were Lorrin's parents OK? She hadn't even spared King Aldon and Queen Mira a thought. She'd hardly even thought about Niles and Lorrin beyond knowing they were alive.

The soldiers didn't challenge her as she passed, but their hands seemed to tighten on their weapons. Elinta wouldn't have fought them if they'd tried. She was too exhausted. Her wounds had stopped bleeding while she'd been flying with Zhayra, but she still couldn't register the pain even after the walk here. It was a wonder she was registering anything. Taking a steadying breath, Elinta stepped into Ford's home, not knowing what she'd find.

King Aldon and Queen Mira stood over the table in the main room with General Nash, General Sonnen, and Shae around them, looking very cramped in Ford's small home. It was much the way she remembered it, with bookshelves stacked to the ceiling with books and scrolls lining the walls.

Lorrin, Niles, and Tamir were also there. The Asali's eyes were more focused now, but he was the only one among them seated. His glowing face was pale. Ford stood next to him, as calm as ever, though his brown eyes softened when he saw her. They'd all changed out of their armour or dirty clothes into something fresh. Elinta looked down at her own. It was covered in Blaine's blood. Just as she knew her face was. Just as her hands were.

Elinta stepped forward, stopping by the table and opposite to the king and queen. They seemed to have missed the action in the streets, looking perfectly collected and clean. Though, on a closer look, there was a smudge of dirt on the king's neck, likely from their flight from the burning palace.

"Elinta," Queen Mira said, her face perfectly hiding whatever she felt at the sight of a *Zearla lurai*. "We're sorry for your loss."

"Thank you," Elinta said, her voice sounding empty in her ears and a little strained from all the smoke she'd inhaled.

Shae made an unimpressed sound but didn't speak.

Ford moved from his place beside Tamir, ducking over to the small sink tucked in the corner before crossing to Elinta's side. He held out a wet cloth in his hands.

"Thank you," Elinta whispered, taking the cloth. She wiped her face with it, shocked at how much dirt and blood came away on the white fabric. There wasn't even any point in using it for the blood on her hands when she'd finished with her face. Elinta dropped the filthy cloth onto the table.

"Now, I think it's time that you and my son told us everything," King Aldon said, his tone even but his body rigid. "It's clear there is more happening than what we believed."

Elinta cocked her head, glad that in this moment she was numb. Fearless. "I am *Zearla lurai*: bonded to a dragon. Lorrin saw that Zhayra, the dragon, is not like what we have all been told to believe and wanted to help us."

Though her words were forward, her voice was toneless. They could not be taken as meaning to cause offense, but they also weren't entirely innocent. She didn't care. What use was there in being delicate now?

King Aldon's face remained neutral, but his hands twitched.

"Prince Mazen Elliar did come to kill Lorrin the night of the Eggslaying." She looked around the group, taking in the cut across General Nash's brow and the bruise blossoming on General Sonnen's cheek. Her healer eyes also noted the way Niles's father held his arm stiffly by his side. Shae was noticeably unharmed.

"But he changed his mind when he saw me," she continued, looking back at the king and queen. "He wants to kill me and Zhayra more than he wants to kill your son."

"Why?" Shae said sharply, as though she'd clearly done something to make Mazen feel this way.

She shrugged though she knew it had to have something to do with the murder of the dragon queen, Zhayra's witness to it, and her being the heir.

"I guess he sees us as a threat."

"Anything more to add?" King Aldon said, looking at his son.

"No," Lorrin said, his back straight. "Just that I don't regret a second of it."

"You all knew?" the king said, looking at Niles and Tamir as well. They both nodded.

Elinta's eyes flicked to General Sonnen. He seemed unsurprised by the revelation that his son was knowingly friends with a kin of the dragons.

"What did Mazen say to you today?" King Aldon said, fixing her with his blue eyes. There was an order in his voice. She wasn't sure which instance he was talking about. She'd spoken a few times with Mazen, but there was only one that he needed to know about.

"He's offered you mercy in the war he intends to wage."

Lorrin's head whipped around in surprise.

"What?" Niles said. But no one in the room even seemed to question if Mazen was capable of bringing war to them. Not even Shae. He'd proved it today.

"In exchange for me and Zhayra, he'll let you all live."

Eight voices rose at once, clambering for attention. Elinta let them, studying each of the people in the room. The king and queen were talking in low voices to one another. Shae's voice rose louder than everyone else's, the woman practically spitting in her fervent hatred of Elinta and in agreement with Mazen's offer. General Sonnen and General Nash, though, seemed to be arguing against her. Lorrin, Niles, and Tamir were speaking too, as much to each other as to the king and queen and even the advisors. Ford was the only one that remained silent. His eyes were locked on her, his face thoughtful. He cocked an eyebrow when she looked at him. She glanced away, unable to acknowledge his silent question.

"Enough," King Aldon said. The voices slowly diminished until the house was silent. "I can see no reason why Mazen would honour this. As you've said, Elinta, he still wishes to kill Lorrin."

"But why should he? Handing over the girl might placate him enough that he abandons that idea, as he already seems to have done," Shae said, looking between the king and queen.

Lorrin's voice was hard with anger when he responded. "We're not handing her over."

Shae laughed bitterly. "The girl is nothing but trouble. You clearly don't know what's good for you, prince."

Lorrin opened his mouth to respond, his eyes flashing, but someone cut across him. General Nash's voice was like a whip.

"Watch your tongue, Shae."

"The king's right," General Sonnen grunted. "We have no guarantee Mazen would uphold any agreement we might make. Not that we would," he added, looking at Elinta.

"What do we care for a dragon and a traitor?" Shae said, her eyes bulging. "If it gives us a chance, it's worth it!"

"No, it's not. He said we could live, but not what the conditions of our lives would be." King Aldon frowned and some of his reluctance slipped into his voice. "As it stands, the dragon Elinta rides is the only one willing to fight *against* Mazen. They might be our only chance of fighting back. Perhaps this is why he wants them."

Elinta didn't respond, letting them believe the king's idea, too. But they were all wrong, thinking this was Mazen's motivation. She didn't stand a chance against him, especially if she was right about the other dragons. But that fear couldn't stamp out the small hope niggling at her, the hope that Mazen could be defeated. If she could keep him away from other Asali, he couldn't be healed. She could stop him. Lock him up.

Shae laughed at the king, shaking her head, but was silenced by the look he gave her.

Lorrin glanced at his father. "You believe what she said about the dragons?"

King Aldon caught his eye. "That's a discussion for another time. But ... I saw the white dragon's reaction to Elinta's brother's death. Whether that is simply because of this bond or a deeper awareness, I don't know, but there is something *more* about it. Regardless, this is the only way."

Lorrin nodded his acceptance, but there was hope sparkling in his eyes, barely contained.

"This is ridiculous!" Shae said.

Elinta decided to play along, her thoughts so far ahead of this group. Mazen was all there was. Mazen and helping them find a way to stop him.

"You need me," she said, staring at the woman. "Whether you like it or not. You. Need. Me."

Then she twisted on her heel and left. She'd heard all she needed to. Done with politics and done with people, she wound back through the city to the one place she knew no one would be.

The palace garden.

CHAPTER
TWENTY-SIX

L ORRIN FOUND HER THERE. It had been late afternoon
when she'd left Ford's place, and now dusk was in the air.
Lorrin looked as exhausted as she felt.

"I wasn't sure where you'd gone," he said, stiffly lowering himself to sit beside her.

She was in the centre of the gardens, having finally found some
semblance of peace among the flowers.

"It was the only place to go," she said. The air had begun to
clear of smoke though a thin wisp still trailed into the air from
the building, the wind kept it away from the gardens.

"I, uh, I found this," he said, drawing her attention away from the flowers beside her. He held out a long blue dagger. Elinta automatically took it from his hands. It shined in the low light, no longer coated in Blaine's blood.

"It's up to you what you do with it."

Revulsion rose in her chest. Both wanting to keep it and destroy it; she shoved the weapon into her healer satchel on the ground beside her. The satchel was almost empty now, its contents used to clean and cover the wounds along her arms and legs. Her *illayas* greaves were beside it.

"Can you," she paused, "can you help me take this off?" She was still in the rest of her armour. Still wearing Blaine's blood.

"Of course," he said softly.

Lorrin scooted behind her and undid the clips that held the armour in place. They were in an awkward spot, and though she thought she could reach them, Elinta didn't have it in her to try, especially now that her wounds had begun to sting.

The clips merely loosened the armour rather than separating it into two pieces, and Lorrin lifted it over her head, and placed it on the ground with her greaves. Battle had made the sparkling armour from this morning almost unrecognisable: with blood covering the front and a large scratch across the shoulder from Vaherin's claw.

"Tamir said he made this for you."

"Yes," Elinta said, staring at her reflection in the metal. At her slitted, white eyes.

Lorrin reached out and tipped her chin up. "I'm sorry."

Elinta hadn't thought there were any more tears in her, but her eyes watered.

"El." His thumb stroked her cheek. She knew it would come away dirty. She was filthy still, despite her earlier efforts to clean her face at Ford's.

Pulling back, she averted her eyes, unable to look at Lorrin's unbridled emotions.

"Is your leg OK?" she asked.

"It's a little sore," he said, lowering his hand, but his voice remained soft. "Tamir offered to fix it, but he needs to rest."

"And Niles?" She still hadn't spoken to him yet. She'd hardly even seen him.

"The same as ever." He grinned, but it faded. "He's worried about you, though."

Elinta looked away, but his hand found hers.

"None of this is your fault."

When she didn't respond, he said, "You saw your father, didn't you?"

Elinta glanced at him in surprise, but he saw the answer in her face.

"It doesn't matter what he said. No matter what you think," Lorrin said, "none of this is on you."

It felt good to hear, but she wasn't sure she agreed. She never should have let Blaine come with her to the city when they knew only something desperately wrong could have caused the smoke she'd seen. At the same time, she knew she never could have stopped him, but the thought didn't ease her pain or guilt.

"I know why Mazen is after Zhayra," Elinta said, the words tumbling out of her before she could stop to consider them.

Lorrin's brow furrowed in confusion. "What do you mean?"

"She's the queen."

"What?" All the breath seemed to rush from him. "The queen?"

"Well, her mother was," Elinta corrected, the words still gushing out of her. "He killed her, Lorrin. And Zhayra saw, and now he wants to kill her too."

"Does anyone else know?"

"No." She shook her head. "I didn't know who to tell. No one can know who she is; she'd be in even more danger."

Lorrin ran a hand through his hair.

"Why did he kill her mother?" Lorrin said, voicing the one question that had been bouncing around her mind since she'd first seen the memory. It had only redoubled since Mazen told her Zhayra was in his way.

"I don't know," she said, frustrated. "But Vaherin was hiding something from them that day. I think they were planning it."

"Where's Zhayra now?"

"In the woods." She'd checked on the dragon earlier, looking through her eyes to see where she was. She'd go to her soon—when she was ready.

Lorrin grimaced. "It's probably best she's not alone if she returns to the city."

"I know," Elinta whispered.

While the royals had tentatively agreed to Elinta and Zhayra staying, it didn't mean that it was safe for either of them. The rest of the city, people who had just been attacked by dragons, hadn't learnt all that she had. They didn't know that the dragons weren't vicious animals, even if that was how they'd appeared today.

Lorrin's eyes trailed to her necklace. "It's beautiful," he said. "Where—"

There was a knock on the door to the gardens, which hung ajar off one hinge.

Niles slipped through the gap. The bruise around his eye had darkened and swelled since she'd last seen him. "Tamir's resting," he said, sitting beside them. He didn't comment on Lorrin's hand still resting on top of hers.

"Promise you're not going to do anything stupid?" Niles said, fixing her with a hard look.

"What? Why?" Elinta asked, startled.

"I don't want you running off to that whacko thinking you're helping us all."

Elinta almost laughed at the idea of Mazen being 'that whacko.' Almost.

"I won't," she said firmly. There was no point to it. Maybe if Mazen would really hold to his promise, she'd consider giving herself up, but not Zhayra. Never Zhayra. But as it was, there was no need to decide. Mazen would return whether she went to him or not. His end game went beyond the two of them.

Niles stared at her for a long moment. "Good," he said, finally satisfied. "Now give me a hug."

He pulled her into him, and she buried her face in his shoulder. When she looked up, Lorrin was watching her with tender eyes. Her hand was still in his. Absurdly, it made a spark of warmth rise in her cold chest.

"I told him all about you," Elinta found herself saying; the words came out muffled against Niles's shirt.

He pulled back. "Really?"

"And you, Lorrin."

The prince grinned.

"He was excited to meet you."

Elinta told them all about her brother. How he'd always looked out for her, how he'd kept their mother's memory alive even when their father wouldn't or couldn't. She told them about his love for horses and his dream of going to Culmar. When she described how he'd introduced himself to Zhayra, Niles and Lorrin both smiled. They were impressed that he'd refused to leave her and stay with their father in safety, and to them, it just proved beyond any doubt that no blame lay on Elinta for what happened to him. He'd chosen his path, and they all knew he wouldn't have changed it even knowing that he would die protecting Elinta.

She'd choked as she described the moment she'd realised what had happened to him. It was with surprise that the words came tumbling out of her. She hadn't intended on reliving them, but it seemed an insult to Blaine not to tell them how he'd died. Niles and Lorrin hadn't seen the moment it'd happened either, but they'd seen Mazen swooping in on Vaherin.

"We thought he was coming to snatch you up," Niles said, the shadow of remembered fear on his face. They fell into silence. Though it was hard to think, without Blaine diving between her and the dagger, she wouldn't be with them now. The blade would have gone straight through her armour.

"Where's everyone going to sleep tonight?" Elinta asked, looking back at the palace in the dimming light. It had stopped burning, but the fire had destroyed a large portion of the eastern side. While most of the building still stood, the damage was extensive.

"We'll work something out," Lorrin said, following her gaze. "It's repairable. But there was a lot lost that can't be replaced."

"My dad and I are gonna stay with you guys tonight," Niles said. "Our house survived, but I don't think he wants to leave your parents."

Elinta's thoughts turned to her own father, and she felt a pang in her chest. His words echoed in her head. *I have no children now.* And she had no family now.

But that wasn't entirely true, as a surge in Zhayra's chest reminded her. As did the hand resting on hers, and the brown eyes that met her own. Elinta thought if she could be reminded of that every day, she might, one day, be OK.

"There'll be another meeting tomorrow," Lorrin said, drawing her attention again. "We need to decide what to do now."

"Just as long as we don't split up again." Niles shook his head. "I hated that."

Elinta had to agree even if she had a nagging feeling they would be safer as far away from her as possible. But like Blaine, she knew they wouldn't leave her. And she didn't want them to. Not really.

She gasped, remembering two people she hadn't heard about yet. "Are Cassia and Aiden OK?"

"They're fine. My uncle got them out of the city when it started," Lorrin said. "Aunt Jaida went to collect them."

"Good," she said, thinking of the twins. They were so young, too young to have seen all that had happened in the city today. She thought of Aiden's smile when he'd asked her to dance at the king's ball, of Cassia's grin as Lorrin pulled her onto his toes, and was glad they hadn't lost them. How many other children weren't so lucky?

A messenger soon arrived to tell them the first and second floors had been deemed the safest places to sleep, so the royal family and the advisors would be moved there. They soon learnt the library had suffered smoke damage, so it wasn't safe to sleep in but, remarkably, the fire hadn't reached it. Any staff members who didn't have homes in the city to go to were to be set up in the dining hall, and any civilians whose homes had been damaged were invited to join them. The king and queen were going to be in their private dining room, but Lorrin wanted to stay with Elinta and Niles, who were to sleep with the generals in another side room.

But Elinta never made it to the room. She lingered in the gardens after Lorrin and Niles left to find some food, graciously taking her armour with them to find a place to store it. Unable to face a night inside the palace surrounded by people who would stare and whisper behind her back, she slipped out into the darkened city. Zhayra was still looking through her eyes, so she blinked twice and felt her ears pop only a second later.

"I'm coming," she whispered, using her dragonsight to find her way to the woods and to Zhayra.

❧❧❧❧

Elinta and Zhayra soared over Nevira in the early morning light. Red and orange streaks painted the sky above the smouldering city. Smoke tinged her nose even up as high as they were, but the haze had lessened. Elinta stared down at the houses, shops, and the palace below her with enhanced eyes. It didn't seem as bad in the light of a new day. Large sections of the city had been damaged or destroyed, including the watch towers stationed on each point of the compass around the city, but people were already out working to clear the rubble. Maybe the palace wouldn't be ready to live in for some time, but the city would go on.

They touched down in front of the palace, a place that had been left clear for Zhayra. The council meeting was due to start in a few minutes. She'd left her arrival as late as possible to avoid all the people. She slid from the dragon's back, ignoring the stares of the countless workers around her, and stood by Zhayra's head.

"I'll see you soon. You'll be listening, right?"

Zhayra blinked once.

Elinta nodded, squared her shoulders, and walked up the stairs and into the palace.

PRONUNCIATION GUIDE

Names:

- Ferran pronounced FEH-RAN

- Zhayra pronounced ZAY-RUH

- Vaherin pronounced VUH-HAIR-EN

- Ciar pronounced KEER (like 'here' with a 'k')

- Raisa pronounced RAY-SUH

- Mazen Elliar pronounced MAY-ZEN EL-EE-ARE

- Aesira pronounced AY-ZEER-UH

- Aisla pronounced AY-S-LA

- Piran pronounced PEER-RAN

- Nakiah pronounced NAH-KEY-UH

Locations:

- Nevira pronounced NEV-EAR-RUH

- Liyarna pronounced LIE-YAR-NUH

- Calaza pronounced CUH-LAR-ZUH

Other:

- *Illayas* pronounced ILL-UH-YAS

- *Zearla lurai ngaran* pronounced ZEE-ARE-LA LER-EYE NG (like Si**ng**apore)-ARE-AN

- *Zetayn nalliyan ayn palla kli ayn karn mai ri/ti* Pronounced ZEH-TAYN NALL-EE-ARN AIN PALL-AH KLEE AIN KARN MY REE. Meaning: "May (the) sun (present) continue to (present) shine on you (male/female)."

- *Zetayn eyan pepyan eka ayn air kli nalliyan* Pronounced ZEH-TAYN EH-YAN PEP-YARN EK-AH AIN AIR KLEE NALL-EE-ARN. Meaning: "May your light (inalienable) (present) return to (the) sun" ('eka' is used despite the contradiction. The Asali consider their light inalienable in life and the use is continued).

More extras can be found on Tiani's website at www.tianidavids.com/extras

The sun will burn brightly tomorrow

Elinta has been left reeling in the aftermath of the attack on Nevira and the losses sustained. Now, more than ever, she's certain that Mazen has to be stopped. But Elinta's bond with Zhayra seems to be merely a shallow reflection of his and Vaherin's. And, if Elinta's suspicions prove correct, the maroon dragon isn't the only one he's bonded to.
But her worries about the bond are put on hold when Lorrin's parents agree to approach the Asali for a temporary alliance. But Liyarna, no longer the safe city Elinta stayed in mere weeks ago, isn't the only place Elinta must visit. There's one more group she hasn't approached. One that hasn't seen Eldras in over a hundred and fifty years. It's finally time for the heir to go home.
As Elinta races to find allies for the final battle against Mazen one question continues to bounce around her head; how did he come to be like this? But Elinta can't help worrying that she might not find a way to stop him before she loses someone else.

The Eldrasian Chronicles book 3 is coming spring 2023

ACKNOWLEDGEMENTS

So, my dedication initially read:

To potatoes. Delicious in every form except one. Looking at you mashed potato.

And really, wasn't that just the best dedication you've ever read? But this series is about fighting; fighting for what's right, fighting for loved ones, fighting fear and sadness, and sometimes fighting yourself. Elinta has a tough road ahead of her, but you can bet she's going to fight. And I hope you do too.

My thanks goes first, once again, to Papa for bringing me here. For giving me this dream and helping me achieve it. For being there for me to cling to in those hard days, and to rejoice with when those days fell far behind.

My editor Carrie Jones! Once again, I'm sorry for any typos here :) Thank you for your enthusiasm and your outstanding advice. I've learnt so much from you.

Taire! I can't believe you managed to capture the image I had in my mind for this cover so perfectly. Your work is unbelievable.

My wonderful beta readers, thank you so much for returning to read *The Dragon Kin.* Your advice, support, and comments are so valued, I could not have gotten here without them.

My broth—I mean, my number one fan ... have you even read *The Dragon Healer* yet? ;)

Mum and Dad, once again for listening to my story gushes.

And you! Thank you for continuing on with me through the series. Please drop a review if you enjoyed The Dragon Kin, every review helps!

The end is in sight and it might be a little ... painful.

Tiani Davids grew up in Victoria reading middle-grade and young adult fantasy, a love that soon expanded to include writing. She now lives on the Far South Coast of New South Wales where she cultivates her passion for reading, writing, and all things Tolkien.

Connect with Tiani online at:

Instagram: @tianidavids

Facebook: @authortianidavids
Website: tianidavids.com
Sign up to Tiani's newsletter on her website to keep up to date and receive exclusive content.

www.ingramcontent.com/pod-product-compliance
Lightning Source LLC
Chambersburg PA
CBHW020332120726
47904CB00002B/375